THE CASTLE OF EARTH AND EMBERS

BRIARWOOD WITCHES, BOOK 1

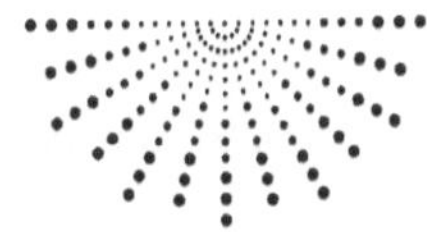

STEFFANIE HOLMES

BACCHANALIA HOUSE

ISBN: 978-19865377-59

❀ Created with Vellum

For James.
You're more than enough for me.

1

MAEVE

"I don't care if we're late," Kelly mumbled as she twisted a strand of cotton candy around her fingers and licked it off. "This diabetic coma I'm about to inhale is a hundred-and-twenty percent worth it."

"Nothing can be a hundred-and-twenty percent worth it," I reminded her, biting into the enormous ball of cotton candy we held between us. The pink fluff dissolved on my tongue. *This is way better than a birthday cake.* "It's a mathematical impossibility."

Kelly made a face at me, her mouth full of cotton candy. "No math on your birthday. Now be quiet and help my finish this sugary fluff, Einstein. We're running late."

My adoptive sister was the only person I let get away with calling me Einstein. Being the a lone science nerd in Coopersville, Arizona, was hard enough without having to deal with a nickname that confirmed to the world I didn't fit in. There was a jock in sixth grade who tormented me with the name. It lasted until I "accidentally" tripped him in chem lab, where he fell hard enough against a bench that his head required stitches. He left me alone after that, but then I made the mistake of chopping my brown hair into a layered pixie cut, and the kids started to call me "dyke" and "lesbo" when they bothered to talk to me, which wasn't often.

Kelly was annoying as hell, but no way was I going to hurt her any more than I already had. So I was stuck with Einstein.

We shoved our way through the thick crowd that had gathered on the fairway. Harried-looking housewives tugged their children from sideshow to sideshow, dishing out tiny plastic tokens like they were prescription painkillers. A long line at the shooting range stretched past the hot dog stand as the high school jocks waited for their chance to show off their shooting skills.

Our parents had told us to meet them at the Ferris wheel twenty minutes ago for some awkward Crawford family fun time. Mom was big on family fun time, especially on birthdays, and *especially* if it included wholesome and PG-rated activities like attending the annual Coopersville county fair, which occurred every year on my birthday. Not exactly a twenty-first birthday blowout, but Kelly could make anything fun. She had dragged me away from our parents as soon as we got inside the gates. She didn't want anyone from school to see us with our parents. It hurt her cred bad enough being the pastor's daughter, but being seen with them in public was just too much.

I couldn't really care less. I'd graduated high school two years ago and I'd been living at home since then, taking advanced physics classes at a community college in Phoenix while I saved money for a real college. I didn't really hang out with anyone apart from Kelly and the folk in my college astronomy club.

Plus, I was checking out of Coopersville in T-minus

forty-three days. My mind flashed to the MIT acceptance letter with a full academic scholarship pinned to the fridge at home. Finally I was getting out of podunkesville and starting my life for real. Goodbye horse manure and creationism class in school and jocks ruling the world – in just forty-three days, I'd be sitting in classes at one of the best schools in the country learning about the universe from top physicists and astronomers.

Hey, gorgeous." Some dumb guy fell in step beside us, interrupting my vision of receiving my acceptance into the NASA graduate space program. "Where are you off to in such a hurry? All the fun is right here."

I didn't bother to slow down. He couldn't be talking to me with my pixie hair (now sporting a vivid pink stripe through the bangs), and my boring hazel eyes. My birth mother had been British and she died during childbirth, so the only thing I had of hers was a name no one could pronounce and skin that burned at the very mention of sun. Not exactly a turn-on for the opposite sex when surrounded by bronzed, blonde Arizona beauties like my sister.

Speak of the damsel – Kelly switched on her hot-guy-incoming smile, but I grabbed her arm and started dragging her away. She shot me a filthy look I pretended not to notice. It was *my* birthday, after all. The guy was hot, I'd give her that – he spoke with a British accent and stood out as much as I did. Dark hair tinged with gold flopped over his face, with broad shoulders and black-and-grey tattoos peeking out from his collar and cuffs, and luminous skin that looked as though it hadn't seen the sun in decades, clear and smooth as crystal.

He also had cold, predatory eyes and a self-satisfied smirk instead of a smile. I already disliked him. But Kelly dug her heels into the dirt, and we ground to a halt. *Fine, whatever.*

"I haven't seen you around before, sugar," Kelly purred, reaching out and touching the stranger's arm in that overly-familiar Arizona way. "You new to Coopersville?"

"I'm just passing through."

"Ah, a wanderer?"

"You might say that." He flashed Kelly his cat-ate-the-canary smirk, but his crystal eyes remained focused on me. A flicker of unease squirreled around my gut.

"We can't talk now," I said, squeezing Kelly's arm. "We've got to meet someone."

"We're going to the Ferris wheel." Kelly batted her eyelashes at the guy. "You want to join us?"

Damn it, Kelly. Forget subtlety. I elbowed her in the ribs. She winced but continued to ignore me.

"It would be my pleasure to escort two fine ladies." His deep, velvety voice caressed my ears, but something about it seemed… off. His accent was almost *too* perfect, like he'd practiced every word in the mirror beforehand. He inserted himself between us, wrapping his arms around our shoulders. His hand snaked down the edge of my tank top and I flinched away. I didn't want him touching me. Kelly shot me a look of 'stop cramping my style.' And I remembered that I was leaving her alone in forty-three days, so I clamped my mouth shut and tried not to think about the guy's arm around my neck.

He kept his eyes on Kelly as we pushed our way through the crowd, but then his hand slipped again, his fingers brushing against my breast. *Oh, no you don't.* I ducked out from under his arm. "Don't touch me, creep."

"Whoa, ease up, sweetheart." He held one hand up in mock surrender, the other arm still firmly wrapped around Kelly's shoulder. I noticed his other hand pressed against the side of her breast. Kelly shot me a look. *Stop being so uncool,* she mouthed.

Whatever. If cool meant having to hang out with this twat (I loved that word; picked it up from a British TV show, and I got to say it a lot because my parents didn't know what it meant), then I was perfectly happy being a square. I thought about putting my foot down and dragging Kelly away, but I knew the guy couldn't do much in the crowded fair, and Kelly could handle herself.

I shrugged. "Three's a crowd. So if you'll excuse me, I think I'll just meet you guys at the wheel. Kelly, just remember what we learned in school about gloves."

Kelly stuck her tongue out at me.

The guy's smirk froze on his lips. Clearly, he wasn't used to women rejecting his charms. "No, that's not how it works. It'll be the both of you, so don't go running off now."

The guy lunged for me. I leapt back, my heart pounding. "Don't touch me!"

A fist came out of nowhere and slammed into the guy's temple. His expression froze for a moment, all smushed against the mystery fist. Then he was flying backward, crashing into the crowd waiting at the duck-shooting booth. People shouted and leapt out of the way. Beer pitchers and cups of Coke spilled, and a kid howled as his corn dog was knocked out of his hand.

"She *said* not to touch her." A deep voice with an even-more-perfect English accent growled from behind me.

"Ow, fuck!" The black-haired twat yelled, grabbing his face. Blood cascaded from a cut above his eye. He tried to get to his feet, but several of the jocks in the crowd shoved and kicked him. Not because they were trying to save my honor, but because they were jocks and that was what they did.

"Hey, thanks for—" I turned to my savior and stopped short.

For the first time ever, I knew what it meant when authors talked about being "mesmerized by beauty," because

I literally could not tear my eyes away from this guy. He stood with tree trunk arms folded, glaring at the twat with emerald eyes pierced with light. They looked like prisms that might shatter at any moment. A soft nose and strong jaw completed a face that would've looked right at home on a men's shaving commercial, complete with a mop of dark, feathery hair that stuck out at all angles, a wild mane I wanted to tangle my fingers in.

Tattoos spiraled down both his arms – intricate Celtic knots weaving over his toned muscles. He wore a black t-shirt with some indecipherable band logo on it, dark jeans, and heavy black boots coated with a layer of Arizona dust. He was staring at me like I was the only thing that mattered in the whole world.

This was the kind of guy who carried around a suitcase of broken hearts. He was the guy all lonely female country singers wrote songs about, except he looked more like a rockstar than a lone ranger. Why was he *here*, at the Coopersville county fair, of all places, and why was he bothering to rescue *me*?

"Are you okay?" he asked, the syllables rolling off that sexy British tongue of his.

"I—" articulation wasn't happening in the presence of such a fine specimen of humanity. "Um..."

My phone beeped. I tore my gaze away from my hot rescuer, and checked the message. It was Mom. The thirty heart emojis at the beginning of the message gave it away without even having to read the "from" bar.

"We're in line. Hurry up!"

Kelly slammed into me. "Who's this guy?" She flashed Mr. British a toothy smile. Obviously, she was already over her infatuation with the black-haired twat. "You saved us from a crazy stalker. What can we do to repay you? Can I buy you a drink?"

Inside, I groaned. *Typical Kelly.* Not two minutes ago she was practically purring on the twat's lap, and now he was our crazy stalker? Well, too bad, she wasn't getting her hands on *my* green-eyed hero.

"You're not twenty-one, remember?" I elbowed her out of the way. Kelly glared at me. Hey, it *was* my birthday, after all. I flashed Mr. British what I hoped was a flirtatious smile. "But I'd be happy to."

"What about Mom and Dad?" Kelly moaned, suddenly desperate to see them now that I had the guy's attention. "We can't just keep them waiting at the Ferris wheel forever."

As if on cue, my phone beeped again. Mom. *"Where are you?"* and about twenty sadface emojis.

I handed the phone to Kelly. "Reply to that. Tell her we'll be there in a second."

"It's your phone. You do it." Kelly tried to shove it under my nose, but I jerked my head away and turned back to Mr. British, who was staring at me with this intense expression that was almost unnerving, if it didn't make my stomach flutter.

"What?" I asked. "Do I have cotton candy up my nose or something?"

Mr. British shook his head, his dark hair waving around his face. "You're just… really beautiful."

That was such a ridiculous line it should have made me snort, but instead, the butterflies in my chest danced like crazy. The intensity in this guy's eyes when he said that… it was like he really believed it was true. It made me feel like a goddess, instead of the frumpy science nerd with a haircut of indeterminable gender that I really was.

My phone beeped again. Kelly glanced at the screen and smiled. "Never mind. Mom said they just hopped on. They want us to wait for them at the bottom, and they'll go again with us."

"I'll walk you," Mr. British said, with a glance over to the twat, who was now having a shouting match with two of the jocks. Mr. British picked up my hand and looped it in his, like an old-fashioned gentleman escorting a lady to a ball. Electricity fizzed up my arm. My gaze fell on his lips again, and my body heated up as I wondered what it would be like to kiss them, all soft and sensual. *I'd make him talk to me with that gorgeous husky British voice, and tell me everything he's going to do to me...*

A loud explosion shook the earth, jolting me out of my dirty thoughts.

I pitched forward. Mr. British caught me in his arms. A sizzle of electric current flared through my body from his touch, immediately extinguished by the searing pain in my ears as the world around me shattered.

The earth pitched, knocking our feet from under us. We slammed hard into the ground, the force driving the wind from my chest. Mr. British wrapped his body around mine, his weight reassuring against me, protecting me from... what? I tried to see through the throng of stampeding, screaming people. An intense wave of heat swept over me, like someone had opened an industrial oven right over top of us. I gasped for air. Mr. British yelled something to me but I couldn't hear it over the roar in my ears.

Mr. British yanked me to my feet, his other arm around a sobbing Kelly. We were swept along with the rest of the crowd fleeing back through the midway. I craned my neck around and finally saw what had happened. My blood froze in my veins.

The Ferris wheel was on fire.

Flames licked their way through the spokes and darted from carriage to carriage. People hung out of the buckets, screaming and crying for help. The whole thing groaned as it buckled in the middle, shooting sparks in all directions.

Someone leapt from one of the top gondolas, and more people screamed as his body slammed into the top of the coffee truck and bounced to the ground. People rushed to him, but he didn't get up.

My heart leapt into my throat. The only parents I'd ever known were on that wheel. I wrenched my body from Mr. British's grasp and took off toward the burning ride.

"Maeve, no!" Kelly yelled after me, but her words were swallowed up by the fire and the fury.

I shoved my way through the crowd, screaming my parents' names. I hit a lull in the crowd and sprinted across the field just as the ground beneath me buckled. With a groan, the whole Ferris wheel toppled over, like it had been shoved by some invisible giant.

No. No, no, no.

I crawled toward the corn dog cart as the Ferris wheel crashed into the ghost train building, sending a shower of sparks down into the midway. Fires leapt from awning to awning, consuming the flimsy fabric of the petting zoo tent in one giant inferno. I noticed someone pulling a sobbing child from a mangled ghost train cart. I picked myself up, ignoring the trembling in my legs, and raced toward the wreckage again.

Mom and Dad are in there somewhere. I've got to find them. I've got to—

I'd just swung myself under the outer ring when a fire leapt up from the ghost train, sending another wave of heat at me. Thick smoke rose from the fires – it wasn't thick here on the ground, but it stung my eyes so badly tears obscured my vision. Everything smelled like a charcoal BBQ.

I stepped back. How the hell was I going to get inside? Loose wires sparked on the ground. In the distance, I heard the faint ring of the fire department's siren.

My weeping eyes caught sight of a figure standing on the

other side of the field. While everyone around him ran in all directions, he stood still, his arms folded, his expression placid as he watched the horror unfold around him. It was the black-haired twat who harassed me and Kelly earlier. His eyes met mine, and he lifted a hand and waved at me.

What the fuck?

He smiled, his white teeth reflecting the glow of the fire. My blood turned cold. A cloud of smoke billowed in front of my face, burning my eyes so I turned away. When I looked back, the guy was gone. All I could see was an enormous black dog loping across the fairway.

With a sickening CRACK, half of the ghost train building fell away. The Ferris wheel groaned. The outer ring slid off the edge of the collapsed structure. I ducked as a live wire swung dangerously close to my head. A gondola dangled just above me, two pairs of legs hanging over the edge of the wooden seat. The owners of the legs weren't moving or crying out.

That could be my parents. I have to—

The Ferris wheel lurched again. I rolled away as the beam above my head crashed to the ground. I scrambled back as the entire outer ring collapsed, folding in on itself like some kind of terrible accordion. Burning hot debris slammed around me as the whole ghost train collapsed, and both structures crashed into the ground.

The force knocked me off my feet, slamming me hard onto the packed earth. My head hit something hard, and stars appeared in my vision. I tried to get up, but the heat rolled over me, paralyzing me in place. Moving only made my head spin worse, and the world around me bubbled and blurred.

I'm going to die... I'm going to burn up right here...

Mr. British's face appeared in my vision. His big eyes

filled my vision, reflecting dancing orange flames. At least the last thing I saw before I died was a really hot guy. I could do much worse.

Then the vision blurred away to nothing, and the world went black.

2

MAEVE

I woke with a start, my eyes flying open. *The wheel. The fire. My parents!*

My whole body tensed, ready to leap out of the way of the wall of fire barreling toward me. But as my eyes took in what was around me, and my body registered smell and light and something soft beneath me —not the hard-packed dirt of the fairground – I realized I was no longer at the fair.

There were no flames, no heat torching my skin, no fiery eyes of Mr. British as he tried to shield me with his body and ended up burning alive before my eyes. I was in my bed back at the Crawford's house, my whole body drenched in sweat.

It was a dream, thank God. My parents hadn't really burned alive on a Ferris wheel. *I should have known. Only in my dreams would a guy like Mr. British be interested in me.*

I rubbed my arms, still feeling the heat of the fire in my skin. I sucked in a deep breath, and the back of my throat recoiled in agony, sending me into a violent coughing fit. It was as though I could still feel the smoke in my lungs.

It had felt so real.

For as long as I could remember, I'd had incredibly vivid

dreams and lucid dreams, where I was aware I was dreaming and able to make my own decisions and choose what happened next (I usually chose to drop everything and float through space or land on Mars. Those were my favorite dreams). But this… this was the worst nightmare I'd ever had.

Sunlight streamed through my open windows, the pale blue curtains flapping in the breeze. Between the windows, Kelly sprawled out on my blue daybed, a pile of fashion magazines and an open bottle of bourbon spread out around her. Her golden hair hung limply over her eyes.

"Welcome to the land of the living," she said, her voice dull and throaty. "You look like shit."

"Nice to see you, too." The words stung my raw throat. Maybe I'd been yelling in my sleep. I did that sometimes, too. I rubbed my head. "I just had the most horrible nightmare. Where'd you get that bottle from? Mom'll kill you if she smells alcohol in here." Our parents never let us have even a drop of alcohol in the house, and you could forget about horror films or Harry Potter books or premarital sex. We weren't even allowed to have Facebook accounts (we did all of these things anyway, but they didn't know that).

Kelly shook her head, and tears pooled in her eyes. Unease stabbed at my gut. Kelly was the strongest person I knew. She never cried. If she was breaking down now… something must've happened.

"You okay, sis? Did we run out of bacon or something?" Kelly always begged for bacon for breakfast.

Kelly shook her head. "Maeve… it's about Mom and Dad. They…" she choked on her next word as fresh tears spilled down her cheeks.

The uneasy feeling intensified. "What happened to Mom and Dad?" I demanded. "Are they okay?"

"Maeve..." Kelly's voice trailed off. She blinked, but the tears kept on coming. "Mom and Dad are—"

She didn't need to finish her sentence. I could read my adoptive sister like a star chart. I *knew*.

My dream wasn't a dream after all.

The Crawfords were dead.

3

MAEVE

*W*hat?
Shit.

No.

Mom and Dad... the Ferris wheel... those lifeless legs hanging from the mangled gondola... The dream that was actually a memory hit me with full force, raw and painful. I squeezed my eyes shut, as if that might somehow reset the clock to before that stupid county fair, and I could beg them to take me to Ruby's Diner or throw a party at the house instead.

Dead.

No.

It can't be.

Louise and Matthew Crawford weren't my biological parents. My real mother died during childbirth back in England, and as far as anyone knew, my real father wasn't in the picture at that stage. My mother had no living relatives, so I was released into the truly delightful English foster care system. I lived in an orphanage for a few years – I don't remember it at all, except in weird flashes in my dreams, which didn't count – before the Crawfords visited London doing their missionary work, fell in love with me at first sight, and somehow found a way to obtain an international adoption. ("It was difficult," Mom always said when I asked her, "but it was worth it for you.") Kelly and I always suspected it was illegal, but we knew better than to bring *that* up.

Apparently, I loved them instantly, too, and I cried for three days when they left the orphanage, before they came back for me. This didn't surprise me – with their hearty Southwestern accents, their eyes that sparkled like the ocean, and their ridiculous eternal optimism that God would sort everything out in the end, they were pretty damn easy to love.

Even when I became a surly teenager obsessed with astronomy and denounced religion with all the subtlety and sensitivity a fourteen-year-old could muster, they never discouraged me. Once, I got sent home from school for refusing to write an essay on the scientific evidence for Noah's flood, and instead of yelling at me, they convinced my teachers to allow me to hand in an essay about the Voyager missions instead. I remembered the day I got my scholarship for MIT – Dad had tears in his eyes as he pinned the letter to the fridge. At his Sunday sermon he managed to mention it at least three times.

How could they just be *dead?* How could such kind and wonderful people be gone from the world? How could their stupid God betray them like that?

The grief crushed against me, pressing in on me from all sides. I gasped for air, squeezing Kelly tight against me as I fought against the invisible force that threatened to collapse me in upon myself, like a black hole sucking in everything around it.

"I couldn't save them," I whispered. The guilt ate my

insides. *If I'd just moved faster. If I'd stayed inside the wheel a bit longer, I might have had a chance—*

The bed creaked. Kelly threw herself against me, wrapping her arms around my shoulders. "You were so brave, running into the fire like that. I thought I lost you, too. And then you wouldn't wake up," she whimpered. "You're all I have left."

Kelly burrowed her head into my shoulder, her tears puddling on my t-shirt. This was all wrong. Kelly *never* cried. I was the wailer – running bawling to Mom whenever Kelly broke the rules of a game. Rules were very important to me.

But not as important as Mom and Dad, and yet now I couldn't muster up even a single tear. I felt numb all over, worn and squashed by the force of the grief. I rested a hand on my chest, feeling my heart pounding against my palm.

"How… how long have I been out?" I asked.

"A couple of days," Kelly sniffed. "I can't… I don't remember exactly. You've been in and out a bit."

Oh, jeez, she's been here, alone, since the accident, waiting for me to wake up. I hugged Kelly to me, holding her close, letting her spill her grief over me, hoping it might draw up some of my own. But it didn't. I remained numb.

After a time, Kelly's sniffles died down, and my stomach growled. I realized that I must not have eaten anything for days. Kelly might not have, either. She could barely boil an egg when she was in full control of her faculties.

"We should get some food," I said, pulling my legs off the bed. Kelly grabbed my arm, her red-ringed eyes burning into mine.

"Don't even think about getting up. That guy said you hit your head pretty hard, and you should be careful in case you have a concussion."

"What guy?"

"That hot British guy you totally blanked me for. He

carried you out of the flames and helped me get you home."

"He did?" I glanced around the room. Mr. British had been in my *room?* If I'd had any chance with him, it would be over now that he'd seen my pink ruffled sheets and the telescope at the window and the rows of dolls sitting on top of the bureau. My eyes fell on the overflowing laundry basket. *Please don't tell me he saw my underwear, too.*

And then I remembered that my parents were dead, and my sister had been on her own since she got that news, and I hated myself for even thinking about a guy right now. My cheeks burned with guilt. *What is* wrong *with me?*

I rubbed my burning cheeks. "Why am I not in a hospital?"

"He said it wasn't a good idea. He said the ER would be full of people from the accident, and we didn't have insurance so it would be expensive, and… he was right. I mean, I saw them carrying away people in the ambulance. He said he could help you, and I… I didn't know what else to do…"

"It's fine," I hugged her again. "You did good."

"I thought he was a doctor or something. He knew exactly what to do. He showed me how to treat your burns." Kelly lifted one of the bandages around my arm. I looked down, but I couldn't see any burn on my skin.

"Wow," Kelly rubbed my arm. "This was all red and blistered the other day. He must be a *really* good doctor."

"Where is he now?"

Kelly shrugged. "He just tied off that last bandage and left. I didn't ask where he was going. I was a little distracted, you know?"

And then she was crying again – big, heaving sobs that shuddered through her entire body. I wrapped her in my arms, pressing my cheek to hers and feeling her tears slide over my skin as if they were my own.

They're gone. They'll never come in at night to say a goodnight prayer with me. They'll never wake us up at stupid-o'clock on a Sunday morning for pre-Church chocolate-chip pancakes. They'll never see me graduate MIT, or win a Nobel Prize, or walk on Mars.

So, why can't I cry?

My stomach rumbled again. "I'm guessing we don't have any food in the house?"

"Don't be ridiculous." Kelly swiped at her leaking eyes. "An endless stream of well-wishers have paraded through the door, each one loaded down with casseroles in all the flavors of the rainbow. Of course, most of them came for the gory details about the accident. It's the talk of the town, but I can't… oh, Maeve, it was so terrible."

"I know."

Kelly sniffed, wiping her nose. "Anyway, you're awake now. I need so much help. There's all this paperwork to go over, and Pastor Tim and Daddy's lawyer keep bugging me. I don't understand what any of them want—"

"Of course I'll help."

"Oh," Kelly drew a couple of envelopes off the nightstand and plopped them in my lap. "You got some mail. One of them's from MIT."

I stared at the college crest on the first envelope. The symbol of my future, the first step toward getting into the NASA space program. Ever since I'd got my acceptance and scholarship, I'd been unable to think about college without excited butterflies in my stomach. A giddy smile would spread over my lips. But now, I felt nothing – the same crushing, harrowing numbness.

It meant nothing without them.

I could see from Kelly's face that she desperately wanted a distraction. "Let's see what they say, then," I said, unsure if it was a good idea to remind Kelly that in forty-one days time (forty? Thirty-nine? I needed to figure that out, stat) I'd be leaving her for Massachusetts and theoretical physics. I slit open the envelope and pulled out a single page.

Dear Ms. Crawford,

Recently you received a letter stating you received the Neil Armstrong Astronomy Scholarship, which would pay tuition fees and a full stipend to complete an advanced degree in Physics or Engineering at the Massachusetts Institute of Technology.

I regret to inform you that this letter was sent in error. Unfortunately, you were not successful in your application and you will not be receiving the scholarship.

This does not impact your position at Massachusetts Institute of Technology, and your place is still being held. I apologize for any inconvenience caused.

Sincerely,

Professor Pauline Breuntas

Head of Physics

I stared at the page until the letters stopped spelling words – they became crude scratches on the page, weird looped hieroglyphs that held some long forgotten meaning.

My scholarship was gone. Without that money, I couldn't afford to go to college at a school like that. Because of the "complications" around my adoption, I couldn't apply for a loan or financial aid. If I took every penny in my savings account, I wouldn't even have enough for one semester.

With one single piece of paper, the last remaining good thing in my life had been taken from me. The dream of being an astronaut I'd had since I was seven shrank before my eyes. But I couldn't conjure up even a single ounce of feeling. Not anger, not sorrow.

Nothing.

Because it all meant nothing.

"Maeve, what is it?" Kelly asked. I didn't want to read the

words out loud, didn't want to speak them into being. I handed her the letter, watching her already stricken face crumple as the impact of the news hit her.

"No," she whispered, her fingers curling around the paper, crumpling it in her rage. "It's got to be some mistake. They can't just *take* your scholarship away. You won that. You *earned* that. I won't let them."

"It's fine," I said. "I'll go back to community college. I'll apply again next year. Maybe I'll get a private loan." But even as I said the words, I knew it wasn't going to happen. This was the last year I was eligible for the full ride scholarship.

"No way. You're not waiting, and the loan…" Kelly didn't want to say it would be hard to get that much money without our parents alive to cosign for it. "I know, we'll sell the house. It's ours now, right? We'll sell it and we'll use the money for your fees—"

I shook my head as I remembered. "Actually, no. This house belongs to the church. Mom and Dad were gifted it to live in only while he was pastor. Now that he's not… they're going to ask us to move out, I bet."

"What?" Kelly screeched.

I nodded, staring at the second letter in my lap. The logo in the corner read "Emily Lawson, Solicitor" with an address in the United Kingdom. On any other day, I might find that curious. But now, it didn't seem important. And I couldn't handle any more bad news at the moment. My chest was already being squeezed in a vise.

Who cares that I just lost the best thing that ever happened to me? Who cares that without the scholarship I'd have to give up my place? Who gave a shit that Kelly and I would lose our home?

My parents were dead dead dead, and nothing would ever bring them back. And I could have saved them, I *should* have saved them, and I didn't.

4

MAEVE

Most people spend the days after their twenty-first birthday with the worst hangover of their life. It was the reward for finally reaching adulthood – the gift of knowing you were no longer invincible, and that all your actions have consequences.

I was spending mine at my parents funeral. In terms of life lessons learned, I'd much rather have the hangover.

But that's what happens when your name is Maeve Crawford and you live a cursed life where every imaginable shitty thing that could possibly happen to a person happens to you. It was almost laughable how little I was surprised.

I sat in the pew beside Kelly while the church band played Dad's favorite worship song. Her hand gripped mine as a fresh wave of tears cascaded down her cheeks. Over the last week, Kelly cried practically every moment she was awake – she sobbed through the meeting with our family lawyer (when he showed us just how little money was in our parents' accounts). She sniffled down the phone to reporters writing piece after sensational piece with headlines like COUNTY FAIR ENDS IN GRUESOME DEATHS and

ARIZONA GOVERNOR CALLS FOR FERRIS WHEEL BAN. She bawled while Pastor Tim (formally assistant Pastor Tim) sat us down to talk about the "next phase of our life," and informed us we'd need to move out by the end of the month. She sobbed while we discussed options with the funeral director, who gently guided us toward closed caskets, given the extensive burns and damage to our parents' corpses.

She cried enough to start the second Biblical flood. Which was just as well, because I still hadn't cried. Not once. I played the memory of the accident over and over, watching the Ferris wheel toppling from the sky, crashing into the tents, the flames tearing through the fairground like demons hellbent on destruction. I heard the screams, smelled the burning, felt the smoke scratching the back of my throat... but it felt like a dream, like some movie I'd seen.

I told myself over and over again how sad it was, how much I'd miss them. But my body refused to cooperate. My tears didn't come. None of it seemed real.

The vise-like grip on my chest hadn't eased. I felt like I was waiting for something to happen, for some sign to tell me what to do next. I had nowhere to go, nowhere to live, no plan for the future. Kelly at least had an aunt she could live with this year while she finished her senior year at high school. (My aunt too, technically, although they never really acknowledged me).

I, on the other hand, was completely untethered.

What the hell am I going to do?

On the raised stage at the end of the vast church hall (our denomination didn't believe in grand buildings like the Catholics, so there was no interesting architecture to distract me) the newly minted Pastor Tim finished the opening prayers, and my parents' friends stood to deliver eulogy after eulogy, talking endlessly about Matthew and Louise's charity work, their mission trips, their contributions to the community.

Then Kelly got up, her whole body trembling as she folded and unfolded the paper containing her own eulogy. I raised an eyebrow at her, asking in sister-code if she wanted me to be up there beside her. But she didn't even see me.

Behind the lectern from which we'd heard Dad deliver sermons every Sunday since I could remember, Kelly cleared her throat. She spoke in one long sentence, her words ragged from grief. She pushed them out in a rush – of our parents' surprise when they found out they were pregnant with her (Mom wasn't supposed to be able to have children, hence me), memories of our childhood, a rambling story about Dad's obsession with The Beatles – eager to have it over with. In front of her, two closed coffins sagged under the weight of the floral arrangements Pastor Tim donated.

I stared at Pastor Tim in his formal black suit, my chest so tight I struggled to breathe, not even able to work up a righteous anger that he was taking away our home. They were very nice arrangements.

~

At the cemetery, Kelly and I hung back behind the crowd, our fingers laced together. The bright Arizona sun beat down on us and beads of sweat rolled down my back, sticking my dress to my skin. Black clothing may be *de rigueur* for funerals, but now I knew why we didn't ever see any goths in Coopersville. The pallbearers moved past us as they made their way down the path toward the family plot. The vise tightened around my heart. I gasped for breath. Kelly rested her head on my shoulder and smeared tears and snot all over the sleeve of my dress.

"You're not crying," she sniffed.

My stomach flipped. I was hoping she hadn't noticed. "Not now. I was before. During your eulogy. You did a great job, by the way."

"Oh." A pause. "Hey, did you ever open that other letter?"

"Letter?"

"That one from the lawyer in England that came for you the other day."

It took me a moment to remember what letter she was talking about. With all the preparations for the funeral, and the whole losing the house and my scholarship and burying my dead parents thing, I'd completely forgotten about the second letter, which I'd shoved in my purse at some point during the week to remind myself to open it.

I fished around in my purse and pulled out the crumpled envelope. "It's right here."

I stared down at the envelope as though it might contain a bomb. Which it probably did. Everything I touched turned into bad news.

Kelly ran her black-tipped fingers over the logo in the corner. "Go on, open it. I could seriously use the distraction right now."

Fine. If it made Kelly feel better, I'd open the damn thing. I flipped the envelope over. Weirdly, it was sealed with a proper wax seal, including a monogrammed shield containing the letter "B" pressed into the wax. I slid my finger under the wax and broke it, pulling the flap open and sliding out several sheets of paper.

On top was a letter, written on the same letterhead as the envelope.

Dear Ms. Crawford,

I trust this letter finds you well. As lawyer for her estate, your mother – Aline Moore – entrusted our office with the articles in her will. Her will included a stipulation that as her only living offspring, at the age of twenty-one you were to inherit her estate that has been held in trust until the time you could claim legal ownership.

This estate incorporates Briarwood House, the surrounding acreage, and the outbuildings and chattels contained therein. The house is currently occupied by four tenants, who wish to continue to reside in the property if you will allow them to do so.

I've enclosed a copy of the deed to the Briarwood Estate. In order to take up ownership of the property officially, you will need to visit our offices to sign the papers, or arrange a signing with a local lawyer.

Should you wish to inspect the estate in person, the tenants informed me that they would welcome your presence in Briarwood House. There are many available rooms and you would be able to take up residency for as long as you wished without breaking the tenancy contract.

Please contact me at your earliest convenience.

Sincerely,

Emily Lawson, LLB.

A second, smaller note fluttered between my fingers. It was handwritten in a messy scrawl that took me a few moments to decipher.

Hi Maeve,

Happy Birthday! I bet this letter has come as a shock! Emily mentioned that you're welcome at the house any time. I just wanted to tell you in non-lawyer speak that we (your tenants) would be chuffed to have you. We're all about your age, and we'd love to turn on the British charm for our new landlord.

My family has lived at Briarwood for the last twenty-one years. My parents were good friends of your mother's.

Briarwood is pretty special. I think you should come see for yourself. Shoot me an email and let me know.

Cheers,
Corbin

I stared at the letters, unable to process what they were saying. "This is some kind of joke. It's like those emails from Nigeria promising millions of dollars if I send them a check for fifty bucks." I turned the first page of the deed. "I'm surprised there's not a voucher for a penis enlargement."

"Um… Maeve?" Kelly tapped her mobile phone. "I just searched Briarwood House. It's… um, well… see for yourself."

She thrust her phone under my nose. I gasped, the first real reaction I'd had to *anything* since I got the news about my parents.

Briarwood wasn't a *house*. It was a full-on *castle*. The square keep jutted out of a rolling hill, flanked by two turrets and an outer curtain wall with a gatehouse. A crisp green lawn punctuated with box hedges and water fountains and beds of wildflowers spread out around it. Off to the side, I could see a later addition and a couple of outbuildings.

Holy shit.

I shook my head. "The letter's not real, Kelly. It's some dumb joke."

"I don't think so," Kelly tapped her phone screen. "That lawyer is legit, at least according to the English Bar Association. And look, this page says that the castle is currently held in trust for the Moore family, with four tenants living on site. Moore is your birth mother's last name!"

"It's a pretty common name. It doesn't mean—"

"You own a castle, Maeve," Kelly squealed. "A *castle*."

Several members of the congregation spun around, tutting at Kelly under their breaths.

I grabbed Kelly's arm and dragged her back from the edge of the crowd. We sat on a bench between two large family mausoleums, and I handed the letter over to Kelly while I scrolled through the Briarwood website on her phone, my chest fluttering with something like excitement crossed with nerves.

"What's this?" I jabbed my finger at the small logo in the corner of the screen, declaring the castle an "English Heritage" site.

"Duh. Weren't you paying attention? This isn't some roadside curiosity like the Winchester Mystery House. Briarwood House is a legit castle, in England."

"England?"

"Yeah, you know, land of Queens and crumpets. That's genuine Lords and Ladies shit right there, and it's all *yours*."

"My mother lived in a castle. Now I own a castle." Nope, saying it out loud didn't make it any less crazy. "But… what do I even do with it?"

"You live there, Your Majesty." Kelly punched me in the arm. "Which is convenient, since you've recently become homeless. Geez, and I thought you were the smart one."

"I can't live there! It's in England! How would I go to college and—" I remembered with a start that I wouldn't be going to college now.

Unless I somehow managed to sell this castle, which I may or may not even own. I don't know how much medieval real estate fetches these days, but I'm guessing it would be enough to pay for my tuition.

"Now she's getting it." Kelly squeezed my arm. "You've got nothing tying you here. You could go over, sign the papers, sell your castle, and live off the proceeds for probably the rest of your life."

"Inflation and taxes would take a chunk," I said. My hand trembled as I read the letter again. *If my birth-mother used to live at Briarwood, then I'd be losing the one link to her that I've had in the last twenty-one years. I'd never had anything of hers, not* even a photograph. Just my name and a story Mom told me about the nuns in the orphanage, who crossed themselves furtively whenever the name Aline Moore was brought up, as if they thought she was a witch or something ridiculous like that.

To see where she lived, to touch the things that she had touched, to maybe find a diary or her letters or photographs…

"I don't know if I should sell it," I said. "It belonged to my birth-mother. She wanted me to have it."

"Then do what the letter says. Go and visit it. Walk the ancient halls. Jump on the tiny medieval beds. And maybe you will find a way to make some money off it without selling it. The website says they run tours. And doesn't it come with a bunch of land? With all the proceeds, you could live in your castle and go to a school over there, like Oxley—"

"Oxford," I corrected her, my mind whirring. I'd never even *considered* a foreign university. I knew the Crawfords would never have had the money to help me with that, even if I could get a scholarship, and international student fees were *insane*. But Kelly was right. With my own castle, maybe I didn't have to worry about that. I could do whatever I wanted…

The problem was, the only thing I wanted was the one thing I couldn't have: for the Crawfords to be alive again.

The idea of leaving Arizona made the nervous butterflies in my stomach crash into each other. Apart from the summer I spent at space camp in Alabama, I'd never even been out of Arizona. Going back to England… to a house – sorry, *castle* – that belonged to a mother I'd never met…

Kelly patted my shoulder. "Don't look so horrified; you don't have to decide right now. Just think about it. You're always Miss play-it-safe, but I don't want you to miss out on this just because you're scared of a change."

"I'm not scared…" I stared down at a map on the tenth page of the deed. It showed the location of the castle in a county called Loamshire, nestled between two towns called Crookshollow and Crooks Worthy. The map was old – not printed off Google but clearly a photocopy of hand-drawn cartography. I admired the intricate border and strange notations dotting the landscape. England looked like an entirely different world.

"You're totally scared. You never do anything exciting or rebellious. Remember when Bobby Kennedy gave us that joint and you made me throw it in the trash and the Hunters' dog ate it?"

I blushed at the memory of having to confess to Mr. and Mrs. Hunter that their dog was stoned. We would've got into far less trouble if we'd just smoked the damn thing. I shot back. "I had premarital sex. That was pretty rebellious."

The sex was with Andrew, this sort-of geeky boy from my community college physics class who was obsessed with science fiction books. We were the two youngest members of the local astronomy club, which meant Andrew and I spent several warm Arizona nights tracking lunar phenomenon from the middle of deserted fields. One thing led to another and we spend most of last year getting funky until he moved away for grad school. The sex itself was underwhelming – the best thing about it had been the thrill of knowing I was breaking the Crawford's cardinal rule, and the fact that Kelly was spitting with jealousy that she hadn't done it first.

Yeah, the teenage rebellion was strong in me.

"So mediocre sex with a physics nerd is the most wild and crazy thing you're ever going to do in your entire life?" Kelly snorted. "Excuse me while I yawn."

I jabbed her in the arm, but her words stung. Kelly was right. I didn't exactly take a lot of risks. I was saving all my risk-taking for the space program. But maybe that was the wrong attitude. Leaving the country to go live in a castle so soon after my parents' deaths seemed like the stupidest idea in the world, but then, so did doing *anything* except crawling into bed and sleeping until it felt okay again, which it never would.

I ran my finger along an illustration in the corner of the map; three small mounds in the middle of a field behind the castle, marked with a weird series of lines and dashes. What did it mean? Did I really want to find out?

I could defer my place at MIT for a semester. It wasn't a big deal. Maybe this was just what I needed. Maybe if I went to England for a little while, I could find the peace I needed to mourn, to cry for what I'd lost, and then I could move on.

"You know what?" I folded the letter and stuffed it into the cup of my bra, the paper rustling against my naked breast. "I might just do it."

5

BLAKE

"What you ask is ludicrous, Daigh." Queen Morgana took a delicate sip from her nectar wine and placed the glass daintily back on the table. One of her sprites darted forward and refilled the cup, flitting back to the wall of the sidhe and pressing her back hard against the earthen walls, her dark brown skin camouflaged perfectly against the dark dirt. "Seelie and Unseelie will never be united."

My gaze swept from the Seelie Queen's attendants (a brownie winked at me. I'd be chatting to her later) to the Lady of Summer herself. From my place at my adoptive father's right hand, I had to turn my head to glance upon her. But Queen Morgana was used to captivating every eye in the room. Her green cloak shimmered with emerald light, casting a warm glow around the gloomy space. A waterfall of golden hair flowed down her back, wreathed in a crown of wildflowers and elder branches. If she was frightened of my father, she did not show it. Her features remained serene, although I noticed her gaze never wavered from his face.

Daigh – my adoptive father and the King of the Unseelie

Court – raised his own cup and took a deep swig. We did not usually have nectar wine in our court – the Seelie brewed it, and they limited our supply, for they knew it set off our dark revels. I usually had to content myself with the horrific Unseelie beer brewed from mushrooms, which tasted about as good as it sounded and sometimes made my vision disappear for hours at a time, giving a new meaning to the term 'blind drunk.'

Everything in the fae realm made me sick. The beer made me blind, the honey cakes made my stomach swell up, the berries made me lose complete control of my limbs and other aspects of my body I won't mention in polite company. Daigh had food brought back for me whenever he sent one of his fae to the human realm, but there was never enough to fully satisfy. The Unseelie thought it was the best fun to mix their fae food into my human supplies and watch as I fought for control of my body. *Haha, yeah, hilarious. With friends like these...*

It was recorded in our annals that one of the human witches – the red-headed one – once said that all fairies were wankers. He wasn't wrong.

There hadn't been a food delivery for me in a couple of days. We could only send one fae at a time into the human realm, and then only for a few hours at most. Each one came back weakened, many without completing their assignment. My stomach growled with hunger, but there was nothing on the feast table that I could eat. That may have been on purpose. Daigh could've procured enough food for me to eat like a prince, but near-starvation was an ideal way to make sure I'd never grow strong enough to usurp his throne or run away back to the human realm. You can't run very fast when you're too weak to lift your head.

Say what you like about my father (and there is quite a lot to say), but he treated me as if I was his true, biological son –

ie. with mistrust and disdain. Weirdly, he'd shown me a great honor tonight by allowing me a place at the table for this unique meeting.

I turned my attention away from the delicious food I couldn't eat and focused on the conversation. My father said this would be an historic day for the fae. I had no inkling what he was planning, but as his words registered, a coldness seeped into my veins.

"An alliance is not so ridiculous," my father was saying. "For years we have let this feud between our courts divide us, keeping our power and our focus inward. But now, the High Priestess of Briarwood is coming to England. This changes everything."

The fae – a bean-sidhe, or banshee – who was tending to the table whisked my untouched plate away and replaced it with another platter. This one was filled with various dried fruits rolled in honey and seeds. They smelled like happiness, but I knew from past experience that eating one of them would have me out of action for a week.

What I wouldn't give to try a curry. My adoptive brother, the prince Kalen, told me about how humans lined up for the chunks of slow-cooked meat drowning in greasy brown sauce. That sounded amazing, like the dogs bollocks, to quote a phrase the fairies had stolen from the witches.

But curry wasn't an option as long as I stayed in this realm. Fae didn't eat meat. They also couldn't deep fry anything. Bread was forbidden, as it symbolized the agriculture that had destroyed England's forests and wild places and led to our imprisonment. It was fruit and vegetables in berry sauces or slathered in honey, three times a day every day, and if you couldn't eat that, you got bruised apples that fell over the orchard wall from Briarwood and occasionally half-eaten pork pies the giant blond witch hurled into the meadow for a laugh.

Dammit. There I was, dreaming about real food and missing all the conversation. The Queen must've said something about the High Priestess, because Daigh was talking again.

"She is within our grasp. My spies overheard the witches' lawyer gossiping in the village. Apparently the girl has decided to take up her place at Briarwood. She will arrive within the week. I think we should be ready for her, take her as soon as we see a chance. We know that she does not know what she is, and from what my spies have seen of her, she's a skeptic who will take some time to be convinced. If we act before she fully realizes her powers—"

The Queen laughed, a tinkling sound like the flow of a river. "*We?* You keep using this pronoun as though we are somehow in this together. Unlike you, the Seelie are content to remain here in our realm, to make our revels amongst the ancient trees and pristine waters. We do not lust after an old world that has been tainted by the human race with their factories and combustion engines and computer chips."

"Are you certain of this? You have been Queen for half a century. Perhaps you should ask your subjects if they wish to roam over mountains and across glades, if they long to stretch their legs beyond the walls of our prison." Daigh gestured to the row of sprites and brownies lining the wall behind the Queen. Faint whispers rose up as they twittered among themselves.

"I do not have to ask them," Queen Morgana simpered, but her eyes flashed with anger. Abruptly, the twittering behind her ceased. "I am the Summer Queen. I speak for the Seelie Court."

I folded one hand across my lap, watching my father's face. He looked as relaxed as ever, but I caught the slight glint in his crystalline eyes. He was planning something, and the Queen was playing right into his hands.

"As you say," Daigh sipped his drink again as if he had no real interest in the suggestion. "I merely point out that now the Briarwood coven are at their weakest. If we combine our forces, we will be able to overpower the spell that keeps us here. My fae have consulted the auguries. We believe this is our time, our chance. And with the girl arriving—"

"I tire of this conversation." The Queen waved her hand dismissively. She picked up one of the honey-coated fruits and slid it into her mouth, her tongue flicking around her green-tinged lips. "Your idea is foolish, and I cannot see you giving up the throne of the Unseelie Court for a human girl, especially not an *American*—"

Daigh smiled. The Queen didn't catch the menace in that smile, but I did. As the Queen reached for another fruit, he flicked out his wrist. His bone knife soared across the table, burying itself in the Seelie Queen's neck.

Her mouth hung open in shock. She grabbed for the knife, but it was too late. The blade exited between her shoulder blades, burying its tip into the back of her wooden chair and pinning her upright. Her hands groped uselessly at the air and a gurgling sound came from her ruined throat. Blood bubbled from her mouth, streaming down the front of her gossamer gown.

Her attendees gasped. Several sprites darted forward, their tiny hands grabbing at the knife handle, trying to wrench it free. One of our soldiers kicked them away.

"You are correct," Daigh grinned, as the life drained from the Queen's eyes. "The witch will not be taking over my throne. She will be taking *yours*."

He rose and, with the elegant strides so ubiquitous of the fae, approached her chair. Sprites and brownies leapt out of his way as he leaned over the table and yanked the knife from her chest. An arc of blood splattered across the table, drenching the food.

The Queen slumped forward, her face smashing into the plate in front of her. Sticky fruit and pale green blood splattered across the tablecloth.

Daigh wiped the blade of his knife with the edge of the tablecloth, and slid it back into his belt. "Send word across our realm," he addressed the courts. "Tell all that the Seelie and Unseelie Courts are now united as one. There is to be no more fighting amongst ourselves. We are unified by a common goal – to reclaim our ancestral lands and rid them of the human scourge, once and for all."

The Court broke out into rapturous applause – some of it genuine, some of it tinged with fear. Seelie sprites leapt into the air, dancing around their dead Queen's corpse, lifting her wildflower crown from her head and placing it atop Daigh's thorny circlet. The boggarts and warriors of the Unseelie Court rapped their claws against their weapons and cheered.

I cheered loudest of all. But not for the reason Dear Father believed – I had no interest in returning the fae to the human realm. I had my own plot involving the indomitable Maeve Moore, and the first part of it had just fallen perfectly into place.

6

MAEVE

What the hell am I doing here?

The question bounced around inside my head as the taxi bumped along a narrow road edged on both sides by towering bushes bursting with bright white flowers in bulbous clusters. The taxi driver chattered on about the bushes – he called them *hydrangeas,* which I knew I'd forget tomorrow because I hardly knew anything about plants – explaining how the flowers bloom green but soon burst into white before fading to green again and dropping their leaves all over the road like an end-of-summer snowfall. "They're a devil of a thing to wash off your car," he said.

I nodded, staring out the window as we clattered past. In the warm sunlight that was so unlike the harsh heat of Arizona, the hydrangea bushes looked pretty alien to me, like everything in this place – fences made of neatly-clipped gorse tangled together into thorny lines, rolling hills that looked like something from the front of a chocolate box, and houses and walls made of beautiful shaped stones or Tudor wattle-and-daub.

I'm in England. Why the hell am I in England? Nerves

41

swirled in my stomach. When I bought the plane ticket and packed my clothes and books, I'd been high on Kelly's enthusiasm and too distracted by my absence of grief for the Crawfords to really think about what I was doing. Now that I touched down in Heathrow and had several conversations with people who talked like Harry Potter characters and was heading out to my very own castle, the full weight of the decision pressed down on me.

I'd really come to a foreign country to live in a castle with four strangers all by myself. If nothing, this little excursion proved to me that Kelly was right – I really hadn't taken enough risks in my life, because this one was freaking me the hell out.

Here we are, luv." The driver turned down a wide driveway flanked by tall oak trees. I pressed my nose to the window to admire the carefully sculpted gardens and espaliered fruit trees spread along a crenulated garden wall. We passed under a stone gatehouse with a sign bearing that English Heritage logo along with some opening hours and a ticket booth. I gathered from the website that we have visitors to one wing of the castle, which helped pay for its upkeep. Thankfully, the castle wasn't open on Mondays, so at least I when I met my tenants for the first time there was no risk we'd get poleaxed by a selfie stick.

The driveway wound on and on through a forested area and then rolling green hills where tiny sheep munched on lush grass. I expected them to be fluffy like cumulus clouds, but they were all scraggly and skinny and covered with tufts of wool.

The driver explained that they were Wiltshire sheep, and their wool fell off during the summer to help keep them cool. "The farmers love them because they're self-shearing." This taxi driver was such a fount of knowledge, I wished I could keep him.

We rose over the crest of a hill, and I got my first glimpse of Briarwood House. *And what a house it is!*

We drove under another stone gatehouse, inside the outer stone wall. The central keep rose like a column from the top of the hill, flanked on two sides by battlements and turrets. I had read on the website that it was an original Norman keep, with the outer walls and Tudor addition added later when the castle became a residence instead of a fortress. Arrow slits and tiny windows wound around the turrets, and crenulations circled the roof of the tower. Victorian mock-Tudor additions jutted out from the entrance, providing a glass conservatory and a small annex and garage. I could see a solar panel array attached to one of the roofs.

Wow.

A castle. *My* castle.

"Right, luv, that will be a hundred and eighty-four quid." The driver pulled up in a small parking area around a dirty fountain. I fumbled in my wallet for the money, counting out the strange notes I'd extracted from a machine at the airport. Was a quid the same as a pound? Was a hundred and eighty-four pounds a lot? I was usually good at math, but I couldn't get my head around the exchange rates. It didn't help that my mind felt like cotton candy after twenty hours on the plane. I'd managed to get a little sleep, but another nightmare about the Ferris wheel woke me and I couldn't keep my eyes shut after that.

I slid out of the car, in awe of the way the huge stone walls loomed over me, pressing me down into the earth. Now I was outside the car, the vibrant colors and scents of the garden assailed me. How was it possible for the air to smell so sweet and green?

Two huge wooden doors on ornate metal hinges greeted me. The driver helped me lift my bag from the trunk and carried it to the door for me. My stomach twisted as I lifted the ancient knocker from its cradle and allowed it to clatter back into place.

Maybe no one will be home. Maybe I won't have to deal with meeting four new people right now—

The door swung open, and I nearly toppled back down the cobbles.

Standing in the threshold was Mr. British – the guy from the county fair. The same guy who had grabbed me and pulled me back from the flames that consumed my parents.

7

MAEVE

"Hello Maeve," he said. "It's a pleasure to meet you."

I opened my mouth to speak, but no sound came out. *No way. No way could he be here. This is insane.*

But it was him all right, looking just as gorgeous as ever in dark jeans, a sleeveless grey hoodie, and his dark hair swept to one side, a few strands flopping over his huge eyes in this totally adorable way. The same tattoos curled up both his arms – in the grey-hued daylight I could see pictures amongst the knotwork – intricate black and grey images of gods and demons battling with short swords and round shields. Around his wrists were lines of what might have been text written in a strange code of long and short sticks. It looked familiar, but my jet-lagged brain couldn't think where I'd seen it before.

Mr. British laughed easily, running a hand through his thick hair. "Don't worry, I get that you're shocked. I'm a bit miffed at the situation, myself. Especially after what happened the first time we met. But trust me, there's nothing nefarious going on. It's just a weird coincidence. Please, come in. Welcome to Briarwood House."

I didn't budge, but I did manage to push out some words. "You… you don't seem surprised to see me?"

Mr. British smiled. "Emily – she's our lawyer – showed me a picture of you, and I realized you must be either the girl from the fair or her long-lost twin sister. I was going to tell you in my last email, but I was worried you might not come if you thought I was stalking you or something. My name's Corbin, by the way. Corbin Harris. I'm one of the tenants. Please, let me take your rucksack. Did you pay the driver?"

"Oh, yeah." I gave the driver a wave as he handed over my bag. "Thank you."

"Anytime, luv." He tipped his hat. Taxi drivers in England were much more polite than back home. I hoped he could afford to buy himself something nice with his hundred-and-eighty-four pounds.

I followed Corbin through the enormous doors, which led under a deep arch into a large internal courtyard. My sneakers slipped against uneven cobbles as we twisted our way through an assortment of outdoor tables and signs directing tourists to a gift shop. I stared up at the sheer stone walls surrounding us on all four sides. A covered walkway around the second story gave access to those rooms, and I could just make out the tops of two towers in the far corners.

Whoa. I *own* this. My mother used to *live* here. It was too crazy to be real.

Across the courtyard, Corbin opened a smaller wooden door with intricate swirling hinges on the wall of the inner Norman keep, and led me into a small antechamber screened with wooden walls where I removed my shoes and lined them up alongside several pairs of scuffed boots and sneakers.

Corbin picked up my suitcase and I followed him into an enormous square entrance hall. A stone staircase swooped up from just in front of the door, flanked by a stunning carved balustrade. My socks scuffed across more uneven flagstones. Every single spare surface of wall was covered with gilded portraits, animal heads, or swords and shields. Corbin pointed up at the ceiling. I expected to see an ornate chandelier, but instead there was a large hole, revealing a glimpse at the painted ceiling of the walkway above.

"See that?" Corbin grinned. "That's an original feature of the Norman keep. If the enemy managed to breach this inner door, the defenders could pour boiling water or pitch down on them."

I shuddered. That was kind of grisly. "Don't tell me this whole castle is riddled with Norman booby traps."

"Not too many. We don't exactly get marauding Vikings attacking these days," he said. "Unless you count Arthur."

"Who?"

Corbin grinned. "You'll understand when you meet him in a second. The castle has been a defensive structure much longer than it's been a residence, so I like that these feature help us to remember its history—" his face broke into this sheepish smile that made my heart skip a beat. "Sorry if I'm boring you. I've lived here my whole life, and I'm really interested in the history of Briarwood House. I help with the tours, which is how we keep the place running without selling ourselves on the streets."

"And you're also a medical miracle worker." I held out my arm so Corbin could see how smooth the skin was. "My sister said you knew just what to do, and I don't have any burns or scars."

"Not a doctor, but I'm good at looking after people."

That didn't seem like a good enough answer, but I decided to leave it for now. "Your parents knew my mother," I said.

Corbin nodded. "You must have so many questions, and I promise to answer them all for you. But you've got to get inside the door first! Come on, the others are chuffed to meet you."

He led me through an arched doorway at the side of the entrance hall, down a short passage of more screens lit with glowing wrought-iron sconces. We emerged into an enormous room. Ceiling beams crisscrossed above my head, hiding a roof gable that was so high I couldn't even see it. The walls were covered with a lime wash that had faded in places, revealing patches of bare stone beneath. Tapestries depicting battles and naked dancing sprites hung from every corner, and more swords hung from the walls and beams, and were even slotted through the wrought-iron chandeliers.

A fireplace that was taller than I was stood at one end, with overstuffed couches and beanbag chairs arranged around it. Above the fireplace was an impressive TV screen, with several gaming consoles and controllers strewn across the mat in a tangle of cords.

My eyes were so busy drinking in the splendor of the room that I didn't even notice the three figures lounging on the couches and talking in low voices until Corbin yelled out, "Look who's here!"

Three faces whipped around, and my eyes darted between them, not sure where to look first. There was so *much* to take in.

First of all, like Corbin, they were all fucking *gorgeous*. I'm talking male model, bodybuilding champion, romance novel cover levels of hotness, and that was with their clothes on.

One hot tenant in my castle was good luck, but four of them? My stomach fluttered. It was like some crazy hedonistic fairy tale. What the hell had I got myself into?

For another thing, they were all grinning at me with beautiful, genuine smiles. They didn't look as though they thought I was some naive girl from the sticks who they could corrupt. Instead, my first impression was of friendliness and… perhaps something more. Or maybe that was just my own heart fluttering in my chest.

Empathy and kindness lurked in their eyes, and I got the sense that they knew what had happened to me back in the States. The press had been all over it, so anyone who searched my name would've been able to stream mobile phone footage of the accident. Somehow, just occupying the same space as them made my breath come a little easier.

A weight I didn't even realize I'd been holding slipped from my shoulders, and the tiniest amount of pressure was released from my chest. I took a step toward them, and for the first time since the fair and all the tragedy that followed, a smile tugged at the corners of my mouth. I felt… *something*.

Maybe this whole living in a castle with four hot strangers thing would b*e exact*ly what I needed.

"Hi," I gave one of those awkward half-shrug, half-wave things when you meet new people and don't know if you should shake their hand or if that makes them think you're an accountant. "I'm Maeve."

"Flynn O'Hagan, at your service," the first guy said with a thick Irish accent as he grabbed my hand, swept into a deep bow, and placed his full lips right against my knuckles. Thick red curls fell over his eyes as he looked up at me. "Tis a pleasure to make your acquaintance at last, Maeve Moore."

Where his lips pressed against my skin, fire whizzed straight down my arm and flared right in my core. I'd never had a guy greet me quite like that before, especially one who looked like Flynn. Sunlight streaming through the high gothic windows caught Flynn's vibrant red hair, making it glow like a golden halo around his head. But unlike an angel, the glint in his blue eyes was pure devil.

And there was something else about those mischievous eyes, those cheekbones like razors. They felt familiar to me, as though I'd seen them somewhere before. On a movie poster perhaps. Flynn was hot enough to be an actor. But somehow I didn't think that was it.

My mouth moved, but I couldn't think of any words. What do you say to a hot Irishman kissing your hand?

"It's nice to meet you, too." I finally managed to choke out. Flynn stood up, but he didn't drop my hand. Instead, he yanked me around the end of the sofa and pulled me down beside him.

"Come pull up a pew and tell us all about yourself. Your accent is *outrageous.* You sound like someone from the telly."

"What's a telly?" I asked, and Flynn burst out laughing – a deep, belly laugh that coursed through his whole body, causing his leg to vibrate.

"A television, luv," Corbin explained. "Flynn, the girl's been in the country less than four hours. You can't expect her to have re-learned her entire vocabulary in that time."

"Yes, I can!" Flynn slid his foot across the table and knocked off a stack of books. "Arthur, where's the booze, mate? We're celebrating Miss Maeve's arrival. This calls for a round."

"All right, all right, hold your horses," snapped the largest of the four guys, who I'd deduced must be Arthur. He wiped a long strand of dirty-blond hair out of his eye, and gave me a wink. His eyes were blue, too – a cold, ice blue to Flynn's deep ocean shade. I was too busy admiring him to respond.

Arthur's blond mane spilled over his shoulders, flowing down his back nearly to his butt. It too shone in the sunlight, rippling like a shampoo commercial as he moved. I longed to run my hands through it. Andrew from Astronomy Club had the same dull buzzed haircut as all the guys in Arizona. The same haircut you got when you joined the armed services, which was not a coincidence in my town.

But back to Arthur, because no way should I even be

thinking about Andrew when I was looking at him. *Wow*. He had this strong, staunch face that said he took no shit from anyone, but his eyes shone with this beautiful kindness that made me want to fall into them and get lost forever. The strength in his features was accentuated by a dark beard, not trimmed like a hipster, but wild and free. An ornate earring dangled from his left earlobe, and I caught the edge of tattoos peeking over his collar and wrists. I saw what Corbin meant by his marauding Viking comment, although to me Arthur looked a bit like a blond Aragorn from Lord of the Rings. A seriously hot Aragorn.

Right now, Arthur was standing behind a large oak bar in the corner of the room, fiddling with some epic glass bottles. He held up a bottle and nodded at me. "Mead?"

"What's mead?"

"It's wine made with honey," Arthur explained. "It's an ancient drink that used to be shared among warriors while they drank in their halls."

Fuck, he really *is* Aragorn.

"Arthur brews it himself," Corbin said, indicating that he'd also like a glass.

"You brew your own alcohol? Does it strip paint off houses?" The football team quarterback brewed moonshine in his dad's barn, and it was shared around at high school parties. I'd never imbibed paint stripper, but I imagined they shared a similar taste.

"It's really sweet. I think you'll like it." Flynn said. "Not for me, though. I'll have a dram of that famed Tullamore Dew whiskey, cheers mate."

"I'll get some tea." The fourth guy – dark-skinned and beautiful, with dreadlocks spilling down his back – got up and scurried from the room.

"Rowan's a mite shy." Flynn settled in the couch, accepting a glass filled with amber liquid from Arthur. "We keep telling him that girls don't bite, but he always makes a holy show of himself."

"Don't be cruel." Corbin helped Arthur with the goblets. "You know Rowan can't help the way he is."

"Who's being cruel? Rowan made eccles cakes this morning. He's a good mate, unlike the rest of you gobshites."

"This is so cool." I took the goblet Arthur offered me and sniffed the pale liquid. It smelled rich and syrupy. "I'm fascinated by fermentation. I used to make kombucha, but no one in my family would eat it because it was 'ethnic.' I tried to make ginger beer once, but it exploded all over the cupboard. I always wanted to try alcohol, but my parents didn't want any alcohol in the house."

"I'll teach you if you like." Arthur raised his own earthenware goblet and clinked it against mine. "Corbin said you were into science, and home brewing is basically just delicious chemistry. We have our own hives on the property, so there is lots of honey."

I turned to Corbin. "How do you know I'm into science?"

Corbin looked uncomfortable. "I… well, I saw the chemistry kit on your desk and the space posters in your room, when I—"

"Right." I gulped. *When he helped carry me home after I nearly died in the same accident that killed my parents, and somehow managed to treat all my wounds and burns so they healed perfectly in just a few days.*

An awkward silence descended on the room. Corbin and Arthur exchanged a glance. I wanted to sink into the floor. *Great, way to bring the conversation to a grinding halt, Maeve.*

"Got the tea." The fourth guy was back. He mumbled his words into the floor as he sat down opposite me, balancing a delicate tray filled with a painted china teapot and tea cups.

"This is Rowan." Corbin nudged the fourth guy with his elbow.

"Hi," I said, watching him lift the pot and fill one of the cups, which he set on the table in front of him.

Rowan leaned forward, dreadlocks flopping over his face. He was dark skinned – black as night and twice as alluring, with a wide, toothy smile that set my stomach aflutter. His hand slid against mine, and when he spoke his soft voice was smooth as silk.

"Hey, Maeve, welcome to Briarwood. It's brilliant to have you here at last."

That *at last* was weird. After all, no one could predict that my parents would be killed and my childhood home taken away and my scholarship rescinded.

My parents are dead. I'm an orphan for the second time in my life.

The force of that realization hit me again, and I jerked away. Here I was, smiling and flirting with these guys in the home of the woman who'd birthed me but who I never met, and all the while on the other side of the earth, the Crawfords lay under six feet of dirt.

And I still couldn't cry. The horrible, consuming numbness clung to my body, and I struggled to breathe against the tightness in my chest. I dug my fingers into my palm, but even that pain felt remote – something that was happening to some other girl in some other place.

Rowan shifted, his gaze falling back to the floor. "I said something wrong. I'm sorry."

I shook my head, tearing my eyes away from him and staring at my palm. My nails had drawn a drop of blood. "No, it's… my parents only died two weeks ago, and I've left them five thousand miles behind me. It's still pretty raw."

"Then it's lucky for you that you're here with these fine lads." Flynn flopped down beside me, his arm slipping around my shoulder and pulling me against him. "We're here to do all the cheering up you need."

"Wait a sec…" I scanned Flynn's face, and suddenly, it came to me. He was a little older, more filled out, more rough-around-the-edges, but it *was* him. "I know where I've seen you before. You went to my…"

"High school," Flynn ran a hand through his wild red hair as he held out his hand. "A few weeks of senior year. You caught me, Inspector Morse."

"Inspector who?"

Corbin laughed. "It's a detective show on the telly, luv. You've got a lot of catching up to do."

"You were an exchange student," I went on, trying to remember the loud, obnoxious boy who'd disrupted my classes and who made my heart beat uncomfortably fast every time I passed him in the halls. "But you had a different name—"

"Same name my mammy gave me, but most of the kids called me Irish, or Red."

"I can't imagine why." I reached up and ruffled his red mop. "I remember you being an absolute terror. I was relieved when you went home."

I had been, in a way. It was much easier to focus on my grades and my MIT application without the hot exchange student distracting me.

"Aw shucks," Flynn grinned wide. "Mission accomplished."

"This is such a crazy coincidence." I took another sip of my mead and tried not to focus on just how close Flynn's leg was to mine. "That I've met two of you before – in Coopersville, of all places. It's not exactly a happening metropolis."

Flynn and Corbin exchanged a look. Flynn started to say something, but Corbin talked over top of him. "It's not as strange as you'd think. Both of us have family in Arizona, so we visit a lot. Flynn wanted to do a year overseas, and it seemed a logical place to go, but it turns out that he doesn't really have the attention space for school. But that's a story for another day. You must be pretty knackered from the jet-lag. Do you want to take a kip?"

I shook my head. Weirdly, as soon as I'd stepped into the house, the weariness of the journey lifted from my shoulders. "Research shows that the best way to combat jet lag is to sync with your destination's schedule as quickly as possible. I'll stay up as late as I can. What time is it now, anyway?"

Corbin checked his phone. "It's just on half twelve."

"I don't know what that means." I didn't know what half the things they said meant. *Knackered. Kip. Eccles cakes.* It was like they were all speaking another language.

"Eleven-thirty, luv."

Arthur gulped down the rest of his mead and slammed the earthenware goblet down on the table. "In that case, we'll give you the tour of your new home. As you would have seen when you came up the drive, the castle is pretty big. We only live in this one wing, around the original Norman keep. Most of the east wing – that's the late medieval and Tudor wing – is reserved for the English Heritage tours, and some of the third floor rooms are empty."

It sounded completely overwhelming. "Lead the way."

The guys all stood, downing their glasses. I raised mine to my lips and gulped back the sweet mead. Warmth spread through my stomach as the alcohol entered my system, and another tiny bit of pressure fell away from my chest. I followed the four guys out of the hall, admiring their asses as they jostled each other to be first through the next door. If nothing else, they were a great distraction – exactly what I needed to feel at least somewhat normal.

A shiver of anticipation shuddered through me. I couldn't wait to see the rest of the house.

8

CORBIN

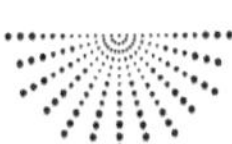

*T*he day we'd waited for had finally come: Maeve Moore was *home.*

Briarwood recognized her presence – the entire castle buzzed with energy, a charged atmosphere that was perfect for working magic. Or perhaps it was just all our pent-up tension unleashing itself. Being in the same room as Maeve lit my body up like a bloody Christmas tree, and I could tell from the way the others moved and talked that they were the same. Even Flynn's flamboyant personality was subdued today.

Maeve Moore; our queen, our goddess, our *priestess.* After everything the fae had done to try to destroy her, she was finally back where she belonged. With us.

Of course, she had no idea who she was or what she was capable of, but we'd get to that. For now, simply having her here was enough to enhance Briarwood's protections.

We exited the Great Hall and crowded into the narrow passage leading down to the old servant's quarters and kitchens. Flynn grabbed Maeve's arm and dragged her toward his workshop, which was outside in one of the Tudor barns. I was happy for him to lead the tour for now, mostly because I didn't want Maeve to see the tent in my jeans.

When I'd seen Maeve at the fairground in Arizona, that had been the first time I'd laid eyes on her since I'd gone to visit my dad on one of his surveillance missions when I was twelve. I had no idea what to expect, but I sure as fuck didn't count on the knock-out beauty standing her ground against Kalen. Every time she moved, her curves swayed like some kind of hypnotic dance. I couldn't take my eyes off her. It took a burning Ferris wheel toppling to the ground to break the spell between us and my protective instincts to kick in. As soon as I touched her to drag her to safety and felt her power leaping through her skin into my own, I was gone forever. I was hers.

But even if she chose me – which I felt certain she would – and our combined powers strengthened the coven, Maeve could never be mine. No matter how desperately my body demanded her. Not after what I'd done.

And now Maeve was here, at Briarwood. We all knew what that meant. Well, everyone except Maeve. But she'd figure it out soon enough, when her own hormones went into overdrive, and she discovered the power she possessed. Flynn and Arthur wanted to hit her with the news today, as soon as she walked in the door. They always did favor the baptism by fire approach. But I'd overruled them – until Maeve's initiation ceremony, until she chose one of us as her *magister*, I was still officially the leader – and Maeve would get a few days, maybe weeks, to discover things on her own.

I hated lying to her, but it was necessary. After all the years of listening to my parents talk about nothing but her, and of arranging her surveillance and listening to the guys tell me stories about her – I *knew* her. Maeve had a scientist's mind – she wanted logical explanations, well-constructed arguments, everything neatly ordered and organized. What we had to tell her was going to sound like a bunch of New Age bollocks, and if she didn't already feel her connection to the castle and to us when she found out the truth – if she wasn't already aware of what was at stake – she'd run as fast as her curvy legs would carry her back to Arizona, and we'd be completely fucked.

Stop thinking about it. I forced myself back to the present. *Just enjoy this time with Maeve while you still have it.*

We followed Flynn down a short path to the barn that had once served as the castle's stables when the castle had been a stately home. Maeve's eyes widened as she took in the high pitched roof and the piles of rubbish stacked in every corner. Flynn called it his Viking horde, but it was – as Maeve would say – trash. Coils of rusty wire, old stained-glass windows with smashed panels, bits of marble tile, old pieces of farm equipment, broken bits of car engines. In the center of the room, Flynn's latest project stood nearly as tall as the beams – a crouching dragon made from scrap metal and stained glass fragments. A single beam of sunlight reached into the room from a tiny, high window, hitting the dragon's stained-glass scales so that it glittered. Maeve walked all around the statue, her eyes wide with wonder.

Damn Flynn and his artistic talent. He always knew how to charm the ladies, and maybe Maeve would be no exception. Would the dragon win her from me? In that moment, it certainly looked possible.

Flynn darted around, his arms flying everywhere as he spun Maeve in circles and pointed out his various projects. Flynn's art brought in a decent amount of income – he could sell a couple a large piece like the dragon and make enough to pay his bills for the year, but he got distracted easily and abandoned projects unfinished.

"What's this?" Maeve asked, pointing to the stepped fountain in the corner of the room. Flynn had fused together three giant cauldrons we'd found in one of the outbuildings and a stone and iron frame to create a series of cascading pools.

"Prepare to be astounded." Flynn reached around and flipped a switch. Maeve squealed with delight as water trickled into the first cauldron, which overflowed into the second, the pressure of the water causing a tiny iron windmill to spin lazily as the water cascaded down into the third cauldron.

"I like to have water flowing when I work," Flynn said. "It drowns out the voices in my head."

Arthur glanced at me and rolled his eyes. I resisted the urge to roll mine back. *Typical Flynn, hogging the spotlight. Time to get Maeve out of here. We agreed – we all get a fair chance.*

We entered the kitchen next, Rowan's domain. Arthur and I hung by the door, giving him this small window to shine. Even Flynn stepped back a bit and kept his stupid comments to a minimum. Rowan squared his shoulders. I could see him mentally counting the spice jars on the shelf as he took Maeve by the arm. None of us – not even Rowan – expected Maeve to pick him, with his strange tics and quietness and obsessions. But he deserved a chance, the same as the rest of us.

Rowan showed Maeve around the space, pointing out the spice racks and explaining his stupidly complicated fridge-stacking system. Maeve listened attentively, and she didn't laugh or poke fun of any of Rowan's OCD tendencies. The tension slipped from his shoulders. She was affecting even him.

"What are you making here?" Maeve peered into the baskets of produce and empty preserving jars on the island.

Rowan's face reddened and his shoulders hunched back up again. I winced. That didn't last long. Maeve looked at

Rowan's face as his jaw locked. He stared at his feet and twirled the end of a dreadlock around his finger.

"Rowan, is something wrong?" Maeve's voice tightened with concern. She reached out a hand to him, but he stepped back, leaving her arm hanging in the air. The awkward tension in the air ratcheted up a notch.

Time to save this situation. I stepped forward and grabbed Maeve's arm, doing my best to ignore the tingle of energy that shot through me when our skin touched. I'd have to get used to ignoring it. I dragged her across the room.

"This is really cool," I said, opening a door at the back of the kitchen to reveal a narrow staircase. "This was installed when the castle was a grand stately home so the servants could rush meals up to the bedrooms without being seen in the main part of the house. It comes up near the staircase that goes up to your bedroom, so it's a good shortcut down to the kitchen if you fancy a nightcap."

"Duly noted." Maeve sashayed across the room and peered up the narrow staircase. "Are the bedrooms upstairs? Can I see?"

At the word *bedroom* passing through her red, pursed lips, my cock tightened in protest. *Don't think about it.* But that was like telling Obelix – the pudgy castle cat – not to think about all the delicious birds sitting in the tree outside the window.

"Sure." I gestured to the staircase. "After you."

Maeve started up the narrow steps, her gorgeous arse hovering inches from my face. I made to follow her, but something heavy slammed into my side, knocking me against the wall. I cursed as my elbow scraped against the rough stone of the wall.

"Sorry mate," Flynn flashed me his devil's grin as he leapt past me and followed Maeve up the stairs. "I didn't see you there."

"I believe you," I mumbled as I followed them up. "Millions wouldn't."

At the top of the stairs, Maeve pressed her hands against the wood panel. "How do you get this open?"

Flynn tried to reach around her to unlock the clasp at the top of the door, but this time, I beat him to it. As I reached around Maeve, she turned slightly to press her back against the wall and her breasts brushed against my shirt, setting off a fire beneath my skin.

Her lips formed an O of surprise, and I couldn't help but mentally fill in that O with the shaft of my cock. I blinked, trying to stop thinking about her like that, trying to remember that it was the magic making me into this *animal*.

The air between us thinned, and an invisible force drew my body forward, my arm brushing hers. A few inches more, and my lips would be pressed against hers—

No. You can't do this. You can't encourage her to choose you.

"Well, isn't this intimate?" Flynn shimmied his way through the gap so that he had his back against the opposite wall, his hands falling against Maeve's hips. If he wanted, he could slide her back so her arse rubbed against his cock, and even though that was totally cheating, I wouldn't even blame him. I was cheating just as bad – my face in hers, my eyes begging for her touch. All I'd have to do was lean forward, press my lips to hers, and it would all be over…

But that's not fair. You all agreed, and it was your idea. She'll choose you in the end – it's the only logical choice to make, and Maeve rules her life with logic.

Maeve's lips parted a little, her breath hitching. The energy pulsing from her body warmed the air around us. It was as though a magnet extended between all three of us, pulling us together. Right now, she had no idea who she wanted more.

The other two guys clambered up the stairs behind us.

Maeve glanced away, and the spell broke enough that I could gain control of myself and pull back. Flynn did the same, and he shot me a look over Maeve's shoulder, a look that said, "how the fuck are we going to last around this bird without doing something unchivalrous?"

Maeve didn't look upset. In fact, her heavy-lidded eyes and ragged breath as her eyes flitted from mine to Flynn's to Arthur's and Rowan's suggested she was pretty into the idea of one of us. Or all of us, who knows?

Stop bloody thinking about it. My fingers brushed against the catch, and I let it off. The door swung out, and all five of us tumbled into the hall in a mess of limbs.

"Here, I'll help you up." Arthur managed to untangle himself first, and grabbed Maeve's hand. Flynn reached for her other hand, but she was already using her hand to leverage herself off the floor. Flynn swiped it out from under her, sending them both rolling across the hallway.

"You guys are nuts." Maeve stood up and dusted herself up. "I'm not an invalid. I can get up by myself."

"Point taken," Flynn mumbled, picking himself up from the floor. There was an imprint of the carpet across his cheek.

"I mean, the way you're acting, it's as if I'm some damsel in distress…" Maeve's words trailed off as she caught sight of the large portrait at the end of the hall. She stepped toward it, her eyes wide.

A shaft of sunlight fell across the frame from one of the small skylights above the hallway, illuminating the figure who appeared to smile down at Maeve from her spot on the wall. It was impossible to miss the family resemblance. The woman in the portrait had Maeve's enormous eyes – although where Maeve's were hazel, hers were an icy blue – and the same bow-shaped lips, lightly colored with red so they stood out from her pale skin like a droplet of blood. Her long brown hair fell in luscious waves down her back, and her hips and breasts swelled from her old-fashioned gown, revealing that hourglass shape that oozed sexiness.

She sat on a chair in the library, a few books stacked on the table beside her. She kept her hands folded in her lap, and on her right index finger, she wore a ring embedded with a citrine crystal. Around her swan-like neck was a larger citrine amulet, and a third stone was set in the diadem that encircled her forehead. Her face was serene, content in her power, and the corners of her mouth turned up into an enigmatic smile.

Maeve reached up with her hands, touching the canvas right against the citrine ring. "Is this… my mother?"

I ran to her side. "Yes, that's Aline Moore. Have you never seen this portrait? The famous artist Robert Smithers painted it. He was a friend of hers, apparently. A smaller copy of it hangs in the National Gallery, but this is the better of the two."

"I just… wow." Maeve's eyes wandered all over the canvas, drinking in the details. "I knew she lived here, but I just never expected to see… wow."

"Do you need a minute? We can all bugger off downstairs—"

"No, I'm fine." Maeve placed her hand over her chest, swallowing hard. "I was wondering if—argh!"

She leapt back as a dark shape streaked across the side table beneath the image, sending a Wedgwood bowl spinning toward the edge. I flung out a hand and managed to save it before it crashed to the ground.

"Obelix!" I growled at the giant ball of black fur.

But Obelix wasn't listening, because he was a cat, and cats didn't listen to the help. He was too enchanted by our newest resident. He perched on the end of the table, stretching out a fat paw toward Maeve in greeting. She stared at the paw, her hand tapping her chest, which rose and fell as she tried to calm her heart rate. I could relate. That blasted cat had given me enough heart attacks to last a lifetime.

"You gave me a hell of a fright, cat," she admonished him.

"He wants to shake hands," Rowan said quietly.

Maeve snorted, but when Obelix didn't retract his hand, she reached out and touched his paw. 'This is ridiculous," she said, but her face burst into a wide smile as Obelix wiggled his paw up and down, his fat body erupting into a loud purr.

Okay, so maybe Rowan didn't have the confidence of Flynn and I, but his ability to teach large furry creatures ridiculously useless tricks might see him win over Maeve yet. If only he could teach Flynn not to be Irish.

"He's adorable," Maeve breathed, rubbing Obelix behind his ears. He collapsed against the table, his eyes rolling back in delight as he shoved his head against her hand to beg for more.

"He's a total pain in the arse," I growled. "But it looks like he has a new favorite human, so maybe he'll stop trying to hog my desk chair."

"Does he like to be picked up?" Maeve didn't wait for an answer, putting her hands under Obelix's shoulders and lifting him against her chest. The cat practically sighed in contentment as he nestled his fat head against her breast. All four of us clenched with jealousy, totally wishing we could be where that cat was right now.

Maeve had been in the house less than an hour, and this is what it had come to? I was officially jealous of a cat. I was starting to regret my decision to keep her in the dark about her power.

"Here are all the bedrooms," Flynn skipped down the hall, kicking open each door with his big, filthy boots. Usually, watching him track soot and sawdust over the immaculate rugs made my hair stand on end and Rowan break out into hives, but today it couldn't bother either of us – not with Maeve here.

Maeve peeked into each of the rooms, taking in mine and Arthur's heavy metal posters, Flynn's enormous Irish flag, and Rowan's immaculate white space in a single glance.

At the end of the hall, a second winding staircase led up into the tower. At the top was a small wooden landing with an arrow slit overlooking the inner courtyard below. Signs on the walls directed visitors to the gift shop and tour entrance. I turned the huge key in the lock and swung the wooden door open.

"This is your room."

Maeve's gasp sent a shiver through my body, right into my cock. I imagined that sound coming out of her mouth as I drove into her, my fingers digging into that gorgeous arse of hers as she bent over the bed I'd chosen especially for her—

"Fuck!"

I spun around in time to see a small ball of flame burst from Arthur's hand, licking the wooden door. He slammed his hand against the door frame, grimacing as he snuffed out the fire before it could catch. He caught my eye and nodded. Apparently, I wasn't the only one struggling to control myself around Maeve. At least Air couldn't burn the castle down.

Luckily, Maeve hadn't seen the flame or heard Arthur's curse. She stood in the middle of the tower room, mesmerized. *We nailed it.*

Ever since our solicitor informed us Maeve would be arriving, the four of us had scrambled to decorate the room for her – mostly led by Flynn, who had an artist's eye for these sorts of things. I had to admit that it looked pretty good. Tall banners hung from the ceiling, painted with Celtic knotwork and figures depicting some of the history of our coven. A dark-framed wooden four-poster bed stood in the center of the room, facing the largest mullioned window, and framed with diaphanous curtains. A second, smaller window was cut low into the wall – right near the floor, and we placed her desk in front of this, with one of the Louis XVI chairs from the other side of the castle angled so it looked out into the gardens below. There was no wardrobe, so Flynn and Arthur knocked up a set of shelves with a hanging rack and baskets and hid those behind an Edwardian privacy screen, also pilfered from the other half of the house. We'd even stuck up some old fashioned astronomical charts I'd found at a local antique shop, and a lamp beside her bed cast a galaxy of stars around the room with a single touch.

Flynn shrugged, as if the hours of work to get it finished were no big deal. "We hope you like it. If not, you're out of luck. It took me three days to paint those banners."

It didn't, actually. Flynn had drawn the designs and Arthur and I had filled them in while Flynn went to the pub. Not that I'm bitter, or anything. I rubbed my knee, which still ached from kneeling for hours with a tiny brush in my hand.

The look on Maeve's face made it all worth it. "All this… is mine?"

"Of course," I said. "You are the landlord. If you want to change any of it—"

"No!" Maeve blushed. "It's perfect. But… all this must've been so expensive. I can't… I don't…"

"Don't worry about it," Arthur said, his back resting against the charred patch on the door. "We all chipped in, and lots of the furnishings come from other areas of the castle, so it didn't really cost that much."

"Please don't feel like you owe us," Rowan added in his quiet voice. "We wanted to do something nice."

Maeve's face twisted, and for a moment I thought she might burst into tears. Instead, she grabbed Rowan, and embraced him. Rowan's body went stiff under her touch, but he softened just enough to pat her shoulder awkwardly. "Thank you, thank you so much."

"I'm bored," Flynn announced. Maeve let go of Rowan and he shot Flynn a grateful look, which was perhaps the first time anyone had ever been grateful to Flynn for anything.

"How can you possibly be bored in this place?" she asked him.

"You mean, how can I stand living under the same roof as my English oppressors?" Flynn wrapped an arm around Maeve's shoulder. "Well, I'll tell you, Maeve, me lass, it takes a fine Irish spirit and my body weight in Guinness just to see me through the day. Speaking of which, I think it's time we hit the pub."

"Flynn, it's *lunchtime*."

"The pub does lunch."

"Rowan was going to cook," I protested. I'd barely even got to show Maeve my library yet.

"The pub is fine," Rowan said quickly, his eyes darting to the door. I realized that he wasn't ready to cook for Maeve yet. Of course. I should have thought. Yet another way I've let Rowan down.

"I'm starving. And I've heard good things about these British pubs of yours." Maeve sniffed the air. "Hey, what's that burned smell?"

I leapt forward, but Flynn was faster, sliding in between Maeve, blocking her view so she couldn't see Arthur frantically trying to put out a fire on the corner of the banner. "That's the smell of these Protestant infidels after I beat them all at pool. Now, to the pub!"

I followed behind the others, my cock already aching with need. One thing was for certain, when Maeve Moore learned how to harness her power, Briarwood Castle was going to be shaking right down to its foundations.

9

MAEVE

I expected us to pile into some rickety English car and drive down to the village, but instead the guys set off on foot across the garden. Just outside the inner gate-house was a small, cobbled path that wound down through the trees. It came out on the edge of a field. I could just make out the village in the distance – a row of houses dotted across the edge of the hill.

I had no idea that England's landscape was *so irregular*. In Arizona, the plains stretched out in all directions, so the horizon was a constant companion – always impossible to reach but right there in your face. Here, rolling hills, quaint villages and ancient trees obscured it.

Corbin swung open a small wooden gate, darting his eyes both ways as he stepped into the field. "Do we own this field, too?" I asked.

He shook his head. "The estate next door – Raynard Hall – technically owns this field. In England, we have something called the 'right to roam' over open areas of land. It means that we're allowed to walk through here, even though we don't own it and it's not a public road."

Wow. In Arizona, if you walked on a farmer's land without permission, he'd probably shoot you. I checked over my shoulder for rifle-toting farmers as I followed Corbin into the field, a delicious shiver of the forbidden coursing through my veins.

We reached the village after a brisk twenty-minute walk that left me puffing. I expected exhaustion to grab me from all the traveling and jet lag, but instead, my body buzzed with nervous energy. The village looked just like the kind of quaint place you saw on English TV programs. Thatched-roof houses lined one long, narrow street, each one hung with handwritten signs declaring their purpose. There was a post office, a tearoom, and a couple of crystal shops. At the other end of the main street (or, as Corbin called it, the high street) were more modern shops with awnings, and something called Tesco that look like it might be a grocery store.

Down a narrow cobblestoned alley was the *Tir Na Nog* pub. I'd never been inside a pub or bar before, and as first experiences went, this one was awesome. Corbin, Flynn, and Arthur had to duck under the low beams that crossed the roof as they descended toward the bar. Dim booths were lit by candles on the tables and wrought-iron lanterns on the walls.

The boys lined up at the bar. Flynn pushed me in front of him. My eyes widened at the long line of bottles and the enormous taps jutting from the rustic wooden bar in front of me. There didn't seem to be any kind of menu. How did anyone ever choose what they wanted?

"Fancy a pint, lads?" A girl about my age with a thick Scottish accent leaned over the bar, her elbows pushing her tits together so her cleavage was practically in Flynn's face. He didn't look like he minded. She wore her fiery-red hair in two long braids, and her wide mouth turned up in a cheeky grin.

"Five pints of your famous ale, thanks Neale, and a couple of menus." Flynn leaned back and squeezed my arm. "We've got a friend with us today."

"Aye, I didn't know you had any of those, Flynn O'Hagan." Neale slammed five giant glasses with handles on the counter and started filling them from a tap.

"I don't even like beer—" I protested.

"This isn't your watery American piss, luv," Corbin said as Neale slid an enormous glass of amber liquid underneath my nose. "Wait until you try a *real* English ale."

Judging by the bitter smell wafting off the top of the glass, I wasn't going to be impressed. I dared a tentative sip, and nearly spat the mouthful back out again. How could people drink this?

Neale flirted with the guys as she poured the rest of their drinks, sharing old jokes and gossiping about people from the village. They clearly came here a lot. This bothered me more than it should. I was starting to feel pretty grumpy until the guys backed away from the bar to find a booth and she turned to me with a conspiratorial grin.

"Welcome to Jolly Old Blighty," she pointed at my pint. "How about I get you something a little more special?"

"Is it more beer?" I groaned.

"I dinnae ken why they ordered you that shite. You're clearly not a beer lass."

"Oh yeah?" I wasn't sure if she was insulting me.

"Aye. I can tell by looking at a person what their poison of choice is, even if they dinnae ken themselves." She pointed to the door as a couple walked in. "He's into the craft beer scam, so he'll order something expensive that tastes exactly like the five-pound pint of piss in front of you, and she'll have a white wine." She called over her shoulder to the couple. "What'll it be?"

"A white wine for the missus, and do you have any of that

Trappist IPA beer, you know, that one brewed by the local monks?" The guy stroked his hipster beard.

"Coming right up," Neale winked at me as she pulled out two glasses and fixed the drinks. "What did I tell you?"

"That's remarkable."

"It's my superpower. That's how I ken you're not going to have another sip of that beer. You want tae ken what your drink really is? I'll fix it for you."

"Sure, why not?"

Neale grinned wickedly as she placed a glass in front of me, poured a clear alcohol in, then topped it off with tonic water and a slice of lemon.

"You're a G&T girl. Go on, tell me I'm right."

G&T? I guessed the T was for tonic, but what was the G? Gin? I'd never had gin before. I picked up the glass and took a sip. It was delicious – refreshing and zesty, with a bit of a kick. No bitterness whatsoever.

"I'm a G&T girl, and I didn't even know it." I grinned back at her. "Thanks."

She waved a dismissive hand. "Aye, I'm a magician. I ken it. Go an' join your fellas and I'll bring over some scran for you all."

I had no idea what scran was, but if it was as good as this drink, I'd be first in line. I was starting to feel a lot better about this Neale. I slid into a seat at the end of the corner booth next to Arthur. The guys raised their glasses with a resounding "cheers," which was clearly something you said in England, and we clinked.

The booth was far enough away from other diners and drinkers we could hear each other talk. And talk we did. Corbin and Arthur regaled me with tales of the castle's history – famous knights and bloody battles and raunchy nobles. Flynn broke in with ridiculous remarks, every word out of his mouth making me burst out laughing, even as the others groaned. Rowan remained mostly silent, his kind eyes studying mine. I noticed that when he spoke up to insult Flynn, or recall a date that Corbin forgot, the others immediately ceased speaking to listen.

Neale dumped huge plates of meat pies (I know, WTF, right? But they were delicious), french fries (or "chips", according to the guys) and mushy peas (not so delicious – Corbin finished off mine). If this was English food, I could live with it.

According to Corbin, the Briarwood lord who added the Tudor wing was a royalist, and hid King Charles in a secret room in the library for a couple of months. "I'll show you the room later, if you like," he said, shooting me that heart-melting smile of his.

"I'd like that very much," I said.

By the time dessert came (Banoffee pie – another first for me, but *definitely* not the last), my nerves disappeared. It was impossible to feel like the frumpy science geek around these guys, with Flynn squeezing my hand and Arthur's thigh brushing against mine, and Corbin smiling and Rowan's soulful eyes never leaving mine. How the hell was I going to survive living with these guys without making a fool of myself?

The history lesson stopped around the Victorian period, and they completely avoided mentioning my mother or how they themselves ended up in the house. Instead, Arthur ordered another round (apparently, people in England bought one drink for everyone in turns) and we debated the merits of various films and TV shows. I hadn't seen a lot of the BBC shows, and anything with violence or premarital sex or magic or science fiction was banned from our house, but Flynn's dramatic reenactments more than made up for my lack of knowledge.

More rounds came, and more food. I had no idea how

long we stayed at the pub, but after awhile, I missed snatches of conversation as I faded in and out of sleep. The jet lag was catching up at last. After my head nodded against his shoulder, Corbin said, "I think it's time we got her home."

The guys stood up, and with a wave to Neale and a promise to return, I followed them out the door. Outside, I was surprised to see it was dusk already, and the cheery gingerbread houses were now shrouded in shadow. The temperature had dropped, and a crisp, balmy breeze kissed my skin. I rubbed my bare arms, wishing I'd thought to bring a sweater.

"Here," Arthur shrugged off his coat.

"No, that's okay. It's not far to walk—" But Arthur was already fitting the coat around my shoulders. It was a long black wool trench, the shoulders sticking out like a tent from my body, and my hands disappearing into the sleeves. I wrapped it around and breathed in Arthur's scent – smoky and sooty, like a bonfire. As he drew his hands away, I noticed dark scars crisscrossing his lower arms around his elbows. They ran around his arm. I wondered what had caused them, but it felt wrong to ask. Arthur noticed my gaze and yanked his arm back.

As we walked away from the shops and out along the country lane toward Briarwood, dusk darkened into night, and the sky opened up above us, the Milky Way splattered across our heads in vibrant steaks. It was completely different from Arizona, with new constellations visible and others obscured. I stopped in my tracks, craning my neck up for a better look.

Someone crashed into me, sending us both toppling into the grass. "Oops, sorry." I turned to help him up. It was Rowan. He accepted my hand, his warm skin sending a tingle up my arm. One of his dreadlocks flicked across my shoulder.

"What were you looking at?" he asked, flipping his dreads over his shoulder.

"Saturn," I replied, pointing out the orb of the biggest planet. "It's so clear tonight that we can see the stripes of her clouds with the naked eye. And there's Venus, and Mars. And there's Virgo – that's my star sign."

"You believe in astrology?"

I shook my head. "Absolutely not. Even if the alignment of the stars could somehow predict your personality, which is pretty damn unscientific, it wouldn't work because modern astrology doesn't take precession into account."

"Precession?"

"Yeah, it's the wobble of the earth's axis."

"The earth wobbles?"

"It does, actually. It's caused by the gravitational attraction of the moon on the equatorial bulge.

Because of it, the positions of the stars in the sky change incrementally every year. Thousands of years of incremental changes have moved the intersection point of the celestial equator and ecliptic – that's the path of the sun – by 36 degrees, which means that when a person is born during the recognized period of time for Aquarius, the sun wasn't *actually* in that constellation when they were born. It's more likely to be Pisces or Ophiuchus—"

"I've never heard of Ophiuchus before."

"It's actually the thirteenth star sign, although not many people use—" I didn't get a chance to explain because a man darted out of the shadows and blocked our path.

"Hello," he said, extending a hand out in front of him, palm facing us. His voice was obscured by a black hood, but it was deep and rich, almost singsong. A black coat – not unlike the one I was wearing – flapped around his tall, muscular frame. From the darkness of his hood, the moonlight flickered off two prisms of emerald light, eyes that reminded me of something, but I couldn't think what.

I didn't think to be scared. I assumed it was some other neighbor out for a walk, but Rowan's body stiffened, his soft face tightening. Tension rose in the air around us, but nothing like the sexual heat I'd felt in the secret kitchen passage with Corbin and Flynn.

Rowan was poised for a fight.

His hand tightened around my arm. "Get behind me," he whispered.

"Huh?"

I heard a shout up ahead as the other guys realized we had a visitor. The grass rustled as they ran back toward us. "Rowan, keep her safe!" Corbin yelled.

"What's going on?" A flicker of fear licked my throat. My eyes fixed on the man standing in the grass. He kept his hand held in front of him, curling a finger toward himself.

"Good evening, Maeve," the man said, his crystal eyes blazing. "If you come with me now, I won't harm your friends."

A lump of fear rose in my throat. "Who are you? How do you know my name?"

The man raised his hand and lifted off the hood. I gasped as I recognized that black hair tinged with gold and the pale, porcelain skin. The narrowed eyes of a predator met my gaze. It was the twat who'd harassed Kelly and I at the Coopersville fair, the one who had waved and smiled at me across the fairway as I'd watched my parents burn.

The force of that realization hit me so hard I physically jolted. I thought that guy had just been some random jerk, but the fact that he was *here*, jumping me in this field... this wasn't random.

He was stalking me.

But why? Who was I apart from a twice-orphaned science geek?

"What do you want from me?" I demanded, trying to keep my voice steady, free of the fear that hurtled through my veins. "Why are you following me?"

"Now, if I told you that, that would take all the fun away." The guy drew his hand across his face in a weird gesture that managed to appear threatening. "And I can tell you'd be a *lot* of fun, Maeve Moore."

"That's not my name," I lied, my heart thudding in my chest. *How does he know that?* "Just tell me what you want or let us pass."

"No can do, I'm afraid." The guy snapped his fingers. The grass behind him rustled, and two more men rose out of the long grass, as if they were emerging from within the earth itself. Both wore identical long black coats and equally sinister smiles.

How come none of us noticed them lying there before? My heart pounded, and I shrunk closer to Rowan. Which was kind of ridiculous. With his wiry frame and quiet nature, I'd probably be the one protecting him.

Let's pray it doesn't come to that.

Rowan's fingers looped in mine and he shoved something into my hand, wrapping my fingers around it. It felt like a twig. "Keep hold of that," he whispered. "Don't let it go, no matter what happens. Don't let him see it."

I nodded, keeping my eyes locked on the twat, who took a step toward me, his sinister grin growing wider.

I caught another flash of black in the grass. My heart hammered against my chest. Was that another one? But no. Arthur stalked toward us, his face set in a determined scowl. Corbin and Flynn were right behind him. The three assailants advanced toward Rowan and I, their hands raised, seemingly unperturbed by the other guys approaching them from behind.

Arthur crept forward, his eyes narrowed in concentration. He raised an arm behind his head. The moonlight glinted off a narrow blade.

Shit. As soon as I saw that blade, my whole body stiffened. None of our assailants had pulled out any weapons. They hadn't actually touched us at all. *Arthur can't really hurt that guy. He hasn't done anything—*

I screamed as Arthur lunged. I braced myself for the blade piercing the man's flesh, for blood and pain, but the guy whipped around and ducked the blow, moving impossibly fast – a black smudge against the inky night. Arthur swung his arm through, yelling something in a language I didn't recognize. The man's hand clamped down on Arthur's wrist, stopping Arthur's blow an inch from his face as if it were nothing. Arthur's face twisted in pain as the guy yanked his arm around, throwing him off balance and tossing the knife into the grass.

"Arthur!" I yelled, stepping forward to help him. Rowan's hand clamped around my wrist, pulling me back.

"Stay with me," he said. "You can't fight them."

"Can you take the heat, fire-wielder?" The man rasped, wrapping his arms around Arthur so that his forearm pressed against Arthur's throat. Arthur's face contorted, and he let out a strangled bellow. He grabbed the guy's arm and for a moment, a bright orange light flared, as though someone had struck a match, but then it was gone and Arthur's body went limp, his eyes rolling back in his head.

No. I'm not watching a guy die in front of me.

I jerked my arm from Rowan's and rushed forward. "Let go of him!"

"Maeve, no!" Rowan tried to grab for my hand again, but I shrugged him away. I reached the guy holding Arthur just as

Corbin leapt on his back. I reached in to help him pry the guy's arm from Arthur's neck. My fingers grazed the guy's skin and a sickening tingle shot up my arm, like a jolt of medicine that made me want to retch. Someone's hands wrapped around my waist and lifted me away.

"He's not worthy of you, Princess," that twat hissed in my ear, his breath hot and ugly on my skin.

"Put me down!" I yelled, kicking my legs back. The balls of my ankles smashed against the twat's shins, but he gave no sign that he even felt it.

"She's a feisty one," he sneered, throwing me to the ground. I threw out my hands, but my chest hit the earth first, driving the wind out of me. I gasped for air, my legs curling up against my stomach.

Rowan's face appeared in front of me, his eyes wide with worry. "Maeve, are you—"

But he didn't even get to finish his sentence. The twat moved in a blur, faster than my eye could follow. In a moment, he'd flung out an arm, catching Rowan across the chest. Rowan sailed through the air and landed with a thud in the grass some thirty feet away.

That... that's not possible.

I coughed, my lungs burning. I tried to push myself up with my legs, but they wouldn't cooperate. The twat grabbed me and yanked me to my feet, crushing my chest against his so his face was inches from mine. Up close, his perfect skin looked wrong, like the skin of an android stretched over a heartless machine beneath.

"Let go of me!" I tried to wrench myself out of his grasp, but his grip was like iron.

"Look at you," he rasped. "You're so *juicy*, full of all that human blood and ancient magic. I just want to eat you right up."

He stuck out his tongue, and ran it along my cheek, its

rough surface scratching my skin. *Gross gross gross.* I tried to jerk away, but my limbs wouldn't move. My whole body locked up, everything frozen in place.

What's happening to me? I tried to cry out, but my tongue wouldn't move, either.

"Delicious." With a final slurp, the twat drew away, a self-satisfied grin spreading over his face. His cruel eyes burned into mine. My skin tingled along his saliva trail.

"Don't you touch her," Rowan's face appeared beside me, his features hard. He placed a hand on my shoulder, and suddenly, I could move again. I kicked at the twat's legs, trying to trip him, but my blows only made him laugh.

"She is ours to touch as we please, *witch.*" The twat spat at Rowan, shoving him away. The twat raised his hand, pointing his palm at Rowan. As I watched in horror, his fingers elongated, the tips curling over into long claws, curled over like the talons of a bird.

But how... this can't be happening. I'm imagining it. It's the jet lag playing tricks with my mind.

It was no trick. The claws reached closer to Rowan's face, sharp points glinting in the moonlight. They were real all right, but how the hell did they get on the end of this guy's fingers?

The twat tilted his head to the side, and laughed cruelly. "Such pretty eyes you have, witch. I think I'll take them."

No. Fuck no. I pushed all of my fear into my arm. My skin grew hot, and there was this weird swelling in my chest, like I'd just started running up a hill and the oxygen was hitting my lungs. I expected him to catch my punch, but somehow, I slipped under him, and my fist connected with his jaw.

The punch was useless, barely grazing his skin. And yet as soon as it connected the twat's face contorted with pain. His whole body sagged and shuddered.

Okay, so maybe I just hit his Achilles' heel. Now was my

chance, without his claw-hands dangling an inch from Rowan's eyes. I kicked out a leg. The shot was too low to get him in the nuts as I'd intended, but I managed to slam my foot into the side of the twat's knee.

His face registered surprise for a moment, and then it twisted with pain as he dropped his hands to clasp his knee. Unfortunately, he seemed to have forgotten that he'd turned his hand into razor-sharp claws. What an idiot. He sliced open his trousers and made a real mess of his knee.

I backed away as the guy fell onto his good knee. Rowan knelt down as well, scooping up a handful of loose dirt from the edge of the trampled path. He pressed the dirt clot to the guy's head, and muttered something in a foreign language.

The twat moaned, his eyes rolling back in his head. "Nice try," he managed to croak out. "But your power won't hold me for long, earth witch."

"It doesn't have to," Rowan growled, his kind voice thick with venom. He kept his hand pressed against the twat's face. Underneath, the guy's skin turned brown and leathery, bits of it flaking off and blowing away in the breeze.

I don't know what made me do it, but I just *knew*. My chest tightened, and I glanced down at my hand that had punched the twat. Inside my fist was the tiny twig Rowan had given me. I knelt down and pressed my hand over top of Rowan's, holding the twig against the twat's face. He screamed, but he couldn't wriggle away.

I focused my mind on that twig and on the dirt clot in Rowan's hand, on the two touching – two parts of the earth coming together. Somehow – and I have no idea why this even *occurred* to me – I knew it was important that I thought about that twig and the dirt and nothing else.

Fear and energy and tingles of heat and light swirled through my body. Bile touched the back of my tongue. But I kept my focus.

The twat's face twisted and sagged. His eyes flashed with anger, and then they rolled back in his head. His body stiffened. He toppled backward, slamming against the ground. His head bounced. He didn't get up again.

I sucked in a breath. *What just happened?*

Rowan helped me to my feet.

"What did we do?" I cried.

"No time for that," Rowan dragged me toward the others. "Come on!"

I stumbled across the field after him, my breath ragged and my lungs screaming. Arthur, Corbin, and Flynn fought the other two guys – the five of them climbing over each other in a whirlwind of flailing limbs. I saw the flash of a white blade under the moonlight and Corbin cried out.

Corbin rolled out of the fray. One of the guys leapt on top of him, sending him sprawling to the ground. Corbin managed to roll over beneath the guy, and he hooked his hand under his shirt and pulled out some kind of necklace which he shoved in the guy's face.

He screamed as the metal necklace touched his skin, then lashed out at Corbin with the same clawed fingers. Corbin wrenched his head to the side as the guy raked his claws through thin air.

Rowan ran over and grabbed the guy around the neck, trying to pull him off Corbin. I stood frozen, unable to move. All I could do was watch the carnage around me.

Arthur and Flynn took down the other attacker. Arthur pinned the guy's arms while Flynn tore open something in his pocket and sprinkled it into his face. The guy screamed, thrashing wildly in Arthur's grip, his foot nearly clobbering Flynn in the face. And then, *poof!* He disappeared.

I squinted into the gathering dark. Yep, the guy was definitely no longer there at all. Flynn helped Arthur to his feet, and the blond giant hunched down to retrieve his knife from the long grass, the stalks bent and broken from the fight.

Meanwhile, Corbin was off the ground. He and the other guy circled each other like two boxers in a ring. The black-coated guy had a long, curved sword made of some kind of white material, almost like the rib bone of a large animal. The white blade shimmered with a pale blue light along one edge.

Corbin's eyes flicked to the other guys. "Arthur!" he yelled, raising his hand.

Arthur tossed his blade through the air. Corbin reached up and grabbed the handle of the knife just as the other guy swung the white sword at his arm.

I gasped. The entire world moved in slow motion, the blade inching closer to Corbin's raised arm, the moonlight gleaming off the sharpened edge. The blue light kissed Corbin's skin, but before it sank into his flesh Arthur slammed into the guy, knocking him sideways and plunging a second knife into his side.

"Arrrrrrgghhh!" the guy bellowed. Arthur leaned his full weight into his, twisting the knife into his flesh. Blood spread out from the wound, but in the dark it looked weird, kind of green. But that was probably just a trick of the light and the green meadow.

The guy's eyes rolled back in his head, and his body stiffened. But before his back had even hit the ground, he also disappeared, his body shimmering away into the air as if it had been made of dust.

I glanced behind me, to where we'd left the twat's body lying in the grass. He had gone, too, although the rustling of the grass behind suggested he might have picked himself up and run.

My head spun. All three of the black-coated attackers had

disappeared. They hadn't just been knocked out – they were completely *gone*.

"Nice one, Aragorn!" Flynn cheered, thrusting a fist into the air, an enormous grin on his face.

Arthur took a deep bow, pushing a knife back into his belt. "It's too bad I left my sword at home. I could have done some serious damage."

"What the hell is going on?" I demanded. "Why are guys jumping out of the grass to attack us? And how in God's name did they do that trick with the claws? And where the hell are they now?"

That was more blasphemy than I'd get away with in an entire *year* in the Crawford house. But right now, it seemed appropriate.

Corbin stood over the place where the last guy had lain and scuffed the earth with his boot. He clutched his shoulder, and I noticed his black t-shirt was torn where the blue-tinged white sword had touched him. Blood – definitely red – ran down his arm. "We need to get going. We don't know if any more might be coming."

As if on cue, the grass rustled behind us. Corbin whipped his head around, then pointed to the house. "Go, now!"

I started to run. Something slammed into me, sweeping me off my feet. I screamed, but a rough voice whispered in my ear. "Hold on." It was Arthur, my Aragorn. He tossed me over his shoulder like I was a sack of potatoes and raced across the field, passing Corbin and Flynn as they stumbled through the long grass.

The rustling behind us grew louder. My heart pounded in my ears. Something snarled, like an angry dog about to attack. "Shite!" Arthur poured on speed, tearing through the gate.

Corbin, Flynn and Rowan leapt through after him, and Rowan slammed the gate shut. The snarling grew louder, and the gate rattled as a dark shape pawed at it. Arthur raced up the path and into the trees before I could get a good look. Flynn puffed in front of me. As Rowan passed us heading up the flagstone steps beside the gatehouse, I noticed his hands were shaking.

The snarls and growls of the dog – it *had* to be a dog – grew faint as we plunged deeper into the estate. It wasn't following us up the hill. But it was big enough it could have just jumped the gate.

We crashed through the inner gatehouse, Corbin and Flynn pulling the heavy wooden doors shut and drawing the bolts. Arthur didn't set me down until we were back inside the Great Hall with the door firmly locked behind us. He dropped me on the couch and slumped down beside me, rubbing his throat, which was raw and red from where that guy had touched him. "There were three of them," he snarled at Corbin, who was digging around behind the bar, one hand still pressed against his shoulder. "How the *fuck* were there three of them?"

"They must be getting more powerful." Corbin drew out a large first aid kit from a bottom drawer and dumped it on the coffee table. He riffled through the contents with his free hand. "They know we are weak right now, and they've had years to plan how to take advantage of that. Maybe we... *fuck*." He winced as he tried to open a bottle of antiseptic with both hands.

"I'll do that," Rowan said quietly, uncapping the bottle and pouring out a little onto a cotton pad. As he rolled up Corbin's torn sleeve, I gasped. A red welt crossed his shoulder, laid on top of three long gashes that tore through his skin, leaving jagged rips that oozed blood. Bits of grass and dirt clung to the skin and his t-shirt. Corbin winced again as Rowan dabbed at the wounds.

"Those rawny bastards." Flynn slumped down in the sofa

opposite, his foot kicking Arthur's knife across the table. I noticed droplets of some green liquid on the blade. Weird, some kind of stain from the grass? "Still, that was exciting. Good thing I'd had that drink or I would've been completely useless."

"You're always completely useless," Arthur shot back. He grabbed a bottle of mead from the bar and filled four cups. "Admit it, you nearly pissed yourself when that pouka showed up—"

"Excuse me?" I held up a hand. "I'm still waiting for an explanation—"

"It's weird they sent Kalen again after he messed up so badly in Arizona," Corbin shook his head. "I don't understand any of this. Fuck, if we hadn't all been there tonight, this could've gone arse over tit."

Arthur flexed his bicep, the bulging muscles transfixing me for a moment. He took a long drink from his mead cup, wiping the edge of his beard with the back of his hand. "As long as you've got me, you'll be fine. It's been an age since we had a tussle with an Unseelie. And three of them in the same night, what a treat."

"Um, guys, what's an Unseelie—"

"You should have stuck that blade right in Kalen's heart," Flynn declared. "That guy is not going to leave us alone."

"We need to figure out how they're getting stronger," Corbin said. "We need to strike now, because if they get too powerful we won't be able to defeat them in our current state—"

"HEY!" I yelled. My voice bounced off the high ceiling, echoing along the vast room. The guys jumped. Arthur splashed mead all over his pants. Four faces turned to me in concern. "Could you maybe fill me in on what the *goddamn hell* just happened?"

I was swearing like a sailor tonight, but swear words were *invented* for nights like this.

The guys exchanged a glance, and then Corbin said slowly, as if he were choosing his words carefully. "What just happened is that we were attacked."

"Brilliant deduction, Sherlock. I *know* that. But what was I attacked by? Those guys were on drugs or something… but I've never heard of any drug that can turn your hands into claws…"

"Not drugs, Maeve." Corbin said, his eyes burning into mine. "I know this is going to be really hard for you to believe, but those guys weren't human. They are fae."

MAEVE

"Not human?" That doesn't make sense. "You mean they're some other species? But… there are no other primates in the world with that level of language ability. I mean, that was *astounding*. What genus and species are they? Why have I never heard of these *fae* in scientific journals? Are they localized in the UK or—" I stopped as I noticed Flynn grinning. "You're teasing me."

Flynn grinned harder. "Not pulling your leg, but I think our little scientist is confused."

"They don't *have* a genus and species, Maeve." Corbin explained. "No scientist can exactly get close enough to study them, for reasons which you discovered tonight. I wasn't kidding when I said they're fae."

"Fae? As in… fairies?"

"The very same."

I studied Corbin's face, waiting for him to crack up laughing, But his pouty lips remained pursed, completely devoid of mirth.

"But… that's just kids stories…" I glanced at Arthur, but

he was nodding sagely. "I stopped believing in fairies years ago… actually, I never believed in fairies…"

"Oh well, then," Flynn grinned at the guys. "You hear that, lads? We're totally safe. Maeve doesn't believe in fairies, so they're going to stop trying to tear our throats out now." He tipped the last of his mead down his throat and reached for my glass. I knocked his hand away. I had a feeling I'd need the alcohol.

"Unfortunately, belief doesn't factor into it one way or the other." Corbin said. "The fae are real, and if you're staying at Briarwood, they're going to be a very real part of your life."

That was such a cop-out answer, but something in the seriousness of his voice made me pause. I remembered that the twat… the fae – whoever he was – knew my name. And that he followed me here from Arizona. A shiver ran down my spine.

I folded my arms. "Okay, so let's say for argument's sake that I believe you about this fairy business. Which I don't, for the record. But let's just leave that aside for now. What do these fae want? Why did they attack us like that? Where did the dog come from? And why didn't they all follow us up the path to the castle?"

Flynn gestured at Corbin with a flourish. "Take it away, mate."

Corbin cleared his throat. "I'll try to answer all your questions, but there's some stuff we can't explain right now. They didn't follow us up to the castle because we've placed magic protections called wards around the boundary of our land. These wards have been in place for many centuries. The fae can't walk on this land, in the same way we can't pass over into their realm. But they want us. They want this castle. It's very important to them."

"I'm sorry, *magical* protections?"

"Yeah." Corbin blinked. "Arthur, Flynn, Rowan and I... we can sort of do magic."

Oh hell. In a small voice, I asked, "Like card tricks, pulling a bunny out of a hat, that sort of thing?"

I knew that wasn't what they meant, but part of me hoped...

"I mean we are witches. We're descended from the ancient bloodlines who used their powers to help the early Britons win the first wars against the fae and banish them to their realm."

I held up my hands. "Come on now. This is getting crazy. Fae, magic, witches... I know you Brits like to poke fun of the stupid Americans, ha ha ha. But if you thought I was going to believe this stuff, then you definitely—"

I gasped back my words as Arthur extended his hand in front of me, palm facing up. A flame burst from his fingers, the orange light casting a strange glow across his skin.

I peered under his hand. Nothing underneath. I grabbed his wrist and felt around his lower arm – there was no wire or ignition or anything hidden against his skin. My fingers brushed over the scars near his elbow, and he shuddered a little. I yelped as the flame leapt up, nearly touching the beam above our heads as a flare of heat crashed against my body.

"Arthur!" Corbin yelled.

"Sorry!" Arthur narrowed his eyes. The flame calmed down a little.

I sucked in a breath. "Okay, I give up. How are you doing that?"

"This is my power," Arthur said. "All witches can control one of the five elements. My element is fire. I can conjure fire at will, and manipulate it." He cupped his other hand, and passed the flame between them.

"Okay, well now I know this is ridiculous because there are only four elements."

"In science, maybe. But alchemists have recognized a fifth element for centuries – the element of spirit," Corbin explained. "But that's not so important now. What's important is that you believe what we're telling you about the fae and about our ability to protect you."

"I don't have to believe this." I folded my arms. "It's *insane*."

"If this isn't true, if we aren't what I say we are, then what other explanation could possibly explain what you saw tonight?" Corbin nodded at Arthur's hand. "Or what Arthur's doing right now?"

"Or this." Flynn held his own hand over Arthur's, his palm pointing down. A trickle of water ran between his fingers, quickly turning into a spout. With a sizzle, Arthur's flame went out.

"Flynn's element is water," Arthur explained. "Because he's such a wet blanket."

"You're hilarious, mate." Flynn shot back. "Maeve, don't let Arthur do the comedy set at my funeral."

"My element is air," Corbin explained. "And Rowan is earth."

Earth. I faced Rowan, remembering how he'd pressed that clump of soil into the twat's face, how he'd chanted something under his breath – a language I didn't recognize. How the guy had recoiled as though the dirt caused him great pain, and how I'd felt *something* as I'd pressed the twig in my hand against Rowan's…

My head throbbed. I rubbed my temples. So many questions, but one burned in the front of my head, one that was vitally important even though their story so far was completely ridiculous. "So, okay. Sure, you're witches. I thought witches were only old ladies with hooked noses or teen girls who dressed like goths, but whatever. That fae guy, why did he know my name? And if he comes from this fae realm, why was he in Arizona on the night my parents died?"

Flynn kicked Corbin's shin, and Corbin cleared his throat again. But before he could say anything, Arthur patted my knee and said. "His name is Kalen, and we've encountered him before. Unfortunately, although we killed his other friends tonight, he lives to hassle us another day. Kalen was in Arizona because he followed Corbin there on his visit."

My body sagged with relief. *He isn't stalking me. This is all just a big coincidence, and there's a logical explanation—*

But Arthur was still talking. "—because Corbin is the leader of our coven – that's the word for witches who work together in a collective—"

Okay, not such a relief.

"I watched *The Craft*. I know what a coven is." Any film or book featuring witches was sacrilegious in our house, so of course we loved them. Our parents went away on a ten day Bible retreat and Kelly and I had binge-watched every Satanic show and movie we could find on Netflix. We spent most of that film mocking the horrific 90s fashion.

"Well, Corbin was the one who found us all and brought us together." Arthur glanced at Rowan. "Some of us had no idea what we even were before we met Corbin. It's only with our coven working together here, with our power focused at Briarwood, that we're able to keep the fae in their realm."

"Fae used to live all over the British Isles," Corbin explained. "That is, until humans came across the seas with swords of iron. People cut down the forests, tilled the fields and built roads through the ancient sacred places. The fae fought the humans, and there were many bloody battles, but in the end the fae lost, and with the help of our ancestors the humans banished them to another realm. They used to escape into our world all the time and cause mischief or chaos, so in the thirteenth century a coven of powerful witches found a spell to seal the fae inside their realm forever. The witches took over this castle in order to guard the entrance to our world. We're all descendants of that coven—"

"Ah, the joys of inbreeding," I said.

Flynn burst out laughing, but Corbin continued as if he hadn't heard me. "—the fae have magic, too. That's how they get the claws. They can focus their magic, and sometimes they can send one fae through the entrance into our realm. But there hasn't been three fae at once for… hundreds of years. So something in the spell that blocks the entrance is faltering, and we need to figure out what."

"Corbin is the biggest, baddest witch of us all," Flynn said. "If the fae get to Corbin, they break us up, and then they might be able to free themselves and walk the earth once again."

"And that's definitely a bad thing?" I asked, cringing as I heard myself entertaining the ridiculous story as if it was something that was real. "It does sound like we humans kind of kicked them off their ancestral land. They have every right to be pissed."

"Except that if they come back into our realm, they're not exactly going to live in harmony with humans. They will raise the Slaugh."

"The Slaugh?"

"In folklore, it's called 'The Fairy Host,' but it's actually a swarm of restless dead – spirits of the most dark and evil people and fae who have been rejected from the heavens and the earth. They fly over the land like a dark swarm of birds, and they bring death and destruction in their wake. The last time the fae escaped and unleashed the Slaugh, we had the Black Death."

Flynn piped up. "Fairies are wankers."

"I studied the Black Death in school," I said. "It was an

assignment about biochemistry. The plague was caused by the *Yersinia pestis* bacteria, which hangs out in rodents and in the fleas that feed on them. It's not caused by some horde of cantankerous ghosts."

"If you say so." Flynn swiped Corbin's drink and gulped it down.

"So fae equals bad. I got that. But you guys know these fae," I remembered. "You called them by their names."

"We only know that guy who attacked you," Arthur said. "Kalen. He's a type of fae called a pouka – he shapeshifts into the giant black dog that chased us to the gate. He's also a prince of the Unseelie Court." Seeing my blank look, he added, "The world of the fae is divided into two courts, each one ruled by royal fae. The Seelie Court are kind of the good guys – they dress in green, and they sometimes help humans, if it suits them. The Unseelie Court are the baddies. They won't hesitate to maim or kill anyone who tries to get in their way. They're the ones who control the Slaugh."

"Although saying fairies are good or bad is a bit unfair," Flynn piped up. "Like I said, all fairies are wankers."

I smiled, but Flynn's strained expression made the smile fade as soon as it appeared. Flynn actually seemed *serious*.

"Iron and smelted metal is poison to the fae," Arthur continued. "That's why they have those white blades – they make them from bone. And that's why I learned to fight with a sword – it can do more damage to fae than bullets or fists."

"That's probably all Maeve needs to know tonight," Corbin said, cutting Arthur off mid-monologue. "She's got that incredulous look on her face that suggests she might stop believing us any second."

"I've haven't actually decided to believe any of this yet," I said. "Except the bit about Kalen and his buddies being dangerous. That part I get."

"We've got the protections in place, so you're safe as long

as you stay on the castle grounds. We can all go in a group if we have to go to the village, and Dora – she's our house-keeper – will bring us groceries and other supplies." Arthur touched my arm. "You've already been through enough. We won't let them hurt you."

I folded my arms. "That's not good enough. If these fae really are going to attack me, I want to learn to fight them off, just the way you guys did."

"That's not…" Arthur looked confused. "I mean, *why?*"

"Why? Because contrary to what our surroundings suggest," I jabbed a finger at the swords dangling from the iron chandelier, "this isn't the thirteenth century, and I don't expect a bunch of guys I just met to be my knights in shining armor. I'd rather learn things for myself."

Besides, this whole move was about doing something completely out of my comfort zone, and swinging a sword around definitely counts.

"I would hate for you to get hurt," Arthur said, rubbing his beard. "I'd feel like it was my fault."

"That's my choice to make. There's more chance of me getting hurt if I don't know how to defend myself, and that *will* be your fault. So you'll teach me to fight?"

"I will," Arthur said. "I have to lead a tour tomorrow morning, but we can start in the afternoon if you like."

"Good."

I settled back into the couch, and a wave of exhaustion rolled over me. The plane ride, meeting the guys and seeing that picture of my mother, the pub, the attack, this stupid story about the fae… it was a lot to happen in a single day. I rubbed my eyes.

"I think I need to go to bed," I said.

Corbin checked his phone. "Yes, of course. You must be utterly shagged."

"I'm guessing shagged means tired? You guys say the *weirdest* things."

"Shagged is a *great* word," Flynn grinned. "It has many meanings. I can enlighten you—"

"Perhaps another day," Corbin said. I barely heard him. It was taking all my energy just to keep my eyes open. Arthur leaned over and wrapped his thick arm around the back of my neck, the other one under my knees. He lifted me from the couch and started walking across the room.

"Come on, let's get you to bed," he whispered in my ear, his beard tickling my skin.

After all my talk about *not* being treated like a medieval princess, I knew I shouldn't let Arthur carry me to bed. But his arms felt so good around me and the ideal of dragging myself up the two steep flights of stairs to my bedroom tower made me want to get right back on the plane and go back to Arizona. Beautiful, flat Arizona. I snuggled in against Arthur, letting the scent of soot and fresh sweat and darkness wash over me.

"Goodnight, Einstein!" Flynn called out.

The other guys called goodnight to me, and I mumbled something back. My body bounced as Arthur ascended first the main staircase, then the narrow, winding stairs leading up the the tower. "Here you are, Princess. Home at last."

"Thank you," I mumbled, barely holding my eyes open.

Arthur planted me in the middle of the enormous bed. He tucked a strand of hair behind my ear. "Goodnight, Maeve. I hope you don't find a pea in the mattress. If you do, blame it on Flynn."

I smiled. "Goodnight, Aragorn."

Arthur hovered for a few moments, like he wanted to say something else, do something else. My heart fluttered a little, and the tightness in my chest tugged against a rising ache between my legs. I focused on Arthur's lips, suddenly transfixed by the curve of them, by the tiny line of bare skin just visible between the pink flesh and his wild viking beard.

What would it be like to kiss him? How would it feel to have Arthur's enormous hands on my body, his tight muscles against my skin? My heart beat faster at the thought of it. Somehow, I knew it would be a hundred times better than anything I'd done with Andrew.

Kiss him. Go on. Just lean over and kiss him.

An invisible force tugged me toward Arthur. The air between us crackled with heat. I wasn't tired any more. I was very, very awake, and very, very aware of Arthur's body only a foot from mine, his huge arms propping him up against the bed, his black metal t-shirt pulling against his broad shoulders.

Kiss him, Maeve.

This voice in my head was completely foreign. Maeve Crawford didn't go around kissing strange Viking boys she'd only just met. Maeve Crawford was the pastor's daughter, the science geek, the girl who never fit in in Coopersville.

But I wasn't in Coopersville anymore. I'd come halfway around the world to find myself. Here, I wasn't Maeve Crawford. I was Maeve Moore, broken girl, mourning girl, and maybe Maeve Moore was *exactly* the type of girl who made the first move, who kissed a hot Viking guy who made fire shoot from his fingers, just because she wanted to.

And damn, did I want to. Arthur's lips parted, just a fraction. His eyes betrayed his own desire.

"Maeve..." he whispered. My name had never sounded so sexy as it did in his deep, husky voice and British accent.

Heart pounding, I leaned forward, my hands on the bedspread, only inches from Arthur's forearms. I half-expected him to pull back, but instead, his whole body jerked as I brushed my lips against his.

A spark of fire shot straight from Arthur's lips right

through my body, reaching right into my chest and wrenching free the vise that had been clamped around me ever since my parents died. I sighed with relief, with the sheer pleasure of his warm touch, of his beard tickling my chin and upper lip.

Arthur moaned, pressing his lips against mine with such force it bent my head back. I pressed back, my lips parting slightly. His tongue slid against mine, warm and soft and delicious.

I breathed deep the smell of him – a hot, smoky scent, mingled with the fresh smell of the sweat he'd worked up fighting off the fae. Arthur reached up, his thick hand grasping my cheek, pulling me against him. I knew that hand could crush me in a moment, and that made him even more sexy.

Heat and emotions raced through my veins, my body begging for release. I reached up my own hand and tangled it in his hair, tugging at his collar, wanting his skin against mine—

My parents are dead.

A rush of sorrow flooded my body as the realization hit me again. Only now, Arthur had released the vise on my chest, and the pain arced through me, raw and unhindered. *They're dead, dead, dead.*

I tore away in surprise as tears sprung in my eyes. Arthur's kiss had unleashed some kind of deluge. I raised my hand to my cheek. It was streaked with rivers of salty tears.

Arthur stared at me, his kind face crumpling. To see a guy that tough, that badass, look so completely crushed would've been totally endearing had I not been in the middle of some kind of meltdown. "Maeve, are you okay? Did I hurt you?"

"No, I..." I gulped as thick, choking sobs clutched my throat. My whole body shook as the grief poured out of me, spilling through my body. "I just... it's just hit me that I'm here… that all this happened because they're dead. My parents are dead. I don't… I shouldn't—"

"Did kissing me make you happy?" he asked.

I nodded, my body wracked by another choking sob. Arthur cringed away, as if my pain physically hurt him. He reached out a hand. It hovered in the air between us. I leaned forward, ready to fall into his arms, to pour out my pain against his body, but he pulled away and stood up.

"I have to go," he whispered. "I'm sorry, Maeve."

"But—" The idea of being alone right now, to sit with this horrible, crushing grief by myself, made me long for the numbness again.

"Hey," Arthur placed a finger over my lips. "This was fun. I want to stay, believe me. But I'm dangerously close to losing control here, and you've had a pretty intense day, all things considered. I don't want to do something we both might regret. But we can pick this up another time, and then," his voice got this rough growl to it that made my insides ache. "You'll be crying out in pleasure."

All I could do was stare helplessly after Arthur as he backed out of the room, his eyes betraying how torn he was. He pulled the door shut behind him, plunging the room into complete darkness.

Alone now with only my pain for company, I collapsed against the sheets. My body shook as I let the tears fall, the beautiful and horrible release of all the sorrow and guilt I'd been stamping down and hiding away ever since that night.

Memories assailed me, dancing in front of my stinging eyes. Mom's cringingly naive attempt to give Kelly and I a sex-education talk, which mostly consisted of her cajoling us to wear promise rings. Dad singing Beatles songs at the top of his lungs as he cooked breakfast for us every morning. Endless Sundays giggling in the back pew with Kelly while Dad delivered his sermons with great aplomb.

The tears rolled down my cheeks, dribbled over my chin, and pooled in my collar bone. *Why?* Why did they have to die? I never got to say goodbye, to tell them how much I loved them for adopting me when no one else would. I never got to say that even though we didn't see eye to eye on a lot of stuff, that I was proud to be their daughter.

And now I never would.

Pale moonlight streamed through the still-open windows, casting long shadows across the room. I lifted my hand up toward the dim light. In my palm was the tiny twig Rowan had given me. Just trying to think about what happened tonight made my temples ache. I couldn't process it through the grief. But that little twig…

Even though objectively, it was just a tiny piece of wood, I knew somewhere inside me that this was *important,* that it carried something of Rowan with him.

I slid the twig under my pillow. Maybe it would bring me peaceful dreams, free of the nightmares that were now playing out in my head. But I very much doubted it.

11

BLAKE

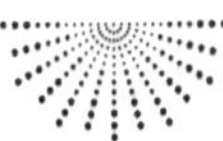

I was on guard duty at the towering sarsen stones that marked the entrance to the human realm when Kalen returned from his assignment. He toppled through the stones in his dog form, legs kicking in the air, mouth foaming. As soon as he hit the earth he shifted back to his preferred shape, but this was not the arrogant prince I'd known my whole life. He lolled and moaned in the dirt, his collar torn and half his face eaten away. Green blood – presumably his own – splattered down the front of his coat. The other two Unseelie soldiers did not follow him.

"Blake," he gasped, dragging his body along the ground. "Help me."

I lifted Kalen to his feet, inspecting the wounds on his face. He'd been burned by something, the skin melted away to reveal the muscle beneath. His eyelid was gone, the other one screwed shut, and that one glimmering eyeball pivoted to stare at me, wide with pain and horror. It looked like elemental magic to me. "You have looked better, brother. How did you obtain these wounds?"

And where are the two guards who accompanied you? Daigh

had given Kalen the simple assignment of taking two fae into the human realm, using both the Seelie and Unseelie crossing stones. This was the first test of the reach of our combined magic, and it had seemed to be a success as, for the first time in decades, three fae crossed into the human realm at the same time. But from the looks of things, it hadn't ended on a high note.

Kalen coughed, splattering blood on my own coat, which I wiped away. "Those Briarwood bastards did this… they got the others."

"You ran into the witches? You were supposed to avoid them so they didn't know of our strength."

"There was an opportunity. We could have taken them down, but they were stronger than we thought."

"That was a stupid idea. Of course they're strong. They've just acquired a powerful witch. Even if she doesn't know what she is, her very presence at Briarwood will increase their power."

"I know that *now*," Kalen shot back. "But if you'd seen them walking across the very field you were hiding in, completely oblivious to your presence, then tell me you wouldn't have attempted it."

I wouldn't have, but I had my own reasons, and he didn't need to know them. "If I'd done it, I would've come back with the girl, and not with two less fae. Now the witches know we have gained significant power. They will be on their guard. Your foolhardy stunt has cost us the advantage of surprise."

He winced. "I am hoping Daigh will not see it that way."

"The king's already in a terrible mood. The Seelie fae aren't stepping into line the way he wishes. You're just going to make his night."

Kalen's ruined face sagged. "Will you return to Court with me?"

"I'm on duty. Oh—" I waved to a figure just rising over the crest of the hill, a fierce bow resting on her shoulder. "There's my replacement now. In that case, I will accompany you back to Court. I wouldn't want to miss the fireworks."

"Vouch for me, brother?" Kalen pleaded. "Remind Dear Father of all my loyal service?"

I smiled, and patted his shoulder reassuringly. Kalen looked a little relieved, which seemed premature to me. If he took my shoulder pat for an answer to his request, that was his own stupid fault.

Word that only Kalen had returned from the foray reached Court before we did, no doubt passed along by the scouts that guarded the road between our land and the old Seelie Court. A few lone fae were still holding out there – led by my friend Laoise – refusing to swear their oaths to Kalen, and they were guarding a stash of nectar wine that Daigh wanted in order to reward his soldiers.

The Unseelie Court held its revels between three *sidhe* in a wide meadow at the foot of the valley, where the two forests of *Tir Na Nog* met. Kalen and I shoved our way through the dancers and brawls. Sprites and brownies leapt out of our way, chittering with curiosity. As princes, we commanded attention wherever we went, and that was especially true now the Seelie Court fairies had joined with us. Fae dressed in both Seelie green and Unseelie black and brown danced around us, laughing and jeering and offering us food. With every step, Kalen shrunk a little further into himself.

"Greetings, Princes," Daigh's voice boomed over the court din. He reclined on a sedan chair held by four groaning far darrigs, while several sprites flitted around his head, peeling fruit with their tiny fingers and feeding them to him. "I see you have returned with fewer fae than you left with. Tell me, where are my loyal and mighty warriors? Will they be joining us in our revels shortly?"

"Um… they will not, oh wise King of Winter," Kalen said, dropping to his knees. I stepped back, wanting a good spot for the show, but not so good that Daigh somehow thought I was defending Kalen. "We met the Briarwood witches in the meadow, and they overpowered us. They are stronger than ever. They—"

"You confronted the witches?" Daigh's voice remained jolly. Only the throbbing vein on the side of his temple gave away his true displeasure.

"I didn't mean to!" Kalen cried out. "We were trying to make it back to the sidhe, and they were traveling across the field from the village. They were right on top of us. We fought valiantly, but they had the girl with them, so we didn't have a chance—"

"Maeve was there?" The king's voice lowered an octave, booming across the glen. The sprites scattered in fright, dropping half-peeled fruit across the ground. "You allowed them to see you? Maeve saw you?"

"As I said, it wasn't my fault." Kalen jerked his head at me. "Blake will speak for me. He knows that I—"

A wet *thwack* emitted from Kalen's head and his protests cut off. A thin wheeze escaped his throat at the same time a line of blood appeared around his neck.

Daigh was no longer sitting in his throne. He stood beside his son, his bone blade at his side, the tip pointed at the ground. The length of the blade dripped with blood. He moved so fast I hadn't even seen him – human eyes cannot process the true speed of a fae.

He'd cleaved his son's head off with such precision that it hadn't even fallen from Kalen's neck.

I let out a breath I didn't realize I'd been holding.

Kalen's eyes glassed over, and with a final wheeze, his

body sagged to the ground, reverting to its dog form. His head separated from his body and rolled across the dirt, coming to a stop at my feet. I kicked it toward Daigh, who laughed his deep, horrible laugh, and kicked it over to Elden, the General of the Unseelie guard. Elden kicked it to Hefeydd, and an impromptu game of soccer broke out in the middle of Court.

The Seelie faeries hung back in horror, wrinkling their faces with distaste as the lines of royal blood marred the dirt. But they were in *our* Court now, where chaos and cruelty reigned.

With the Court thus occupied, I slipped back from the crowd and made my way to my father's throne. Daigh reclined once more, polishing his sword against his black cloak, smearing his son's blood down his shirt. I knew, objectively, that the sight of it should make me sick, but I'd seen Daigh kill many princes in my lifetime. He could always bear more children, and the life of a prince was only worth as much as his duty and loyalty to the Court.

That's why I intended to make myself the worthiest of all.

"You were wise to be rid of him," I murmured in my father's ear as I reached for a platter of grapes and handed one to him.

"I am disappointed," he said, allowing me to place the grape on his tongue, while he held up the blade to inspect the edge. "Kalen was one of our finest warriors."

"A warrior is no good if he cannot follow instructions."

"True." Daigh slid the sword back into his scabbard, and patted my knee. "He was so unlike you, Blake. I always expected you to be a great disappointment. It would not have been your fault, given your lineage. But you have borne your time here with great strength and loyalty. I noticed that Kalen tried to pull you in to defend him."

"A foolish move on his part. What he did was moronic."

And you're just as moronic, if you believe this flattery imbues my loyalty. It may work on your fae, but I am not fae. I kept those thoughts to myself, and pressed my advantage. "So how will we proceed, now that the witches know of our advantage?"

Daigh gave a shrug, as if it were neither here nor there. "We will follow in Kalen's example, send more warriors to bother them near the castle. Meanwhile, while their attentions are elsewhere, we will continue with the plan as conceived."

"Excellent idea, my King." I bowed my head, hoping my platitudes had been enough. "And with Kalen now without his head, who will you send to lead the first mission?"

"I was thinking of sending you, Blake."

Yes. I tried to keep my grin solemn, so he wouldn't realize just how much I'd been counting on obtaining command. "Thank you, Dear Father."

"That is, if you feel you can handle it. This will be the first time you return to the human realm since you came to live with us. There will be many temptations. It may be hard for you to return to us, especially if your mission takes you past a curry shop."

It was a joke, but a pointed one. I bowed my head again. "You have shown me great favor, Dear Father. To have been allowed to live in the fae realm, to have been given the value of your centuries of knowledge… it is worth more to me than a hundred curries. Even though the portal now allows me egress, I will not betray you."

Not yet, at any rate.

"You do yourself great honor, Blake." My father's emerald eyes bore into mine. "Do your duty well and you will be rewarded handsomely in the new fae world."

"Thank you, Father. I will make you proud." I bowed and slunk away, fading into the press of fae bodies gyrating in their revels. I pushed my way through the crowd, stepping over the mangled body of Kalen's canine corpse, and pressed my back against the dirt wall of the sidhe. I took a moment to assess my situation.

Kalen's stupidity had given me a couple of key advantages. It would have alerted the witches that the fae were increasing their power and could now send more warriors into their realm, so when it came time to reveal myself, I'd be more likely to gain their trust. Most importantly, his place had opened up for the expeditionary force to the human realm. After Kalen's fuck up, Daigh wasn't going to trust just anyone, and I'd proved myself more than trustworthy.

This could work. If everything went according to my plan, I would draw the witches in, and my chance to get to Maeve would come, all while fulfilling Daigh's plan and remaining in his good books. It was a win win win, and all the wins belonged to me.

12

ROWAN

Even downstairs, we all felt the shudder in our bodies as Arthur kissed Maeve. My whole body tingled with electricity and I shoved my hands under my thighs to stop myself lashing out when Arthur came back. Flynn looked as murderous as I felt, his pale skin reddening as his hand trembled around his glass. Corbin's expression fell. He looked completely defeated. Of course – he expected Maeve to choose him. We all did.

It wasn't fair. All three of them had a fair shot with Maeve. They talked her ear off at the pub, took over the tour of the house. I'd managed about four-and-a-half sentences in the kitchen before Flynn whisked her away. They *knew* that I couldn't talk to her when they were around, that she'd never look at me with them joking and being larger than life. And then Arthur went swinging his sword around and being the chivalrous knight. And now she'd chosen and it didn't matter how I felt.

I barely even had a chance.

Arthur returned a few minutes later. He wasn't smiling

nearly as much as I would've been. "Go on," he said, slumping down on the couch. "Ask me about it."

"Let's go to the library," Corbin said. "We have a lot to discuss."

We filed down the hall to the library. I stopped at the door, as I always did, unable to step foot in the room until I had counted the spines of all the books on the cabinet on the right. As earlier, when we'd taken Maeve on a tour, there were 194.

I exhaled the breath I'd been holding.

I was grateful that the others hadn't pointed out what I'd been doing to Maeve during the tour, but I guess it didn't matter now.

They waited for me to finish and take a seat next to Flynn on the leather chesterfield. Corbin sat behind his desk, leaning forward on his muscled arms. With his stern face, he reminded me of a school principal. I'd seen a few of them in my life – when I was forced to attend school – all stern-faced and furrowed brows as they tried to get me to talk, to explain why I did the things I did, to find out why I didn't have shoes or a lunch box or where a bruise on my arm had come from or why I wouldn't give a home address. They usually had bookshelves in their offices, and I just counted the books until they stopped asking questions. But that wasn't going to work here.

"So tell us all about it, you lucky bastard," Flynn said, breaking the tense silence between us.

"She didn't *choose* me," Arthur sighed. "She kissed me, but she hasn't chosen me yet."

"Why not? You bite her or something?"

Arthur frowned. "It wasn't about me and her. I don't think it mattered to her who kissed her. I just happened to be the one who carried her upstairs. Come on, she's still reeling from the deaths of her parents. She started to cry, and I realized I needed to get out before I tried to take things further."

"How do you know she didn't choose you?"

"I know because we can all still feel the pull of her," Arthur glanced at each of us in turn, his eyes lingering on mine. "If she'd truly chosen me, surely the tension would have gone away?"

I rubbed my arm, my fingers grazing over the raised scars on my wrist. Fire burned under my skin. Arthur was right. The spell hadn't been broken. We were all bound to her until she chose one of us.

My other hand slipped into my pocket, fingering the condom I kept there. Corbin had given us each a huge stack when he first heard Maeve would be visiting Briarwood. We all knew what her presence would do to us. Even with the coven's magic working on me, I knew I'd never be using any of mine. But I kept it in my pocket because... I didn't know why.

"I think you're right. So, we have a problem," Corbin said, leaning forward, his eyes gliding over all of us. When they met mine, I looked away.

"I'll say we have a problem," Flynn piped up. "I'm randy as a goat with Maeve around, and you three are totally cramping my moves. I don't do crossed swords, so—"

"Mate, you're crazy," Arthur said. He'd taken his usual spot in the enormous wing-backed chair beside the globe – the only chair in the room that comfortably sat his enormous frame. He leaned forward and lifted the lid off the globe beside him, revealing several alcohol bottles and glasses inside. He grabbed a whiskey and poured himself a glass. "She barely looked at you all evening. And she may have kissed me, but she's definitely got eyes for Mr. Saved-me-from-the-runaway-Ferris-wheel over there."

"And Rowan, Mr. Give-a-lady-a-twig-and-she'll-be-yours-forever," Flynn clapped me on the shoulder. "Smooth move with the stick there, mate. I couldn't have done better myself."

"I was just trying to keep her safe," I mumbled into my chest, my cheeks flaring with heat.

"This spell is making it bloody hard to remain a gentleman," Arthur added. "But as the only one who's kissed her, let me say right now that it was worth it."

"If we could be serious for just *one moment*," Corbin snapped. "We're already *painfully* aware of the situation with Maeve. She will choose when she's ready. In the meantime, we just have to—"

"—walk around with permanent tent poles?" Flynn adjusted his pants. I glanced away. I didn't really want to think about my friends and their stiff cocks. Thinking about my own was bad enough.

I'd been hard since Maeve first walked into Briarwood. Part of that was the magic that bound us to the castle and the coven. Because we were still so young, the magic did weird things to our hormones. It couldn't make us want something we didn't already desire, but it enhanced our feelings tenfold. A hundredfold. For me – who struggled to talk to girls on a good day – this was going to make some kind of connection with Maeve practically impossible.

But I was the one who saved her in the field. We worked magic together to disarm Kalen. We had a connection... didn't we?

I jumped as Corbin slammed an enormous volume down on his desk and started flipping through it. "Maeve's choice is the least of our concerns right now."

"We destroyed those fae, no worries," Flynn said. "Old Aragorn over here managed to get two with that dagger of his. I don't see what the big deal is."

I wanted to smirk at Flynn's adoption of Maeve's nickname for Arthur, but there were serious things to deal with.

"The big deal is that there were *three* of them. Can anyone ever remember three fae at once before?"

I shook my head. The others did the same thing.

"I can't either, and I don't think it's been written in the histories since the Middle Ages." Corbin turned the page. "When you combine that fact with Kalen's appearance at the fair the other week, and what he managed to do to Maeve's parents, what we get is a very dangerous pattern emerging. The amount of power the pouka must've drawn from killing all those people might be what gave him the power he needed to bring two fae with him tonight—"

"—but the question is, can he do it again?" Arthur finished.

"Exactly. Now, I think our first step should be—"

"We should tell Maeve the truth," I whispered.

The others whipped their heads toward me. I jerked my head down to my chest, unable to meet Corbin's angry gaze. I stared at the ground, counting the threads of the fringe along the border of the carpet. *One... two... three...*

"We already discussed that, Rowan," Corbin's voice rasped with barely concealed annoyance. He hated that I was questioning him because I'd never done it before. I didn't particularly *want* to be questioning him now. Corbin was everything to me – the person who'd given me a real, wonderful life. I usually deferred to him for everything. But when I thought of Maeve's stormy, beautiful face as she'd demanded a rational answer to all her questions, I *knew* I was right. Lying to her now would only endanger her.

... ten... eleven... twelve...

"That was before there were fae coming after her," I mumbled, still staring at the floor. "Daigh knows exactly who she is. He's already tried to kill her once."

"Walk the scenario through, mate. You've met Maeve now, so you can see what she's like. Analytical. Scientific.

She's having a hard time believing what she encountered *tonight* were actually fae, and she saw and touched them. If we tell her she's a powerful witch who will lead our coven in a great battle against the fae, what do you think she'll do?" When I didn't answer, Corbin filled in for me. "Because I think she'll jump on the first plane back to Arizona and command us to never speak to her again. And that means she's dead meat, and so are the rest of us."

"I don't like lying to her," I murmured. *Twenty-two... twenty-three... twenty-four...*

"Neither do I, but it's best for now. Are we in agreement?"

... twenty-seven... twenty-eight...

"I think it's best, for now," Arthur said.

"I agree with Aragorn," Flynn added. Of course he did.

"Stop calling me that," Arthur growled.

... thirty-two... thirty-three...

"Right, that's settled. *Again.*" Corbin took my silence as agreement. Or perhaps he didn't, because this wasn't a democracy. A coven always had a leader, and for now – until Maeve knew who she was – he was ours. "Now, let's move on to the fact that, for whatever reason, the fae have suddenly got a fuckton more powerful, and what we're going to do about it."

"We need to protect Maeve, at all costs," Arthur said.

"Agreed. Flynn, we need more swords and daggers and iron objects. You should start with a charm to protect Maeve. Rowan, since that twig of yours worked pretty well, you could work up some more earth-based charms and spells. We should expect more of these attacks. And maybe we find a way to keep Maeve in the castle as much as possible. I don't think she should go into the village without at least two of us with her at all times."

"I'm teaching her to fight," Arthur said, a hint of pride in his voice.

"Yes, you are." Corbin's tone said what he thought of that. "And I will hunt through every book in this library and try to figure out how the fae might be using the deaths from the fairground accident in order to break through the protective spells. If they can get that many fae into this realm, then it might not be long until they can get into Briarwood."

We broke up. No one really wanted to talk. Even Flynn had nothing to say. We each went our separate ways. My room was at the end of the hall, directly beneath Maeve's. I lay in bed staring at the ceiling, counting the crossbeams and the stones around the window, as I always did, and imagining her up there, laying across the bed, her pixie hair splayed out around her face, that shot of pink bright against the pillow. My whole body buzzed with want of her.

She hasn't chosen. She kissed Arthur but she didn't choose.

Usually I was content to sit back and let the other guys make the decisions. On movie nights, no one asked me what I wanted to watch. When we ordered Indian food, I just got what the other guys chose. I was so happy to have an actual family – guys who looked out for me and tolerated my quirks – that I didn't want to do anything to jeopardize it.

But Maeve… I wanted her to choose *me*. And that meant I was going to have to step on some toes. I knew I barely had a chance, but for once in my life, I had to try. Arthur had his intensity, Flynn would make her laugh, Corbin would protect her the way he protected all of us, but maybe there was something I could offer… something the other guys couldn't give her. Something she desperately needed.

If only I had a bloody clue what it was.

13

MAEVE

*E*ven after I eventually stopped crying, sleep didn't come as easily as I hoped. Chalk it up to jet lag (my body thought it was eight in the morning), grief, and all the excitement and mystery of last night. Plus, my new bedroom was bigger than the Crawford's *entire house*, and it echoed in weird ways and a cold draft blew in from the window and my parents weren't sleeping at the end of the hall and my body hummed with need after Arthur's kiss and…

nothing was the way it should be.

I tossed and turned in my huge bed, mulling over everything the guys had told me. The memory of that guy – Kalen – licking my face made my skin crawl. I remembered his sharp claws raking for Rowan's head, and how he'd moved so fast he'd appeared to be in two places at once.

Fairies. What nonsense. Fairies were from storybooks. The trashy fantasy novels Kelly loved to read (she had dozens of them stuffed under her mattress – the Crawfords would have a heart attack if they knew she read books containing both witchcraft and premarital sex) were filled with stories of alluring and tricksy fae. They were just some made up mythology – a way for farmers to explain away ruined crops or mothers to assuage their grief over babies that died of disease.

And yet... *the claws... the teeth... the weird green blood... the way they moved and spoke.* Corbin was right with his question – if they weren't fairies, then what the hell had I seen in the field last night?

It could be an undiscovered, undocumented species. That did pop up every now and then. What about that article in last month's *New Scientist* about a new hominid species that supposedly interbred with homo sapiens during their migration to Australasia? I wondered what DNA testing on Kalen would reveal.

Last semester I completed a paper on theoretical physics that was absolutely fascinating. One of the tenets of theoretical physics was the idea of a multiverse – that everything within our cosmic horizon of 46-billion light years could just be one universe among many others. And in these different universes, the physical properties could be completely wackadoodle. There might not be any electrons. Gravity might work differently. Fairies might exist. All things were possible in the multiverse.

I'd written my essay about the controversy around theoretical science and observation. We can't observe the multiverse, so any theories made about it can't be tested. There were scientists out there who believed we should totally rethink the whole scientific method to account for this.

"Should the success or failure of an idea come down to the fact it helps us account for the data?" I'd asked in the closing paragraph of my essay, indirectly quoting the cosmologist Sean Carroll. I got an A+ on that essay.

Maybe I just needed to apply a little theoretical physics to this fairy situation.

Perhaps when the guys talk about this gateway to the "fairy realm," *what they're actually talking about is a wormhole that moves between the multiverse? That theory has been postulated many times, although it raises so many questions about Hawking radiation and the information paradox, but—*

—but it could *explain how fairies can enter our world while not actually being observable.*

Excitement bubbled inside me as the theory formed in my mind, and I started to ask myself questions after question to refine it. Did the wormholes only work one way? Was the existence of exotic matter from the other universe preventing the wormholes from collapsing the "protective magic" Corbin kept going on about? That would explain why only one fae might be able to go through at a time, but if more exotic matter stabilized a wormhole...

I rolled over and punched my pillow. Dammit. I was never going to sleep if I kept thinking about theoretical physics. I might as well give up now. "Fine, you win," I growled at the moon out the window. If I was going to spend the night thinking about wormholes and fae instead of getting my much needed sleep, then I was damn well going to arm myself with information.

I fished my laptop out of my bag and opened it. I typed the words "theoretical physics existence of fairies" into the search bar, but an error box flashed up. I needed Briarwood's wifi password.

Argh! In all the craziness, I hadn't even thought to ask the guys for it. I slammed the laptop shut and shoved it across the desk.

I thought about Corbin's library downstairs – all those shelves of old books, many of which he'd said had been in the castle since its earliest days. There probably wasn't much about theoretical physics, but they might have observations of the fae from other residents of Briarwood I could use to form my theory.

Maybe I'll even find observations from my mother.

I crawled back on the bed and hugged the comforter to my chest. With everything that had happened, I hadn't really stopped to think about the fact that I was in my mother's home. She had walked these same halls, maybe even slept in this very same room. Who was she, that enigmatic woman in the portrait?

Had she run into fairies, too?

14

MAEVE

I woke with a start. Sunlight poured across my bed, blinding me. Everything felt wrong. The comforter was a different weight to the one on my bed, I seemed to have about ten more pillows than I was used to, and the room felt so empty.

And then I remembered… I wasn't in my room at the Crawfords' any more. I was in the tower room at Briarwood Castle. I was there because the Crawfords were dead.

Dead, dead, dead.

I touched my hand to my cheek, remembering how I'd cried last night after Arthur kissed me. My eyes and nose stung from all the tears, but it was a good kind of pain. For the first time, I'd actually felt the raw fury of grief.

Now, the numbness ate away at my body once again, and there was a teeny bit of excitement peeking around the edges of it, which was concerning. I was supposed to be at Briarwood to mourn and sort my life out, and I'd only been here one day and I was more confused than ever. Lusting after all my housemates, kissing Arthur, being attacked by strange men with crystal eyes and fingers that turned into claws…

... and this room... my room in my house...

I rubbed my eyes and sat up, gazing in wonder at the space around me. The guys really had gone all out. They couldn't have guessed better at my tastes. I slid out of bed and went over to the desk. A huge stack of books on the end caught my eye, all science titles. A note was pinned to the top.

"For when you decide to return to your studies – Corbin."

My cheeks glowed as I read the note. I ran my fingers along the spine of the first book – a selection of essays on astrophysics. But how did Corbin know what I was going to study? Maybe the lawyer had told him...

Another note caught my eye, pinned to the wall beside an amazing piece of art I hadn't noticed yesterday. It was a round lattice of metal leaves and vines, all twisted and folded around each other. I stepped closer, and my heart thudded as I realized what it was.

A star map.

Each tiny leaf marked the position of a star in the English sky. Hidden in the vines were animals, each one intricately sculpted from iron – a scorpion, a pegasus, two fish... *the constellations.*

A note was pinned to the bottom. I peeled it off.

"I'm calling this piece 'frolicking.' Fancy a frolic, love?" - Flynn

I smiled. Of course it was Flynn.

A divine smell wafted under my nose. I looked down and noticed something on the small table below Flynn's note – a tall, thick beeswax candle, the wax mottled with swirls of red and orange. I picked it up and sniffed it, inhaling the heavenly scent of musk and cardamon. A small box of matches and a wrought-iron candle-snuffer sat beside it, along with a square of paper.

The paper simply read, "From Arthur" in a beautiful old-fashioned cursive script. My heart soared. I sniffed the air again. That amazing smell wasn't only coming from the candle. I turned around, scanning the room. But where—

A tray of food sat on the bedside table. Scones piled high on a plate beside porcelain bowls of clotted cream and beautiful chunky strawberry jam. I remembered that Rowan was the cook, and wondered if he'd baked them himself.

Did the guys sneak in here this morning and place these gifts? My cheeks flushed. I hope they didn't see me with the sheets kicked off. I slept naked.

My chest fluttered. Or maybe I *did* hope they saw me. Maybe I hoped that very much.

I lathered up a couple of the scones and bit into one. Mmmmm, heavenly. All buttery and soft and fluffy. Why didn't we eat scones in America? They piss all over pancakes any day of the week.

When I finished the scones, I tossed on some clothes, and took the tray and my laptop bag down the back staircase to the kitchen. When I opened the hidden door, I was surprised to see Rowan standing at the butcher's block, expertly cutting up a stack of tomatoes and throwing them into a giant pot.

"Hey, you're awake." He smiled at me as I leaned over the table and gave him a small hug around his waist. He smelled like warm spices and fresh vegetables. His warm smile melted me like a buttery scone. "Do you want a cup of tea? I can put the kettle on."

"Sure." I shrugged, suddenly nervous. "I've never actually had tea before."

Rowan leaned across to the sink and meticulously scrubbed his hands before flicking an electric kettle on and assembling some teacups. "I hope the breakfast was okay. I think scones are much nicer warm from the oven, but I didn't want to disturb your sleep after that long flight."

"The flight wasn't the half of it." I yawned, collapsing into the high stool opposite him and sliding my tray onto the bench. "It's *everything*. I think my brain is even more tired than my body. I'm still struggling with the whole fairies are real and my housemates beat them up thing, but I think I've come up with a way to resolve it. The scones were delicious. Did you bake them?"

He nodded, returning to his work. "I do most of the cooking around here." I waited for him to tell me about his skills. Most guys loved an opportunity to show off. But Rowan just kept cutting tomatoes and placing them into the pot, his gorgeous lips moving as he counted under his breath.

Finally, the silence got a bit weird for me. "What are you making?"

"Tomato chutney. We've had a glut of tomatoes from the garden this summer, and I want to preserve them so we can keep enjoying them over the winter."

"How very forward-thinking of you."

"I like when everything is planned out," Rowan said without looking up. His voice sounded a bit strange, but I might've imagined it. "I don't like surprises. The tea's ready."

The kettle whistled. Rowan washed his hands again, then poured out the hot water and fiddled around with spoons and milk and saucers before presenting me with a cup of caramel-colored weirdness.

"Me neither, usually." I sniffed the tea, wondering why so many people could like something that smelled like wet dirt. "Every year at Christmas time I would bribe my sister Kelly with candy to sneak into our parents' room, find the presents they hid in the closet, and tell me what they all were."

"Why didn't you go and look yourself?"

"Duh, because I didn't want to get in trouble." I raised the cup to my lips and took a sip. *Gross.* It *tasted* like wet dirt. I reached across the table and grabbed a small tomato from the stack and popped it into my mouth. The tart fruit popped on my tongue, bursting with flavor and rinsing away the taste of the tea. "That tomato is delicious! But yeah, that's why I'm a scientist, I think. I like to know things, to understand them. Surprises mean that I haven't figured things out yet. But four guys sneaking into my room this morning to leave thoughtful, beautiful gifts totally doesn't count. That was an awesome surprise."

Rowan looked up again, and the smile on his face lit up the whole room. "Want to help?"

"Maybe in a sec. Could you tell me the wifi password? I want to look up some info on the fae. I have many questions."

"Oh, the password is briarwood with a capital B and zeroes for o's. But you'll find much better information in the library. Ask Corbin to show you. We have a huge collection of occult and folklore books."

Somehow, that didn't surprise me one bit. "Okay. Where's Corbin?"

Rowan shrugged.

"Fine." Somehow, now that I was downstairs talking to Rowan, my theory didn't seem as important. I got the feeling that these moments with the quiet boy were precious. "I'll help you. What do I do?"

"Nothing until you've washed your hands."

After washing my hands, Rowan handed me a knife and a bowl of freshly-picked bell and chili peppers. He showed me how to cut them to get all the seeds out. As he maneuvered the knife to demonstrate the correct technique, I noticed how precise his cuts were. Always three cuts, never any more or any less. "With the chilis, we want to keep the seeds," he explained. "That's where all the heat comes from, but the pepper seeds are just woody. They taste like shite."

Shite. I loved the way Brits talked.

"Got it." I elbowed Rowan out of the way and started to

massacre a chili. Rowan watched me mangle the fruit, his expression twisting uncomfortably. At one point, he was even gripping the table as if he was holding himself back from reclaiming the knife and banishing me from the kitchen.

"Right…" he gulped. "I'll just go back over here and leave you to it." He shuffled his own chopping board further around the butcher's block so the mountain of produce and enormous pots obscured his view of me. He started chopping… *one, two, three…* always that same rhythm, and he didn't say another word.

As I chopped and scraped, I kept darting glances over at Rowan. He had his dreadlocks tied back in a tidy bun high on his head, and I noticed a single hoop earring dangling from his left ear. The earring was carved with a delicate knotwork pattern. He wore a long sleeve sweater, even though warm sunlight streamed in from the high kitchen windows. At his wrists, I could just make out the edges of tattoos creeping toward his hands – more knotwork by the looks of it, and that strange stick writing I'd noticed on Arthur's ink. He was skinny, but toned, his shirt pulling across his shoulders as he made light work of the mountain of tomatoes. I loved the way his brow furrowed in concentration as he worked. There was something so sexy about a guy wielding a knife and being perfectly comfortable in the kitchen.

Once, Rowan caught me looking, and gave me a full smile. My heart did a little flip-flop thing. He was so not the usual type of guy I'd go for – there were very few black people in Coopersville, and none that looked or acted anything like him – exuding such softness while also being a little odd. He was really gorgeous, and he intrigued me.

I am crazy. It's a supremely bad idea to get all hot and bothered about any of my new housemates… and I already kissed Arthur. Now I'm contemplating a move on Rowan. Am I insane?

Maybe. Maybe it was grief making me do these weird, un-Maeve things. Maybe it didn't matter why.

"Hey Rowan." I dumped some oddly chopped peppers into the pot. "How did you end up living at Briarwood? I mean, you're not a cousin of mine or something?"

Rowan stared into the pot. "Can you cut them a little more square? I really like them to be square."

"Why, does it affect the taste? And you didn't answer my question."

I was kidding, but Rowan didn't look at me. His voice went very quiet. "We're not cousins. I'm an orphan, too. My parents were friends of your mother. She gave the house to Corbin's family to look after, and they let the rest of us live here, too."

"So you lived here your entire life?"

Rowan shook his head. His chopping speed increased a bit. The good vibes between us completely disappeared. I waited for him to elaborate, but he didn't. Instead, he frowned at his tray of perfectly-chopped tomatoes.

"Not square enough," he said, sliding a tray of tomatoes into the trash.

My heart lurched. I'd upset him. Of course, if he was an orphan, talking about his parents would upset him. That's what normal people do when they lose their parents. Not cold, unfeeling bitches like me who could barely muster a tear until a guy kissed her.

"I'm sorry, Rowan. I didn't mean to bring it up." He shook his head again, and started lining up more tomatoes on his board. I stared down at my own, unsure of what to do next.

"Mmmm, something smells delicious," a deep Irish brogue rumbled against my ear, breaking the tense silence. Flynn stuck his head over my shoulder, his cheek pressed against mine as he peered down at the pot. My face tingled where his skin touched mine. How could a guy that fit and toned feel so smooth and soft—

Get a grip, Maeve. It must be the grief causing me to lose my mind. Only a minute ago I was thinking about how hot Rowan was, and now I'd jumped to Flynn. I had sex on the brain 24/7. I ducked under Flynn and swatted him with the spatula. "Out of the kitchen unless you've washed your hands."

"Or I'm in for the caning of my life, eh?" Flynn grinned, darting out of reach of another swing. "Sign me up, Miss Maeve. I bet you're handy with a cane."

"Take your dirt out of here," Rowan said softly. "Maeve, thanks for your help, but I can finish up. You should start on your research."

I started to protest, not wanting to leave things with Rowan strained, but Flynn grabbed my hand and dragged me into the small informal living room opposite the kitchen. The guys had turned it into a rec room with a huge pool table, a TV only slightly smaller than the enormous one in the great hall, and a set of vintage arcade games.

"You've been here one day and Rowan's allowing you to help him in the kitchen? We've been friends for ten years and he won't let me even fry a bloody egg. Girl, you are all kinds of magical."

I held up my clean hands. "Clean hands, that's the trick."

"Ah, then I'll be out of luck." Flynn held up his palm, which was smudged with black coal dust from his forge. "I hope you keep talking to him. It's good for Rowan to talk to girls."

"I think I might have upset him. I was asking about his parents and Briarwood—"

"Never mind Rowan. He's a little messed up about some stuff." Flynn's eyes brightened. "Did you get my gift?"

"I did. I loved it like you wouldn't believe. You're really talented."

"I know. And devilishly handsome, too, don't you think?" Flynn struck a pose, and I laughed. "I told Corbin you win a lady's heart with art, not with stuffy books about science, but he wouldn't listen."

"I *like* stuffy books about science, but I like art, too."

"And you like sword-wielding warriors, too?" Flynn lifted an eyebrow. My cheeks flushed. He knew about me kissing Arthur. Or course he did, they probably all knew. Guys always talked about that stuff.

"Um… yeah. I am multifaceted in my interests. People can like all sorts of different things." I thought about the four different guys in the house, and how I already liked each of them for different reasons. The flipping in my stomach and the way my skin tingled suggested it was *more* than like. "Sometimes you don't have to choose."

"If only thing things were that simple." Flynn gestured to the pool table. "Do you want a game? I'm bloody hopeless. Corbin tells me it's all about math and angles or some shite, so you'll probably be brilliant."

I shook my head. "As much as I'd love to hit your balls around a table—" Flynn snorted and my skin glowed, knowing I'd made the trickster laugh "—I actually want to do some studying."

"It's *summer.* Birds are singing. The river bank is warm. Pints are being pulled at the pub. Why in the Holy Mother Mary's name would you stay inside studying when you're not even at uni?"

His last words stung. I remembered the cold letter from MIT informing me my scholarship had been rescinded. Right now I should have been meeting my dorm mates and finding my way to my first classes instead of bumming around inside an English castle. The option of selling Briarwood was still there, but even after one night I wasn't sure if I'd be able to part with it. I didn't want to mention it to the guys just yet. "I actually wanted to see Corbin, but he's not around. Maybe you can help me? I'm looking for some more information on these fairies. In particular, about the gateway between their realm and ours."

"Do you actually believe what we told you?"

"Theoretical physics could explain it all, so tentatively yes. But I need more information in order to prove out my theory."

Flynn grabbed my hand and yanked me down the hall. "Right this way! Flynn O'Hagan will show you everything you need to form your crazy theories."

"But the library's that way—"

He grinned. "But this will be so much better."

"There!" Flynn gestured triumphantly at a small mound in the middle of a field, just beyond a low stone wall that marked the easternmost boundary of Briarwood.

"It's a hill." I frowned, leaning against the wall and struggling to catch my breath. I'd followed Flynn across the entire Briarwood estate, down behind the sculpted gardens teeming with tourists, through the thick hedge of wild roses that gave the castle its name, down through the back fields and across the edge of a tiny wood. He skipped over the uneven ground with ease, his long legs making light work of the distance, while I huffed and fumbled along behind him.

I wish I'd thought to bring a drink. I'll have to get a lot fitter if I want to pass the physical to join the space program.

"That's not a hill." Flynn threw up his arms, as if he was totally exasperated by me. But he was grinning. "By the Mother Mary, it's a *sidhe* – an ancient burial mound. These sidhe are scattered all over the United Kingdom and Ireland. Every one of them is an entry and exit point to the Fae kingdom, although most have been blocked off with magic so the fae can't use them."

"Who's buried inside?"

"We don't know. The grave was robbed many years ago. It's probably some ancient king of the *Aes Sidhe*. That's what the fairies call themselves. Their race ruled over England before the humans arrived with their weapons of iron and pushed them all into the realm of *Tir Na Nog*, which I only remember because it's also the name of our fair pub." He grinned at me as he plopped down in the long grass behind the wall, pulled a paper bag filled with candy from his pocket, and offered me a piece. "See? Practical research. This is better than a stuffy old book."

I accepted a hard ball covered with sugar, and popped it into my mouth. *I can't believe I'm looking at a wormhole into the multiverse. It looks just like a pile of dirt to me.* "If this is where the fae cross over into our world, can we walk through it and go into their realm—*omigod.*"

My taste buds screamed in protest. The candy was so sour it turned my mouth inside out. I spat it out in the grass in disgust, and Flynn burst out laughing.

"You've got to be careful with boiled sweets. Some of them have a mighty bite. And as for the portal, we can't get near it," Flynn said. "Just as they can't pass through the castle grounds, so we cannot pass through the door into their world. If you and I were to walk into the sidhe, all we'd see is an empty chamber."

Interesting. So the wormhole will only transport matter based on certain parameters. What differentiates a fae from a human, based on matter? Surely for them to function in our universe they must contain the same electrons?

"So the fae come and go from this same point? They can move both ways through the wormhole—"

"Get down."

Flynn's voice changed. He threw his arm around my shoulders and shoved me into the grass, laying his body down beside me. I tried to lift my head to see what he'd seen, but Flynn pushed my head down. My ears pricked, the hairs on my arms standing on end. Flynn's skin was warm and soft against mine. My breath hitched.

What's going on?

Flynn inched closer, and flattened some of the grass in front of the wall. There was a gap in the stones wide enough for us to see through. He pointed at something in the field below.

Two green-cloaked men wandered across the field, heading toward the hill… sorry, the *sidhe*. They carried a small lump in their hands wrapped in blankets.

"Stay right here," Flynn whispered. "Don't make a sound."

Before I could ask him what the hell was going on, he'd leapt over the wall and raced toward the figures.

16

MAEVE

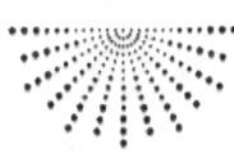

My breath caught as I watched Flynn stroll across the field toward the fae. Something told me this was very, *very* dangerous. I remembered last night that it had taken all the guys working together to take down our attackers. At least these guys were Seelie – I remembered that the Summer Court wore green, and weren't generally antagonistic.

I can't believe I'm sitting here, acting like this fae nonsense is real. But even so, I shuffled closer and pressed my entire face into the wall. Flynn slowed his pace, stepping in front of the two figures. He held out his hand.

The fae looked up. The one holding the bundle stepped back, while the first leaned forward, hissing through his long, sharp teeth.

"Stay away, human," The fae hissed, loud enough so I could hear. "You are forbidden to prevent us from accessing the gate."

Flynn shrugged. "Maybe I'm a rebel. Maybe I don't care about the rules. What have you got in the bundle?"

"A little gift for the fae king," the first fae replied.

Flynn grabbed for the bundle. The first fae leapt in front of him, snapping and snarling. Flynn waved his hand in front of the fae's mouth.

"Cor, you need some breath mints! You smell fouler than a protestant's shitter." Flynn raised his hands behind his head. "I'm not going to break any rules, Seelie. I just want to see what you've got."

The fae snarled, but the second fae tapped his friend on the shoulder and whispered something in his ear. The first fae stepped aside, his lips turning up into a cruel smile.

Don't look, Flynn. It's a trap or something. Why else would they change their mind and decide you can see what they've got?

The fae held out the blanket. Flynn slowly reached forward with one hand, the rest of his body tense. He flipped a corner of the blanket over, revealing a tiny baby's face, all screwed up with sleep.

I gasped when I remembered what Corbin had said last night. *They steal children and take them away to become slaves in their court.*

"This is a human baby," Flynn said, his voice burning with anger. "You've stolen it."

"Don't worry. His mother won't even miss the little tyke. We enchanted a pumpkin to appear as him. They never notice the difference."

"You're Seelie. Why would your rulers command you to do this? How will you get the baby back to your realm?"

"So many questions," the first fae said, flipping the blanket back over the child, who squirmed in his arms. "You're an inquisitive one."

Even from here, I could sense the anger rolling off Flynn. "You can't take this child. I won't let you."

"Are you going to fight us, water witch? Are you going to try and bar us from our right of way?"

"Maybe," Flynn smirked. "You're not the only one who

can break the bloody rules." He raised a hand to the sky and uttered a single, strange word.

Nothing happened. The fae watched the sky, smirking. A single white cloud bobbed over the edge of the wood that stretched along the far side of the sloping field, like a fluffy sheep trotting along on the breeze. A few moments later, the cloud was twice the size, and the edges grayed as they grew heavy with water. The cloud spread over the sun, and the temperature dropped. Rapidly.

I rubbed my arms as a frigid wind blew down the valley. The raincloud billowed overhead and the heavens opened up.

A torrential downpour pounded down, the full force of the water focused over the mound. Thick droplets pummeled the earth around the mound, forming deep puddles across the field. Even from my position back behind the wall, water drizzled over me, sticking my clothes to my body. Down the slope of the hill, I could see water cascading down the stone steps leading into the sidhe, pooling there, lapping against the stones as the sidhe filled up. A few moments later, the water flooded over the top step and a puddle spread over the ground.

"That is against our laws, water witch," the first fae growled, wiping its matted hair from its eyes.

"Not even close," Flynn lowered his arm and flipped his head so the lock of red hair over his eye stuck up at an odd angle. "You guys are perfectly capable of swimming down to your doorway, but I don't like your chances of getting that baby through without drowning it, and you know how much your king is going to *love* a dead baby."

"You will be sorry!" The fae spluttered, holding the baby to his chest. It wailed and flailed its tiny arms, annoyed at being held under the cold shower.

"It's not so nice when your own tricks come back to bite you, is it?" Flynn smiled back.

The fae looked like he was going to attack, but then he leaned back on its heels and an evil smile played across its lips. I glanced behind Flynn, where the fae's eyes rested, and saw something that turned my blood cold.

A face emerged from the water flooding the sidhe, followed by a pair of broad shoulders clad in a black cloak that didn't seem to register the fact it was submerged. The fae gasped in a couple of lungfuls of air.

"Is this what passes for an English summer?" he called out in a deep, singsong voice, like a tenor warming up before a concert. He rose out of the water, shaking himself off like a wet dog.

Even through the driving rain, I could see he was hot. All the fae I'd seen so far were beautiful – with that perfect skin and those crystalline eyes – but even by their standards this guy was out-of-this-world. Wavy hair framed his face and streamed down his back, thick and black and shimmering with streaks of silver. His cheekbones stood in high relief – two razors slicing across his face, drawing the gaze down his aquiline nose to those pouty, sexy lips and strong jaw. A drop of water collected on the tip of his chin. His coat pulled in all the right places, and a gleaming white sword on his belt declared him a warrior. Emerald eyes blazed, their depths unfathomable. An aura of raw power radiated from his body, slivers of that power plunging into my chest and pounding between my legs.

Stop thinking like that. That's an Unseelie, and he's dangerous. In fact, Flynn's probably in trouble. I should go and find the others.

But without Flynn, I'd barely remember the way back to the castle. If the fae decided to attack, by the time I got back, it would be too late. I hadn't brought my phone down with me, and I didn't have any of the guys' numbers anyway. *The best thing to do is to wait here and hope the element of surprise will give us an advantage.*

The Seelie fae bowed to the new arrival. "Welcome, your Highness."

My teeth chattered. I crawled closer on my elbows, heart pounding. This wasn't good. This was three fae against Flynn. *But wait, why is that Unseelie here with the Seelie? I didn't think they got along or worked together at all.*

Flynn whirled around, his eyes bugging out of his head as he registered the black-clad figure. The grey clouds parted and slid away, revealing the clear blue sky and pounding heat of the sun beyond. "I've never seen you before, Prince."

"It's true, we've never had the pleasure." The dark fae extended his hand to Flynn. "I am Blake, Commander of the *Aes Sidhe*. What seems to be the problem here?" he asked in a bored voice.

"This witch… he has blocked the entrance."

The fae named Blake grinned. "It's only water." He kicked a spray at Flynn. "And it is a *mighty* hot day. I think you'll find a solution to this problem presents itself."

The two fae glanced at each other, then they both dropped to their knees and started to slurp at the puddle, gulping down the water. Flynn summoned another raincloud, but the fae who came out of the water raised his own hand to the sky, and suddenly Flynn was on the ground, clutching his head and howling with pain.

"Flynn!" I cried, leaping to my feet and vaulting the wall in one go.

I took off down the hill toward them, aware that I had no weapon and the twig Rowan gave me was still sitting conveniently under my pillow.

The two fae didn't even look up from their thirsty work, but Blake met my eyes with his – two emerald lakes, clear and bright as crystal. I fell into them, my steps grinding to a halt, stunned into inaction, as though I was trying to claw my way through an invisible wall.

What the hell is this?

"Well, well," the dark fae said, smoothing down the seam of his coat. "What have we here?"

"Get away from him!" I yelled, balling my hands into fists. My words came out shrill, panicked. I tried to push my way toward them, but that invisible wall kept me back.

Blake grabbed Flynn by the neck and jerked his body like a puppet. Flynn's eyes rolled back and his mouth hung open. "I hear your request," Blake said, his voice like syrup. "But I don't see how you will follow it up should I decide not to obey."

"I've got powers the likes of which you never encountered before, pal." I shot back. "If you don't want to feel the wrath of the Arizona state under-21 competitive chess champion, you'd better back the fuck off."

"Such language, and in one so young and beautiful," Blake tsked, flopping Flynn's head from side to side. I pounded against that invisible wall, but it didn't do anything except send shooting pain up my arms. "And that accent... they really don't teach you to speak properly in America."

I stepped back, panic rising in my chest. My sneaker caught the edge of something hard. I kicked it with my toe. *Metal.* Some kind of tool. Maybe heavy enough to do some damage.

Blake stepped toward me, dragging Flynn behind him. He pressed his hands against Flynn's temples. Flynn's eyes clouded over, and his face kind of crumpled, like the skin was about to slide off the bones. Something crackled under the fae's fingers, giving off a sugary sweet scent as Flynn's face contorted in agony.

"And your vocabulary... tsk tsk. You're on English soil, so you need to learn correct English. A shag is a bird *and* descriptive of being overtired *and* a delightful naked activity. A rubber erases pencil marks and doesn't prevent childbirth." Blake took another step toward me, dragging Flynn's limp body alongside him. If I was right, he'd just stepped over the invisible barrier, but I had no way of knowing for sure. "To you, trousers are pants, instead of the sexy scrap of fabric underneath. Tell me again, what do you call—"

CLONK.

The spade connected with the side of Blake's head. His emerald eyes remained fixed on mine, but the rest of him wobbled. His hands slid from Flynn's cheeks, and he toppled forward, hitting the ground hard. He didn't get up.

"In Arizona, we call that a spade, motherfucker." I grinned.

"Maeve—"

I dropped the spade and rushed to Flynn's side. He'd fallen with Blake, his body bent over backward. His skin felt cold and clammy. He slid his hands around my neck and allowed me to pull him to his feet. A lattice of dark spiderwebs spread across his temples and forehead, radiating out from where Blake touched him.

"What did he do to you?" I cried, draping his arm around my neck. Flynn's weight dragged me over, but I managed to pull him a little way up toward the hill.

"Don't worry... get... the baby..." he whispered, each word a ragged breath.

I whirled around, just in time to see Blake crawling toward the sidhe, the baby tucked into the crook of his arm. The other two fae had already disappeared down the staircase, which was now only ankle deep with water. Blake turned back at the entrance to the mound, his crystal eyes meeting mine. He shot me a lopsided grin that might've been vaguely attractive if he hadn't just tried to kill my friend. The baby cooed in his arms.

"I'll be seeing you around, Miss Arizona, Water Witch," he called. "If I were you, I'd keep practicing your chess moves. Because next time, I'll show you just how important a pawn can be."

I hurled myself toward Blake, but he disappeared down the steps, his coat fading into the darkness below.

"We're too late," Flynn croaked. He leaned hard against me, barely able to support his own weight.

"What did he do to you?" I stroked the lattice of red lines across Flynn's freckled cheek.

Flynn's eyes darkened. "I have no idea, but I feel like I've been run over by a train and then another train. But… I guess we just met Blake, prince of the Unseelie Court."

17

FLYNN

My legs shook so badly I could barely hold myself up. Maeve had to drag me back to the castle. Whatever that Blake character did to me, it was fucking *wretched*. I didn't even have the energy to make a joke about shags.

The whole encounter weighed on me as Maeve wrenched and jerked my pain-filled body toward the castle. Nothing made sense. Seelie and Unseelie were there together, and they were both working to steal that baby. Blake seemed incredibly powerful, but who – or what – was he? We knew all of the Unseelie princes by name, so why had we never heard of him before?

And where the bloody hell were the others? Corbin could usually sense when one of the coven was in danger. Why hadn't he come?

Maeve dragged me past the walled kitchen garden and in through the buttery door. Rowan glanced up in shock, dropping a tray of bread on the floor. "Wipe your feet!" he yelled.

"Rowan, get the others." Maeve dragged me into the kitchen. "Flynn's been attacked!"

As soon as Rowan's eyes met mine, he registered that something was wrong. He darted up the hidden staircase, calling out for Arthur and Corbin, but there was no answer. He dashed outside, calling at the top of his lungs.

Maeve pulled out a seat at the butcher's block and poured me into it. I grabbed the edge of the bench to steady myself, gasping at the exertion. I hadn't been this buggered since that time Corbin decided we should all run a half-marathon to get fit for battling fae and I'd stopped at the pub halfway through to re-fuel.

"Hey, no fair," I murmured as I started to slide off the edge of the stool. "You stuck me on a chair made of jelly."

"Jell-O," Maeve whispered as she wrapped her arms around me and hefted me up again. "It's pronounced 'Jell-O.'"

I let out a laugh that made my ribs ache. "Fecking hell, don't make me laugh, woman. I think I've just pushed a rib through my spleen."

"Shite, Flynn." That was Rowan. He skidded back into the kitchen. I could feel his hand on my face. "I found the others. They were down in the meadow, fending off a fae attack of their own. What happened? Who did this to you?"

"Blake," I whispered. That was probably all the description I was capable of. My eyes fluttered shut and much as I tried to pry them open, they were definitely stuck that way.

"Who's Blake?"

Mother Mary. Maeve was leaning over me. I could get a glimpse down her shirt if only my eyes would work. What the hell did Blake *do* to me?

"Apparently he's a new Unseelie prince. We were by the sidhe meadow behind the castle. These two Seelie fae were stealing a baby, and Flynn tried to stop them. Then Blake showed up and he grabbed Flynn's head and kind of shook him and there was this smell like candy apples and he did *that* to Flynn's face."

"My precious face," I moaned.

"Hold on." Rowan clattered around the kitchen, slamming glass bottles and containers down on the butcher's block. "Keep him still."

More footsteps clattered into the room. "What did Flynn do now?" Corbin yelled. Figures he'd assume this was my fault.

"He *was* trying to save an innocent child from the fae and they did this to him." Maeve shot back. "And if you want to do something useful instead of standing there like an idiot, you'll come here and help me hold him."

I cheered inwardly. This bird had spunk. No one talked to Corbin like that. But sure enough, his hands slid around my middle, and his thick chest replaced Maeve's busty one. Not nearly as pleasant, but definitely sturdier.

"Hold on, mate." Corbin whispered in my ear. "We'll put you right."

Rowan was crushing something with his mortar and pestle. "I've never seen this before," he said. "This isn't any fae magic I've heard of. If I didn't know any better, I would say this was a spirit attack."

"That's what I'm seeing," Arthur said. He leaned close and I could smell his meady breath on my face. "My mother described a spirit attack in her diary, and she said it left similar marks."

"But the fae can't manipulate the elements the way we can," Corbin said. "It doesn't make any sense."

"Unless this new surge of power they've got has somehow given them that ability," Arthur said. "You're the historian, Corbin. Have you ever read anything about this?"

"Not that I can remember, but I'll hit the books again today and—"

"Aragorn's beard is tickling me," I croaked out.

"Guys, give him some space." Maeve's voice cut through

like birdsong over a nest of hornets. Just her presence calmed the pounding in my head. Instead of feeling as though I'd been knocked about the a giant sledgehammer, with Maeve's hand on my shoulder, the sledgehammer only felt medium-sized.

"Hold still," Rowan swiped something wet and gritty across my cheeks. "This may sting a little."

"Bah, you English can't handle pain. My superior Irish blood has withstood decades of bloody slaughter. I can handle a little sting—" Okay, maybe that wasn't a *little* sting. Maybe it was a fucking huge sting. Maybe it felt like my face was being eaten by acid. Blinding pain seared across my vision. I gritted my teeth.

"Well, that's one way to shut him up," Corbin said with a smile in his voice, the bastard.

My hands flailed to hold something. Maeve slipped her fingers in mine, and the warmth of her skin radiated through my arm, reaching right up through my neck and into my face, rolling over the fire in my skin and taking away some of the heat. She squeezed my fingers and I squeezed hers back.

"I hope this works." Rowan said, his voice worried.

"What the fuck have you done to me?" I managed to choke out. He didn't have to sound so bloody *uncertain*.

A few moments later, the sting faded a little, and I managed to regain some function in my face. I found I could move the muscles in my mouth enough to twist them up into a semblance of a smile. I tried to blink, and found that it worked. Light flooded me as the kitchen came into view. Four concerned faces stared down at me.

"How do I look?" I croaked out. I raised my hand to my cheek, feeling the gritty paste on my skin.

"Kind of shite," Corbin said.

"Like a creature from the black lagoon," Arthur added.

"I think it's an improvement," Corbin said.

"I'm just so glad you're okay." Maeve wrapped her arms around me, pressing her head into my shoulder. I reached up and rubbed her back, my hand gliding over the strap of her bra and instantly sending my thoughts to a bad place.

"I've never been better." I turned to Rowan. "How long until I completely heal? I can't rely solely on my charm and good graces to pull in the ladies." *One particular lady,* I thought but didn't say.

"I wish I knew. I've just used the standard healing potion for spirit attacks. It seems to be working, but I have no idea what the properties of this new fae magic actually are." Rowan stammered over a few of the words. This was probably the most words he'd ever spoken at once since I met him four years ago. "If this were a standard spirit attack from another witch, it would take a few days for the signs on your skin to fade, and of course, your mind will be pretty weak and vulnerable—"

"So no different than normal, then?" Arthur grinned.

I stuck my tongue out at him. "This is the thanks I get for trying to be chivalrous."

Corbin sighed. "Now that we've got our Flynn back, can we get the full story of what happened?"

I started to tell them about taking Maeve to see the sidhe, but my head throbbed and I found myself unable to think of the right words. I collapsed back against Maeve's arms while she finished the story, carefully describing the scene in detail.

"So it's confirmed, then." Arthur said as she finished her description of clonking Blake over the head with that shovel. "We have one bad-ass bird on our side."

"I was damn lucky that spade was there, and I still didn't manage to save that poor baby. How could they take it, anyway? I thought you said humans couldn't pass through the barrier between worlds?"

"Today is confirmation that's no longer the case." Corbin

said. "But we don't know how or why—" His face lit up with that stupid look he gets when he discovers some dumb fact in a history book and has to share it with the rest of us.

"What?" Arthur demanded.

"To the library!" I cried, in my best Batman impersonation. Corbin was already running for the hall. Maeve helped me down from the stool, and I leaned on her and Arthur as we trudged down the wide hallway.

By the time we entered the library, Corbin was already throwing books and newspapers around, mumbling under his breath. I wanted to tell him that if he couldn't find what he was looking for, it was because his filing system was shite (Corbin was rather proud of his filing system), but the walk down the hallway had exhausted me so much I was struggling for every breath.

"Ah-hah!" Corbin held up a section of the local newspaper, his cheeks flushed with triumph. "I knew I'd seen something before. Look at this." He laid the paper out on the coffee table, holding down the corners with little brass weights like a complete twat. We all leaned in.

"Do you mean, half price vibration machines?'" I pointed to an ad in the top left corner. "Because honestly, mate, I didn't want to say anything, but you're looking a little hefty around the middle. Too many of Rowan's mutton pies—"

"I think I liked him better when he was in too much pain to talk," Arthur said.

"Just a modicum of seriousness while we do this would be appreciated, Flynn." Corbin pointed to an article in the middle of the page – a local mother appealing to anyone who had news about her missing baby. Apparently, the child had been kidnapped from its crib in the middle of the night.

"This was two weeks ago," Corbin said. "I hadn't connected it to any fae activity because I had no idea they were powerful enough to kidnap children again. This last time they tried this was centuries ago, when the coven at that time was particularly weak—"

"If the fae have taken two babies, what does that mean?" Maeve asked. "What are they going to do to them?"

"It means that they're more powerful than we thought," Corbin frowned. "As to what they'll do, we don't know. That's what I'm trying to find out. My guess is that they need the children for some kind of spell. The fae were known for stealing infants to raise as their own – they didn't usually kill them. But if we want them back, we need to find the fifth." He said this last bit with a pointed look at me.

"The fifth?" Maeve looked confused.

"Covens can have as many people as they want, but certain numbers make for stronger magic," Arthur said. " When my parents were in the Briarwood coven, there were eleven members. We're supposed to have at least five people in our coven, each one specializing in a different element. We need a wielder of each element in order to complete our circle and give us the ability to do more complex spells. Currently, we don't even have practitioners of all the elements."

Maeve pointed around the room, her finger landing on Rowan, Arthur, Corbin, and then me. "Earth, Fire, Air, Water… looks like you're all set to me."

"Don't forget the fifth element," I croaked. "Spirit."

Maeve sighed. "I was hoping you'd forgotten about that."

"Just because your science books don't talk about it, doesn't mean it doesn't exist." I rubbed my cheek. "According to Rowan, it was spirit that marred my beautiful skin."

Maeve collapsed into the chesterfield beside me, rubbing her temple. "So you're telling me there is some mythical fifth element that can melt people's brains?"

"My brain isn't melted!" I cried. "It's just a little bollocksed up."

"We don't know all the details about exactly what spirit can do," Corbin said. "There aren't that many spirit users around. Elemental magic is passed down genetically, and spirit users tend to be the witches burned at the stake. Some spirit users can speak to the dead, some can see the future, others can poke around in people's heads and alter their thoughts or visit their memories or dreams, which was probably what this Blake fairy was trying to do."

"Your mother was a spirit user," I piped up. Corbin shot me a look, but I ignored it, the same way I did most of the things he said or did.

"My mother?" Maeve shook her head. "My mother wasn't a witch."

"Do you know that for a *fact?*"

"Flynn's just fooling around," Corbin said quickly. "You can't believe anything he says."

The relief on Maeve's face made my heart skip. I realized then that maybe Corbin had a point about her. She was dealing with this whole fae thing pretty well, but that was entirely different from finding out that she wasn't what she thought she was.

"I was literally just figuring out how to resolve this whole fae realm thing using theoretical physics, and now you tell me there's a mysterious fifth element that certain people can manipulate? When it rains, it bloody pours with you lot."

I laughed at her use of the word *bloody*. "Be careful, love. We'll turn you into one of us yet."

If only she knew how true that was.

"If that means I get to eat jam scones every morning, then count me in," she laughed. "So you just need to find this fifth magic user and you'll be able to close the wormhole—I mean, gateway—again? But shouldn't they just be the son or daughter of the last member of the coven? Can't you just look them up on Facebook?"

"It's not as easy as that. Many of the witches in the original coven are dead." Corbin looked nervous. I glanced at Rowan, who stared at the bookshelf, his lips moving as he counted the volumes along the shelves. "I was lucky, my parents taught me about magic and showed me how to control my powers. But these others grew up being forced to suppress their abilities, or not even knowing their magic existed. I spent most of my adult life searching for them and helping them control their powers."

"We haven't always been easy to find," Arthur said. I was pleased when he didn't elaborate.

"The last person is proving particularly difficult," Corbin said, rubbing his shoulder where the fae attacked him the other day. "Both their parents were members of the Briarwood coven, but they died twenty-one years ago, and their infant son vanished. There's no record or sighting of them since. I keep an eye out for news items that might suggest an unintentional use of spirit magic, but so far, nothing I can connect to the fifth. But perhaps it's time to renew the search —Maeve, what's wrong?" He broke off as Maeve bent over the table, carefully studying the article with a weird expression on her face.

"I just thought of something," she said. "Could that Blake guy have actually been human?"

Corbin shook his head. "You said he came out of the sidhe. Humans cannot cross over into the fae realm, so there's no way."

"But we saw them take the baby back with them, so they must be able to now. Maybe that's why you never saw this guy before – maybe he's been in the fae realm all along, but he couldn't come through the gateway." She wet her gorgeous lips with her tongue. "That would explain why he had this… spirit power. He's actually a human with elemental magic."

"That's…" Corbin looked completely flummoxed, which I had to admit was a very good look on him.

"And it explains how I was able to hurt him!" Maeve exclaimed. "A hit with that shovel probably wouldn't have touched a fae, not with the speed they move. But Blake went down like a sack of potatoes."

"Fiddle-de-dee," I sang, which was my standard response whenever someone brought up potatoes. My head pounded, and a wave of exhaustion swept over me. Battling the fae and having my brain probed sure did a number on the body.

"It makes sense, but it doesn't make sense," Arthur said. "You said the others referred to him as a prince. If he's an Unseelie prince, how could he be *human?*"

Corbin went to a bookshelf and started pulling books down. "We're already dealing with something highly unusual, with more fae coming through the portal, the baby-stealing, and now the Seelie and Unseelie working together. We need more research…"

Corbin's voice faded into the background as my head throbbed. I leaned against Maeve's shoulder, my ear pressed against her neck. Her blood pulsed, the beat of it steady and reassuring. I breathed in the scent of her, fruity and light. Not only was she insanely hot with all those curves, but she had saved my life today, *and* made a joke about Jell-O. She was basically perfect. Total girlfriend material.

Pity I was a useless boyfriend. Flirting and shagging and joking around I could do – in fact, I was the fecking *boss* at those things. But Maeve's grief was fresh and raw and written all over her face, even as she dealt with all this fae bollocks we kept throwing at her. She needed someone who could dig deep inside her and heal that grief. And that wasn't me. It would never be me. I couldn't touch pain like that without falling off the edge myself.

By Holy Mother Mary she had me all tied up in knots.

Those pouty lips, that short haircut with the pink streak, the satisfied look on her face when she clonked Blake with that spade... her dark eyes flicked to mine, and her hand rested against one of her full tits, and I imagined those tits free, her nipples hardening in my mouth. My dick strained against my jeans, and that made my head spin, and the whole effect was like the best kind of inebriation mixed with the worst kind of hangover.

The magic acting on Briarwood drew me toward Maeve, but if that was all it was, I'd step back and let one of the other guys have her. That would be the best solution. But Maeve was special, and the idea of giving up the chance of shagging her to a bunch of Englishmen didn't sit well with me. This was winner takes all – and Maeve was one hell of a prize.

Plus, I didn't like losing to the other guys. Corbin I could live with – he was Mr. Bloody Perfect, after all – but Arthur? No fecking way.

We were getting closer to D-day – the day Maeve found out what she truly was, and the day she'd have to choose among us. And even though I knew it was a bloody stupid idea, I was going to do whatever I could to make sure she chose me.

1 8

MAEVE

I sprawled across the sofa in the great hall, staring up at the ceiling beams and hanging swords criss-crossing over my head. The fire blazed beside me, warming my naked skin. My eyes felt heavy, and a taste of honey lingered on my lips. I'd been drinking mead, and somehow I'd discarded all my clothes. But why wasn't I in my room? Where was everyone else?

A hand snaked across my stomach, the touch lighting my skin on fire. Flynn's face appeared in front of mine, his face smooth again, no trace of the fae's magic on his temples. The firelight flickered in his bright blue eyes, making his freckles stand out. His wicked smile gave me flutters in my chest.

"Maeve, you have to choose," he said. I started to ask him what I was choosing, but he smothered my lips in his.

The kiss took my breath away, hot and smoky and full of raw passion. The fire in Flynn's lips seared straight to my sex, which pulsed with an urgency I'd never experienced before. I nibbled his lower lip, and the moan that escaped his lips made my whole body shudder.

A mouth closed over my nipple, the tongue swirling

around. My eyes flickered past Flynn's face, and there was Rowan, his dark eyes raw with hunger. A loose dreadlock fell over his face, tickling the bare skin of my stomach. His tongue lapped around my nipple, sending a shiver of delight through my body. His delicate hands traced lines along my collarbone.

"You have to choose, Maeve." His voice trembled against my nipple. I moaned against Flynn as shivers rocketed along my body. Rowan's dark skin against mine was the perfect contrast.

A mouth closed around the other nipple, and rough hair tickled my skin. "You have to choose, Maeve." Arthur's kind eyes penetrated mine.

Oh yes.

Three guys, all touching me, all worshipping my body with their hot mouths and daring fingers. Their eyes burning with lust, with need, with the knowledge that I wanted them just as much as they wanted me.

Another hand stroked my leg, starting from my toes and walking across my skin. The fingers weaved and danced over my skin, along my thigh. My body ached as the fingers darted closer, closer…

"You have to choose, Maeve, luv." Corbin. His husky voice rippled through me. He pressed his lips against my throbbing clit.

I threw my head back and howled. The pleasure wound its way through my body, tearing along my limbs. Corbin's tongue stroked me gently at first, growing the ache inside me. I bucked my hips towards him, begging for more. He responded by attacking me with his tongue, hammering my clit in furious strokes until I screamed, my limbs jerking and my head spinning from the force of the orgasm that tore through me.

Flynn kissed along my neck, finding my lips again and

assaulting my mouth with his. "When Corbin's done," he whispered, "I'm going down there. I bet you taste better than a fine Irish whiskey."

But Corbin didn't stop, not even after the heat in my veins cooled. The boys continued their ministrations, their tongues and hands roaming every inch of me until the ache rose within me again, hard and eager.

"You have to choose, Maeve." A deep voice boomed.

Something pressed between my legs. A hardness. I moaned and arched my hips, ready for whoever it was who wanted to take me.

Why do I have to choose? Why can't I have them all?

A thick hardness thrust into me. The room swam. I cried out as it slid inside me, my body filled, my cravings sated. My whole body worshipped by an ocean of lips and hands.

"You have to choose, Maeve." That deep, rumbling voice again. But it wasn't the voice of one of my boys. It was familiar, but who…

My eyes fluttered open again, and I was staring over Flynn and Arthur and Rowan and Corbin, their naked bodies draped over me, and into the eyes of Blake, the black-clad fae who had come through the wormhole.

He bucked his legs back, thrusting his hips forward and driving himself deep inside me. My whole body convulsed with pleasure. *Oh god, the feeling of him…*

Blake's crystal eyes caught the light of the fire, gleaming with mischief. "I told you we'd have some fun together. This version of a shag is much better, don't you agree?"

I bolted upright, throwing myself off the couch. I landed hard on the floor and spun around, ready to face the fae.

My heart pounded. How had Blake gotten into the castle? How had he found his way into this… whatever it was, without my boys killing him? Was he manipulating their minds?

I breathed hard as my eyes adjusted to the sudden darkness. My bedroom came into view. I tugged my feet out of the sheets, where they'd become tangled. Yeah, I was definitely in my bedroom, the curtains drawn against the cold moon. I listened. Apart from an owl hooting outside, the house was completely silent.

It was a dream, that's all.

But it had felt so real… I touched my nipple, still feeling the scrape of Arthur's teeth against my skin. My core still ached with need of them all, and tingles ran down my legs and covered my clit from Corbin's tongue. And inside… I ached with longing. For Blake? But that was crazy. For all of them? That was… perverted.

You're going mad with grief, Maeve. I rubbed my thigh, trying to get the desire out of my veins. *Of course it was a dream. You may like all the guys, but you barely even know them, and no way would you want them all together like that. That's just sick and perverted. And Blake at the end? Why the hell was he there, after he hurt Flynn like that?*

But the buzz in my body and hardness of my nipples told another story. I'd just dreamed about my first sixsome. And I liked it.

I liked it a whole *hell* of a lot.

MAEVE

I tossed and turned for a while, the vivid images and sensations of the dream still whirling around in my head. Eventually, I must've drifted back to sleep because I woke up the next morning to the sun streaming through my windows and the heavy weight of Obelix snoozing on top of my feet.

Obelix jumped down and disappeared down the stairs, yowling at the top of his lungs for breakfast. I yawned and sat up, rubbing my eyes. The haze of jet lag that had hung over me the last couple of days had gone – and the numbness in my chest had slid away a little more as well, leaving me raw and a little nervous.

I pulled on a pair of jean shorts and a cap-sleeved t-shirt and padded downstairs. Voices echoed through the castle as the guys joked with each other in what I was learning was their typical routine. I tried to follow their voices, but sound traveled weirdly in the enormous spaces and heavy-duty stone walls, and I still didn't know my way around all the rooms. I peeked in the kitchen, and they weren't there, although the neatly stacked dishes beside the sink and a fresh basket of vegetables told me Rowan had been at work.

I tried the rec room, but they weren't there, either. "Hey guys!" I called out. "I'm Dorothy, lost in the land of Oz. Help me find my way to breakfast!"

Corbin called back. "We're out on the porch."

I followed their voices through the winding halls, taking a wrong turn out into the internal courtyard where a line of visitors waited for the first tour to start, before finally locating the door that would take me out onto the sprawling porch at the back of the castle, overlooking the garden and the rolling fields and the wood, and the wild Crookshollow Forest beyond. Rowan bent over the table, setting down platters of savory muffins and scrambled eggs. Corbin handed around plates – his arm still a little stiff from where the fae had hurt him – and Arthur handed me a flute of pink Champagne.

"I thought life couldn't get any better than waking up to freshly baked scones," I said, accepting the glass and taking in a deep whiff of the fresh, buttery and bacony muffins. "But you proved me wrong."

"We wanted to give you something special." Arthur's thick fingers brushed mine. "To welcome you to Briarwood. Plus Rowan informed us you don't like tea."

"I don't know how you can drink it! It tastes like dirt." The guys laughed. "But seriously, we've already gone to the pub, and all those presents in my room… if I didn't know any better I'd say you were buttering up your landlord. Do you want me to put in air conditioning or something?"

The guys exchanged a look. Finally Corbin said, "Everyone at this table knows what it feels like to lose someone. We just want to make sure Briarwood is a safe place for you to mourn or… do whatever you need."

"Although, now that you mention it…" Flynn grinned,

rubbing the red lattice on his face. "I always thought the castle would be much improved with a pool."

Four faces stared adoringly at me. I blushed, reeling in their kindness and in the news Corbin had just shared with me, that they'd all grieved for someone they loved the way I was doing now. If only they knew about the filthy dreams I'd had about them all the night before. Thank God none of them had that crazy spirit power that could see into people's dreams.

If spirit magic even *existed*. I still had my doubts. I hadn't quite figured out how witches and elemental magic fit into my multiverse theory yet.

Arthur swept my chair out for me, and I settled in. "Thanks, Aragorn." I beamed, and Arthur bowed. The boys started passing plates around the table, and I helped myself to two muffins and a giant pile of scrambled eggs. Rowan even had homemade chutney (another new British word I learned) in a tiny bowl, and I dumped a glob of that on top and dived in. "So, aside from my postponed sword fighting lesson, what's on the agenda today? More fairy-slaying?"

Rowan looked surprised. He looked up from cutting his muffin into perfect squares. "You decided to believe us?"

"Based on the empirical evidence I've seen so far, ignoring the existence of the fae is just willful ignorance. I have come up with an explanation of sorts that I can live with, for now. And I'm going to help."

"Help us?" Corbin lifted an eyebrow.

"Yes, If you want any hope of defeating the fae, you need to take a scientific approach. And that begins with a full study of them. No offense," I nodded to Corbin, "but those books in your library are total trash. There's no ethnological or anthropological studies of the fae. Well, luckily, you happen to have a scientist living with you."

Arthur rubbed his chin. "I'm not sure you quite understand what you're getting into. Science is all well and good, but it's never won a war."

"Yes, it has, actually. Scientists have been key to massive breakthroughs and victories in numerous wars. Bayer's invention of synthetic tire rubber kept the entire German army moving after the Allies cut off their supply of natural rubber from Southeast Asia. The invention of ultrasound was vital to detecting U-boats in World War II. The trireme made the Athenians the rulers of the sea and were imperative in their victory at—"

"Okay, okay, okay." Arthur held up his hands. "I'm beaten."

"Go on, Einstein," Flynn leaned over the table, his fingers dancing on my hand. "Tell us what you need."

Hearing Kelly's nickname for me in Flynn's musical Irish brogue sent a wave of pleasure through my body. "Um… I've been working on a scientific theory that might explain the fae. Unlike other theoretical physicists, I might actually be able to test some of my hypotheses. I'd like to get some scientific instruments and set them up around the sidhe. And I'd also like to interview each of you about your experiences with the fae. No fantastical accounts," I glared at Flynn. "Just straight up ethnographic information that I can compile into a study. And I want to see all your research on this fifth coven member."

Corbin looked uncomfortable. "Why?"

"Why? Because you're the only one who's looked at it. You might be missing something really obvious, and a peer review will highlight that. Because if finding this witch is as important as you say, then you'll take all the help you can get, even from a college physics dropout from Arizona."

Corbin glanced at Rowan, who was staring at his plate, not saying anything about as loud as a person could. I knew there was more to this "fifth" story than Corbin was letting on, and damned if I was going to let him keep it from me.

Corbin cleared his throat. "Fine. We'll sort all that out for you. Now, should we finish this delicious breakfast?"

"Way ahead of you." Arthur was already squirting a generous swirl of something called HP sauce over his eggs. He passed the bottle to me and I sniffed it. *Gross.* Why couldn't Brits just use ketchup like the rest of the civilized world?

I'd just taken a bite of the warm, cheesy muffin when an elderly woman in a black dress strode briskly across the porch toward us, a feather duster resting against her shoulder. "Master Corbin?" she called out, her voice flat and harsh. "There's someone arrived to see you. She's waiting in the reception hall."

My eyes widened. This must be the woman Arthur mentioned the other night. *We have a maid? Cool.*

"Oh, thanks, Dora." Corbin stood up. "I'll bring her out."

The maid – Dora – shot me a filthy look. "Who is your guest? You don't usually let them stay for breakfast."

Whoa, there's a loaded comment. I glanced at Corbin. How many girls *did* he bring back to the castle? It hadn't occurred to me before, but now that I thought of it… these guys were all smoking hot and actually genuinely nice, which was not a common combination. Girls must fall all over them. I remembered Neale flirting with them at the pub. Had Corbin slept with her? Had any of them?

It didn't make any sense, since I'd only met these guys two days ago and, apart from Arthur, none of them had made any indication that they wanted to take things to the places they'd gone in my filthy dream. But a possessive knot twisted in my stomach at the thought of the guys being with anyone else. Now that I was here with them, I wanted them all to myself, which was totally crazy, right?

Right?

Corbin wasn't giving anything away. "Dora, this is Maeve. She's going to be living with us from now on."

"And who does she belong to?" Dora frowned at me. *Wow, what a cow.*

"I can speak for myself," I said, a little frostily. "And I don't belong to anyone."

"American," Dora sniffed. She turned to Corbin. "Don't let her steal any of the silverware."

"*Thank you*, Dora. That will be all."

Dora bustled away, unable to resist another loud sigh as she stomped into the house. I gave Corbin a sickening smile. "Well, she's *adorable*."

"She's as old as this castle, and twice as formidable. But she's not so bad once you get to know her." Corbin stood up. "I'd better go get Emily."

As soon as he left, Flynn let out a whoop. "Grumpy guts has gone, let's get this party started."

"Um…" Before I knew it, Flynn had pulled a portable speaker from somewhere and plugged in his phone. A minute later, weird humping bass noises shook the table. I dropped my fork and stared at Flynn in horror.

"I'm sorry, this is *music?*"

"This album just dropped this morning. It's this wicked drum and bass out of Dublin."

"Can you stick it back in?"

Rowan snorted. I noticed he was placing each little muffin square on his tongue one at a time. I wondered how his OCD tendencies handled the irregularity of scrambled eggs.

"Come on, Flynn," Arthur growled. "Turn that shite off."

"Arthur only likes brutal Scandinavian death metal," Flynn shot back, turning the sickening noise up another notch.

"It's *black* metal, actually," Arthur shouted over the din, thumbing the intelligible logo on his black t-shirt. "And that's not *all* I like. I'm also into folk metal, thrash metal, symphonic metal, doom metal—"

Flynn wrinkled his nose. "Forgive me for not recognizing the diversity in your musical interests."

"At least metal doesn't sound like the speaker is throwing up—"

"Guys!"

We whirled around. Corbin stood on the edge of the deck. Beside him, a blonde bombshell wearing the tiniest pencil skirt known to humankind shot all my boys (and I was already thinking of them as my boys) a sultry smile.

"Emily!" Flynn dropped his speaker and rushed over to give the woman one of his customary hugs. Arthur took the opportunity to unplug the phone from the speaker, a feat for which I was eternally grateful.

My gratefulness wore off when Arthur too rose and embraced this woman, her tiny, perfect breasts pressing against his chest. The hug lasted a few seconds longer than I expected, and jealousy flared in my chest as I wondered if they'd had some thing together.

A shag. I reminded myself of the British term. *I wonder if they've shagged.*

"Maeve, I'd like you to meet Emily, our family lawyer." Corbin brought her over to the table, his eyes flashing with delight. "And your lawyer now, too."

"Nice to meet you," I plastered a smile on my face. Somehow, when I imagined the person who wrote me that letter about Briarwood House, I'd pictured a middle aged, slightly round matron with a grizzled face from too many years fighting against the glass ceiling, not this graceful creature, this perfect example of feminine beauty.

Emily shook my hand. "Maeve, it's lovely to meet you.

I've brought along all the papers for you to sign to officially pass Briarwood's ownership on to you. It's funny, but I always pictured you as a blonde. You can never tell with names in letters, can you?"

Her greeting tugged at me, a weird annoying feeling that something wasn't quite right. But I didn't have time to ponder it further, not while Ms-Perfect-Tits was waiting. I extended a hand and shook it.

"Come join us for breakfast," I heard myself saying, plastering a fake smile on my face. "We probably have a lot to discuss about my mother's estate."

"Oh, yes, please," Emily beamed, and slid herself into the empty chair beside Rowan, touching his arm in a familiar way that made my skin crawl. "It's been an age since I had Rowan's home cooking. I'm hopeless in the kitchen, too busy at work. Ooh, is that HP sauce? Arthur, you naughty boy. All right, send it this way."

Emily and the guys started to gossip about some dude – Ryan Raynard – who owned the adjoining property, called Raynard Hall, and was apparently this uber famous reclusive artist who hadn't been outside in years. I shoveled down the rest of my breakfast, which now tasted like cardboard, and tried not to be such a bitch. *Just because Emily's pretty, and she knows my guys, and she's hanging around the castle like it's her second home, doesn't mean that she's slept with any of them, and even if she has, it's not any of my business...*

I slid back in my chair, and it hit me. What was wrong with what Emily had said. She thought I was a blonde. She hadn't recognized me. But how could that be, when Corbin had seen a picture of me that she'd shown him?

One of them was lying to me. But was it Emily... or Corbin? And why?

ARTHUR

I grabbed two wooden swords from the collection in the hatstand and led Maeve out into the apple orchard at the back of the garden. The orchard was hidden from view behind a high stone wall – ideal, since I didn't want any tourists to see what we were up to. I'd made that mistake once, and the next day we had two Health and Safety inspectors up at the castle asking me about protective equipment (apparently a suit of armour wasn't considered good enough) and if I needed a fairground licence for my "sideshow."

"What are those for?" Maeve asked as I handed her the sword. "This isn't iron. I can't hurt a fae with this."

"No, you can't, but if you don't practice with these first and learn the basics, you won't be able to hurt a fae with the iron one, either." I stepped back from her and held my own sword out in front of me, showing her how to grip the hilt with both hands. "This is a wooden replica of a two-handed sword of English design. Later – if you still like me – I'll show you how to fight with a smaller, single-handed sword and shield. But two-handed is good to start with. You hold your hands here and here," I demonstrated my grip on either end of the hilt. "This grip enables you to pivot the sword through different holds. We call these *wards*."

"Like this?" Maeve mimicked my swing.

"Exactly." My heart thudded in my chest, and I extended my stance to make room for my stiff cock, hoping Maeve wouldn't notice. I'd had this vivid dream about her last night – she was lying naked in the middle of the Great Hall and I was sucking her nipple and she made these mewling sounds at the back of her throat. Now I couldn't look at her without remembering the curve of her breast and the taste of her skin.

Which was good, because I wasn't sure I wanted to remember the rest of the dream – all my other friends naked around me, and some random guy in a black coat I'd never seen before.

Seeing Maeve swing that sword brought it all back, especially if Maeve insisted on being all warrior princess. I shifted my leg. This was going to be one *long* lesson. "That's how you control the weapon. Most swords have a ball-or triangular shaped pommel, and you can use this for pivoting as well, but some of them have a spike, which is great for doing this."

In a flash, I slid in close to her, wrapped my sword around hers, knocked it aside, flipped mine over, and drove the pommel into her face, stopping an inch short of hitting her eye socket. To Maeve's credit, she didn't shriek. Instead, she blinked twice and her muscles relaxed against mine. This close, her sweet scent danced over my nostrils, and it was all I could do not to pull her closer and taste her again.

How the hell was I going to survive these lessons without giving in to the pull of her? We were only ten minutes in and already I was imagining taking her up against one of the apple trees, her shapely legs curled around me, her hot wetness clenching my dick—

"Show me how to do that," Maeve breathed. She blinked again, and her chest brushed against mine. I sucked in a breath and turned my pelvis away from her. Damn, this was going to be hard work, but I had to let Maeve come to me if I was really the one she wanted. That's what I'd agreed to, and no way in hell would I go back on my word to the guys.

It took all of my willpower, but I dropped my hold and stepped away from Maeve. "That comes later. Today we're doing basic stances and crosses, and then we'll do a little bare-knuckle fighting. Now, follow me closely."

I drilled Maeve on some basics, and explained the importance of distance and timing when in a fight with swords. I made her repeat the drills over and over, hoping to kick in her muscle memory.

"Where did you learn all this?" Maeve asked as our wooden swords clattered together. I'd gone easy on her in the beginning, but as she got better, I added more force behind my blows. She defended with equal force.

"From Youtube videos, mostly." I said, swinging again. "And studying sword fighting manuals written by the medieval sword masters. I was involved with a historical martial arts club in Crooks Worthy for a while, but I had to leave last year."

"Why?"

I hesitated. I didn't want to tell her why. I didn't want her to think less of me.

"Arthur, why?"

Maeve sensed my hesitation through my sword and used it to push my weapon aside and slide in close. My sword hung uselessly out to the left and her face drew up against my chest, her breath hot against my neck.

"I don't know what to do from here," Maeve said, her voice breathy. "But I think I got past your guard."

I gulped. Her sweet scent invaded my nostrils, spinning around my head, making my senses all wobbly. The only thing that was working was my cock and it pressed painfully against my thigh, desperate for escape. I gulped. "Yeah, you did. Good work."

The fire licked at my veins, that all-too-familiar force drawing me closer. Maeve's dark eyes widened, and she wet her lips. Her face poised inches from mine. My chest burned. *Kiss me, dammit. I want you so bad, and it's more than just the coven's magic talking. You're a wonder, Maeve Moore—*

Maeve tore herself from my arms and drew back, her breath coming out in ragged gasps. I felt her absence as a pain in my chest, a longing to be close to her.

"This isn't teaching me how to fight," she declared, her chest heaving. "Now, let's do that move again."

We backed up to our starting places. Maeve raised her sword to her shoulder, holding it pointing to the sky, her hands tight into her shoulder, the way I'd shown her. I came at her with a huge swing and a bellow. You should always make a lot of noise when training someone to fight, especially if they're a woman, because real fights are noisy. It teaches them to be aware of more than one sense. When women are attacked, they usually go completely silent, which isn't ideal because making noise may alert someone that you're in trouble.

Maeve swung the sword down to meet mine, blocking my blow and waving the tip dangerously close to my face. We practiced it again and again, and I was chuffed at how well she was doing.

We switched sides, and Maeve attacked me. Other girls I'd fought with – back at the medieval club and my earlier martial arts classes – who would go so softly that it was hard to defend their half-hearted blows, but not Maeve – she threw her whole weight behind every swing. She was so committed that she leaned too far forward into her next blow, so when my sword came down I accidentally slapped her across the cheek.

"Ow!" She staggered back, clutching her face.

I dropped my sword and ran to her, gathering her in my arms. "I'm sorry. I'm so so sorry. Did I hurt you badly? Is it bleeding?"

"It's fine. I'm fine…" But when I tugged her hand away, I could see an ugly welt forming on her cheek. Streams of tears rolled down her cheeks. My stomach churned. I'd done this to her. I'd hurt her.

This was what I did. I lost control and hurt people. The familiar burning in my chest rose up, like an enormous burp desperate to be free. Only instead of wind it would unleash the fury I kept locked away inside. Panic clouded my vision as I shoved it back down. *This is why I haven't had a girl since I came to Briarwood. This is why I only train by myself. This is why I would be the absolute* worst *choice for Maeve. How can I help her learn to tame her powers if I haven't even tamed my own?*

"I'm sorry," my voice cracked. "We'll stop now. This was a stupid idea. I don't want to hurt you any more."

Maeve laughed, wiping her face. "No, these tears aren't because of you. Seriously, Arthur, this barely hurts."

"It looks bad. We should get you inside."

"No, *listen*. I was thinking about my parents, about how they always wanted me to be athletic. Everyone in Arizona plays sports. My Dad was high school quarterback. Kelly was on the cheerleading squad. Mom played on a church baseball team. They went to the state championships every year. But I refused. I was hopeless in gym class – I can calculate the circumference of a sphere but I can't catch one for bollocks."

"Nice use of bollocks." I wiped a tear from the corner of

her eye. "You're a fast learner."

"Hey, languages are a lot like physics – once you learn the rules it's just a matter of getting the nuances right. I haven't quite mastered the nuances of shagging and shagged and shagging around, but I'll get there."

"Wait until you learn about bollocks vs the dogs bollocks. But you were saying about your parents?"

She sniffed. "Just that they were always on at me to do something physical. My Dad would always say, 'Chess club is not a sport, Maeve.' And now here I am, learning how to fight with swords like a real medieval knight, and they would have hated it but also been proud at the same time, and I just…" she wiped her face again. Her whole body crumpled against me.

"Hey," I stroked her hair, trying to ignore the beautiful sweet smell that rose off her or the way her body fitted so perfectly against mine. "It's okay to cry."

"You don't understand," she sniffed. "I *haven't* cried. For weeks I've been this big ball of numbness, and everyone's been looking at me, expecting me to show some emotion. But it's like their loss was so great that it took everything away, even my ability to *feel*. And then I came here and met you guys and learned about fae and kissed you and cried the other night and now I'm feeling *too much*."

Bloody hell, she was even beautiful when she cried. Maybe *more* beautiful. Everything I knew about Maeve and her brilliant, analytical mind said that this outburst was rare for her. It was actually an honor to be the shoulder she chose.

Don't waste it. Say something reassuring, you bellend.

"Everyone grieves in a different way," I said. "You have to give yourself permission to do whatever it takes to get yourself through the pain. And then you have to forgive yourself for all the shit you end up doing because of it."

"What do you mean?"

"I didn't cry either when my mum died. I was too angry. I had this fire inside me, burning with rage that the world had taken her from me."

"When did she die?" Maeve tucked a strand of pink hair behind her ear, her big hazel eyes boring into mine.

I hesitated. No way did I want to talk about Mum, especially not with the fire dangerously close to flaring up in a bad way. But I remembered when I first met Corbin – only months after he lost his brother Keagan – and how angry I was, how I'd lashed out at him when he'd found me, punched him out, broken his nose. Corbin brought me to Briarwood, and in front of the fire in this big, empty castle, he told me the story of his own pain. It poured out of him – all the guilt and loss and the hopeless, crushing loneliness. I took it into myself and wore it as my own, and his pain pushed out my own, and for a while things didn't hurt so much.

That was why I stayed, I think, in the end. Because being around Corbin, and seeing him wear his tragedy like a badge of honor and turn it into passion, made my own pain fade to the background. Here, I had more control over the fire.

Maybe… maybe I could be that for Maeve.

I sighed. "She died when I was eight. Her and my dad, they fought all the time. Big screaming fights that shook the walls and sent me cowering under the bed. They were both fire elementals, so they had these terrible tempers. Mum was better at controlling it – she channeled the fire into her artwork, into her charity work. But Dad pushed his into his fists, which he then swung at Mum, or at me."

"Oh, Arthur." Maeve wrapped her arms around me, squeezing me tight. It reminded me of Mum. When the fire burned inside me, and she could see I was about to blow, she'd hold me and squeeze me and whisper funny stories in my ear. She didn't want me to learn to deal with it the way Dad did.

Maeve touched my arm, right near my elbow. "Is that where you got the scars?"

Shite. "No."

The fire crackled inside me, pushing against my fingertips. I moved my hands off Maeve's shoulders so if a flame flared up I wouldn't accidentally burn her. I sucked in a deep breath, and continued, hoping I'd distract her enough that she wouldn't ask about them again. "Anyway, they were screaming at each other in the kitchen, and I could hear crockery smashing, and then Dad was the only one screaming, only his screams were different. He howled at me to call an ambulance, so I dialed 999 and then I went downstairs and saw her body slumped against the kitchen floor." I shuddered at the memory. "He hit her and she fell and smashed her head open on the granite bench. And just like that, she was gone."

"I'm so sorry." Maeve buried her face in my shoulder. I breathed in the sweet scent of her hair. Already, the tension in her shoulders had lifted a little. This was working.

Which was damn good, because it was tearing me open. A short flame burst from my hand, and I quickly slammed my palm against the grass to snuff it out. *That's enough of that.* "It's fine. It was a long time ago. I told you because I want you to know that I remember what it was like, the way the grief seeps into every aspect of your life, how the whole world's eyes bore into you, expecting you to react a certain way. How your own body betrays you because it hurts so damn much."

"Yeah." Maeve rubbed my shoulders. "How everyone you see suddenly seems different, like their lives are completely separate to you, because they couldn't possibly understand how the knowledge of it follows you everywhere."

"That's what's so brilliant about Briarwood." I stared up at the tops of the trees – the sprawling apple trees loaded with fruit, the towering oak and ash that lined the edge of the garden. "Here, we live in another world. The outside world doesn't bother us. It really is like we're part of some far off, fantastical world. Everyone in this house came here to heal, no matter what they told you."

"Maybe I'll heal, too, but not if I'm kept in the dark. Corbin is hiding something from me." Maeve studied my face, those dark eyes not missing a thing. "You all are, I think."

"Do you trust us?"

She hesitated, then nodded. "I know I shouldn't. It's ridiculous, since I've known you for all of three days. But something in my gut is saying that I can trust you. I don't usually listen to my gut without empirical evidence to back it up, but you guys did save my life the other night, so I guess that's enough for now. Yes, I trust you."

"Then trust that Corbin will tell you everything when the time is right." I thought of the letter sitting in the top drawer of Corbin's desk and of the tear-streaked girl in my arms. What would it do to Maeve when she read that letter?

But she was so strong, so much stronger than any of us imagined. All these years we'd watched her from afar, protected her, and we didn't know her at all. But I wanted to, and not just because of the magic.

Maeve changed the subject again. "How did you come to live at Briarwood?"

"I was the first of us that Corbin found when he decided to put the coven together again," I said, choosing each word carefully. "He was fifteen. I was fourteen and I… I was hell-bent on bollocksing up my life. I lived with my Dad, who'd told the police my mum slipped on the wet tiles and got away with it. He'd become an even bigger dick, and I couldn't look at him without seeing what he did to Mum and how he'd lied to get out of the consequences. I was so angry, and I couldn't control the anger. I had nowhere to channel it. Kids were always mean to me at school, because I was so big, and I hated sports like rugby. I read lots of fantasy books and watched horror films and played Dungeons & Dragons, and… that wasn't the done thing."

Flashes of memory snatched at me – of Lance Holmes smashing a case of D&D figurines I'd laboriously painted, and stealing my clothes in the middle of the night and flying them up the flagpole so I had to go into the quad completely naked while everybody in school sniggered at me. "This kid Lance, we used to be friends in junior high, but by the time we went to high school together, he had it out for me. He knew all these stories from when I was younger, when I couldn't control my magic. He spread this rumor that I was a pyromaniac who'd killed my mother, that I was unstable. I came into the classroom one day and he was telling people she must've done something to me as a child to make me like this, and that I should be locked up, and I—"

A flame flickered on my palm. Maeve gasped. She reached out to touch it, but I shut my fingers around it, snuffing it out.

"It'll burn you," I said. "That's what being close to me does. It burns people. That's what Lance found out. I *lost* my shit. The fire burst out of me before I could stop it, and it caught on Lance's uniform, and he was screaming and thrashing around. He had serious second-degree burns by the time they put him out."

I searched Maeve's face for a sign of the horror she must be feeling, for the realization that I was a monster. Her mouth fell open a little, but her bright eyes widened, staring at me with such empathy, I had to fight against an urge to fall against her, to wrap her up inside my bulk and keep her close forever. Instead, I sucked in a deep breath, steadying myself against her apparent willingness to accept my darkest secret, and continued.

"They wanted to send me away. The press came knocking at the door, wanting the inside scoop on the 'Firestarter.' Dad didn't even like me that much anyway, and I didn't think he wanted the press looking into our past, so he left. Just walked out one day and never came back. I had no one to speak for me. None of my relatives wanted me. They thought my mum was kooky, and that she'd made me crazy. I was going to be locked away in an institution, but then Corbin appeared with this fancy lawyer from London who somehow convinced the judge that there was no evidence I'd started the fire. So they let me free, and Corbin asked me to come live here."

"And you came, just like that?"

I gestured up at the imposing facade of Briarwood. "Wouldn't you? You don't get second chances very often in life. I was lucky enough that Corbin gave me this one."

"Oh, Arthur. I'm so sorry." Maeve nestled her head against my shoulder. "I know what it's like not to fit in. My school was sports-obsessed, too. And Christ-obsessed. My own parents believed the universe was six-thousand years old. Can you imagine what happened when I told them I wanted to be an astronaut?"

"I cannot imagine that." Mainly because the idea of being something other than a screw-up who played too many computer games never occurred to me. But something about being close to Maeve made me believe anything was possible.

Every inch of my body demanded that I kiss her. My lips stung with the memory of the taste she'd given me. But it wasn't enough. I didn't just want Maeve's body. I didn't just want her because of the magic, because of the need to make the coven whole. I wanted her because she was amazing, and even if it damn near killed me, I wouldn't touch her until she thought I was amazing, too.

*A*rthur and I lay under the apple trees for the rest of the morning. I thought he'd kiss me again. The hunger in his eyes certainly desired it. But his words and his touches were almost more intimate.

Every time my fingers grazed his, or his breath tickled my skin, I thought of jumping him and pressing my mouth to his again. But something held me back. Lots of things. The dream. The fact the guys were all hiding something from me, that Corbin at least knew who I was before I arrived at Briarwood. The look on Rowan's face this morning. Emily's tinkling laugh.

I thought about what Arthur said to me, about how he'd lost control. My chest throbbed – not with tightness, but with a weird nakedness, as if Arthur's story had opened a gaping, bleeding wound through which all my pain and grief now poured.

Arthur said Briarwood was a place of healing. I pressed my hand to my chest, feeling the sorrow throbbing behind it, knowing in my heart this was only the beginning of a great unleashing. I felt sliced up, pieces of me chopped off and scattered on the wind. I'd lost pieces when the Crawfords died, more pieces when Pastor Eric took our house away, and more when MIT rescinded my scholarship. Maeve Moore nee Crawford was just bits of flesh and misery, clusters of lamenting electrons floating in the cosmos. But maybe in this place, where fairytales were real and there was a hot guy around every corner, maybe I could put all the pieces back together again.

Arthur placed his arm around me and my body flared with desire. The wound in my chest gaped a little wider as the ache between my legs rose up to meet it. *Oh, bollocks.* Such a great phrase. It rolled off the tongue even better than *goddammit.* Bollocks seemed an accurate descriptor for this situation I found myself in. I shifted my weight around, trying to shake away the sensation, but I accidentally brushed my thigh against Arthur's crotch, and his breath caught on his lips, and that only made things worse.

Great, now I was more confused than ever. What did I even *want* from Arthur? He wasn't the kind of guy I'd usually consider dating. I shouldn't even be dating anyone. I didn't know how long I'd even be staying in England. What would happen to us if I had to sell the castle? Not to mention the fact that I was a scientist and he was… was a blond-haired Aragorn who could shoot fire from his palms. It was stupid. It would never work.

But the flutter in my chest and the ache in my stomach begged to differ. My parents chastity teachings hadn't rubbed off on me – I didn't have to date Arthur to… to *shag* him. It didn't have to go anywhere. It could be my wild English fling before I settled down to a life of equations and working my ass off to get into the space program.

The idea had its merits, but was I ready for sex? Would it tear open the wound in my chest so I bled my sorrow everywhere? Would it break me apart completely? And was Arthur even the right guy for that? He said himself that he burned whoever he touched. And the others…

"What are you thinking about?" Arthur asked, his breath tickling my ear. "Your face went serious all of a sudden."

I'm thinking about jumping your bones. I'm thinking that you're the first of the guys at Briarwood to spill your guts to me. I'm thinking that if I let you in, you'll burn me, and maybe I'll like it, and maybe it will turn me to ashes.

I shrugged. "I'm just trying to square up everything I learned about the fae and your coven with my multiverse theory. There's a lot of thinking I have to do, and I'd really like to start setting up some equipment and writing this all down. I need to formulate a proper hypothesis."

"Can you explain this theory of yours to me, in really, *really* simple terms?"

I was still trying to demonstrate the multiverse theory to Arthur using daisies I'd picked off the lawn when Flynn called us for lunch. We ate out on the porch again – Flynn said it was a rule in England that you couldn't waste a single day of sunshine because we only got a few. Rowan had made some traditional English dish called Toad-in-the-Hole, which sounded disgusting, but was actually delicious; beautiful, thick homemade sausages cooked inside a giant savory dough and smothered with a thick gravy. I had three helpings, all washed down with some HP sauce (it was starting to grow on me) and a glass of elderflower cider Arthur had made. All the other guys had cider except for Rowan, who had a cup of steaming tea.

"I've compiled some research you might find interesting in the library," Corbin said to me. "If you give me a list of the implements you want, Arthur and I will run into town and grab them this afternoon."

It was on the tip of my tongue to ask about why Corbin

was lying about where he knew me from, but I decided to hold off until we were alone.

I shook my head. "I have to come with you. I really need to choose this stuff on my own. I'll be fine," I glowered at Corbin's drawn face. "Arthur's already taught me tons of sword moves, and if you all come with me, I'm sure we'll be fine. We could even take a taxi – they're not going to try anything out in the open, surely."

"I don't like it," Corbin frowned.

"Oh, go on, you grumpy bastard." Flynn speared the last piece off Corbin's plate and shoved it in his mouth. "We can't stay locked up here forever. My arms are about to fall off from all the hammering I've done in the forge this morning. Us Irishmen start to turn green if we don't set foot in a pub every twenty-four hours."

"Wag off, Flynn," Corbin growled.

"I think we should go," Arthur said. "Maeve's been telling me about her theory, and I think there might be something to it. Any knowledge could potentially give us an advantage against the fae, and right now we need everything we can get."

"We could talk to the girl," Rowan mumbled into his chest.

The guys fell silent. "What did you say, mate?" Corbin asked.

"The woman whose baby went missing yesterday. If she saw anything weird, she wouldn't tell the police. But she might tell us."

"That's a brilliant idea," I said. Rowan beamed. "It's settled. We're going to town."

"Not today though," Corbin said, pushing his chair out and collecting the plates. "We have a surprise for you this afternoon."

"Another surprise?"

"This one was all my idea," Flynn said. He grabbed my hand and dragged me around the side of the garden, where a flat lawn stretched out toward a low topiary maze. A series of metal hoops had been shoved into the pristine lawn, creating a weird zigzagging course. Flynn grinned as he handed me a flat-ended mallet. "You're a little like Alice, fallen through the rabbit hole into a strange new world where everyone says bollocks and Irishmen are the rightful rulers. So I thought we could play some croquet, and then Rowan's made a proper high tea – finger sandwiches and scones with jam and clotted cream and all that guff."

"But—" It was on the tip of my tongue to say we couldn't play croquet when the fae had stolen two babies and were pushing their way further and further into our realm, weakening the wormhole between the multiverse. But Flynn tilted his head to the side, and the smile he gave me made my heart somersault.

"Look, we're still no closer to getting those wee ones, so I figure we need a distraction. Recharge our batteries and all that. I have a present for you, too." Flynn opened my palm and pressed something into it – a round medallion on a leather cord, its surface covered with knotwork and that stick writing Corbin and Rowan had on their tattoos. "I made it for you this morning. It will help protect you from the fae, and if you pressed it against their skin, you'd probably do a fecking load of damage."

"Flynn, it's beautiful." I ran my fingers over the surface. Flynn clasped it around my neck, and I placed my hand in Flynn's and let him walk me across the yard, his flirty humor making my skin flush and my body light.

The multiverse could wait.

My eyes flickered open, recognizing the tapestries on the wall and the blazing fire. I was in the Great Hall. I must've fallen asleep.

It had been an intense day, between meeting Emily, signing the papers declaring me official owner of Briarwood, sword fighting and crying with Arthur, skipping around the garden while Flynn chased me with a croquet mallet, devouring a stack of Rowan's scones, and then holing up in the library with Corbin to start poring through the ancient books about the fae. We worked for hours, mostly in companionable silence, and although I started making notes for my ethnographic project, we hadn't managed to find much that would be useful in our current predicament.

I must've fallen asleep in front of the TV or something. But why do we have the fire going? It's the middle of summer.

I sat up, rubbing my eyes. All the overstuffed couches and mismatched coffee tables and gaming consoles were gone. Someone had even got rid of the bar. The room was bare, apart from the velvet chaise lounge I reclined on. It had been placed in the center of the room, directly under one of the wrought-iron chandeliers.

But... but how did the guys move all this furniture without me waking up? And why would they do that? Are we spring-cleaning the castle or something?

"You have to choose, Maeve." Corbin walked past the fire, circling my couch. I jolted with shock as I took in his complete nakedness – every inch of Corbin's muscled, tattooed body was on proud display. His broad chest tapered into a narrow waist and tight, toned thighs, the muscles pulling and rippling as he moved. Between his legs, an enormous cock stood proud and erect, the head purple with desire.

"Um…" My words dried on my lips. An ache of wanting surged in my stomach, flaring between my legs. *Damn. Imagine that body pressed up against mine, my fingers running over those tight abs, stroking that enormous—*

My eyes barely recovered from the beauty of Corbin when Arthur fell in step behind him, also completely naked. If Corbin had the body of a Greek hero, than Arthur's was the body of a Viking warrior – his muscles were even larger, bulging from his body like hard rocks. Tattoos of knots and serpent dragons encircled his arms and upper torso, and along the inside of his thighs and arms were thin, white scars. He'd freshly oiled his beard and braided it into two long strands that curled out from his body, with bright-colored beads carved with those stick-like symbols tying the ends.

His beard wasn't the only thing that curved. His huge, hard cock – even bigger than Corbin's, if that was even possible – had a slight upward curve to it. Would that rub in all the right places when it was inside me? I ached to find out.

"Gggg…" My sex pulsed with need, suddenly aware of

how hollow I felt, how desperate I was to be full, but with whom?

Flynn came next, skipping like the fool he was, his whole face lit up with that dazzling devil's grin. He was leaner, more wiry than the others, but still toned. Freckles scattered across his chest and down his arms. Unlike the others, he only had one tattoo – a woman's face on his chest, right above his heart.

My eyes darted to his cock, which wasn't as long as Corbin's or Arthur's, but was thick and inviting with reddish veins around the already engorged head. I licked my lips, wanting to run my tongue along the length of him, taste his Irish meat.

Flynn's sparkling eyes met mine. "You have to choose, Maeve."

I cast my eyes around for Rowan. He emerged from the shadows at the corner of the room, and followed the others to move around my couch. His dark skin glowed in the crackling firelight, sleek like a panther stalking its prey. The dreadlocks around his face were pinned back with a silver brooch covered in knotwork. The rest streamed down his back, the beads on the bottoms clattering together. His cock swung between his legs, surprisingly bigger and longer than all of the others. Rowan stared at the ground, his lips moving as he counted something on the rug. When he finished, he looked up, and the hunger and wistfulness in his eyes nearly broke me completely.

The guys circled the couch, inching closer to me with each round. My eyes didn't know where to look, drinking in the sight of all those bulging muscles and gleaming cocks, all erect and waiting for *me*.

Corbin touched me first, sliding my robe off my shoulders, his fingers like fire against my skin. *When did I change into a robe?*

I sat up, swinging my legs over the edge of the couch as the robe pooled around my body. I was naked underneath. Corbin's eyes widened as he took in my body. His hand skimmed over my collarbone, my breast, the edge of my stomach. His fingers fluttered over my thigh, and the ache burned hot inside me. I pressed my legs together and dug my toes into the thick rug.

"May we touch you?" he asked, his voice husky with need.

I moved my legs apart, giving them a full view. "Don't be shy."

Arthur didn't wait another moment. He lunged at me, his eyes wild with hunger. He pressed his mouth to mine.

The kiss burned right through my body, reaching inside me and twisting my insides around. Arthur's huge hands cupped my breasts, grazing my nipples with the coarse surface of his fingers. I gasped against his lips as his rough touch sent shivers right to my core.

Arthur bent me back against the couch. He dived between my legs, nibbling my thighs, teasing me to the very edge. While he danced around the one spot that throbbed with need, Corbin climbed up beside me, his lips devouring mine. Behind his head, Flynn shuddered as his eyes wandered over my body, and his hands reached out to stroke my skin.

Hands slipped over my breasts, cupping each one. A freckled hand, a black hand. Corbin's tongue danced in my mouth, while another pair of lips – Rowan's, I think – kissed a trail down my neck. The circle closed around me, my guys worshipping my body, touching my heart, tearing open my chest and spilling all my pain and sorrow upon the velvet couch.

My guys lay me right back, folding their bodies around me. Hands and lips and tongues flew everywhere. Arthur's long hair tickled my skin as he kissed along my inner thigh, inching closer and closer to the ache that demanded attention. I gripped hard muscle, holding them tight. *Don't stop. Don't ever stop.*

Hands gripped my thighs, pulling my legs apart. The ache throbbed inside me. *Please, please, I want all of you. I want everything you have to give me.*

And then I was sinking, sinking, and the lips against mine grew hotter and hotter, and the world swirled. I pulled back, and got a good look at the guy I was kissing.

It wasn't Corbin – it was Blake.

I gasped, but whether it was surprise or pleasure I could no longer tell. A sound pierced my ears – a shrill, rhythmic ringing that drew me back from the moment. The edges of Blake's face wobbled, and his voice sounded far away.

"What's happening?" I choked out, but my words sounded weird, like I was speaking underwater. The shrill ring in my ears intensified, drowning out the pleasure pulsing through my veins. The room, the boys, the lips and tongues and fingers all faded away as an inky blackness devoured my eyes.

Blake's grin followed me as I slipped away into oblivion. "Welcome to your wildest dreams, Princess."

MAEVE

I woke with a jolt. My eyes adjusted to the dark, and I saw that I was no longer in the Great Hall, but back in my own bedroom. My hands gripped the sheets, bunching them into knots around me. My whole body was covered in sticky sweat and the ache between my legs still throbbed, my pussy desperate to be filled.

What the hell was that?

Okay, so I was officially a nymphomaniac. Being around these guys all day, every day, was making me mad with lust. And kissing Arthur again seems to have made it *worse*.

I knew, logically, that dreams were just my brain throwing up random images and sensations during the REM sleep stage, perhaps as a way of processing information that I encountered throughout the day. It stood to reason that my dreams might be particularly vivid or disturbing after I'd witnessed my parents dying like that.

But why was my mind going back to that same fantasy – that orgy in the middle of the Great Hall? And why was that Unseelie, Blake, always there, always right in the center of things?

The shrill noise pounded in my ears. I glanced around, my heart pounding. If it was a dream, how did the sound follow me into—

My phone. The screen lit up, and it vibrated across my nightstand, the ringing piercing the din. I grabbed for it, noting my sister's picture on the screen and the time in the corner; 2:28AM.

"Kelly?" I cried, jamming the phone to my ear. "Are you okay? What's wrong?"

The fae were in Arizona the night my parents died. Corbin said that pouka Kalen was after him, but what if they went after Kelly next? What if—

Kelly laughed, although her laugh sounded a little wooden. "I'm fine, Einstein. Boy, do you sound weird. Did I wake you up from a nap or something?"

"It's after two in the morning! Of course you woke me up."

"It is? Oh crap, sorry! I thought I had this time zone thing right. It's supposed to be the middle of the afternoon."

I groaned. *Typical Kelly.* I'd explained the time zones to her a hundred times before I left, and even downloaded a conversion app onto her phone. But that was my sister for you. We'd been texting back and forth ever since I'd arrived, but I hadn't had a chance to talk for more than a couple of minutes. Now, the sound of her voice sent a wave of longing through me. I missed Arizona. I missed fry bread and cheese crisps and the horizon following me everywhere and there not being any fae. I missed being a normal twenty-something science nerd with normal crazy Evangelical parents and normal science-nerd problems. And most of all, I missed Kelly.

"Yeah, well…" I rubbed my eyes and turned on my bedside lamp, illuminating only one small corner of my enormous room. "I'm awake now. So go on, tell me what's up."

"I just wanted to talk to you." Kelly's voice cracked a little. "I'm living with Aunt Florence and Uncle Bob now. They made up a fold out couch in the den. Every night I go to sleep staring at the corner of the pool table. They've been great, but..."

"But you don't really belong there?" My chest tightened again. I understood. Everything at Briarwood had been amazing so far, but it felt as though I was out of time. And I'd met Bob – Matthew Crawford's arrogant radio preacher older brother who was convinced he was the direct word of God – enough times to know he wouldn't know what to do with a strong-willed teenage girl like Kelly. Every time we came back from Bob and Florence's house, our parents would get extra-strict for a couple of weeks, trying to live up to Bob's ridiculous Godly standard.

"Exactly. Bob confiscated my phone and most of my clothes. There's no internet, no TV, but Uncle Bob does bible study with us every night where he basically talks about how it's a woman's purpose to serve her man and have babies, *and* they're trying to make me march in an anti-gay parade."

"Yikes. Kelly, I'm so sorry. It's only for this year, though."

"I know. I tell myself over and over. And the first week of school was *weird*. Everyone was so *nice*. No one wants to talk to me in case they say something wrong. I made a joke in math class and no one laughed, so then I threw a pencil at Jake Skipper and Mr. Daniel saw but didn't even give me a detention." She sniffed. "It's just so messed up."

"Kelly, I'm so sorry." I hated myself for her tears, her pain. "I should be there with you. I'd put Bob in his place. We've all each other's got. We should be facing this together – the Crawford sisters against the world."

"No, Maeve, *no*." Kelly said firmly. "Don't you dare come

back. If you do, I'll never talk to you again, and then what would be the point of being stuck at Uncle Bob's house without my scintillating conversation to keep you from going mad?"

I laughed, tears rolling down my cheeks. "But you're hurting—"

"Of course I am, you ninny. My parents were killed. But you being here isn't going to make me hurt less. In fact, it would be worse, because I'd know that I was holding you back from a zany English adventure. Now, go on, tell me about the castle. No, tell me about the hot guys!"

I grinned despite myself, the memory of the last dream echoing across my mind. I'd mentioned in my texts that the four tenants were actually totally hot dudes, and ever since Kelly had been hounding me with suggestive emojis. She was getting almost as bad as Mom with the emojis—

No, don't think about Mom. Instead, I described each of the guys in detail, starting with Corbin, and finishing with Arthur. I wasn't sure if I should mention the kiss, but when it got to it, I couldn't help it.

"Omigod!" Kelly squealed. "He sounds absolutely scrumptious. You've got to send me pictures. I am so jealous right now. You're living in a castle with four hot guys and are being kissed by a blond Aragorn. Are you dating yet?"

"Kelly, I'm not in any state to date anyone, especially not someone who is technically my tenant." But at the thought of it, I couldn't help smiling. I told Kelly all about the tower room, and all gifts the guys gave me, and Rowan's breakfasts and the pub and learning to sword fight and playing croquet with Flynn.

"I'm so jealous," she said, her tone wistful. "It sounds amazing."

"It is, but it's also… weird." I ached to tell her about the fae, but I knew that was a terrible idea. She wouldn't believe me, which made sense, since I still wasn't sure I believed myself. "There's a picture of my birth mother in the hallway. She looks a lot like me, only way prettier."

And last time I looked at it, I heard a voice talking to me, but let's not mention that.

"I bet *Arthur* doesn't think so."

"Shut up," I grinned, cradling the phone in my arms. We talked for a little longer, Kelly's voice making my chest ache a little. She sounded so clear, as if she was just in another room, and not thousands of miles away.

After we finished the phone call, my eyes were wide open. No way could I go back to sleep now. I pulled on my robe and padded across the bedroom and down my narrow, winding staircase. My throat itched from all the talking and laughing – a glass of water or juice would definitely help. As I padded down the hall toward the secret staircase, I noticed a shaft of moonlight from one of the tall windows falling across my birth mother's portrait.

No, not moonlight. I peered out the window into the courtyard below. A square of light from the library downstairs stretched across the cobbles, casting a faint glow along the rows of ancient stones. Through the window I could make out Corbin's broad shoulders hunched over his desk, a stack of books piled high beside him.

He must be working all hours, trying to figure out how to stop the fae.

I thought of going down there to see him, but the memory of Corbin's touch in my dream stopped me. I pulled away from the window and my gaze flickered back to my mother's portrait. I stood in front of it, gazing up at her. The citrine jewels on her finger, necklace and diadem glimmered as though they were more than just paint splashed on a canvas. Her lips – so like mine – curled back into that mysterious smile.

Her eyes aren't the same as mine. Mine were hazel, with that weird shattered glass effect around the edges that Kelly once said was like looking into water. Hers were a cool, clear blue, bright and vivid and totally enchanting.

"I wish I'd been able to meet you," I said, my voice echoing down the silent hallway. The portrait stared back with that same alluring smile. A heavy weight crushed my chest – the pain of a different life I might have lived if she'd still been alive, and of another person who moved on and left me behind.

Silent tears rolled down my cheeks. I let them fall, tumbling off the end of my chin and splashing into the carpet. *Everything's so messed up. I wish I had someone to talk to, someone who understand what it's like to lose everything, what it feels like to not trust what you've seen with your own eyes—*

Talk to me, Maeve.

I leapt back from the painting, grabbing the sides of my head. *That did* not *just happen. A weird, singsong voice that wasn't my own did* NOT *just talk to me inside my head.*

I listened hard, tugging thick handfuls of hair until my scalp ached. But the voice didn't come back. The castle remained as still and silent as death.

Okay. Now I'm imagining things. That's great. Way to add another dimension to this totally fucked up mess I've got myself in.

I stared at the image for a long time, until I stopped seeing my birth mother – she became a conglomeration of pigment and geometric shapes and tones. I let the weight and history of Briarwood wash over me, the high stone walls embrace me, coddling me, keeping me safe. Even if my life was "complete bollocks" as Flynn would say, at least I had this place, and while I was here, I could never truly be alone.

Sighing, I tore my eyes from my birth mother and went down to the kitchen to find myself a snack.

~

"How will you get this woman to talk to you?" Corbin linked his arm in mine. Behind his back, Flynn glowered at him and gave him the finger.

The woman he was referring to was Jane Forsythe, who had lost her baby to the fae, although she didn't know it was them yet. Corbin had put in a quick call to Emily this morning and managed to wrangle Jane's address out of her – it was such a small town pretty much everyone used Emily's law firm. Getting that address meant stomaching twenty minutes of listening to Corbin flirting over the phone, which turned my stomach in jealous knots. Although watching Flynn make funny faces behind Corbin's back made it slightly easier to bear.

My four guys now walked in a diamond formation around me – Arthur at the front, huffing and sweating in the ankle-length coat he wore to disguise the short sword he had sheathed on his belt. Corbin and Rowan stood either side of me, the ends of Rowan's dreadlocks flicking the bare skin on my arms as he walked. Flynn pulled up the rear. He sang some weird, somber Celtic song at the top of his lungs.

"I'll think of something," I said. "My parents used to visit grieving widows and sad old people all the time as part of their work and they'd often drag me along. I should be able to get her to talk."

"I don't like you going in alone," Arthur huffed, his hand flying instinctively for the hilt of his sword.

"We won't get anything out of her with you four standing around looking menacing. Besides, I have my protections." I placed my hand in the deep pocket of my denim overalls, brushing the handle of the short knife Arthur had given me, wrapped in a short Latin incantation scrawled on a piece of parchment from Corbin. In the other pocket was the small twig from Rowan and the medallion Flynn made me.

We walked under the enormous gatehouse marking the entrance to Briarwood, dodging between cars arriving for the morning English Heritage tours, and turned onto the country lane. Arthur insisted that if we were going to walk, that we take the main road instead of the shortcut through the field. I didn't blame him – he'd run into the fae twice in as many days in that field, and here on the road we'd be visible to passing cars and other people's front windows. "The English are nosy neighbors," Arthur said, as he waved to a lady pruning her rose bushes across the road. "That makes for as good a fae protection as we could hope for."

I nodded my agreement, but mostly because it was nice to walk with them along the lane, between the towering oaks and the hydrangeas with their puffy flowers. We passed thatched-roof cottages and grand manor homes. Birds chirped and somewhere in the distance a donkey brayed. It was all very idyllic.

Just before we reached the village high street, Corbin turned us off down another narrow lane. He stopped in front of a small cottage, the front garden crowded with bright flowers. From the looks of it, it had once been an outbuilding for one of the larger estates – a classic Tudor wattle-and-daub, with window boxes bursting with purple flowers and runner beans snaking up the garden trellis. No one was outside, and the curtains were drawn across the front windows. I pushed my way through the wooden gate and snaked up the path, the guys right behind me.

A horseshoe and a bundle of sticks that looked suspiciously similar to the twig in my pocket hung beside the doorway. I fingered the bundle.

"They're from the rowan tree," Corbin said. "Rowan is supposed to help keep the fairies away."

I smiled over my shoulder at Rowan, who dared the slightest of smiles back. "He does a bloody good job. Now, all of you, go wait at the end of the path. She won't open the door if she sees you all out here."

My boys exchanged a glance. I knew they didn't like it – especially Arthur – but they obediently moved away to stand at the cottage gate, the tops of their heads only just visible over the large primrose bush beside the gate. I took a deep breath, smoothed down my hair, and knocked on the door.

I heard footsteps stomp toward me. A few moments later, a woman flung the door open with such force it slammed into the wall, shaking the tiny cottage.

She looked about my age, which was terrifying because I knew she had a kid and although lots of girls in Arizona had kids in high school, I somehow imagined women in England were all proper and waited until they'd finished their degrees at Oxford and found some rich Earl to marry. She looked a mess. Her eyes were ringed with red circles, and her straight brown hair stuck out at all angles, as though she hadn't brushed or washed it in days.

"I *said*, I'm not talking to any more bloody reporters," she snapped, her mouth curling into a scowl.

'I'm not a reporter, ma'am." I extended a hand to her. "My name is Maeve Crawford. I'm from the… ah, the local Women's Welfare Group. We're a support group for single women facing hard times, and I wanted to come over and see if you needed anything."

Jane Forsythe sagged against the doorframe, her snarky demeanor disappearing in a flash, replaced by a face so broken with sorrow I thought I was staring into a mirror of my own soul. "No, I…" She shuddered, but her voice remained firm. "I need my child back, but you probably can't help with that."

You might be surprised.

Jane turned her head away, and my heart thudded as I realized she was crying and didn't want me to see. "Would you like me to come in?" I asked. "I could make some coffee… I'm sorry, I mean, tea. You drink tea in England, I always forget. And maybe I could do some dishes, put some laundry away, just make life easier. I really do just want to help."

"Do you get a Girl Guides badge for this?"

"Yes, I do," I answered automatically, hoping I was reading her right. "It's called the Assisting Distraught Mothers badge. The picture is of me buried under a pile of diapers and housework while you drink three bottles of wine simultaneously while cabana boys fan you with palm fronds."

Jane gasped with laughter, her face completely shell-shocked at the expression of mirth. I guess that was what happened when your child went missing. My heart ached for her. She held the door open a fraction wider. "Come in, but if pictures of my house turn up on social media, I will hunt you down and make you choke on that badge."

"Deal." I liked Jane already.

Inside, the cottage was just as messy as I'd expected. Days of teacups and empty takeout containers littered the kitchen. Flies buzzed around lazily, unsure of what to feast on first. Clothes were strewn everywhere. My foot kicked a toy rabbit that lay face down on the floor. I picked it up and stared into the smiling bunny face. *Her baby might've dropped that while the fae stole him away.*

Jane threw herself down in a sofa and pulled a photo album onto her lap. Inside were pictures of a smiling, chubby baby who looked exactly like the one Blake had taken through the wormhole. Which didn't actually mean much, since I couldn't tell any one baby apart from another.

I went into the kitchen, put the pot-bellied kettle onto the stovetop and fiddled with the knobs on the oven before figuring out it was gas, so I had to light the element as I turned the knob. While the pot boiled, I cleared all the containers off the counter, dumped all the old tea bags and open chocolate bar wrappers into the trash, and ran some water to wash the coffee cups... sorry, *tea* cups. Jane just flipped the pages of her photo album and stared off into space.

I flubbed my way through the tea-making process (what went first? Milk? Sugar? When did you take the teabag out? Rowan showed me but I couldn't remember a thing because his eyes were so beautiful and tea was so gross) and set it down in front of Jane. She took the mug and sipped. Either I'd got the tea right or (more likely) she was too sad to taste anything – either way, she didn't spit it back in my face. I took a sip of mine. *Yup, still tastes like dirt.*

"The kitchen's looking a bit tidier," I said, wondering how I could get her to talk about what happened. "I'll wash our cups and things before I leave, so at least you won't have to worry about ants."

"Thank you," she said, sliding the book off her lap and back on the table. It was open to a picture of Jane with her baby in a long flowing gown, in front of a beautiful gothic church.

"Wow," I said, touching the edge of the picture. "Your little girl is so beautiful."

"Connor is a boy," Jane said, her mouth wobbling.

"Shit!" I clamped my hands over my mouth. "I'm so sorry. I didn't mean... I just thought with that gown..."

"It's fine," Jane smirked. "At least I know you're definitely not a reporter. So you don't baptize babies where you come from?"

"Arizona, and yeah, we do, but it's a pretty simple affair. The church I went to – my father was the pastor so I had to go – didn't believe in ostentatious ceremonies. We just did them as part of standard Sunday service. Splashy splashy, there you go."

"Well my parents believe in doing things the *proper* way, which means stuffy, stiff-upper-lip, Church of England bollocks." Jane jabbed the picture with her index finger. "I didn't even want to do it – I had Connor out of wedlock, so I'm not in God's good graces – but my mother insisted. She filled the church up with all her friends, and then wouldn't speak to me for months afterwards because Connor screamed the place down and puked all over the vicar's vestments and he refused to finish the ceremony. Bloody hell, he was only *three months old*, what did they expect? And of course, when I actually need her, she's too busy with the annual garden show to—" Jane gulped, then shook her head. "Anyway."

"Can I ask… non-reporter to mother, what happened the day Connor disappeared? All the ladies at the Women's Group are gossiping about it, and I didn't know who to believe."

"You don't believe the gossips," Jane growled. "That's my advice."

"Sorry, I know it's a personal question, but—"

"Yeah, it damn well is."

She glared at me, and I felt about ten inches tall. Here I was trying to dig information out of a grieving mother. If the roles had been reversed, I would've clocked her one, and she would've deserved it. My cheeks burned with shame.

This was a bad idea. We'll have to find another way to get information about the fae.

I set my cup down and stood up. "I'm sorry. I crossed a line. I'll see myself out."

"Wait."

I froze. Jane looked up at me, and in her face I read a tumult of emotions – anger battling with harrowing sorrow, duking it out with the overwhelming desire to unload on a friend. I gave her what I hoped was a kind smile. "I lost my parents recently in a terrible accident. I heard what happened to you and I thought, this girl understands."

"I haven't lost Connor," she snapped. 'He was *kidnapped*." She flapped her hand at the chair, and I sat down again, before she changed her mind. "I've told this story a hundred times to the police and the reporters that it's stopped having any meaning, and at least *you* cleaned the kitchen.

"I put Connor down to bed at six pm, like usual, then came out here to watch telly." Her fingers grasped the edge of the chair. "I had a glass of wine – *two glasses*, and before you say anything I'm formula-feeding, so it's okay – and I was falling asleep, when I realized *Midsomer Murders* had just started, but I hadn't heard Connor cry yet. That was odd. He doesn't settle easily, so I usually only get forty-five minutes to myself, and this had been two hours. I went to check on him. The door was shut, which was odd because I usually left it halfway open, but at that stage I thought a draft had just pushed it closed but then..." she took a deep, shuddering breath. "Then I pushed the door open, and I saw these... these *things* lifting Connor out of his bed."

"What did they look like?"

Jane rubbed her head. "Look, just so you know, the police think I was so drunk I can't remember what I saw. But I *know* what I saw, and that was these weird little creatures – like enormous dragonflies with clear wings that buzzed a mile a minute. Their bodies were long and green with skinny forearms and hind legs, and faces that looked eerily human, with hair like moss. They almost looked like tiny fairy sprites from story books, which I know sounds mad, but—"

"It doesn't sound mad at all," I whispered. "What happened next?"

"They flitted around, lifting my baby out of his crib, but

they seemed a bit listless, maybe like they were in pain. I tried to grab Connor off them, but they bit or stung me, and it hurt so bad." She rolled her sleeve up, showing me a scattering of nasty gashes and bites on her arm. "I kept fighting and fighting, but they were so strong, and they got him out of the window. By the time I'd run out the front door after them, they were completely gone. And they left behind a... a pumpkin in the crib." She scowled. "A pumpkin with a smiling face painted on the side, in blood."

"Yikes." I shivered. What a horrible thing to witness.

Jane shrugged. "The police think the kidnapper might have used a drone to scoop Connor up through the open window. Apparently, there's been a similar case of drones used in a kidnapping case up in Scotland. They've taken Rory – that's Connor's father – in for questioning. But that's bollocks, too. Rory's a complete tosser, no argument, but he wouldn't do this. It's too... dramatic, too *gothic*. But that only leaves me with two possible explanations – my tea was drugged, or I've gone crazy."

I leaned forward and touched her knee. Jane jerked back as though I'd slapped her, but then she relaxed. I withdrew my hand. "I believe you. About the creatures."

"You do?" Suspicion crept into her voice.

"I've been living up at Briarwood House. I've seen some weird stuff around here, too."

"Like what?"

"Like a guy who attacked me in the field beside the castle. He had claws instead of hands. That's why I wanted to talk to you. I think we may be able to help each other."

"How?" She was sounding suspicious again.

"There's lots of old books in the library at the castle. They've got information about things that look like the creatures that took your baby."

"So show them to the police," Jane said, but her dark eyes

sparked with interest.

"If the police were trying to convince you that you were drunk, then I don't think they'll take these books seriously."

Jane tilted her head to the side. "Am I going to take these books seriously?"

I shrugged. "Back in the States, I was a physics major. I was going to MIT. I don't believe in anything I can't scientifically measure. And I'm taking these books seriously."

"MIT, huh?" Jane gave me a sardonic smile. "You certainly are a Jill-of-all-trades. I'd like to see these books."

"Sure. Come up to the castle any time. Tell the ticket office you're there to see Maeve Moore, and they'll point you in the right direction."

"I thought you said your name was Crawford?"

I sighed. "It's a long story, and I've got to meet some friends. If you feel like getting out of this place, just stop by at Briarwood. I'm there all the time."

"Thanks." Jane couldn't quite stretch the corners of her mouth up into a smile, but she made a real effort.

I stood up, making as though I was about to leave. I glanced toward the narrow staircase at the rear of the room, and the hallway beside it. A mother wouldn't have a nursery up that steep staircase. That meant Connor's room would be downstairs. I knew Jane wouldn't appreciate me looking in, but maybe... "Do you mind if I use the bathroom before I go?"

She nodded. "Sure. It's out the back door."

I was totally confused about her instructions until I headed down the short hallway and realized there was no bathroom in any of the other rooms – only a small alcove that contained a sewing machine, and another doorway that was closed. Bright red wooden letters on the door spelled CONNOR. I tried the handle, and it clicked open. I pushed the door open as quietly as I could, and peered inside.

A white crib sat under the mullioned window, which was now locked up tight. Toys lined the bureau, and old-fashioned bunnies in coats and bonnets and capelets romped across the wallpaper. Another old iron horseshoe hung over the crib. With a pang, I noticed a selection of story books lined up on a tiny bookshelf. The first book was titled FAIRY STORIES.

I couldn't see anything that seemed like a clue, but I focused on taking in all the details, so I could describe them to the guys later. My heart pounded. All it would take was Jane to come back here and I'd destroy all the trust I'd just built with her.

I backed out of the room, pulling the door shut behind me. I grabbed the back door and opened it as I clicked the nursery door shut to disguise the sound. At least I'd found the bathroom.

The cottage was so old it didn't even have an indoor bathroom. A small outbuilding had been erected just three feet from the back door – a modern replica of the wattle-and-daub construction with hanging baskets of flowers dangling from the eaves. I could see the edge of a basin through the half-open door.

It looked safe. *No fairies.* I stepped out and pushed the bathroom door open all the way. *Might as well make a pitstop.* I closed the door and turned away from the mirror to the toilet.

"Well, isn't this cozy?" A deep voice growled against my ear.

My heart leapt in my chest. I spun around, my hand flying to the knife in my pocket. Hot fingers encircled my wrist, pinning my hand.

Blake's lips pulled back into a self-satisfied smirk. "We meet again, Princess."

My heart hammered against my chest. Blake placed his back against the door so that I couldn't escape the bathroom without somehow getting through him. His bulk and hard muscles suggested that was unlikely. With his other hand, he reached into my pocket and pulled out the knife. "Nice blade," he said, twisting it this way and that. He dropped my hand, but I didn't bother to reach for Flynn's coin or Rowan's twig. Something told me they wouldn't do any good.

"How can you touch that?" I demanded. "It's made of bronze."

"Please." Blake's crystalline eyes sparkled as he twirled the blade on his finger. "Don't patronize me. I know you've figured it out by now."

"You're not fae."

"Bingo." I gulped as Blake placed the knife against my throat. The cool blade slid over my skin. My whole body stood on edge, the world standing still, the only thing existing that cold metal and Blake's shimmering eyes.

"Please…" I begged.

"It's all out in the open," Blake said, his voice casual, as if he was discussing the weather. "You know my secret, and after everything we've shared, I know all sorts of things about you. I know how you like to be kissed along your neck, right against this blade—"

Bake took the blade away, and I let out a breath, only to suck it back again as he pressed his lips against my neck. Against my terror, my own body betrayed me, brimming with hot desire at the soft touch of his fiery lips. Lust ripped through my body, and that familiar ache throbbed between my legs.

What the hell is happening to me?

Blake kissed a trail up the side of my neck, his lips brushing my earlobe, sending delicious shivers through me. "I know how you writhe when that blond Viking runs his tongue along your inner thigh, and how you love the dreadlocked one to suck your nipple so hard you—"

"Stop," I choked out.

Surprisingly, Blake stepped back. The air between us sizzled with sexual tension. I gripped the toilet roll holder to stop myself leaping against Blake, like a magnet seeking its opposite. My chest heaved. *What the hell is going on?*

Blake looked a little flummoxed himself, as much as a human pretending to be a fae could look flummoxed. His smirk faltered a little, and he scratched the back of his head. A black curl fell over his eye. "Your wish is my command."

"If that's the case, give back Connor."

"That's out of my control, I'm afraid. If it's any consolation, Jane's son is being well looked after."

"He's damn well not. He's in the hands of the fae, and you're planning to do something evil with him."

"Evil, are we?" That smirk grew wider. "My, how you have got the fae all wrapped up in a lovely little package."

"Your friend Kalen keeps trying to kill my friends."

Blake's eyes flashed with something that I might've mistaken for anger on someone with actual human emotions. "I took care of him for you."

"What?"

"Let's just say he won't be barking up your tree again." Blake snorted at my blank expression. "he's dead, Princess. He's popped his clogs, he's pushing up the daisies, he's cashed in his chips, whatever that means. The Unseelie played footy with his severed head, and my team won. If that act of selflessness doesn't get me into your good graces or your knickers, then I'll just give up right now."

"No, you won't," I sighed. "Look, why are you *here*? If you're going to do to me what you did to Flynn, just get on with it. I'll scream, and bring the entire Briarwood coven down on your ass."

"I'm not going to hurt you, Maeve."

"Wait, how do you know my name?"

Blake's smirk widened. "Ah, I see your friends have taken liberties with the story they gave you. It shouldn't surprise me."

"Have you come to steal me away to your realm, like Connor and the other baby?"

"I'll steal you away wherever you want to go," Blake growled, his voice caressing my insides, making the ache pound with frustration. "But alas, I'm nowhere near strong enough to take you back with me, even if I wanted to. No, I've come to give you a friendly warning."

"You're not my friend."

"I'd very much like to be."

"And this is how you start a friendship? By hurting Flynn and stealing babies and trapping me in a bathroom and invading my dreams?" I hadn't meant to say that last bit, but the sensation of Blake's lips on mine, of his cock pounding deep inside me, came back to me, as vivid and visceral as if they'd really happened.

"Is that what you think is happening?" Blake laughed. "Oh, Maeve. You don't know what you are at all. I didn't invade your dreams, sweetheart. You're the one who pulls me in."

He's lying. It's just some fairy trick designed to confuse me.

But something that he said made me hesitate. He said the guys hadn't told me the whole truth. I knew that because of Emily not recognizing me. But I'd been too distracted by croquet games and sword fighting lessons and Viking kisses and theoretical physics to make the guys tell me the *truth*.

A surge of anger flared in my veins. *I've been an idiot.* Letting the guys lie to me because of this stupid, schoolyard crush I had on all of them. *Well, not anymore.*

I'm getting some answers, one way or another.

"What is your warning?" I asked Blake.

"Only this; the fae courts are now united. Their combined power will eventually break down the gateway between our worlds. And take it from someone who's been there, you don't want to find out what comes out from that gateway."

"You almost sound like you want me to stop them."

Blake nodded. "That's one thing that I want. The other things…" His finger traced a line of fire across my cheek. "Maybe you'll find out one day soon."

Oh, bollocks. My body responded again, and I tilted my chin towards him. Blake tucked a loose strand of my bright pink bangs behind my ear, his fingers sending shivers through me.

"Why, though? Aren't you a fae prince or something?"

"Appearances can be deceiving." Blake withdrew his fingers, his lips pursing. "Until next time, Maeve Moore."

"No, wait—" I grabbed for him, but he disappeared, his body shimmering in the air as his form dissipated into nothing. I swiped my arms around the bathroom, convinced it was some kind of trick, but Blake was nowhere to be seen.

I did my business, my whole body tingling, and went back into the house. "I've got to go," I said to Jane. "But you're going to be… I mean, that is…"

The corner of Jane's mouth turned up a bit. "Yeah, I know what you mean."

I whipped my phone out of my pocket. "I'll give you my number. Don't forget to come up to Briarwood whenever you want."

"Hey, if you think it'll help find Connor, I'm there."

As soon as I shut the front door behind me, the guys peeked out from behind the primrose bush. Arthur took one look at my face, and frowned. "What's wrong? What happened?"

"What's wrong is that Blake just appeared in the bathroom, is what's wrong."

"I'll kill him," Corbin growled, surging forward, his hands balled into fists.

"No." I grabbed Corbin's collar, yanking him back. "We're leaving."

"Why?"

"Why? Because I'm not going after Blake until I know for a *fact* that he's really on the wrong side of this, and right now I'm not sure. I'd be a damn sight more certain if you guys stopped lying to me."

Corbin's lip twitched. "We're not lying—"

I held up a hand. "Save it. We've going into town to get the equipment I need, and then, when we get back to Briarwood, you boys have some explaining to do."

2 5

MAEVE

I set down my bags on the table in the Great Hall. Luckily, Crookshollow had this reputation for being the most haunted village in England (apparently, over two hundred witches were burned during the height of the witch trials – a bit of a sobering thought considering who I lived with), which meant that the local tourist shops sold ghost-hunting equipment that was actually semi-decent. I wasn't hunting ghosts, of course, but it would monitor fae and wormhole activity just as well.

"Do you want help setting these up?" Flynn asked, pointing an EMF meter at Arthur and making a 'woo woo' noise.

"No," I grabbed the meter out of his hand. "I want you all to tell me what's *really* going on."

Flynn glared at Corbin, who looked miserable. He leaned against the doorframe, as if he intended to make a quick escape. Rowan perched on the end of the sofa, his big, kind eyes following me as though he were in awe.

Arthur moved toward the bar, but I held up a hand. "No

drinks. This isn't a celebration. I want the full story, right now. You guys haven't been straight with me."

"We've been completely honest with you, Maeve," Corbin said.

"No, you haven't." I glared at Corbin, who stared at a spot just beyond my shoulder. "You said you recognize me because your lawyer sent you a picture. But that's not true. When we spoke to Emily yesterday, she didn't recognize me. And today, Blake spoke my name. He *knows* me. And..." I paused, hoping I'd be able to talk about this without revealing exactly what happened. "He's seen my dreams."

"What?" Corbin looked shocked. "That's not... that doesn't..."

I folded my arms. "So I'm done with half truths and this 'you're not ready' bollocks. I want the full story, unabridged, footnotes included. Go."

"What were these dreams about?" Corbin demanded.

"I'm asking the questions here."

Arthur looked up, tucking a strand of long blond hair behind his ear. For a warrior, he looked almost sheepish. "Are these dreams about all of us in the Great Hall, um... *together?* You and me and Corbin and Rowan and that Irish git and... Blake?"

My face flushed. "How... how do you know that?"

"Because I've had the same dream, a couple of times actually."

Corbin stared at his friend. "And you never thought to mention it?"

Arthur's kind eyes flashed with annoyance. "I didn't know anyone else was having it! I didn't exactly think it was polite to tell our landlord I was dreaming about her being the center of a sixsome—"

"How do we know it was the same dream, though?"

Corbin said. "Maybe you're just having similar feelings, because of the kiss and—"

"In the last one, all the furniture was gone, and you were on a red-velvet couch, wearing a silky robe," Arthur said to me, the tips of his own ears turning a little red. I nodded, my cheeks burning.

This is not happening. But it was. Arthur continued. "We were parading around you, completely naked. Corbin tore the robe off, and I was the one who was—"

"I've had the dreams, too." Rowan said, his quiet voice strained. He stared at his hands, his fingers drumming a repetitive rhythm against his palm.

My cheeks burned even brighter. How the hell was this possible? And why did it have to be *those* dreams Arthur and Rowan saw?

"So why haven't Flynn and I had these dreams?" Corbin demanded.

"Actually…" Flynn lifted his hand. "I think I might've been in on that second one, with the… ah, parade? I thought it was just my filthy mind. I love you mate, but I'd prefer if you didn't touch me bollix like that."

"So why haven't I had any of these dreams, then?" Was it my imagination, or did Corbin sound a little jealous?

"You were up late in the library," I said. "I remember the light being on last time I woke up. I think we all have to be asleep at the same time. Blake seemed to believe they were my dreams and I pulled him into them, but how I did that I have no idea."

"Why didn't you tell us before?"

"For god's sake, Corbin, because I thought it was just a dream. This is supposed to be *my* interrogation. You guys, start talking, now."

Corbin sighed, rubbing the side of his head. His usual controlling demeanor gone, he looked like someone had just slapped him across the face. A flash of guilt hit me before I remembered that he lied to me, and I pushed it down.

"Okay, okay," he said. "It was going to come out sooner or later. We just wanted to protect you for as long as possible. But this dream thing confirms it."

"Protect me from what?"

"From yourself," Corbin's face strained. "Maeve, you're a witch. And not just any witch. You're a spirit user. You're the most powerful witch in England, and the only one capable of holding off the threat of the fae."

"**W**hat the *hell*?"

Of all the things I thought Corbin might say, that was *not* one of them.

I'm not a witch. This is absurd.

Corbin sighed. 'We didn't want to tell you like this. I knew you wouldn't believe it, and after everything you've gone through – with the Crawfords' murders – the last thing we wanted to do was to upset you more."

"Well, I'm pretty damn upset, okay!" I yelled. "And what do you mean, murders? It was just a fluke accident."

Corbin shook his head. "That fae, Kalen, who was at the fair that night, came to Arizona to find you. To kill you. That's why I was there – I had to make sure he didn't succeed. I've been protecting you ever since you were sixteen, since my parents handed the duty over to me."

I slumped down on the end of the couch, my head spinning. What Corbin was saying… it didn't make any sense. "Protecting me?"

"Yeah, we all have. That's why you remember Flynn, the exchange student. That was his shift watching you. The year before that, Arthur was a janitor at your school. I've been a student at your community college for the last four semesters, but I didn't pass your first year physics paper, so I had to switch to history." Corbin dared a small smile. "You're way too clever for me to keep up with."

I didn't even register the compliment. The implication of Corbin's words sank in, turning my blood to ice. "You've all been… stalking me?"

"We prefer to think of it as being bodyguards from a distance," Arthur said, his voice shaky.

I thought of the tower bedroom they'd decorated, how they seemed to perfectly judge my taste. *Because they've been watching you through windows and spying on your private moments.* The thought turned my stomach, but not as much as what they were saying about me being a *witch.*

"We didn't want to interfere with your life, to give you this burden before your time," Corbin said. "So we stayed in the background, just keeping watch for the fae, as my parents did before me. We never saw any fae activity around you – it would take an enormous amount of power for them to appear in America – until the night your parents were killed."

I remembered how that fae – Kalen – tried to drag Kelly and I toward the Ferris wheel. A flash of the fire seared against my eyeballs. The screaming of the crowd, the groan and crack of the wheel as it collapsed, the acrid smoke burning my throat as I tried to run inside to save my parents. I remembered Kalen waving at me from across the field, his expression smug, and how the smoke had obscured him as he shapeshifted into the dog. He must've rigged that explosion, with the idea it would take out my whole family. Cold settled all over my body.

I hate the fae. I hate them more than anything.

"I am so, so sorry, Maeve," Corbin's voice changed. Gone

was his 'history professor' tone as he recited the facts. Tightness clawed at his words, as though he struggled for breath. I dared a glance at him, knowing it would melt a tiny bit of the ice, and was surprised by the depth of the pain in his eyes. "When I saw Kalen walk up to you and your sister, I thought that was his move – that he was trying to lure you away. I never could have predicted he'd bring down the wheel. I never—"

He choked on his words, whipping his head away so I could no longer see his face. Flynn stood up. I expected him to say something cutting to Corbin, but instead, he went across and tapped his friend on the shoulder.

"You okay, mate?"

Corbin shook his head. I wondered what was going on with him – his face had paled. His hands balled into fists at his side. Was it something more than just guilt over letting my parents die?

Good. I folded my arms. *Let him feel guilty. It's his fault the fae were drawn to me.*

Flynn glanced at me, and gave me a smile that contained none of his usual mirth. "Allow me to continue the saga. Where were we? Yes… we had to watch over you, because you're the daughter of Aline Moore, who was the fecking best witch of her time."

I glared at Flynn. "You said my mother was a witch before."

He nodded. "It's true. She was the High Priestess of the Briarwood coven, which is why she wears those jewels in the portrait upstairs. All of us—" he swung his arm around the room, indicating the other guys "—are the children of one or both parents who were also part of that same coven."

Flynn started to say more, but Corbin cut him off. He wouldn't look at me but he still wanted to be the one to talk about the history. "There was an attempt by the fae twenty-one years ago to break open the gateway and enter our realm. The Briarwood coven – our parents' coven – fought them off and sent them back, but at tremendous cost. My parents lived, and Arthur's, but Flynn lost his father and Rowan both his parents. We don't know who your father was, but since he would have been a member of the coven, we presume he died also. Your mother was pregnant with you during the attack. Leading the coven through the powerful spell took too much from her, and she went into premature labor. My parents helped to bring you into the world just as Aline passed away, but not before she gave them specific instructions."

"And what were these instructions?" My voice dripped with sarcasm. "To polish the cauldron? To feed the black cat? To de-bristle the flying broomstick?"

Corbin cringed. "They were about you, Maeve, and the power she passed down to you."

"This is absolutely ridiculous! You've all been reading those Harry Potter books too many times. My mother was *not* a witch and I don't *have* any powers."

"Then how come you're pulling us all into your dreams?" Arthur shot back.

I rubbed my bare shoulders with my hands, keeping my arms folded across my chest, as if their presence would keep in all the anger and confusion from pouring out of the wound they'd opened up.

"If you truly have been spying on me for my entire life," I growled, "then you must know by now that I need empirical evidence if I'm going to believe anything as fantastical as this. If you can't give me that, then I'm getting straight on the next plane back to Arizona."

Corbin shot Rowan a look that was pure 'I-told-you-so.'

"And if we can make you believe this?" Flynn asked, his voice hopeful. "Will you complete our coven?"

I just glared at him, until his buoyant expression withered away.

"The library," Corbin choked out. He stood, still not looking at me, and trudged out of the hall. I glared at his back, but followed after him, the other guys clattering along behind me. We passed rows of gilded portraits, and I half-expected the grim faces of the castle's former owners to start moving and talking.

In the library, Corbin walked across to his enormous desk, opened the top drawer, and drew out a small envelope, sealed with wax similar to the one Emily used. He came back and handed the envelope to me.

"This is from your mother," he said, still refusing to meet my eyes. "She wrote it on her deathbed. She gave my parents strict instructions to ensure her daughter read it once she turned twenty-one."

I turned the letter over in my hands, my fingers brushing the yellowed edges, the dust gathered around the seal. MAEVE was written across the front in a florid, ostentatious script.

"We haven't read this letter," Corbin said. "It's for your eyes only, Maeve. If you want to tell us what it says afterward, then we're happy to listen. But it's yours to do with as you wish."

I clutched the letter to my chest. *Aline, my birth mother.* I held in my hand something she'd touched, the first piece of evidence that she even knew I existed. My heart pounding, I slid my finger under the seal and cracked it, pulling out a single sheet of faded paper, filled with tiny lines of that same cursive script. My knees wobbled, and I tumbled onto the couch, no longer certain I could hold up my own body weight.

Reverently, I smoothed it out on my knee, and started to read:

My dearest Maeve,

My dear friend John has just presented you into my arms, and you are the most perfect creature I have ever laid eyes on. I have passed many hours of my life by the pond at the bottom of Briar Wood, watching the swans float across the glassy surface, their necks held up in graceful arcs. I thought no other creature of such beauty existed, but you have proved me wrong.

There are so many things I wish to tell you, but there is so little time. I will die tonight, of that I am certain. I saw my own death many years ago. The power of premonition is an ugly gift, and I pray that you will not inherit this curse from me. Your own powers will take some time to manifest (for unlike the other elemental powers, spirit develops from puberty and won't fully manifest until you turn twenty-one) and it's possible you may not yet even be aware of them by the time you read this letter.

I imagine you have many questions for me – about your powers and your heritage. Your father was a traveler – he sought out our coven and stayed at the castle for some time to help us keep the fae hordes at bay. He went missing shortly after you were conceived. I came out into the garden one night to find his shoes empty by the gate at the edge of the field. We never saw nor heard another trace of him. I fear the fae got him, destroying his body to claim his great power for themselves.

Because of the things our coven has done, the authorities will not allow my dear friends, Bree and Andrew Harris, to adopt you. They will fight for you, but they will lose – this I have already seen. You will be placed into an orphanage, and your adoptive parents will take you far away from Briarwood and your heritage, your curse. This too I have seen.

Without your power, the coven will never be strong enough to fight back the Slaugh. The fae know this, and so they will eventually come for you, even as safe as you are with your new family. Bree and Andrew will keep vigil over you, to protect you from their attacks until you receive your own powers.

I have done all I can to keep you safe, my beautiful daughter. I wish you to have a wonderful life, the life I never had – twenty-one years to be carefree, to be normal, before you are tied to this terrible duty.

You have my heart.

Aline, your mother.

I set down the letter, my head spinning. I could practically *hear* her speaking inside my head, her voice wispy and melodious. She spoke of future events as if she knew they were coming, but even if this so-called spirit element existed, *precognition* was impossible.

My mind whirred. Theoretical processes and ideas buzzing around in my head... *unless we are talking about retro-causality, where causality is reversed to allow an effect to occur before its cause. But that's really just a philosophical thought experiment laced with pseudoscience...*

"I need evidence," I whispered.

"The letter is evidence," Corbin said.

"How do I know this letter is actually written by my mother, and that it was written the date she said it was? It could be forged. Anyone could handwrite a note and stain the paper with tea." I sniffed the paper. "Okay, so this doesn't smell like tea, but there are other ways to make paper look old. Before I can take any of *this*—" I gestured to the four of them and the note in front of me "—seriously, I need to know unequivocally that this is real."

"Tell me you didn't just use the word unequivocally in a sentence," Flynn moaned. "I'm going to need to carry around a dictionary just to talk to you."

Corbin rummaged around in his desk. "Hold on a sec," he muttered as he sorted through a stack of documents. "It's here somewhere..."

"Maybe if you learned the proper Queen's English instead

of your bastardized Irish gaff, you wouldn't need so much help with the big words," Arthur said to Flynn.

"Suck me bollix," Flynn shot back, waving his middle finger at Arthur.

"Ah, here it is!" Corbin held up a paper. Flynn snatched it from his hand and slapped it triumphantly in my lap.

"Read it and weep, Einstein," he grinned at me. "There's your unequivocal proof."

I stared down at the document. It was a deed for Briarwood Castle and grounds, stating that the property was to be held in trust for me until I came of age at twenty-one, and that the descendants of the other coven members were welcome to use it as a residence or for business purposes without paying rent, as long as they also "protected me from harm." The document was signed by my mother and witnessed by a 'Bree Harris' and a lawyer from Emily's firm. I checked my mother's handwriting against the letter. They were identical.

"I can show you Aline's death certificate, and the papers from the orphanage, authenticated and all," Corbin said. "But I think you know what this means."

My temples throbbed. *This can't be true.* But there it was, the empirical evidence right in front of my eyes. My mother wrote that letter, and she wrote it before she could have possibly known the Crawfords would adopt me and take me to America.

My mother was a witch. *I* was a witch.

"I'm the fifth," I whispered, trying to hold my trembling hands in my lap. "I'm the fifth you've been looking for."

"You are more than that, Maeve," Arthur said, his kind eyes boring into mine. "You are our High Priestess."

CORBIN

Maeve took the letter and went to her room, slamming the door behind her. I cringed as the sound echoed around the castle.

One by one, the guys all disappeared off to their various activities – Arthur to practice his sword fighting, Flynn to bang around in his workshop, and Rowan to pick herbs in the garden. I stayed hunched over the desk, the Briarwood coven's *grimoire* open on the desk in front of me. But every time I tried to focus on the scrawled words and vivid drawings, the ink blurred in front of my eyes. My thoughts wouldn't focus on anything but the horrible, twisted expression on Maeve's face when she found out her adoptive parents had been murdered.

Murdered... and I hadn't been able to save them. I'd been so distracted by seeing Maeve on her twenty-first birthday and knowing that soon she'd be coming into her power. I thought we'd made it – twenty-one years without the fae finding her and trying to kill her. When Kalen grabbed hold of her, I didn't take the time to think, to assess the situation. I acted on impulse, and my impulse got Maeve's parents killed.

More innocent lives I couldn't protect.

I buried my face in my hands. Across the room, the grandfather clock ticked down the seconds. If I didn't figure out what spell the fae were trying to pull off, I'd soon be adding a lot more innocent lives to my already impressive tally.

"Corbin."

I jerked my head up. Maeve stood in the doorway, her hip jutting out in a confident stance. She wore a simple black sundress covered in a pattern of cherry blossoms, the swoop of the skirt drawing my eye to her shapely legs and those incredible hips. She crossed her arms and stared at me with an expression that was half rage, half curiosity.

I gulped, rubbing my eyes. Had I been asleep? I'd barely managed a couple of hours the last few nights. This was a particularly bad bout of insomnia. I'd been so distracted with the books, I hadn't even noticed before how tired I felt, how my head throbbed under the strain of the dim lamp that lit my desk. The light from the windows had faded, and I had to squint to make out Maeve's features from across the room.

Books always did that to me, and languages. Time stood still while I patiently caressed them into giving up their secrets.

"You didn't come down for dinner," Maeve said. She held up a plate. "Flynn was showing off his face. It's nearly healed, which is pretty amazing. For not-doctors, you guys sure have the magic touch."

"We do our best." I rubbed the spot on my shoulder where the fae's claws and blade cut me. Even though the wounds had healed, the skin still itched a little. Maeve waited for me to elaborate, but I didn't. I *really* didn't think Maeve was in a place yet where she could deal with the idea of healing spells, especially not since I'd used them on her.

"I called and called for you," she said. "You didn't answer, so I brought you up some leftovers. It's this weird pie that's filled with meat, which makes no sense to me but it was delicious, so what do I know?"

"I… I didn't hear you." I glanced at the clock – it was half eight. *How is it half eight already? I only sat down a few moments ago.*

"I know. I've been watching you for ages." Maeve sashayed across the room, placing the plate on the corner of the desk. "You look exhausted. What are you doing?"

I'm still trying to figure out what spell the fae are trying to perform," I explained, pointing to the pictures in the book. "It's hard because their magic is very different from ours. I'm hunting for references to spells they performed in the past. This is our coven's *grimoire*. Or rather, one of them – we've filled up a few volumes over the centuries. The fae have made magical assaults on our realm before. I figure if they've tried anything like this in the past, our ancestors would've explained how to defeat it."

"Grimoire?"

"It's a spell book, passed down through the generations. Each coven writes down their own studies, magical workings, incantations…" I turned a page, and showed her an entry written in my own chicken scratch. "Each coven appoints one member to act as historian. I wasn't going to trust Flynn to do it for us."

Maeve bent over the page, staring at the boxes and branches I'd drawn across the page. "This is some kind of family tree?"

"Sort of. It's tracing the lineage of the coven, and which descendants might carry the magical genes." I pointed to the boxes. "Here's me and my parents, and my other siblings. My mum is an Earth witch, and Dad's an Air witch – so we have a range of different elements. Arthur's mother is Fire, which is a dominant gene, so I always knew he'd have the fire ability. That's why I started searching for him first."

"Who are these people?" Maeve pointed at five other names written alongside our parents'. I noticed she didn't mention the big blank space next to her mother's image.

"Other members of the last Briarwood coven. I was trying to trace them all, find out if they had children who exhibited elemental powers. The last coven was quite large – fifteen members at its height – but many of them were killed in the last battle with the fae. Those who were left either couldn't or didn't want to perform magic again, so they all lost touch."

"Except your parents."

"Yeah." I pointed to two of the names I'd joined with a dotted line. I needed to distract Maeve so she wouldn't ask me more about my family. "Colleen and Darren Beckett. They were the second people I tried to track down. The more spirit users a coven has, the stronger it becomes. They were both spirit users, and according to the coven records, they had a child the same year my parents had me. Spirit is a recessive gene, so—"

"So any child they had would also be a spirit user?"

"You really are brilliant, you know that?" I grinned at Maeve, who beamed back at me. Her scent invaded my nostrils – sweet and fresh, like the first summer blueberries picked straight off the vine. Just having her so close to me wiped away my exhaustion. "Colleen and Darren weren't recorded among the dead after the fae attack, and I managed to track them to a house in Wiltshire. Unfortunately, they don't live there anymore. No one did – the place was condemned after no one would buy it, given the gruesome murder-suicide that happened inside."

"What?" Maeve's mouth hung open, her lips curling back. For a horrifying moment, I imagined what it would be like to slide my cock between those lips, to feel her tongue run down the length of my shaft…

The air between us heated up, and I became painfully aware that the edge of her breast grazed my arm. From the sparkle in her eyes, it looked like she did, too…

I cleared my throat. "It seemed that shortly after they moved there, Darren shot Colleen in the head, and then killed himself with the same gun. But the weird thing is, the police records didn't make any mention of a child."

"That is weird." Maeve's words came out hushed, breathy. Her eyes smoldered. My cock pressed urgently against the fly of my jeans.

"Maeve…" *Danger, Will Robinson.*

She draped herself over the arm of my chair, her bangs flopping across my shoulder, brushing my skin, making all sorts of filthy visions dance across my conscience.

Don't make a move you can't take back. Never forget what you are guilty of.

"Corbin, I've been thinking…" Maeve drew a pattern on my knee with the tip of her finger, tracing a line of fire across my skin that shot straight into my cock.

"That sounds dangerous." *This is dangerous.* Maeve had that look in her eyes, the look that said she was ready to act on her urges. And as much as I wanted her, as much as I thought I'd be the best candidate for *magister*, she absolutely should *not* choose until she knew everything.

"This spirit power I supposedly inherited from my mother, would it have anything to do with how I've been able to control everyone's dreams?"

"I don't know. Spirit does occasionally manifest as dreamwalking and dream powers. So, ah, what happened in this dream of yours?"

The flush on her cheeks told me all I needed to know.

"You were all in them. You all kept saying I had to choose, and I… I didn't want to."

Oh sweet bollocks. My cock strained at the idea that Maeve wanted something so explicit, so kinky as what the guys had hinted at happened in those dreams. *It hadn't been done in so many generations, but—*

I wish like hell I'd fallen asleep the other night. I want to see every filthy corner of Maeve's mind.

Okay, it was time she knew the rest, before the strain in my cock tore my whole body apart. I flicked back through the pages in the grimoire, flipping between herbal recipes and birthing rituals. "I want to show you something," I said. I located the page I was hunting for and let the book fall open.

Maeve's lips pursed as she took in the drawing. It was a highly detailed scene, drawn by one of the grimoire's earliest owners – a witch named Agnes from the Middle Ages. It showed a troupe of witches – mostly men, but a few women – all naked and writhing against each other in a great, heaving orgy. In the center of the image was a voluptuous woman reclining on a sofa, her head thrown back in ecstasy as five men pleasured her body. Her hands were wrapped around two hard shafts, and a third was being held out for her waiting mouth to accept, while the other two men penetrated both her holes.

Usually, seeing that picture had no affect on me – it was just an historical curiosity from a time when the church's puritanical ideas about sex hadn't quite penetrated pagan society. But now, I couldn't help but seeing Maeve's long neck bent back, her body writhing in ecstasy as the members of our coven worshipped her body.

And her expression didn't help. Maeve stared at the picture with wide eyes, her lips rounding with an O of understanding as she took in the details of the erotic scene. My gaze darted down to her cleavage spilling out of her thin dress. A dark nipple – hard and round – jutted out from the fabric. Maeve's hand gripped my knee hard, her fingers brushing within inches of my—

Oh bollocks. Be strong, Corbin.

I took a deep, shuddering breath, and continued, reminding myself that it was my responsibility to give Maeve this information. "Unlike Judean religions, where the male desire for progeny dictates all carnal activity, in pagan rituals like ours, a woman's pleasure is vital to the success of all magic. The High Priestess is the center of a coven's power, and therefore, her orgasm is the height of the ritual. Does this look like your dream?"

Maeve nodded, biting her lip in this way that drove me totally crazy.

"In the old days of the coven, everyone participated… like this image. It's the best way to raise the power needed for complex rituals. But as Christian ideas became more ingrained, covens stopped practicing polyamory. In order to be truly strong, the High Priestess chooses a *Magister.*" I glanced at Maeve, but she was still staring at the erotic drawing. Something flickered across her face. "The magister is like the second-in-command – a trusted counsel and powerful witch in his own right who pairs with her in the rituals. Most high priestesses in the last two centuries opted to make their magisters their chief consort and draw their power that way."

Maeve's fingers trailed across the high priestess, tracing the line of her ecstasy. "So is this why I'm dreaming so… so…"

"So *filthy?*" I laughed, but the sound came out more high-pitched than I expected. "Ever since you got here, this whole house has been in a constant state of arousal. Your power has already begun to grow now that you're back inside Briarwood's walls. All the members of the coven can feel it, and we're drawn to you. That's why there's this tension in the air."

She gave a throaty laugh. "I thought that was just me."

"It's *definitely* not just you."

I placed a hand in my pocket and withdrew the condom, setting it down on the table in front of her. "I made sure all the guys had some," I said. "So that if you decided to choose one of us as a consort, we'd be ready."

"What if I don't want any of you as a consort?" Maeve's words were angry, but the look in her eyes was pure hunger. "What if I'm angry with all of you for lying to me, and I want to shag some random dude I meet at the pub?"

"You can do that, of course." I tried not to let my face show how much the idea of her being with someone who wasn't me appalled me. "Whoever you sleep with – whether they be mortal or witch – will increase your powers. The important thing is that you orgasm, and the more times the better."

I let that little nugget of information sit in her mind. Maeve blinked, her face bone still, but her eyes exploring all the possibilities of what I'd just said.

"How do I choose?" she asked, her voice tight.

"By creating a blood bond. I can show you the ritual if you like—" I grabbed for the grimoire.

Maeve wrapped her hand around my thigh, snaking her fingers closer to my throbbing cock. I groaned as her fingers scraped along my bulge, sending arcs of fire into my skin. I dropped the book.

When she spoke, her voice was choked with desire. "I'm no Christian, Corbin, and I don't want to choose *any* of you. Right now, what I want is for you to fuck me senseless."

28

MAEVE

hose words – so crass, so forward, so *totally* unlike me – had barely left my throat when Corbin mashed his mouth against mine. His fingers wove through my hair, wrapping around the back of my neck and pulling me against him.

My whole body hummed with need as I climbed on his chair, straddling his body and wrapping my legs around him. Corbin moaned against my lips as he ground his hardness into me, and the heat in my veins surged to feel the size of him through his jeans.

Corbin's tongue pummeled mine, assaulting my mouth and leaving me gasping for breath. His teeth tugged at my lip, biting a little. I yelped at the pain, but my protest turned into a murmur as his fingers snaked down my sides, grazing my already hard nipples through my thin dress.

His body against mine... it felt so good, so right, so powerful. Heat surged down my arms, drawing my hands to explore his skin, to cup his chin, tangle my fingers in his hair, drag my nails over the skin at the back of his neck until he shivered with delight. Corbin ground against me harder, and

I mashed my weight against his, the ache inside me begging to be filled with him.

Never in my life had I wanted something as much as I wanted Corbin inside me, right now. And that included the telescope that I'd begged the Crawfords to buy for Christmas for *six* years.

Corbin tugged his lips from mine, trailing kisses along my neck, leaving a blaze of shimmering flutters in his wake. His hands tore at my dress, finding the zipper, his fingers stopping just short of grabbing the clasp.

"You definitely want this?" he asked, his eyes blazing. Just his breath touching my skin made my body pulse with need. "You don't want to wait until—"

"Correct. I don't want to wait."

Corbin's fingers closed over the zipper and he yanked it down. I lifted my hands and he pulled the dress over my head. I was dimly aware that I should feel nervous about what Corbin thought of my body, all the lumps and curves and bulgy bits, but then his lips were around my nipple and all thought ceased.

I moaned as Corbin's tongue darted across the sensitive bud. Just like in my dream, he licked and sucked and teased me until I yelped. But this was a hundred times better than any dream, because I was awake, and my body was on fire, and Corbin Harris smothered me in pleasure.

His mouth still wrapped around my nipple, Corbin picked me up as though I was made of paper, and laid me back across the desk, draping me over the lewd drawing in the open grimoire. I went to sit up, but he pushed me back down. Corbin's hands shoved my thighs apart, cupping me under my ass. His face twisted into a look of such exquisite joy that it shook me inside and out. Before I could say anything, he dived between my legs.

His tongue found the source of the pounding, throbbing

ache, and he attacked it with the possessive dedication he gave to everything in his life. He drew long strokes across me, then touched only the tip of his tongue to that spot, vibrating it in place and reducing me to a gibbering mess as an orgasm tore through me.

At least, I *think* it was an orgasm. My whole body shuddered and jets of molten pleasure flared through my veins. The world spun and red dots appeared in my vision.

"Whoa," I moaned. I wanted to say it was my first, that I'd definitely never had one of those with Andrew, but all that came out, again and again, was "whoa, whoa."

"Plenty more where that came from." Corbin grinned, his mouth finding mine once more. He leaned over me, one hand cupping behind my neck, while his other hand reached between my legs again. He pushed one finger inside me, stroking my wall as his pinkie snaked up and swirled around that spot once more.

Moments later I died and was reborn again in a fire of pleasure and ecstasy. My body slipped off the side of the earth and plunged into nothingness, weightless and breaking into stardust. I clung to Corbin until the trembling subsided and my veins stopped burning up in the sun.

"That's two," he grinned. "Can you feel anything magical?"

"Mmmmm." I held him. "I feel like I just saw the center of the Sun."

"I mean, can you feel your power?"

I closed my eyes, drawing myself into my body, searching for some deep-hidden power. But I didn't even know what I was looking for, how I was supposed to feel. All I knew was that warmth pooled in my limbs, my brain surged with disjointed thoughts and half-articulated flashes of brilliance. I knew there was an ache in my belly and between my legs that still demanded to be sated, and that was more important than anything else right now.

"Maybe it needs a little something extra," Corbin said. I nodded, reaching down between us and grabbing the belt of his jeans. I slipped the buckle through my fingers and tore it open. Corbin moaned as I reached inside and drew him out.

I lifted my head so I could see his cock, and wasn't surprised to see he was exactly the same as in my dream. Huge and long and glorious. I wrapped my fingers around his shaft and gave him a stroke. Corbin's eyes fluttered closed, and he growled deep in his throat.

Corbin's hand was on my thigh again, and with his other hand he reached behind me and grabbed the condom from the desk, ripping it open with his teeth and rolling it over his bulging dick. I helped him roll the condom on, then leaned back against the book. Corbin spread my legs again, and entered me with a deep thrust.

I cried out as half Corbin's length slid inside me, filling the ache that had begged for this for so long. I wrapped my arms around him, digging my fingernails into his back. Corbin gripped the end of the desk with one hand, the other holding up my thigh, his fingers spread across my ass cheek.

"You feel amazing," he puffed, as he drew out and then sank into me again, our bodies moving together, rising and falling with each long, glorious thrust.

He kissed me, his tongue playing at my lips as his body moved against mine. My legs fell open, begging for more of him. My ass rubbed against the edge of the book. *Is this disrespecting the Briarwood grimoire?*

No. I thought of the erotic drawing upon which we were grinding. *If anything, this is exactly* what *that book is for.*

The desk creaked as Corbin thrust harder, building up a steady rhythm that made the ache inside me pound with anticipation. He angled my ass up and thrust in deeper, filling me, giving me exactly what I needed.

I clawed at his back as the ache climbed inside me, the pressure like a pot reaching the boil. Corbin ground his pelvis against mine, driving deeper still. His thrust tore through me, sending the pot screaming as it boiled over, and molten hot pleasure poured through my limbs. My muscles clenched and unclenched around him, clamping onto Corbin's cock as I rode the third orgasm until the room swirled in a haze of color.

Corbin stiffened, his muscles clenching. He buried his face into my neck, his teeth scraping my skin as he shuddered with his own orgasm. His body tightened into knots, a snake coiling to strike, and then, with a cry, he pounded into me one final time and collapsed against me.

"Shite," he whispered, his arms encircling me. His thick muscles embraced me, keeping me warm.

I giggled. "You Brits and your quirky words. I can't wait to tell my sister I just had my first *shag* on foreign soil."

Corbin's eyes warmed. "How did you rate it, Maeve Moore?"

"A solid ten out of ten."

Corbin sighed. "You've no idea how chuffed I am to hear that. Are you tired? I'll take you up to bed."

"I don't know if I am tired, but I'd like to go to bed."

I snuggled against Corbin's chest as he scooped me in his arms like I was a little kitten, and wobbled out of the library. He wasn't as steady on his feet as Arthur, cursing as he stubbed his toe on the bottom of the stair, but the kisses he trailed across my face while he carried me upstairs were uniquely his own.

Corbin pushed the door of my room open and laid me out on my bed. He stared down at my naked body, his eyes filled with a mix of awe and desire and sadness.

"I am not worthy of you," he said.

"Don't talk bollocks." I grabbed him, yanked him down,

forcing my tongue between his lips. It only took a moment for him to yield to me again.

Corbin always looked after everyone else, and he never asked for what he wanted. He just thought about what was best for the coven, even if it left him without anything at all. Where was his family? His parents were the ones who watched over me until Corbin was sixteen, and from the way he talked about them, they were still alive. So why weren't they still here at Briarwood, helping him fight off the fae? There was more than enough room for everyone. And why did Corbin think he was 'unworthy' of me? Why did that impossible sadness flash in his eyes when he thought no one was looking?

It was there now, creeping in at the edges, even as he kissed me. Of all of us, he had the most to lose if the coven failed, because it was *his* coven, rightfully. He may think that I was the High Priestess, but I knew the truth – I was just a science nerd from Arizona who had somehow walked into a fairy tale where nothing made sense, except for the fact there were four guys here who cared about me, who wanted me as much as I wanted them, and I'd be damned – I mean, *buggered* – if I was going to give up this opportunity.

I'd decided, after I went back to my room and read my mother's letter again, that I was wrong to expect everything at Briarwood to be explainable by science. I expected everything to be wrapped up in a nice little theory, but everything that happened over the last few weeks has taught me that life doesn't work like that. Maybe I still didn't quite believe all this stuff, but I did trust my gut, and my gut wanted to be here at Briarwood, helping my guys fight for everything this castle represented.

All Corbin's talk of orgies and orgasms. That image of the Priestess, so lost in her ecstasy, so different from the "purity pledge" lectures Mom had given Kelly and I. So free of guilt and shame, such a celebration of atoms colliding and electrons firing, of beautiful chemistry coming together and making sparks fly. Sex had never really appealed to me before, because I'd always framed it as a tool of the church used to control people, especially women. But not anymore.

I'd come to Briarwood to push through the grief of losing my parents and find my way again. And if sex with hot English witches would help me find my way again, then damn, I was not going to question it.

I pulled Corbin down and wrapped my body around him, giving in to my inner witch once more.

~

I stood at the gate to the meadow, the barrier between the safety of Briarwood and the outside world. Moonlight lit the grasses, shimmering with a light dusting of dew. My foot kicked something hard. I bent down, and held up a scuffed boot. It was enormous – a man's size.

"Nice night for a walk, Princess."

I dropped the boot in surprise. Blake reclined against the gate, leaning over so his face was inside Briarwood's territory, that self-satisfied smirk plastered across his pouty lips.

"This is my dream. It can be whatever type of night I want it to be," I said, staring over Blake's shoulder at the red-tinged moon. After a moment, a huge cloud rolled across the sky, obscuring the moon behind a wall of grey fog.

"Nice one," Blake whistled. He held out his hand, and I took it, daring someone to come and stop me. *It's my dream, I can walk with Blake if I want to.*

I opened the gate and slipped out, joining Blake in the field, beyond the protection spells preventing the fae from hurting me. I should have been terrified, but instead, a sense of liberation surged through me. *This is my dream. I control it. If the fae want to come get me here, I'd like to see them try.*

Blake and I walked in companionable silence down the path toward the village. I had so many questions I wanted to ask him – namely, how he came to be a human living in the realm of the fae – but as I studied his razor cheekbones and smooth porcelain skin, each one died on my lips. That smirk never left Blake's face, and I hated to admit that the idea crossed my mind that if I kissed him, it might get a genuine reaction out of him. I hated the fact that my lips itched to try it.

Blake stopped in his tracks, yanking my body around so I was facing the castle. Briarwood towered over the landscape, her turrets jutting out from the hillside, telling everyone for miles around who was in charge here. Blake tightened his fingers around mine. "I want to show you something."

"What?"

"Your kingdom, Princess."

He raised his hand to the sky, and chanted something in a low-singsong voice. The world around us changed, swirling and shifting, everything wobbling like I was looking through warped glass. After a moment, the surface smoothed out again, everything solid once more. I stood in the same field, looking up at the castle, but everything was different.

Instead of fresh, dewy grass beneath my feet, the earth was dry and parched. The neat hedgerows that circled the castle had grown into an imposing fortress of spiked bramble, so high that only the top of my bedroom tower was now visible. Dark clouds covered the sky, completely obscuring the moon and stars. These clouds hung low, and seemed heavier and denser, as though they didn't hold water vapor, but something much more sinister. A sickly orange glow lit up the horizon and my throat burned as I breathed in the acrid, sooty air.

"Welcome." Blake swung his arm around the air, a sardonic smile crossing his lips. "Behold the future realm of the fae."

"But this is earth…. what did you do to it?" This had to be a trick, an Unseelie Court glamour. The fae realm was supposed to be bright and beautiful, full of luminous light and beautiful glades and never ending revels.

But the fae shook his head. "Not me, Princess. *You* did this. You burned the skies and poisoned the air and turned the very earth itself to dust. You are responsible for this destruction."

"Me?" My stomach churned. *It can't be true. I didn't do this. I wouldn't even know how to do this.*

"Oh, sorry – not you *specifically*. I mean the human race." Blake tossed back his head and laughed, the sound hollow. "Although as High Priestess, you definitely contributed." He pointed to the glow along the horizon. "I think that might've been your handiwork."

"What is it? Why does it grow like that?"

"Duh, because it's radioactive." Blake grabbed my hand and yanked me forward. I let him drag me off in a different direction. In front of us, a towering hedge of briar and brambles jutted out of the field. "If you want to know why the Unseelie King is making his move now, it's because he too has seen this vision. Although I saved this next bit just for you."

We pushed through an arch cut into the brambles. On the other side stood a sight so gruesome it sucked the air from my lungs.

The smell hit me first. A familiar scent like BBQ pork

invaded my nostrils, all the more horrifying because it reminded me of Arizona summers when my parents were alive and not the grisly sight before me.

Set into the ground were six long, pointed wooden stakes, pointing up toward Briarwood and propped up with small frames. Skewered on four of the stakes were four charred, broken bodies, their limbs bent and twisted. One had its hands cut off and strung around its neck. Black patches on the earth beneath the stakes revealed they had been burned *in situ*, while still alive, their faces frozen in open-mouth, bug-eyed terror.

I stood in front of the first, choking back bile as I searched his face for some sign that this was an illusion, that it was Blake's idea of a twisted joke. What I found instead turned my heart to ice. The eyes that stared back at me – their lids burned away – were the same vibrant blue that had laughed at me from the other side of a croquet hoop. How those eyes survived what had been done to him, I could not guess. Probably it was for my benefit. A faint covering of fire-red hair still covered his burned and disfigured skull.

Flynn.

The other faces swirled around me and I recognized them all – Corbin, his beautiful vivid eyes poked out, Arthur, with his hands swinging from a rope in an invisible breeze. And Rowan, my beautiful Rowan, his ears lopped off, his body twisted where the stake pierced his chest.

My boys. My precious guys.

Bile rose in the back of my throat. I tried to turn away, but my body froze. Every grisly detail etched itself on my memory. My head throbbed, my chest tightened. I choked as the contents of my stomach sprayed themselves all over the dead ground.

Blake pointed to two stakes at the end of the line. "I bet you can't guess who they're for?" He grinned.

No. This is just a dream, just a...

But it didn't feel like a dream. It felt... important. Vital. It felt like some truth I already knew but didn't want to see. And now I was being forced to see it in all its grisly glory.

I felt to my knees. Only instead of hitting the cold, charred earth, I fell through it, toppling into the darkness. The world spun around me, and though the stakes and their bodies disappeared from view, those tortured faces never left me.

I woke with a start, sweat pouring down my body. A hand stretched across my stomach. *Corbin.* His body cupped mine, his soft lips grazing my shoulder, the sheets tangled around us, cool against our warm skin.

He's safe.

I stroked his cheek, relishing the smoothness of his flesh, trying to unsee the horror of his ruined face under my eyelids, but knowing it was probably never going to happen. I took several deep breaths, trying to get my heart to return to normal.

I stared at the ceiling for a time, wanting to wake Corbin up and tell him about the dream. But his face was so peaceful, I couldn't bear it. There was not a trace of that dark pain in his expression. So rarely was Corbin granted quiet of mind in this house, I didn't want to bring him back to reality.

But that didn't help me – the dream haunted me, and I knew I wouldn't be going to go back to sleep any time soon.

I slipped myself out from under Corbin's arm, pulled on my silky robe, grabbed the empty water glass from my bedside table, and tiptoed down my spiral staircase and into the hall.

Getting anywhere in this huge castle took time, and I was wide awake by the time I descended the secret staircase to the kitchen. I was surprised to see the lights on and Rowan hunched over the bench, shirtless, his muscles rippling as he worked an enormous ball of dough. Flour dusted the surface of his skin, the particles glimmering in the light like a fine layer of glitter.

"Rowan."

He jumped when I spoke, but his face broke into a smile as he looked up and saw me.

"I didn't hear you come down. I hope I didn't wake you up, with the lights and… and…" Rowan swiped a few of his dreadlocks over his shoulder, leaving a trail of white flour across his dark cheek.

"I couldn't sleep. I… I had another dream." I paused.

His face was impossible to read. "Like the others?"

I shook my head. "No. This one was a nightmare. I'm still a little shaken up."

He patted the stool at the island beside him. I sank into it, watching as he continued to knead the bread with rhythmic thrusts. His lips moved as he counted each push and pull of the dough, the way he counted many things. I wondered if he always counted while kneading bread, or if it was something he was doing because I was here.

I was just about to ask him about the counting when Rowan mumbled into his chest. "You were with Corbin?"

"Yeah… I…" I couldn't continue.

Rowan's face twisted, a weird mix of happiness and pain. "That's fine. That's okay." He stopped kneading and pulled out a stool on the other side of the island. He sank into it, clasping his hands in front of him, still staring at his chest. Something twisted in my gut as I took in his hunched shoulders. *I've hurt him.*

"Are you upset about me and Corbin?" I reached across the table to take his hand, but as soon as my skin touched his, Rowan drew away.

He shook his head. "It's as it should be. Corbin's the

leader here. He should be the *magister*. He's the one people always fall for."

"People?"

"Girls," Rowan whispered, wrapping a floury arm around himself. With a sinking heart, I remembered the way Emily flirted with Corbin, and how he and Neale bantered back and forth. "Corbin has a lot of girls because he can just *talk* to them. He wants to protect people, and girls love being protected."

"Not me." I jabbed my chest. "I'm pretty good at protecting myself these days, as long as I have my trusty spade."

Rowan snorted. I hoped it was the start of a laugh, and not directed at me.

"Corbin told me a lot of stuff tonight, about being the High Priestess, and how I gain my powers. I'm not saying I believe any of it, but… it fits, you know?" I reached for his hand again, and this time he didn't pull away. My fingers stroked his knuckles, and even the light touch sent another tingle of desire through my body. "I've been feeling so weird since I arrived at Briarwood. I came because my life in Arizona was taken away from me, and I thought maybe going somewhere completely different would help me move on. But now… let's just say Briarwood is starting to work its magic on me. I think you know a little about what that's like."

"This castle is built on the embers of our pain," Rowan said. "But when you mix those embers with fresh earth, seeds of new life can grow."

"That's beautiful." I turned Rowan's hand over, slipping my fingers between his. Rowan's arm jerked a little, but he still didn't pull away. I stared at his face and for a moment he looked up, and his green eyes darted about in panic. I wanted so badly to peel away the layers of him, to see the person that lurked beneath the tics and counting, the person who'd been so deeply scarred that Briarwood wasn't even enough to heal him, that he had to withdraw within himself, to a world of his own order.

"Maeve…" Rowan's voice shook. He tugged on my hand. I tightened my grip, wanting to keep the mesmerizing connection of our bodies as long as possible.

"I've seen the way you look at me, Rowan. I wouldn't say no. You don't think you're worthy of me because you think I'm this High Priestess, but I'm telling you as Maeve Moore, fellow weirdo, that even without this coven magic acting on us, I would shag you in a *heartbeat*."

Rowan gulped. He yanked his hand away, his eyes wild with panic. "That's not true. Don't say things like that."

"Look into my eyes, Rowan." He shook his head, staring at the lump of dough on the counter. "It *is* true. I didn't choose Corbin. We slept together, but I didn't choose him. There might be other options and right now… I'm not ready to choose anybody."

I reached for Rowan's hand again, but he shoved both his hands into his lap. "Tell me about the dream," he said, taking a shaking breath.

"Blake was there, but it was just the two of us this time. He said it was his turn to show me something, so I think I might have been in his dream and he was controlling it. We were standing in the meadow, looking up at castle. Only, nothing was right. Everything was charred and burned and dead, Briarwood buried beneath walls of thorns. The ground was parched, the sky poisoned with radiation. Even the air tasted different, thick and gross."

Rowan didn't say anything, but he did look up at me, his blue eyes flashing.

I continued. "Blake said it was our fault – humans were responsible. He said the fae were coming for us because the king had seen this vision. Then he showed me these stakes in the ground and on them were—" I gulped as Rowan's beautiful face was replaced by the charred image – his ears gone, his skin burned away, revealing bone and muscle. I gulped again, feeling the bile rise in my throat. "—you guys. The four of you. You had been pierced through the chest on stakes and burned alive."

"No, Maeve..." Rowan leaned across the table. He still didn't touch me, but his eyes were wide with concern. "That must've been horrible. What do you need?"

What do you need...

If I'd been talking to Corbin or Arthur, they'd be flipping to solution-mode, trying to figure out what the dream meant. Flynn would be making some kind of joke to distract me from the memory. But Rowan knew that laughter couldn't erase the horror. He only wanted to help me find a way to cope.

Rowan had been through something so terrible, so utterly horrific, it had shaped him into a person who instantly recognized the slivers of that same pain in others, and he tried to give them what he'd never been given. But right now, I didn't need anything... except Rowan. I wanted to give him a little of what he needed right back.

I slid out of my chair and walked around the island. Rowan stared up at me, his eyes large, almost frightened, but desperate to help me take away the burden I carried.

"I need *you*," I said, and pressed my lips to his.

I expected Rowan to jerk away, but he didn't. At first, he completely froze, his body stiffening as the warmth of his lips flowed into me. His fear made me bold. I wrapped my arms around his neck, sinking against him, parting his lips and sliding my tongue inside.

He moaned against me as piece by piece the tension in his body unraveled, and he sank into the kiss. His own tongue wound around mine – tentatively at first, and then exploratory.

So different from Corbin, so gentle and kind. I breathed in Rowan's unique scent – fresh bread and bright herbs, smells of home and hearth, of earth and embers.

I tangled my fingers in Rowan's dreadlocks, fanning them out around us, letting them become a curtain that hid our pain. I watched his face as he deepened this kiss and his own eyes flickered open. They saw me watching and the panic leapt into his body, stiffening him, clamping his lips shut.

But I wasn't going to let Rowan off that easy. I kept kissing him, stroking his face, playing with his hair, pouring everything I had into convincing him that I *did* want to be with him.

The tension eased from Rowan's shoulders, and he shuddered against me as he raised a shaking hand to my cheek, his fingers lightly tracing my skin, filled with wonder and awe. Heat rose up in my body, responding to his tenderness, eager and waiting for Rowan to unwrap me like a birthday present he'd waited all year for.

I shuffled forward, straddling Rowan's chair, pinning him between the chair and the island. Panic flashed in Rowan's eyes, but it turned to desire as I reached down and placed my hand over his crotch. Under his jeans he was hard, and even without seeing him I could tell that the naked dream I'd had about him was accurate.

The ache crept across my stomach, pulsing between my legs, begging for release. I worked my fingers along Rowan's belt, pulling out the loop, popping the button of his jeans, and tugging on the zipper.

I want to feel him in my hand, stroke him until he loses control, until he stops believing that he isn't worthy of this.

My heart raced as my fingers grazed the size of his cock, and Rowan shuddered. *What the hell am I doing?* I'd literally *just* come from shagging another guy and here I was, making out with Rowan, trailing my fingers over his flour-dusted torso, ripping his pants off so he could take me in a manly fashion.

What I'm doing is driving it out. All the grief. All the fear. This was exactly why I'd come to Briarwood for, to destroy the grief. All I needed to do that was this beautiful boy with pain in his eyes and his enormous, glorious black cock.

Rowan's fingers walked up my spine, leaving a trail of shivers across my skin. He buried his face into the side of my neck, nibbling and groaning into my collarbone as I pulled his cock out halfway and wrapped my hand around it.

I stroked him slowly, using the pre-cum on his head as lubrication as I slid my hand along his shaft, feeling the slight curve of it. Rowan's eyes burned into mine, open the whole time as though he wanted to commit every second we had together to memory.

His hands slid down my shoulders, pushing away the silky robe. It glided down my arms, revealing the tops of my breasts. Rowan reached for them, drawing them out one at a time, his face reverent, worshipful. He bent down and placed his lips over my nipple, his touch so soft, so light.

A moan escaped my throat and I leaned back and tightened my fingers around his cock. Rowan's tongue glided across my bud, already hard as a pebble and he suckled lightly, sending shivers through my chest.

He moved his lips to the other nipple, licking and sucking with the same aching gentleness, while using his fingers to play with the first. A trail of white flour granules extended across my chest, a swirl of glistening stars in the Milky Way. I dropped Rowan's cock, unable to keep my grip on it when my body hummed with so much electricity.

Rowan lifted me with surprising ease given his size. I let my arms hang limp and the robe slid completely off me, pooling on the floor at our feet. Rowan's mouth formed a silent O as his eyes swept over me. Never in my life had I felt more like a goddess.

He sat me down on another stool and knelt in front of me, his eyes never leaving mine. His hands caressed my body – soft and reverent – as though I were a nymph he couldn't believe was real. He trailed kisses along my thighs, his dreadlocks teasing and tickling my skin. I arched my back, bringing myself closer to him. Rowan dipped his head, tasting me with a long stroke of his tongue.

His lips lit me on fire, sending flames straight to the ache in my stomach. He drew his tongue back and stroked me again, his eyes trained on my face, watching and reveling in my reaction. The raw sensuality of watching him as he licked me in my most intimate spot nearly sent me over the edge.

He licked with rhythmic strokes. Of course he did. This was Rowan. He kept meticulous time, never altering his steady pace until I could anticipate each glide of his tongue, and the knowledge of it drove me closer... closer...

When my orgasm came, it crept along my veins like a hot flush, slow and languid before bursting forth and consuming me – a thousand stars dying in a cosmic blaze inside my body.

Behind Rowan's head, I could see a row of bread loaves all lined up along the windowsill, each one on its proofing cycle. Rowan, the Earth-user, the one who made the garden grow and the food delicious and who would move the earth itself.

My body rocked and shuddered, the fire retreating into a warm glow. Rowan wrapped his arms around my middle, resting his head on my thighs and staring up at me with eyes heavy with want. "Do you want to stop, beautiful?" he whispered.

I shook my head. "I want you inside me."

Rowan leapt to his feet and embraced me, his body warm against mine. Our skin – milky white and smoky black –

warmed each other as our limbs twisted around together. Rowan's lips met mine, urgent and yielding, but still so soft, so kind, so different from anything else I'd ever known. His hand stretched out across the table, grabbing his wallet – the surface also dusted with flour, like every other part of him. Inside, he drew out a condom.

"Corbin gave this to me. I never expected I'd need it," he said, a laugh in his voice.

I took it from him and tore it open while he shuffled out of his jeans and boxers, adding them to the pile of clothes on the floor. I stifled a gasp as I took in his body – not because his thin frame was more muscled than I expected, but because of the scars that traced over his dark skin. Thick welts across the fronts of his thighs, their surface lighter and slightly raised. Faded splodges that might have been burn marks on his lower torso. It looked like someone had tortured him.

I traced a line across one of the scars and Rowan shuddered, his eyes filling with pain. "I know I'm ugly," he whispered. "If you don't want—"

"You are not ugly," I said, grabbing his cock and rolling the condom over the tip, my fingers dancing down his glorious shaft. He was so long the condom wouldn't even go down the whole way.

"And you are the most beautiful girl I've ever seen," Rowan whispered. I fell against him, my legs fitting over him. I held his cock while I got myself into position, then sank down against him. We both moaned as his thickness entered me, sliding in halfway as I closed around him, my body not yet prepared for something so big and thick.

Rowan kissed me, his tongue seeking mine. His eyes burned into me. I used my heels against the island to rock back, driving him deeper. With each inch I managed to take inside me, the intensity of the sensation grew. *So much... so much of him, and all for me.*

With a final thrust, I took in the last inch, my muscles contracting around his length. The slight curve in his shaft touched me in places that had never been touched. The ache built again, just from the sheer excitement of having him completely inside me.

Rowan's fingers trailed up my spine, and I gripped his flour-dusted shoulders as I drove up with my feet, sliding up his shaft and then grinding my hips back down against him, pushing him deep inside me.

Sitting together like this felt so intimate, wrapped up in our own cocoon of bodies. Rowan gripped my ass with his hands and thrust up to meet me each time I came down. We moved slowly, and I felt every shudder of his cock, every inch of it caressing me inside.

My second orgasm came quickly, a total shock. The pressure rose like a tornado out of nowhere, and consumed me. I slammed down on Rowan's pelvic bone, tossing my head back as my walls convulsed around his thickness, my own body pulsing with release. Rowan pressed his hand against my stomach, as if he hoped to feed on the ache through my skin.

Rowan's mouth fell open in a silent gasp as his body shuddered against mine and his huge cock jerked out his own orgasm. Even with the condom, I'd never felt a guy come with such intensity before.

We collapsed against each other, gasping aloud as our bodies flooded with warmth. Rowan stroked my back, his fingers leaving tingling trails as his touch set my hairs on end. He nuzzled against my cheek. To my complete surprise, he looked down at our bodies, still pressed together, and burst out laughing.

"What?" I glanced down. There, across my stomach, was a

perfect impression of Rowan's hand, fingers splayed, rendered in white flour. Like the mark of Saruman on my pale skin.

I laughed too, wrapping my arms around Rowan and kissing his soft cheek. "Some people just give hickeys."

We slid apart, and Rowan disposed of the condom while I pulled on my robe and tied it around my waist. I watched his wiry frame bent over the trash, and the reality of what just happened hit me.

Two guys.

I slept with two different guys in the same night.

I rubbed my eyes, unable to believe that it was real, that I'd really done that. What would Mom and Dad say if they knew? I may not have shared their views on religion, but I'd always thought I was with them about not being a wanton slut. And yet, here I was, standing in the kitchen, where the food was prepared, having just had my fifth orgasm of the day. *What would they—*

They can't say anything, because they're dead.

And there it was, the reason. *I'm in pieces, every part of me scattered across the cosmos. I am ash and dust and I wish I could put myself back together again but I don't know how and when I'm with these guys, it feels as though being broken is okay, it's allowed.*

But it will never bring the Crawfords back. It will never heal me. I'll never be whole again.

Rowan straightened up, and he must've seen the look on my face, because his own face fell. "Maeve, are you okay?"

"No, I mean, yes. I mean, I—" My words choked on a sob. My pain reflected in Rowan's eyes, and I couldn't bear it. My gaze fell to the scars along his thighs. *I can't do this. I can't bear his pain as well as mine.*

"I'm sorry," I breathed, as I turned on my heel and fled for the stairs, tears streaming down my cheeks.

Everyone grieves differently, Arthur said. *You have to give yourself permission to do whatever it takes to get yourself through the pain. And then you have to forgive yourself for all the shit you end up doing.*

Arthur's grief had driven him to hurt someone. Rowan's pain had given him the furious need to control. And me? The loss of my pastor father and god-fearing housewife mother had driven me into the arms of two of my new housemates.

In the *same* night.

Was that slutty? I had no idea. I didn't have a moral barometer, but I'm pretty sure it was. I could call Kelly and ask her, and I knew I would soon. But for the moment, my head was too messed up.

Corbin was still sleeping in my bed, so I padded through the empty great hall and slipped outside into the courtyard. The night air brushed my body, fanning the robe across my bare skin. A thin line of red snaked across the corner of the sky – sunrise was not far away.

I slumped into one of the overstuffed bean bags, and

stared up at the sky, mapping the constellations I recognized. I wondered if I would be able to find a local astronomy club.

But why? I wiped a tear from the corner of my eye. *I'm not going to MIT. I won't be getting into the space program. My parents won't be watching me graduate with honors.*

Nothing in my life was turning out the way I hoped. Now what was I? A slutty witch living in a castle in a foreign land, trying to protect the world from a fae invasion.

I laughed as fat tears rolled down my cheeks. This time, I let them fall. The whole thing sounded completely ridiculous. Because it *was*. I could barely even think about what I'd learned and seen over the last week without wanting to commit myself. Maybe I should?

I wasn't sure what I believed any more. I didn't really think I was a witch, but I couldn't deny that I'd definitely been feeling the heightened sex drive Corbin had referred to. The fact my pussy still ached from having two different guys inside me spoke to that.

The fae were real enough, and the portal, too. I'd seen them go inside that sidhe and disappear. They absolutely had stolen two children.

The dreams… those I couldn't explain. The memory of what Blake had shown me plagued on my mind – the gaping, horrified faces of my guys, the charred earth, the broken sky, the two empty stakes waiting for their next victims…

If what Corbin told me was true – if *all* this was true – and I do nothing, then that vision was our future. Even if all this was some hallucination I invented in my grief, then fighting the fae may help me heal. Either way, Jane needed her son back. There was everything to gain by fighting, and nothing to gain by closing my eyes and pretending this wasn't happening.

The red streaks across the sky turned golden in hue, and

light crept across the courtyard, bringing clarity to the darkened corners and cracked stones. I wished it would bring the same clarity to my life.

"Maeve?" A voice called to me from above.

I glanced up. Corbin's head hung out of the tiny tower window, the breeze ruffling his dark hair. "You've got a text."

"Throw it down!" I yelled, leaping to my feet and holding out my hands.

Corbin flung my phone into the air, and in a display of skill and dexterity I'd never before displayed in gym class I managed to catch it. The screen showed a number I didn't recognize. I read the text:

It's Jane. The police called off the search yesterday. I don't know what to do, and if I stay in this house a moment longer I'm going to get very brassed off. You said I could come to the castle? I'd probably better wait until the sun has actually come up.

I texted her back.

Come anytime you want. I'm awake.

A moment later, my phone beeped again.

Good. Expect me in twenty minutes.

"Maeve, come back to bed," Corbin called down.

"Or stop yelling across the courtyard," Flynn's head appeared over the side of the second-floor walkway. "Some of us are trying to get our beauty sleep."

"An extra hour isn't gonna help you, mate," Arthur called down, sticking his head out from the other side. "Hi, Maeve. Why are you up so bloody early?"

"She was helping me with the bread," Rowan called up. I whirled around. Rowan stood in the doorway to the great hall, properly dressed now in jeans and a t-shirt, a familiar dusting of flour along his forearms obscuring his intricate tattoos. He glanced at me with a concerned look, but his eyes didn't linger.

"Now that we're all here…" I waved my phone. "Jane's coming over. The police called off the search for Connor. I told her she could look at our books."

"Do I have to put on pants?" Flynn called back.

"Yes," the other three guys chorused.

"It's really your decision," I added.

Flynn huffed. "Fine. But there better be a dram of Irish whiskey waiting with my breakfast for this. The nerve of forcing an Irishman out of bed before noon." His head disappeared over the rampart. Corbin and I exchanged a look and I burst out laughing.

~

"And you think this is what took my son?" Jane frowned at the book open in front of her.

I nodded, smoothing down the page of the yellowed folklore book. Different types of fae were depicted on the page, each one with a description of their traits and whether they were Seelie or Unseelie. "I know it sounds crazy, but I saw them with my own eyes. They took your son through a *sidhe* – that's a doorway into their own realm. I tried to stop them, but it didn't work."

Behind me, Corbin clambered down the ladder with another stack of books in his hands. His expression said he thought showing these to Jane was a bad idea, but I admired the fact that he didn't try to challenge me. Corbin believed so strongly that I was supposed to lead this coven that he was casting aside his years of leadership without a thought. Or maybe it was the fact that no one who saw the bags under Jane's eyes and the fury etched across her face would be able to withhold anything from her.

Jane turned the page, peering down at a woodcut of

fairies stealing a human child in the night and replacing it with one of their own. Her expression was unreadable. "I've seen pictures like these before. My grandmother used to tell me stories about the fae. She believed in all sorts of superstitions."

"You had sprigs of rowan at your front door," Corbin said, kindly. Jane's face flushed briefly.

"Yeah, and horseshoes in most all the rooms. Those were my grandmother's traditions, and I kept them up even though I think they're naff. According to her, fairies don't like rowan or iron. It's actually her cottage I'm living in. She left it to me when she died a couple of years ago, as well as all the furniture and gardens. I had no idea she'd done that until a lawyer came to see me, but it kind of made sense. She and my mother don't exactly get along. No surprise, because my mother is a cow, but Grandma always had a soft spot for me. I just wish she'd been able to meet Connor…" Jane trailed off. "I'm rambling."

"Rowan's making some of his amazing hot chocolate," Corbin said. "Nothing seems as bad after a glass of hot chocolate."

"Anyone who says that hasn't had their baby taken by fairies," Jane snapped back, but her eyes were a little warmer.

Something occurred to me. "There was a horseshoe over Connor's bed."

"Yes," Jane said. "How did you know that?"

Guilt flushed my skin as I remembered that I'd been snooping in Jane's house. Before I could confess, Corbin piped up. "An iron horseshoe should have deterred the fae. Climbing into the room and taking Connor would have been extremely painful to them. So why did they do it?"

Jane slammed the book shut and dug for the next one. "You guys are the experts. You tell me."

"You said they seemed listless," I remembered. I pulled a book from Corbin's stack and settled into the corner of the sofa. "That might have been the effect of the iron."

"And what was with that pumpkin?" Jane wrinkled her nose. "With the scrawled-on face?"

"Fae would often leave behind an object that they charmed with glamour to look just like the child," Corbin said, flipping through another folklore book. "There's stories from Ireland of mothers realizing their children had been taken only when their baby suddenly turned into a vegetable and by then it was too late. I wonder if you distracted them before they could finish the glamour spell and they decided just to take Connor and run for it."

"Why choose Connor, though?" I asked. "Surely there would have been other children without horseshoes who'd be easier to kidnap? Do you think there was a reason they specifically wanted Connor—"

"That's them," Jane said suddenly. She jabbed her finger at an image in Corbin's book. "That's the creatures who took Connor."

"Spriggens," Corbin read. "I've never seen these guys before. Something as small and delicate would usually not be able to penetrate the doorway between our worlds."

"These are Seelie," I said, pointing to the description. "I guess that confirms it. The Seelie and Unseelie are working together, just like Blake said."

"Say I believe this is true," Jane said. "Say I'm shit out of options and all the crazy talk is starting to sound like the only reasonable explanation of what happened. How does this help us get Connor back?"

In response, Corbin dumped a bunch of books in Jane's arms. "That's what we're doing here," he said. "Somewhere in these books and diaries is a clue to the spell the fae are trying to perform with these children. If we can find it, we can figure out a way to stop it."

"So I'm going to save my son by reading?" Jane asked, raising an eyebrow incredulously.

"Well…" Corbin shrugged. "Yeah. You don't have to help if you don't want—"

"No." Jane dropped down into Corbin's wingback chair behind the desk and opened the first book on the stack. "I'm a fast reader."

Corbin looked like he was about to say something about his chair, but he snapped his mouth shut and plonked down on the other end of the sofa.

Silence prevailed, the only sounds in the room the rustle of pages and the slurp of hot chocolate. I skimmed through two folklore volumes written by previous residents of Briarwood and a dull-as-dishwater herbal manual before my hand fell upon a small book. *Principles of Spirit Magic*, the title declared in faded gothic script.

My heart thudded in my chest. The guys said I was a spirit user like my mother. But I knew very little about what that actually meant. Apart from the dreams, I hadn't really done anything particularly magical. Not that I really believed any of this. But maybe the book would have something useful.

I opened it up, flipping through the pages until I came to a section called DREAMWALKING.

The power of dream walking manifests itself in different ways, depending on the witch and how he/she chooses to wield it. It is one of the rarest types of spirit magic and is not well understood.

A witch may use her powers to enter the dreams of another, to bring people into her own dreams, or to transport her body through the dream-realm to other places, times, or spiritual planes.

"Guys," I cried excitedly, leaping up so fast that Obelix,

who'd settled himself between Corbin and I on the sofa, shot me a filthy look and returned to licking his bollocks.

Bollocks. Such a multi-faceted word.

"Watch out!" Corbin steadied his mug of hot chocolate. "Did you find something?"

I grinned. "I think I know a way we could get Jane's baby back."

CORBIN

"Corbin, I need every book you've got on dreams and dreamwalkers." Maeve instructed as she paced back and forth across the library. As soon as she'd shown me the passage in the book, I'd grasped what she was getting at and called the others into the library. Thankfully, Flynn was wearing pants.

Maeve started passing out the volumes she'd already found. Everyone lined up to help (except for Jane, who had to go check in with the police about Connor's case). Funny, no one was ever this enthusiastic about research when *I* needed a hand. "Right, you guys, I'm looking for a spell to manipulate a dream, or… and I can't believe I'm saying this… to use dreams to astral-project."

"Whoa, Maeve. Getting your freak on." Flynn grinned.

"No, Flynn, I'm trying to save an innocent life." Maeve was not in a joking mood. "Even if we can't figure out what the fae are trying to do with Connor or the other baby they took, we can at least try and get them back—"

I barely heard any of the conversation, so mesmerized was I by Maeve stomping across the library like she owned it, which I guess technically she did. Her skin glowed with the faintest trade of white light. And my attraction to her grew and swelled with every breath she drew in between her bow-shaped lips. I glanced across at Arthur and he nodded. He felt it, too. The hum in the air, the sizzle of untapped potential magic waiting to be channelled.

Maeve didn't realize it, but she was already gathering her power. I couldn't believe that only hours earlier, I'd had her over that very desk she leaned across right now, our bodies entwined together, her power feeding from mine—

Maeve waved her hand in front of my face. "Earth to Corbin? The books… I need them."

"Um… right." I pulled her over to a shelf on magical lore. "Hold out your hands. This could get heavy."

"Ooh," Maeve breathed out as I dumped a heavy volume of dream magic into her arms. "Luckily I've been doing those workouts with Arthur or that would've sent me through the floor."

You've been doing more than working out with Arthur, I noted, but didn't say it aloud, not with Jane in the room. Maeve's power had grown far too much for her to have just been with me – she'd shagged someone else. But old Aragorn wasn't giving anything away – his hands in his pockets, his forehead furrowed in thought as he peered over Maeve's shoulder, his beard tickling her collarbone…

Stop being an idiot and get back to work. I opened the book in front of me, flipping through the pages of spells. *Maeve didn't choose you. She has a right to be with whoever she wants, and you have no right to get all possessive just because she slept with you first. And if she had to shag someone else, then one of your best friends makes a bloody good choice, considering the advantages it's going to have when performing spells—*

No matter what I told myself, that growling, gnawing

feeling in my gut wouldn't let up. I glared at Arthur again as he turned the page for Maeve. *Bastard.*

Focus. I flipped open my book, turning my body away from the desk so I didn't have to look at Arthur and Maeve. Now I faced Rowan and I noticed his gaze was fixed on Maeve, too. Poor Rowan, he didn't have a shot in hell.

I scanned the pages, searching for any spells about dreams or astral-projection. Unfortunately, none of the ancestors of the Briarwood coven had a degree in Library Science, so they hadn't thought to index or catalogue their spells. I'd made a start on it, but it probably wouldn't be finished in my life-time. We had to search through every page on every book, and the chances of finding what we needed were—

Hang on a sec.

The image in my book showed coven members asleep, draped naked over logs and rocks in the middle of a forest. Above their heads, they danced with a horned demon in a dream. My eyes darted across the spell, translating the mingled English/Latin text. My heart leapt in my chest. "I've found something, but it's not easy."

"Of course it fecking isn't," Flynn rolled his eyes. Everyone crowded around the sofa. Maeve draped herself over the arm, her leg brushing mine and sending all sorts of distracting thoughts through my head.

"So this is a dream projection spell," I explained, moving my finger across the loopy writing. "According to this, one dreamwalker can pull other witches into a dream of their choosing. If the dreamwalker has the ability, they can use that dream to move to different places on earth."

"Sounds dangerous," Arthur said.

"Oh yeah, she's a real bastard," I jabbed the page. "The dreamwalker needs enough power to sustain the dream for all the other witches. And, the witches within the dream must return to their bodies in the waking world before they wake up or they'll be stuck in the dream forever. Plus, it doesn't say anything about using dreams to *cross the multiverse*."

Maeve wrinkled her forehead. "I don't understand, so are we in a dream or in the real world? We have to be in the real world to affect it, surely?"

"Not according to this," I said. "Have you got one of your physics books handy? Maybe it's a quantum thing."

Maeve shook her head. "We are *way* past the point where quantum theory will help."

I glanced at her in surprise. For Maeve to say that about science… she really *was* starting to believe. Maeve stared at the spell with a determined glint in her eyes. "For this to work, you'd all have to be asleep at the same time."

"I can't fall asleep if Arthur's in the room," Flynn complained. "He snores like a truck driver."

"I do not!" Arthur shot back.

"I can mix a sleeping draught," Rowan whispered.

"Can you make it taste like a glass of whiskey?" Flynn grabbed the book from my hands and started reading out the words he recognized. "The rest of this spell seems pretty easy, as long as Maeve can get her witch on for long enough."

A frown crossed Maeve's face. "We know I can pull people into a dream, but I don't want anyone else to do this. I want to try. I want to help get Connor back, but you don't all have to risk your lives to do it, too."

"Don't talk bollocks," Flynn said, shoving the book back into my arms. "This is the first piece of serious magic our complete coven will perform. I want to see what we can do."

"I'm in," Arthur said.

"And me," added Rowan.

I glanced around the room. A surge of pride coursed through me to see the determined faces staring back at me.

Our coven. It took me seven years for find them all and bring them here to Briarwood. When it came down to it, every one of them had no problem risking their lives to do the right thing and I loved them for it.

I stood up and threw my arms around Flynn and Maeve, bringing them together into a group hug. Maeve wrapped her arm around Rowan and drew him in, and Arthur's thick arms nearly encircled us all. My grin stretched ear to ear as I yelled, "lets kick some fae ass."

MAEVE

"**W**hat *are* you doing?"

I squealed with shock, dropping my end of the couch. The leg landed on my foot, sending a shooting pain up my leg. On the other end, Arthur winced as the opposite leg slammed into his shin.

We both whirled around. Dora stood in the entrance to the great hall, casting her frown around at the furniture pushed up against the walls and the rolls of tapestries propped up in the corner. She folded her arms across her black dress and tapped her orthopedic shoes against the stone floor.

"Just um… a little spring cleaning." I winced, rubbing my foot.

"It's not spring," she snapped. "And *I* do the cleaning. Those tapestries are over four hundred years old, young lady. You don't know how to properly handle them—"

"That's why we've left them for you to take care of," I gestured to the tapestries.

"How kind of you," Dora said in a voice that implied it wasn't kind at all.

The two of us stared daggers at each other until Arthur coughed awkwardly. "Hey, um… Dora, there's some mold on the curtains in my bedroom. Shall I help you lift them down?"

"Certainly, Arthur, that will be lovely." She turned on her heel and stomped off toward the staircase.

Arthur sighed and set down the end of the couch. "I'd better go help her."

I nodded. "Looks that way. I don't know why she doesn't like me."

"I'm sorry about Dora. She's been cleaning Briarwood for Corbin's family since he was in diapers. Most of us don't have families or don't see our families, so I think she sees herself as kind of a grandmother. She doesn't like it when we bring girls here. Corbin even had a girlfriend for a while, and Dora would only refer to her as 'that woman.'"

I shrugged. "Hey, my father was a preacher. I know over-protective parents when I see them. She thinks I'm a bad influence on you boys." My mind flashed back to last night, to Corbin pounding into me, to Rowan and I moving together on the kitchen stool. *Bad influence is damn right.*

He kissed my forehead. "You can be a bad influence on me any time."

Arthur darted off to occupy Dora. I tried to shove the couch toward the middle of the room myself, but it was too heavy. I poked my head out into the courtyard and yelled, "Corbin!"

Footsteps clattered across the ramparts. Corbin's head appeared over the railing around the covered walkway, his dark hair mussed up as though he'd been bent over a book. "You rang, m'lady?"

"Help me!"

A few moments later, I leaned my shoulder into the couch arm, trying to throw my weight behind it, but the damn thing barely shifted an inch. I cursed at it, and a deep voice behind me growled, "I don't see what the problem is. My view of the situation is bloody brilliant."

I glanced up. Corbin leaned against the doorframe, his eyes fixed on my ass, which I'd stuck right out to try and move the couch. A warm flush coursed through my body, but I folded my arms and gave him a stern look.

"I'm glad we sent Jane home so she didn't have to see this chaos. Dora arrived and she's not happy about the mess in here, so Arthur's gone to distract her." I kicked the sofa. Bad idea. A second, even sharper pain shot through my leg. "He's left me to deal with this beast on my own."

"At your service." Corbin trotted over and lifted the other end with one hand like it was nothing. We shuffled the couch into the center of the room with the others.

"Job done." I collapsed onto the couch where, in a few hours, I'd be falling asleep as part of my first spell. A spell where I'd have to somehow drag my four coven-mates into my dream and then take us into the realm of the fae… a place where, by rights, we shouldn't even be able to go.

A flutter of fear flickered across my stomach. I pushed it aside. I'd read the book on spirit magic cover to cover, and Corbin had even shown me a couple of simple spirit spells my mother had written in. Staring at her loopy, cursive writing made a lump rise in my throat, especially when I thought about the portrait in the hallway I hadn't glanced at since I'd heard that weird voice. I'd never got the chance to know my mother, but through this weird power she'd given me, for the first time in my life I felt like we were connected.

I only hoped I'd inherited her skill along with her power.

Corbin lay down beside me, turning his body to face mine and wrapping his thick arms around me. I snuggled into his warmth, and that growing sliver of doubt shrunk away to almost nothing. Corbin's strength was his protectiveness. He was used to putting others needs first. His family, the other guys, and now me. He believed I could do this, and his belief flowed into me. Maybe that was what Air users like him did – they exuded this *presence* into the air around them, so that it flowed into everyone they came into contact with.

Corbin's lips found mine and I welcomed the kiss, reveling in the heat of his lips, the way my whole body tingled and thrummed as his tongue slid over mine.

"You slept with someone else," he said, his gaze intense. It wasn't a question.

I nodded. I was about to say that it was Rowan, but then I decided not to. Instead, I said, "Does that bother you?"

"Not as much as I expected it to," he said, his hands stroking my face. "But a little. I thought… well, last night was so amazing, I thought… I hoped you'd choose me."

"Why do I have to choose anyone?" I said boldly. The image of the orgy in the grimoire flashed in front of my eyes.

"Be serious." Corbin pressed his lips to mine, our mouths opening against each other, our tongues entwining. His kisses stole my breath, and I forgot what it was I was daring to propose, instead wrapping my legs around Corbin and enjoying the shivers that coursed through me as his hands explored my body.

"Share that?"

I snapped my head back. Flynn's face dangled a few inches from my face, his mouth set in his customary cheeky grin.

Corbin swore. "Bloody hell, Flynn, you made me bite my lip."

"Tell me bollix." Flynn vaulted over the back of the sofa, squishing his body behind me. Now, I was sandwiched between Flynn and Corbin, the meat in the world's most delicious sandwich. Two hard bodies pressed against mine, and the ache inside my pulsed with desire.

I hardly dared to breathe. My eyes locked on Corbin's. His face read equal parts annoyance and desire. Flynn's hands danced along my bare arms, raising the hairs on my skin.

What's going to happen next?

What do I want *to happen?*

My body knew the answer to that, even if my brain was still stuck on the idea that I was going to burn in hell for all this.

"Go on," Flynn urged. "Don't mind me."

Corbin hesitated for a split second, his eyes searching mine. My heart in my throat and the throb inside me begging for more, I nodded. Corbin leaned forward and pressed his lips against mine. The ache in my core flared to life, harder and hotter than ever.

Something scraped along my neck. Flynn. He kissed along my collarbone, his teeth brushing against my skin, sending delicious shivers right down my spine.

Two guys, each one with their hands on me, with their erect cocks pressing into my thighs, my hips. Each one different – Flynn's hands rough from his work in the forge, his red curls tickling my skin. Corbin's fingers smooth as silk, his kisses hard and urgent. Each one sending flares of pleasure through my whole body.

This is just like my dream.

Well, in my dream, it was *all* the guys, each one pleasuring me in his own unique way. But two guys was a pretty damn good start... *this is amazing.*

Flynn's hand slid further down my arm, his fingers trailing over the bottom of my t-shirt. He lifted the fabric up and I gasped against Corbin's lips as Flynn slid his fingers against my stomach. Everything felt more raw, more intimate, with the two of them, knowing that the other was watching.

"You okay there, Einstein?" Flynn whispered against my earlobe.

I moaned in response, bending my hand beneath his arm and running my fingers down the bulge in his pants, encouraging him to keep going. Corbin's lips devoured mine, his kiss fierce. He dug his fingers into my thigh, pressing me against his hard cock. Flynn's fingers slid higher, skimming the bottom of my breasts.

"Mary Mother of Jesus, she's not wearing a bra," Flynn breathed. Now it was Corbin's turn to moan as Flynn's hand closed over my breast, lifting up the bottom of my t-shirt so Corbin could see Flynn's hands playing with my nipple.

I leaned back against Flynn, giving Corbin more room. He bent down and pulled up the rest of my top, freeing my second breast. Corbin bent down, his mouth clamping over the other nipple.

Oh my Goooooood...

A mouth on one nipple, the tongue flicking at my sensitive bud. Flynn rolled my other nipple between his fingers, pinching it slightly. Now that my mouth was free, he bent my head back and covered my lips with his. Flynn's kisses were like him – light, fluttery, the kind of kisses that swept a girl away.

I can't believe this is happening. Please, don't let it stop.

The air around us sizzled with heat. I relaxed into the sensations, feeling their kisses and caresses through my whole body, relishing the warmth of being surrounded with them. One question burned in the back of my mind.

How far will this go?

As if he heard my question, Corbin slid his hand down the outside of my thigh, bringing it up between my legs, underneath my skirt. His fingers brushed over my panties.

The lightest touch, but it sent a fresh wave of pleasure through my body.

In response, Flynn's tongue rammed into my throat and I devoured him with all the passion that swirled around inside me. Corbin's fingers snaked under the edge of my panties, and he pressed one finger against my throbbing clit. I shuddered, already so close to climax—

"Um, guys?"

Shit. Hell. Bollocks!

Corbin sprung off me like he'd stuck his cock in an electrical socket. Flynn sank back into the couch, somehow thinking he could camouflage himself in the purple cushions. I stuck my head up over the top of the sofa, dreading what – or who – I was going to see.

Rowan stood in the doorway. For once, his eyes weren't on the ceiling, his lips weren't moving as he counted the swords. Instead, his gaze bore into mine, his expression completely unreadable. My cheeks blazed as I yanked my top down, covering my breasts. The ache had gone, replaced by a terrible churning in my stomach that somehow, I'd hurt him.

Rowan's eyes never left mine. He said, his voice calm but emotionless. "The draught is ready."

I gulped. No time now to sort this out. I couldn't worry about Rowan or Corbin or any of the guys. I had to focus on trying to do the one thing I still didn't entirely believe I was capable of.

I had to perform real, honest-to-God *magic*. It was time to do my mother proud.

33

ROWAN

here was no mistaking what I'd just walked in on. Maeve's vest was around her shoulders, those gorgeous tits of hers bouncing free. Flynn's hand pinched her, and Corbin had a face full of tit, which made my blood boil because I knew exactly how great a place that was to be. Corbin's hand was up her skirt, and from the way she was moaning and quivering, he was touching her just the way she liked. When Maeve had looked up and seen me, her heavy lidded eyes showed only desire.

Corbin and Maeve and Flynn. Seeing them together like that *should* disgust me, make me seethe with jealousy, shouldn't it? That was how people felt when someone they liked was with someone else. *Two* someone else's.

But that wasn't what I felt at all. Not after Maeve had said what she'd said to me last night. *You don't think you're worthy of me... but I'm telling you... even without this coven magic acting on us, I would shag you in a heartbeat.*

I trusted Maeve implicitly and I believed her words, even though they were completely foreign to me. Maeve wasn't the first girl I slept with – there were girls at the shelters and on the street, high on anything they could get their hands on and desperate for some kind of feeling. That was me, too. But that had been mechanical, a means to an end, a way to numb myself for an hour or two, a way to score the next hit. With Maeve... that was the first time I actually *felt* something.

Seeing her with her breasts naked, her head thrown back in ecstasy... I was feeling it again. My own fingers itched to run over Maeve's soft skin, to be the one lying with her back pressed against my chest, *my* fingers teasing her nipples.

I wanted Maeve, and I thought that maybe, *possibly*, I would love her one day, if I was even capable of that emotion. But I loved Corbin, too, or as close to it as I was able. And Flynn and Arthur. They were my brothers. Corbin saved me. He got me off the street, even when I didn't want to come. He brought me to Briarwood. He paid for my first cooking class. He was the first person in my life to believe I was worth something. Seeing him with Maeve like that – knowing that for once he wasn't thinking about who he had to protect – made me happy.

I just wanted him to be happy.

But where did that leave me? Maeve said she didn't want to choose at all. *But does that mean what I think it means?*

"I'll get Arthur," Flynn darted off. Maeve shot me a sad look, then slunk away, smoothing her skirt down.

I slid the silver tray in my hands onto the small coffee table we placed in the center of the circle. On it stood five small shot glasses of foggy brown liquid, each one spaced evenly from the last (I measured). In the center I placed a tall glass filled with salt and a red candle tied with sprigs of rosemary and rowan. Beside the candle were four bracelets, which Maeve had woven earlier from locks of our hair. These were how Maeve would pull us into her dream and ensure we stayed locked with her.

Everything we needed for our ritual, all nearly arranged in a perfect circle.

Corbin came up behind me. "Rowan, I—"

I hated to see that look on his face, that fallen look that said he thought he'd hurt me, that he'd give up this one for me if he thought it would make a difference. But it was also a look that said he knew I didn't have a shot.

For once, he had things *wrong*.

"I wish it had been me," I said.

"I know," Corbin looked so forlorn, it almost made me burst out laughing. "It should have been you, Rowan. I wanted that, you know, right? Even though the magic makes me want her, too. This just sort of… happened. I know even know what I was thinking – she slept with me last night, and then she went and slept with Arthur, too. But I'll stop. I promise that I'll stay away from her from now on. She's yours. I just…. I just lost it a little, and then Flynn jumped in and I got carried away—"

"No," I shook my head. "I wish it had been me, instead of Flynn. Me, and her, and you."

I'd never seen Corbin look so… *lost*. "Um…" he gulped. "Right."

A hundred unsaid things passed between us in that moment.

"And it wasn't Arthur who slept with her last night," I couldn't resist adding. "It was me."

Corbin looked stunned, and I had to admit, I liked seeing him look like that. He opened his mouth like he was going to say something, but no sound came out. A hundred thoughts whirled around in my head – images of him and me and Maeve – but I couldn't find the words to articulate them, to make him understand. Instead, I counted the cracks on the wall behind his head.

"Rowan—" Corbin started.

Footsteps on the staircase broke our bond. A moment later, Arthur appeared at the door to the Great Hall, dressed in his medieval garb – a long tunic and linen breeches tucked into enormous leather boots. A leather belt slung around his waist held his two-handed sword and two shorter blades. Flynn dashed in behind him, dressed like a normal person but wearing an enormous iron medallion around his neck.

"Right, we got rid of Dora," Flynn announced. "I convinced her there was a special sale on silver polish over at that bargain store in Crooks Crossing. Now, where's my dram? I want to get under before Arthur's snoring starts."

I pointed to the silver tray. Flynn picked up one of the glasses to inspect it, his brow furrowing. Then he set it back down, deliberately off-center. Because he was Flynn.

Corbin picked up the salt and raised it, then hesitated. He glanced at Maeve. "You should be leading this."

"I don't know what to do," she admitted. "Please, I need you to take charge of the ritual. Let me focus on the actual dream walking."

She knew just how to give Corbin what he needed. He grinned as he raised the salt again, and said his blessing over it. He offered the salt to the four corners – the north, south, east, and west. Then – while we chanted the invocation we all knew by heart – Corbin sprinkled the salt in a circle around the sofas and beanbags Maeve had arranged around the center of the room. He left a small gap in the salt.

Arthur lit the candle and passed it to Corbin. The woody scent of rowan – the tree of protection from which I'd been given my name – filled the room. Corbin walked clockwise around the circle again, holding the flame high as he spoke the invocation once more. He stepped through the gap he left in the ring of salt, closed it off with the last granules in the glass, and set the candle back down on the table.

Maeve gestured to the couches and beanbags. "Shall we make ourselves comfortable?"

After what had just happened on that sofa, I doubted anyone would be getting comfortable there. Corbin looked ready to jump out of his skin. Flynn kept glancing between Corbin and I and Maeve was biting her bottom lip, her usually-neat pixie hair sticking out all angles. I suspect her nerves were more to do with what she was about to do. Maeve didn't strike me as the type of girl who bothered with regret for what she had done.

Probably a good thing. There was plenty enough regret in this castle to go around.

Flynn was the first to sit, grabbing his shot glass from the tray, flopping down on one of the beanbags and crossing his long legs on the table. "I'm ready for the best night's sleep of my life."

"Why, is Corbin's mother out of town?" Arthur said, picking up his own glass.

"Ask me bollix," Flynn shot back, and downed his glass in one gulp. "That was a terrible joke."

Corbin sat down on the end of the sofa, picked up his own glass, and tossed it back. He set the glass back down, his mouth twisting into a grimace "I wish that tasted as good as your hot chocolate, Rowan."

Maeve picked up the last two glasses and handed one to me. Her hand brushed mine, and a cloud of bright thoughts assaulted me, quite out of character, really. She held up her glass, and it took me a moment to realize she wanted me to toast her.

I clinked my glass to hers and tipped the liquid down my throat. It did *not* taste like hot chocolate.

Maeve threaded the four bracelets onto her wrist, turning them to admire the different colors – Corbin's dark, silky hair, Arthur's blond, Flynn's vibrant red. Mine was just a single dreadlock, with a bead on the end. She gulped back her drink, and immediately stifled a yawn. "I hope it's a better sleep than last night. I was so wound up, I barely got a wink."

On the couch behind her, Corbin choked, his eyes wide. I smiled at Maeve, but the draught already tugged at my facial muscles, making it a little lopsided. I settled back into the sofa beside Corbin, remembering how bright Maeve's eyes looked as she rode me last night, how much I wanted another night like that with her.

And maybe, with Corbin, too...

That was the last coherent thought I had before I slipped beyond the veil of sleep.

3 4

MAEVE

The four boys fell asleep first, slumping over the sofa arms, their heads lolling to the side. Flynn was right; Arthur *did* snore, his huge body shuddering with each outward breath.

I longed to move around them, to touch their faces and feel the warmth of their skin, but the draught was starting to work its way through me. My brain fogged over. I stared at the corner of the room, watching the cracks in the lime wash wobble. I tried to lift my arm, but it was like an enormous weight was tied to it.

This is insane. You've just taken a drug you don't understand. You can't seriously believe you can do magic. Dreams are just the brain's responses to REM sleep—

Don't think about that. Concentrate on where you want to go. Think about the fairy realm... the sidhe... the wormhole across the multiverse...

My eyes fluttered shut, and darkness enveloped me. My body slipped over the edge of consciousness.

I opened my eyes. Bright light poured over me, and it took a moment for my retinas to adjust and discern the shapes around me.

I lay in a bright field of tall, lush grass. Wildflowers of every shape and color swayed in a gentle breeze. The grass wafted over my bare legs, tickling my skin, fresh and light and beautiful.

Why am I sleeping outside? Why am I—

Then I remembered what I had come to do, and where I (hopefully) was. Slowly, worried that sudden movement might knock me out of the dream state, I got to my feet, and peered across the meadow.

I stood at the bottom of a wide valley. Sweeping forests drew up on either side of me, the high treetops disappearing into dense, fluffy clouds. At the end of the meadow, a series of sidhe peeked out. Smoke puffed from bonfires, and the faint sounds of music and laughter wafted on the breeze.

Okay, the first part of the plan was a success. I was pretty sure I was now in the fae realm. I had crossed the multiverse in my sleep. I could deal with the theoretical physics behind that later. Now, I had to bring my guys with me.

I glanced down at my wrist where the four circles of hair encircled my arm. I unwound the end of the first one, pulling a single hair from the bundle. It was dark hair, wavy and almost black. *Corbin.* As I unwound the bracelet, I imagined it as a rope in my mind, pulling Corbin from his place flopped over the sofa in Briarwood into the meadow.

"Maeve, you did it."

I whirled around. Corbin sat on the grass behind me, his face shining with pride. I threw my arms around him, relishing the solidity of his form. He was definitely *here.* I brought him into the dream with me.

"Now for the others," I tugged at the bright red bracelet. A few moments later, Flynn shimmered into view, a little further down the valley.

"Einstein." Flynn ran up and embraced me, his grin wide. He pressed his lips against my earlobe. "I wish you were naked, like the other dreams."

"Down, boy," I pushed him away, but I was smiling. *So far, so good.*

Arthur was next. His blond hair fell through my fingers as the bracelet unraveled and he appeared next to Corbin, dressed in his medieval garb, his scabbard splayed out on the grass beside him, but neither his sword nor knives were with him. A deep crease marred his cheek.

"I think I fell asleep on the ground," he said, rubbing his shoulder. "My body hurts."

"It might be that beer bottle I left under the beanbag," Flynn said.

"I hope you're fucking kidding," Arthur grumbled, rolling his shoulder.

"Mate, I never kid about piss."

"You're a bloody wanker, Flynn." Arthur's hand reached for the hilt of his sword. He frowned as he discovered his sword wasn't there. He immediately rose to his knees, searching through the grass. "Where is it?"

Corbin frowned, his hand clasping the belt of his jeans. "My button is gone, too. I think maybe there's some kind of spell that prevents metal of any sort from passing into the realm."

Flynn glanced down at his chest. Sure enough, his amulet was gone. He looked crestfallen. "It took me hours to make that," he sighed.

I plunged my hand into my skirt pocket – sure enough, my knife and Flynn's amulet weren't there, but I still had the twig and Corbin's paper. They would have to do.

"Forget that, what are we going to do without my sword?"

Arthur grumbled. "Do you plan on knocking them out with your Irish wit?"

"Hey, give me a hand here." I was trying to unravel Rowan's bracelet, but his dreadlock wouldn't pull apart. Sticky wax coated my fingers, and all I managed to do was pull tufts off.

"Try this," Flynn offered, holding his hand over the bracelet. A few drops of water fell from his fingers. The water was surprisingly warm, and it made the wax soft and easier to handle.

"Thanks for doing something useful," I grinned at Flynn.

"For once," Arthur mumbled.

"You can wag right off. I'm always useful," Flynn shot back.

I managed to unravel the bracelet and Rowan appeared beside Corbin, his face lighting up as soon as he saw us. He stumbled forward, his baggy pants catching in the long grass, and embraced me. The warmth of him gave me strength.

Every part of this dream felt so real, from the grass swishing around my legs to Rowan's lips pressing against my collarbone. I reminded myself that this wasn't an ordinary dream – it was an astral-projection into another universe. And I'd somehow managed to do it. Possibly.

"What do we do now?" I asked, glancing around. We had no real plan beyond this point.

"Our best bet is to get closer to the sidhe," Corbin pointed to the mounds. "It sounds as though revels are taking place. We can sneak through the trees and hopefully get closer without being seen."

"How do we know they're not holding Connor somewhere else?" I pointed into the twin forests and down the valley. "He could be at any of their main population centers—"

"Unlikely," Corbin said. "The realm is deceptive – it looks

enormous, but it's only a glamour fooling your eyes. When the humans first banished the fae here, their witches made the realm small enough that it could be easily guarded. It's one of the reasons the fae are so desperate to escape. The borders are only a few miles away. The Seelie and Unseelie courts are practically right on top of each other. Come on."

We crept into the trees and made our way down the valley, staying as far back from the edge of the meadow as we could, in order to hide in the thick forest. Not that it did much good. We were about as obvious as a herd of elephants shopping at Walmart. Every few feet Arthur's heavy boots snapped a twig or Flynn yelped as something prickly stabbed him in the arm.

"Could you lot be *any* noisier?" Corbin snapped. "I don't think every fae in the vicinity heard you yet."

"Can't Maeve just dream us up some non-noise-making boots?" Flynn complained.

"I don't think that's how this dream works—"

"Sssh," I said, my ears straining. "I hear something."

The guys stopped in their tracks, crouching down behind me. I peered through the trees, and could just make out the tops of several *sidhe* in a clearing down the valley. Between the towering mounds – their entrances uncovered and bedecked with garlands – danced the fae.

I gasped as I took in the sheer number. There were hundreds of them, all shapes and sizes, all the monstrous and beautiful creatures I'd seen in the pages of Corbin's books. Green and black coats twirled around each other, laughing and singing.

"This doesn't make any sense," Corbin whispered from beside me. "Those are Seelie and Unseelie fae dancing together. This shouldn't happen. The two courts hate each other. We know they're working together, but this—"

"That is all you'll see of our revels, *witch.*"

I spun around, my heart in my throat. A fae leapt out of the trees, darting straight at me. I kicked out a leg and caught it in the stomach, but as it sprawled out on the ground another one grabbed me from behind, twisting my arm until I cried out.

"Corbin!" I yelled, but I was too late. Out of the corner of my eye, I saw Corbin go down, several fae piling on top of his body, holding him in the dirt while they tied his wrists with a thick vine. I couldn't see the others anywhere, but I could hear Flynn yelling and branches breaking as they crashed through the forest.

Arthur crashed through the trees, bellowing as he tried to shake off an ugly fae whose sharp teeth latched onto his arm. Arthur lurched toward me, fumbling for his scabbard, but of course there was no longer a sword there. Five other fae piled on top of him, and he too went down in a fury of fists and teeth.

Remembering one of the wrestling tricks Arthur taught me, I sank against the fae who held me, letting him think I'd given up the fight. His grip loosened as he tried to drag me away, and I took the chance to sink all my weight into a kick to his knee.

The fae howled, dropping me as it fell to the dirt, clutching its knee. My own foot stung, but I tried to ignore the throbbing as I flung myself toward Corbin. I grabbed the nearest fae and tried to tug its spindly arm from around Corbin's neck, but for such a tiny creature it held on with surprising strength.

More fae swarmed on top of us. They tore me from Corbin, dragging me back, wrapping my wrists in the thick vines. I kicked and screamed and twisted my body, but there were just too many.

"Hello, Princess."

My body went rigid. I looked up.

Blake stepped out from the shadows of the trees. He wore the same black tunic and trousers as always, the long coat swirling dramatically around his legs. A great curved wooden bow rested on his shoulder and a set of arrows in a woven quiver sat diagonally across his back. He looked totally badass. Hope surged in my stomach.

"Blake!" I cried out. "Help us. We have to get to the—"

Blake snapped his fingers, and sound fled from my throat. I kept moving my jaw, pushing air past my vocal chords, but no sound came out.

He's taken my voice. But why would he do that, unless... unless he's been lying to us the whole time.

My whole body went cold. This was bad. This was very, *very* bad.

"Shall I finish them, Prince?" asked one of the fae, a tall, willowy guard dressed in a green uniform with the same flawless skin and crystalline eyes of the black-clad fae who first attacked up in the Briarwood meadow. "They have invaded our lands and spied on our rituals. Their deaths will be our greatest victory!"

"We can drink our nectar wine from their skulls!" another piped up.

I held my breath, but to my momentary relief, Blake shook his head. "These are the Briarwood witches. We cannot take such actions, justified as they are, without orders. I say, if they are so desperate to find out our secrets, we should indulge them." Blake nodded to his sergeant. "Take them to the King."

3 5

MAEVE

The fae dragged Rowan and Flynn from the trees, binding their hands with vines and throwing them down beside us. Corbin managed to tug a hand free and smacked one of the green-guards in the face. Hope surged within me as he swept out a leg and toppled another two green-guards.

The surge of triumph soon faded as the fae overpowered Corbin again and forced some kind of drink from a water-skin down his throat. A moment later, Corbin's head nodded against his chest. He was sound asleep.

Rowan looked worried. "That's a powerful sleeping draught." He whispered to me. "If we're not able to wake him up soon, he might remain asleep forever."

They threw Corbin on a makeshift stretcher made from gnarled branches and a bed of woven vines, and forced us to march behind him down toward the barrows. As we came out of the forest, I noticed tracks winding through the undergrowth – steps fashioned from stones and roots leading in all directions, lit with dangling lanterns that flick-ered in the gloom of the woods. Above our heads, platforms in the trees swarmed with fae – and baskets swung on vines between the platforms, carrying food and skins filled with liquid.

They marched us down between the barrows, along stone-lined dirt paths between dancing, jeering fae. Many held aloft platters of cakes and honeyed fruits, the cloying scent of all that sweetness mingling with the acrid smoke of a blazing bonfire.

The guards lined us up along one side of the bonfire and tossed Corbin's body off the stretcher into a heap at our feet. Fae darted in to kick and bite him, and I tried to scream at them to stop, but whatever Blake had done to hold my throat was still in effect.

"Show me the humans," a deep voice boomed.

The fae fell silent. I whipped my head up, my gaze falling on six wizened old hags wearing green and gold robes, each one holding one corner of an hexagonal litter, upon which sat a resplendent throne of vines, bedecked with garlands of flowers in dazzling jeweled tones.

And upon that throne sat a man whose presence *exuded* power. The air around him crackled with energy. It tugged at me. His eyes – like a pair of glittering emeralds – held me rapt, the curve of his smile strangely familiar, even though I'd never seen it before. My feet shuffled forward, desperate to reach him, to throw myself at his feet.

"I am Daigh, ruler of the united fae courts. I demand to know why you have breached the veil of our worlds," the king roared, his voice soaring over the crowd of silent fae, booming off the surface of the drum skins, tearing through the narrow paths and on up the valley.

"Not *technically*," Flynn shot up. "You see, we're actually dreaming right now. So this isn't *me* in the flesh you're talking to, it's just a dream image and—"

I tried to choke out a scream as a guard stabbed his bone

knife into Flynn's shoulder. Flynn howled and dropped to his knees, clutching the deep wound. Blood pooled between his fingers, and his face collapsed with pain. No one stepped forward to help him.

The fae king – Daigh – didn't flinch. A tiny sprite flitted around his head, holding up a wooden cup. The king took the cup and sipped, that familiar smile turning up further. "You seem real enough to me."

"Don't hurt him anymore!" Rowan said. "He's no threat to you. None of us are."

The king's eyes flicked to Rowan, then back to me. Once more, that weird stab of… of *something*… twisted in my gut. It wasn't fear, although there was plenty of that, shuddering through my limbs. It was this tugging, crawling sensation that I should be able to put something together.

"Ah, they have brought with them the *American*," Daigh sniffed. "I always detested that accent. I can see why my son silenced you. It's a shame to hear such linguistic atrocities from your lips, but in time, I'm hopeful you can be corrected. Maeve Moore, would you like to explain why you have broken the treaty to step into our realm?"

I was no longer surprised that this king knew my name. All the other fae seemed to. I pointed at my throat. Blake waved his hand, and with a gush of air my voice returned. "We came to take back the children you stole from Crook-shollow," I said, pronouncing each word carefully, ensuring all the muscles worked as they were supposed to. "That is against our accord. You have broken the treaty first."

"Treaty," Daigh snorted. He spat a mouthful of wine on the earth in front of us. "What you call a treaty, we call *slavery*. We call *unlawful occupation*. We've been trapped in this dwindling world, the shadow of our true birthright, by you colonialist usurpers. We have watched – helpless and seething – for centuries as you humans scoured the earth, tearing down the forests and building roads and shopping centers," the king screwed up his face as though he'd tasted something disgusting. "You have squandered the paradise you unrightfully took from us, and we refuse to honor the laws between our people that were designed purely to contain us while you took what you wanted for yourselves."

"What's all this bollocks?" Arthur narrowed his eyes.

"This *bollocks*, Fire Witch, means that we're no longer content to rule over this dwindling valley while humankind poisons our rightful home. Your weapons of iron imprisoned us here, and your historians allowed us to fall out of knowledge, to become creatures of myth and superstition. But we have a weapon the likes of which you cannot even imagine, and unlike you, we are content to lie in wait until the time is right for us to return to our rightful home, to put back the damage you had done."

"You're dangerous," Flynn yelled. "You hurt innocent people. You steal their children and drown sailors and lead ramblers into the woods to starve. You couldn't live alongside humans without hurting us, so don't talk bollocks about your rights being violated, *especially* not to an Irishman."

"Is not anyone dangerous when their homes are threatened?" The King glowered back. "When the barbarian hordes descend over the hillside, swords raised, murder in their eyes? What would you do, Water Witch, to save your precious castle?"

"But that was centuries ago!" Flynn yelled. "Millions of humans live peacefully here in England now. You can't just push them all out of their homes."

"Oh, I don't plan on forcing you all to go live in France," the fae king said. I waited for him to explain what he did plan to do – he seemed to be into that old-school I'm-the-villain-so-I'll-reveal-all-my-plans-right-before-I-kill-you vibe. But Daigh waved his hand, as if the conversation were boring him. He addressed his nearest guard. "Throw them outside. Let the court faeries have their fun with them. Return through the gateway and compel a human to enter their castle and destroy their human bodies. Burn them all like the witches they are."

"No!" I cried, adrenalin pulsing through me.

"Maeve," Rowan spoke my name in his quiet voice, trying to soothe me. But it was no good. Panic rose up in my throat. I'd read the spell – if their bodies died while they were in the dream with me, their spirits would be trapped in the dream forever, unable to leave, unable to wake up, unable even to adhere to external logic.

The king smiled. "Ah, that loosened her tongue." He jabbed a long, thin finger at me. "Of course, you will spare Maeve from the fire, but you must return her body to me. I'm keeping her."

He's what? My gaze fell on Blake, standing behind the throne, the flickering lantern-light shimmering off the silver-streaked black hair that streamed down his back. That coldness in his eyes, the sheer ease with which he'd tricked me… that was what happened to a human who was kept by the fae.

'I'm not staying with you," I spat, struggling against the fae that held me.

"You do not have a choice."

"But why?" I asked. "What if I gave my life for one of them? Why keep me? I'm the least powerful witch."

The king's lips curled back, flashing me the coldest, most haunting smile. "Because, Maeve. I am your father."

ARTHUR

"**M**aeve!" I yelled, struggling against my captors as that Blake fae swept in and dragged Maeve away. She called after us, tears streaming down her beautiful face, but her father – her *father*, what the fuck? – bustled her away so we couldn't get her. My heart shattered into pieces as I reached for her, unable to get near her.

The green guards of the Seelie Court had learned their lesson from handling Corbin. At least twenty guards pounced on me, holding my arms down as they tightened my bonds. I lifted my head, searching across the barrows for Maeve, but she'd already been lost in the sea of green and black.

The guards dragged us away from the fire and dumped us in the middle of a clearing. Around the edge hundreds of fae gathered, passing wooden cups and plates of fruit and honey cakes between them. They stopped when they saw us, hands frozen halfway to mouths. Whispers circulated. I caught the gleam of bone knives glinting under flickering lanterns. All eyes fell on us.

"These are the witches who've kept us imprisoned here

for centuries," the guard cried. "Our righteous and noble King has ordered their deaths. See that justice is done on behalf of all fae."

The crowd moved around us. One of the fae struck out at Rowan, slashing a claw across his face. Rowan cried out as blood flowed down his cheek.

"Get away from him," I growled, heaving my body up and throwing myself at the fae. I knocked him to the ground, but with my hands tied behind me I could do little more than flay about like a maniac. Two far darrigs landed on my back, claws slashing at my shoulders, and threw me down on my face, sitting on my legs so I couldn't get up again.

I wish I had my bloody sword. Corbin was probably right and there was some spell that destroyed or repelled anything iron from entering. I'd have made a spell like that if I were a fae. I hoped like hell the blade was at least back at the castle, so I could be buried with it. *Flynn made that for me for my twenty-first birthday—*

Wait a second... I have an idea.

Corbin was on one side of me, out cold. *Bloody lovely, just when I actually needed him to be a know-it-all git.* I managed to toss the fae off and roll on to my side, jabbing Flynn in the leg.

"Oi, you lay off me!" Flynn yelped. "It's bad enough those little blighters are going to string us up by our nuts—"

"Just shut up and listen to me. This is just like a lucid dream, basically? We can control certain things. We can make stuff happen?"

"I don't bloody know! I think Maeve is in charge, not us." Flynn jerked his head back just as a fae jabbed at him with a bone knife. The blade skimmed his collarbone, making a long, shallow cut. "Blessed Virgin Mary, that stings like a mother fucker—"

"Maeve!" I yelled, hoping like hell my voice carried over

the laughing and shrieking of the fae. "Give me a sword!"

A fae came over and kicked me in the head. Loud ringing pounded in my ears, and the sounds of the revels dulled and dimmed. *My sword...* the single thought pushed through the pain as the fae kicked and bit me, again and again. *Maeve, I need my sword...*

I had no idea if she heard me, but I had to hope she did.

A sharp pain arced up my side, momentarily blinding me. I rolled away from the source of the pain, my body moving slowly, so slowly. Something heavy landed in my fingers. I closed my hand around it, hoping it was some part of a fae I could mangle, but knowing things were rapidly turning against me.

My chest soared as I felt the familiar weight of my leather hilt. *My sword. I don't know how she did it, but Maeve bloody got it here for me.*

And now I'm going to seriously fuck up some fae.

The fae kept up their attacks but I stopped trying to fight them. Instead, I inched my body forward, climbing up the blade, placing my hands over either side of it and rubbing the vines against them.

A moment later, the sword cut through, and I popped free. My hand fumbled for the hilt again. My fingers closed around it, and I tensed.

Another fae leapt at me, bone blade raised high. I rolled over on my stomach, using the momentum to swing my arm up. The sword sang through the air before its heavy weight swung down. The blade sliced through the fae's arm, lopping the limb off below the elbow.

The fae stared, eyes bugging, as its severed arm flopped to the ground. He only started to scream when a fountain of green blood spewed from the stump.

The cry was taken up by the other fae, who leapt back from us, their eyes wide with fear.

"Iron!"

I leapt to my feet, landing in a strong stance. Ignoring the throbbing in my head, I swung the sword in a wide arc. The fae darted away, desperate to avoid contact with the blade. Not one of them even stepped forward to help the one I'd maimed, who clutched his stump and howled. Iron and metals made from it were poison to the fae. That was why the blade slid through them so easily.

Two more darted forward, trying to grab my arms. I took a nasty slice out of one's shoulder, and it collapsed, shrieking with pain. The fae leapt back further, cries of panic echoing through their ranks.

"Stay back, you poxy bastards!" I yelled, waving the sword one last time before turning away to saw through my friends' bonds. Flynn's shoulder was in a bad way, his arm hanging limp and useless. Dried blood caked one side of Rowan's face, and his usually tidy dreads jutted out in all directions.

And Corbin… even after I cut away his bond, he still lay there like a corpse. Rage burned inside me as I realized what that might mean.

I turned back just as the fae started to creep forward again. A tall flame rose from my hand. I gathered the power within me, forming the fire into a glowing ball. I lobbed it into the crowd of fae, watching in satisfaction as it caught on clothing and garlands, sending three fae rolling to the earth, their bodies ablaze. The fae rushed about, gibbering and panicking as flames leapt through the crowd, catching on clothing and skin.

That's for Corbin, you bastards.

I raised another ball of fire in my palm, holding it aloft. "Listen to me!" I yelled at the panicking fae. "Now, I want to know exactly where the king has taken Maeve, and if you don't want your entire court to burn, I suggest you tell me, *now.*"

*M*y *father.*

Daigh waved an arm, and his litter turned away. Smooth hands grabbed me, and Blake dragged me with him, following behind the litter. Several of the green-guards and other fae in long black cloaks fell in step beside him.

"He's… he's joking," I choked out.

Blake shook his head, his face impossible to read. I realized I believed it. After everything that I'd discovered about my life, my past, over the last weeks, nothing took me by surprise any more. Of course my father was a fae, and not just any fae, the king of the violent Unseelie Court. *It makes perfect sense.*

We drew up beside the litter. Daigh chuckled, and in his smile, I realized the cause of the weird feeling – it was recognition. I'd seen his smile before… in the mirror. "We fae are tricksters, but in this case, I am being entirely truthful. Your mother and I had an arrangement. We met under the light of the full moon, down in the Briarwood meadow, for a 'roll in the hay,' as you humans like to say. Unconventional – a fae and a witch – but we both wanted a child, and that desperation does play havoc with the mind, to the point where even the unthinkable becomes desirable." Daigh clicked his tongue on the roof of his mouth in a way that made me shudder. "And your mother, in the heat of the moment, she bucked against me like a little filly in the stables—"

"Don't talk about my mother like that," I growled.

"Like what?" Daigh laughed. "Like a *whore*. You humans do so relish that word – a word with the power to discredit a woman, to render her impotent even as you grant her the sexual appetite of a tigress. Your mother knew exactly what she wanted and she took it – she would have made an absolutely *enchanting* fae. The only thing I do resent is the fact that she trapped me in this forsaken place and hid you from me. But I waited. I knew you would show yourself when you came of age. As it was, I didn't even have to wait – those hapless witches of yours led me right to you."

"Well, you didn't manage to kill me, so I would think the title of hapless should go to yourself."

The litter halted outside the entrance to an enormous barrow. This one was on the outskirts of the revels – the door framed with garlands of vivid blue and purple flowers that gave off a pungent, sickly-sweet scent. The king stepped down, his pointed leather boots hitting one of the litter-bearers in the face as he crossed the threshold. Blake dragged me inside after him. The king whipped his head around, and fixed me with a perfect, pearly smile. "Whatever made you think I was trying to kill you?"

I gulped. "The Ferris wheel… my parents…"

"They were *not* your parents," the king said, his voice suddenly stern. "Come, daughter. From here, you will rule over your own kingdom. Those humans could never give you anything that compares to that."

I dug my heels into the dirt floor, but Blake was much stronger than me. He simply scooped me up – thrashing legs and all – and carried me into the sidhe. The round chamber was lit by the glowing beeswax candles set in enormous chandeliers made of bleached bones – femurs and shoulder blades and pelvic bones forming intricate, almost Rococo-esque filigree that cast jagged shadows across the dirt floor. Some of the bones were animal – enormous creatures, the likes of which hadn't been seen on earth for millions of years – but others were clearly human and fae.

The dim candlelight could not hope to penetrate into the darkest corners of the vast room. A vaulted ceiling rose above us, crossed with twisted vines and hung with yet more garlands. In the center of the room a pair of thrones stood – one larger than the other, both made of twisted vines and bleached bones and covered in cushions of ivy.

The king sank into the larger of the thrones, pushing his crown further up his forehead. His glittering eyes caught the light. He patted the cushion beside him. "I achieved *exactly* what I intended when I got rid of those people and your scholarship and your house."

"You took my scholarship—" Rage burned inside me. *Of course, I should have seen that a mile away.* Without the scholarship and my parents house, I had nothing tying me to Arizona, so it made perfect sense to go to England. Corbin's letter played right into Daigh's hands…

Blake dumped me in the chair beside Daigh, but I crawled out of it, toppling to the floor. *Bastard.* Like hell I was going to sit beside that man, not even for a moment. Every terrible thing that has happened in my life could be tied back to his evil, and he dared to sit there grinning me like he was the cat and I was a saucer of cream.

A circle of guards closed in around me, but they didn't

make a move to touch me. "It was I, not your witches, who returned you to England," Daigh said. "You are in your rightful home, ready to take over your destiny as the rightful Queen of the fae."

This is insane. "I'm not the queen of anything. I'm not a fae. I'm a witch. That's how I managed to project the whole coven into the fae realm through my dream."

The king laughed. "Do you think if witches had the power to cross over into our realm, that we would still be here? No, dear daughter, if that were true humans would have journeyed here long since, pillaged this place of all its beauty, and turned it into another outlet mall or theme park. No, it is your *fae* side that has brought you here, that kept you hidden from us."

"I'm not a Rubik's Cube. I don't have *sides.*" There was a commotion behind me, and several of the king's attendants disappeared from the dark room to investigate. I almost imagined I could hear cheering echoing from outside, and my heart sank to think that they might be cheering because my boys were being killed.

Maybe Blake's vision was coming true after all. Maybe I'd find my guys impaled on stakes, their mangled bodies burned beyond recognition.

Speaking of Blake... I glanced behind the king, but I could no longer see Blake there in the gloom. I climbed to my feet, peering over the heads of the fae, searching the dark corners of the cavernous room. *Where is he?*

"It is my hope that over time, you will fully embrace your fae side," the king said. "You will learn to be happy here. Blake has found that he can survive in *Tir Na Nog,* even though our food is poison to him. But once you restore us to our rightful place, you will have all the human slaves you could need to bring you your favorite delicacies."

"I'm not staying here," I protested. "I'm not helping you. I'd sooner *die*."

"You won't have a choice." Daigh – my father – waved away one of his attendants, who was trying to whisper something urgently in his ear. "My fae have killed your precious witches. Your power alone will not be enough to hold us back. My soldiers are on their way to your world now. They will have their human agent return your body to us. Once we are in possession of your body, we control you—"

"You don't control *shit*."

My heart soared as Arthur rushed into the room, his arms raised above his head and a terrible look of rage and vengeance on his face. The glint of the lanterns shone off the blade of his sword as he swung it down, cutting up the first line of Seelie guards who tried to halt him.

His sword. How the hell did he manage to find that?

Great and terrible was my Arthur's rage as he slashed that weapon into fae flesh, staining the dirt floor with green blood. He bellowed as he hacked and slashed, his feet darting and weaving, his body poised and graceful – performing his dance of death. The room erupted into chaos as the screams of dying fae filled the air, and guards and court fairies trampled over each other in their haste to make for the one exit.

My chest swelled. *My Aragorn.*

Behind him came Flynn, his fists whirring through the air, a bone knife raised high. He may not have had Arthur's skill with a blade, but he had a brawler's anger and he fought *dirty,* sweeping out legs and kneeing crotches and smashing his fist into noses and throats. He followed in Arthur's wake, cleaning up his mess as they moved around the perimeter of the room.

And behind them both, staying close to the wall, was Rowan. His face was drenched with sweat and blood as he held Corbin's stiff body up and dragged it behind him, Corbin's arm slung over his shoulder.

"Kill them!" The king roared at his panicking fae, but no one seemed to hear him. I rose to my feet and rushed toward my boys, but my feet stuck fast to the ground. I yanked and yanked at my legs, but they wouldn't move.

Daigh's eyes glinted in triumph. He held his hand out in front of him, the palm pointed directly at me. "You will not be going anywhere with them," he spat.

"Touch Maeve and we'll hurt your prince," Arthur roared.

I whirled around. I don't know how, but Flynn had Blake under his arm. Blake's own arm hung limp at his side, a jagged cut across his shoulder the likely cause. Blake's eyes bore into mine, cool and surprisingly serene, as Flynn's bone blade pressed up against his throat.

"You're making a mistake," Blake warned.

"Shut up," Flynn growled, pressing the blade against Blake's skin. A thin line of red blood streaked across Blake's throat.

The king laughed, wiping spittle from his jaw. He waved his other hand at Flynn. "Fine. Kill him if you must. It is of no consequence to me."

"I will," Flynn yelled, pressing the bone blade deeper into Blake's throat. Blake tried to say something else, but all that came out was a strangled cry.

My chest lurched. "Flynn, don't," I said, not really sure why I was trying to save the guy who'd betrayed us. I tried to fling myself toward them, but the king still held me glued in place.

Panic rose in my throat, and I realized with startling clarity that I was watching the beginning of the deaths of my boys. As good as Arthur was, soon there would be reinforcements, and a single shot from one of those deadly recurve bows and he would never swing a sword again. I couldn't see a way out of this, unless...

Unless I gave myself up. Unless I did what the king asked.

"I'll do it!" I yelled at the king. "I'll do whatever you want. I'll stay here with you and rule your kingdom, but you have to let the guys go free."

"Maeve, no," Arthur growled, sliding his blade into a sprite who tried to latch on to his hair.

The king grinned. "Ah, so she does see reason. That's my girl. I'm sure that if your gentleman puts down his iron weapon we shall be able to come to some kind of arrangement."

"Arthur, put down the sword." My voice wavered. My whole body trembled. *I can't believe I'm doing this.*

The idea of staying with Daigh, of becoming like the fae, turned my stomach. But if I wanted to save my boys, I didn't have a choice.

"Arthur, Flynn, *please*," I begged. Tears streamed down my face. "This is the way it has to be. He killed my parents just so I'd come here. I can't have your deaths on my conscience, too. Please..."

"He's a fae. You can't trust him," Flynn hissed, pressing that blade harder into Blake's throat. "Even if he is your father, it doesn't mean anything to him. He's going to let his own son die."

"Perhaps you would take his place?" The king asked Flynn. "Blake's not my biological son. He's just some baby I stole before I was banished here. I thought he'd be a fitting lover for my daughter once she came of age. But if she has found more worthy suiters, I obviously have no need of him."

"Unlike your boy here, we don't need your help to find a girl," Arthur stepped forward, slicing through a horned fae that stood in his path. "You're not getting the earth back, no matter how many fae you send after us."

Two black-clad fae leapt at him, but instead of attacking them, Arthur flicked his sword back over his shoulder, slashing a vine that rose to the ceiling. His blade sliced clean through it. The vine whipped up over their heads, and my gaze followed it up, realizing with a start what Arthur had done.

Now free of its rope, an enormous bone chandelier crashed to the ground, right on top of Daigh's throne.

The throne collapsed, and Daigh was flattened to the ground by the weight of the chandelier. He moaned as a scapula pinned his chest. A heavy arm of bones crossed over his legs, bending his knees at impossible angles. Green blood poured from a deep wound on his head. His mouth hung open, but all that came out was a bubbling, strangled gasp.

Fae rushed forward to help their king, but one swing of Arthur's sword cut them down and sent them back against the walls.

I collapsed to the ground, my feet free. I picked myself up and ran over to the guys, flinging Corbin's other arm over my shoulder and taking some of the weight from Rowan.

"Maeve…" Daigh managed to choke out, his eyes rolling back in his head.

"She's not yours to take. If you want Maeve, you're going to have to get through us first," Arthur slid his blade through the king's hand, driving it deep into the earth.

Daigh's wheezing scream sliced the air. Smoke curled from the edges of the wound as the iron did its work, poisoning his skin and drawing out his magic. Arthur stepped back, whipping another bone knife from his belt.

"Get it out!" Daigh yelled as he tugged at his hand, but the sword held him fast to the ground. The skin around the blade withered and curled up, like dead leaves in fall. The fae quivered against the walls, too afraid to touch the iron blade.

"Maeve," it was Arthur, his hand on my arm, pulling me toward the door. "Let's go."

"You don't have to tell me twice!" I lifted Corbin higher on my shoulder. Rowan and I raced behind Arthur as he pushed his way through stunned, terrified fae and out into the crisp moonlight.

We raced for the trees behind the sidhe, crashing through the undergrowth, no longer caring how much noise we made. My chest heaved as I struggled to carry Corbin's dead weight... *oh God, I hope he's not dead. Please, don't let him be dead.*

The sky darkened overhead as we ran, darkness creeping in much faster than was natural, but I guessed nothing was truly natural here. Arthur bowled through the trees ahead of us, his enormous limbs tearing leaves and snapping branches, clearing our way. If only he knew where the hell he was going.

Flynn huffed behind us, dragging Blake along, his blade still pressed to Blake's throat. Blake tried to yell something, but his words turned into bellows of pain as Flynn socked him in the jaw.

All around us, fairies leapt and danced through the trees, chittering to each other in their foreign language. They stayed well back, nervous around Arthur, even though he no longer had his sword. But I could see they were closing around us like a crab's pincers. Soon we'd be completely surrounded.

"What the fuck do we do?" Flynn yelled.

"We have to keep going," Arthur said. I could barely see his outline ahead through the gloom. "We're heading to the valley, but I don't know how to get back to the place we came in."

"There's no bloody point," Blake yelled. "You need to get to the gateway—"

His words cut off as Flynn punched him in the jaw again. "Shut your pie hole, or I'll shut it permanently next time."

The chittering grew louder, more focused. The fae were coming.

"Arthur," I moaned. My arms and legs burned. Beside me Rowan puffed, his entire body drenched in sweat. Corbin's body snagged on every branch and bramble.

Maeve, listen to me. Blake's voice reached my ears, but the sound wasn't coming from behind me. It was inside my head. How the hell was he doing that? *You have to listen to me. I can hide you, I can save you, but you need to trust me.*

"No way in hell," I muttered out loud, my breath coming out in ragged gasps as I struggled on another few steps. I screamed as an arrow whizzed past on my left, burying itself into a tree trunk.

Fine, die here in the forest riddled with arrows like a porcupine. That's your prerogative. Or, you could hide in the enormous hollow log up here on the left, and I'll cast a glamour to lead them in the wrong direction, and you and all your merry men can live to be fools another day. Your choice.

Was I supposed to trust this guy after he betrayed us, exposed us to the fae? He was clearly playing games with me, just like his father… *our* father, I reminded myself with a shudder. But he had a point – the fae were getting closer. We wouldn't outrun them. I glanced around, searching the gloom for a place to hide.

Hollow log… hollow log… *There it is!* I caught a glimpse of an enormous fallen log jutting out across the forest floor. I pulled Corbin toward it, dragging Rowan along with me. Sure enough, rot had hollowed out the log so we could fit inside, and with the direction the fae were coming, there was a chance they'd head right past without seeing us.

"Arthur, Flynn," I hissed. "Get in here."

Rowan and I dragged Corbin inside, his legs scraping over the rotting wood, pulling up curls of bark. Flynn followed, his arms tight around Blake and his hand clamped hard over his mouth. Arthur crouched on the end, his bone blade raised, ready to make a last stand should this not work.

Please let it work.

The fae host thundered through the forest, flitting between the trees or swinging from the branches like monkeys. Flickers of white sliced through the trees as slivers of moonlight caught their bone blades, and their teeth and claws gnashed and tore at the trees. My whole body shuddered with fear.

I crouched as low as I could in the log, pressing my body into the damp bark and wishing like hell it would swallow us up and take us back to Briarwood.

No. Not until we find what we came for.

I held my breath as the fae passed us by, their grisly host moving deeper into the forest. As soon as we could no longer hear them, Flynn breathed a big, dramatic sigh. "That was close. Good job spotting the log, Maeve."

"It wasn't me. Blake was the one who saw it. He sort of… told me about it."

"What the fuck?" Flynn released his hand from Blake's mouth.

"Yeah, I'd be very interested to know how you did that," Arthur said, training his knife on Blake's chest.

Dried blood splattered Blake's face and his breath came out in ragged gasps. Flynn's knife had bit into the flesh of his neck, and Blake winced as he opened his mouth to speak, his hand flying to his throat. He glanced at me, his eyes wide, begging for me to vouch for him.

"Remember how I said he was a spirit user?" I said. "Well, it seems one of our powers – or at least, one of Blake's powers – is telepathy. I heard his voice inside my head, telling me about the log. He was right. He helped us, so maybe we shouldn't try to stab him."

"You sure it was him?" Arthur frowned.

"Oh yeah," I remembered Blake calling them my 'Merry Men.' "It was definitely him."

"But why is he trying to help us now when it's his fault we're in this mess in the first place?" Arthur demanded.

"I'd like to know that, too," I glared at Blake. "You took my voice."

"Only because you were about to reveal that I'd helped you," Blake coughed out. "Bloody hell, you're not very good at this subterfuge thing. Come on, we need to get out of here. They'll figure out you're not ahead of them soon enough."

"Will you take us to the children?" I said. "We probably all need weapons if we have to get through more of those guards." I turned to Arthur. "Speaking of weapons, how'd you get your sword back?"

He arched an eyebrow. "You gave it to me."

"No, I didn't."

"Yes, Maeve, you did. We were in trouble. I was wishing inside my head that you could find a sword for me. I just had this idea that if you could hear me, and since you control the dream, that you could make it happen. And then the hilt just appeared in my hand."

I folded my arms. "Arthur, I was a little busy dealing with my *father*. I didn't have anything to do with it."

"But—"

"We don't have time for this," Flynn piped up. "We need to go back for the children."

"You're in luck, witches. I'm going to make your whole night." Blake gave me a weak grin. "I already moved them to a safe place. The fae back at the sidhe are guarding two pumpkins charmed with glamour to look like the babies. I've got the real tykes here in the forest. But we have to hurry."

"He's lying. He'll just lead us back to the king."

Blake snorted. "After what he did, you think I want to go back to that prick? I've lived for twenty-one years in this hellhole where everything is literally poison to me. I want you bastards to take me back to Briarwood with you."

"That's not happening," Arthur folded his arms.

Blake folded his. "Fine, then I'm not helping."

"We're wasting time arguing with this wanker," Flynn held up his knife. "I'll just kill the gobshite."

"No, stop!" I shoved myself between them, my fingers gripping Flynn's wrist, holding the knife back. "Don't hurt him. He's a human, not a fae. He's a spirit user who has helped us. I think we should trust him."

"He may not be a fae, but he's been raised by them," Flynn growled, trying to wrench the knife from me. "He's given us no reason why we should trust him, why we should follow him."

"You should follow me because I'm your one shot of getting out of here alive," Blake said. "There, you've got your one reason. Can we get going now?"

"Let him go, Flynn." I tried to pry his arm from around Blake's throat. Flynn's muscles relaxed under my touch, but not enough that I wasn't still worried he'd kill Blake.

Flynn's expression wavered. "He nearly got us killed!"

"No, I saved you from getting your arse beheaded on the spot," Blake said. "When they took you back to the barrows, I was figuring out how to get you out of there. I was *just about* to step in and free you all, but your barbarian friend there got all stabby with that iron blade and sorted that out for me. Now, if you don't mind…" he slipped out Flynn's grasp and clambered for the log's entrance. "We need to hurry."

"I'm also curious why you're helping us," I said.

"I told you," he said. "Back at Jane's house. I explained it all."

"You really didn't."

"Fine. I'll explain when we're safely back in your realm. But if you want to bring those babies back with you, we need to go now."

Flynn forced Blake to walk in front of us, his knife pointing into Blake's spleen with every step. Blake led us back the other way, deeper into the forest. He followed no path. My stomach twisted with nerves as I realized that without him, we'd never find our way back out again. My hand patted the stone in my pocket. Maybe we wouldn't have to get out again. As long as Blake was taking us to the babies—

Blake stopped, his head tilted to the side. "We're here," he said, scanning the forest around us. He pointed ahead at a beautiful ancient oak tree, the trunk gnarled and twisted. Steps had been carved into the enormous tree and moss hung in long garlands like streamers. Blake darted up the staircase and reached into a hollow in the tree.

"This your clubhouse?" Flynn smirked up at him.

"Yeah," Blake pulled out two tiny bundles, balancing them carefully in his arms as he clambered back down the staircase. "I needed some place to get away from the court and the princes and those damn intolerable drums. Here they are."

He passed a tiny bundle into my arms. I peeled aside a corner of the blanket, and a squishy sleeping baby face peeked into view. It opened one tiny eye, then the other, peering up at me with intelligent curiosity.

Connor. I was pretty sure it was Connor. Babies kind of looked alike to me, but I recognized a bit of Jane's brashness in his gaze. My chest soared. We'd done it. We'd found the babies, and they were alive, and safe.

Now we just have to get them home.

Flynn had the other baby in his arms. He made cooing noises and tickled it with a long, freckled finger. Something about the look in his eyes tugged at my chest, and made a lump form in my throat that wouldn't dislodge.

"What next?" Arthur asked me. He faced away from us, into the forest, his hand gripping the hilt of the bone sword he'd taken from one of the guards he'd slain. Even as his eyes scanned the forest for danger, his hand reached up and stroked Connor's cheek. The baby cooed, and the lump in my throat grew larger.

"How do you normally get to the human realm?" I asked Blake. The spell hadn't exactly been clear on how we got back. I'd figured it would be obvious once we got here, but so far – like everything else in the fae realm – it was anything but.

He shook his head. "There's a gateway, but that's a sure-fire way to separate your head from your body. By now, they'll be guarding it heavily. Your only hope is to go back the way you came – through the dream."

"Oh, right."

"Maeve?" Arthur asked.

I stared down at Corbin's lifeless body, my heart racing. "I just… I'm not really sure how to do this. The spell didn't exactly explain how to return. Corbin usually figures this stuff out, but he's…"

"Okay, right." Arthur rubbed his head. "Usually when you want to reverse a spell you have to actually… *reverse* the spell. So we just backtrack through the same steps we took to create the spell. You need a lock of each of our hair." He whipped his hand up, and his blade chopped a long lock of gold hair. He dropped it into my hand. "You tie those around your wrist, then we all go to sleep, I guess, and you drag us back."

"Do we go to sleep, or wake up?" I asked, as Flynn carefully cut off two tiny locks of the babies hair and placed them in my hand. "Aren't we all asleep now?"

"I don't feel asleep," Flynn said. "I can't wake up if I'm not asleep. And I don't exactly feel like a nap right now."

"Shut up for a minute. I have to think." I had theorized that what I was doing when astral-projecting was moving my consciousness through the multiverse into one of many possible realities, one of the "Many Worlds" postulated in quantum phenomena, in which theoretically a counterpart of my own consciousness resided. There was an idea in theoretical physics that dreams were windows into events occurring in an alternate world seen through the eyes of our counterpart consciousness. But since my consciousness was *here*, in the dream, then which world was I really existing in, and in which world was my counterpart consciousness? Was I asleep, or awake?

My brain hurt. This was where Corbin would really come in handy. He had a way of being able to translate my theories into magical practice. I rubbed my temple, trying to play through the scenario in my head.

"We have to wake up," I said, firmly, although I wasn't really certain at all. "Or, rather, I have to wake up, and pull the rest of you back with me. Quick, everyone, give me a lock of your hair."

Flynn lopped off a loop of his red curls, then bent down and chopped off a lock of Corbin's dark hair. Meanwhile, Rowan tied one of his dreadlocks around my wrist and he plaited the other three together to create one loop.

I turned to Blake. "Wake me up."

He grinned. "I knew you were going to ask that, Princess."

"You got us this far. And I know you can do this, too. You got inside my head before. Do it again. Wake me up."

He shook his head. "You don't know what that could do. Besides, I don't want to knock about inside your head. It's scary in there."

"Just do it, *Prince*," I threw his title out. "Get us out of here, and as soon as we're back, we'll find a way to free you from the king. We owe you one for everything you've done."

Blake smiled. "Careful. You don't want to be in the habit of owing favors to the fae. We tend to collect at really inconvenient times."

"You're not fae."

"Now *that* is a matter of interpretation." Blake's eyes pierced mine and something shifted in my head. At first it was an itch at the back of my skull. Then the itch spread, becoming a dull, throbbing ache. Random thoughts and memories flared up – Louise Crawford coming out of the kitchen with an enormous rainbow birthday cake, eight candles burning on top, Kelly and I singing in the worship choir, me having a screaming argument with our science teacher after she insisted creationism was a valid scientific theory.

"Wha—" I started to say, but the memories stole my voice. They flooded me, pouring over me like water, swirling over my joints, pressing between my ribs, cocooning me in parts of my life I desperately wished to forget.

My parents texting me to meet them at the Ferris wheel.

Me, screaming at that stupid fae, Kalen, when I should have been with them, the wheel falling, burning, buckling. The people screaming. My parents bodies burning. *All because of me.*

The air crackled with heat. The smoke seared my throat. Every part of my body shook with the horror of it, as though it were happening again. It *was...*

A nightmare. Blake had dug deep into my brain and fed me my worst nightmare in Technicolor.

Behind every tortured face, between the mangled struts of the wheel, through the thick smoke of the fire, Blake's eyes blared – fierce and determined, heedless to the pain they brought with them.

A dark void opened up in the ground beside me, swelling in size until was a great gaping hole in the earth. Trees and roots disappeared into its depths, sucked away into oblivion. The Ferris wheel toppled in after it, and the ghost train, and my parents' burned, charred bodies.

Clutching Connor against my chest, I met Blake's eyes. The connection between our minds sizzled – and a sharp pain tore through my skull. I screamed as Blake's fingers tore deep into my consciousness, pulling out all the grief and guilt I carried with me, and threw it at me in a cannonball of sorrow and torment.

My body shuddered as the pain hit me, and whether it was physical or mental pain I no longer knew. They were the same. I burned up in the horror of my life, torn open by my own internal horror.

"What are you doing to her?" Arthur grabbed Blake's arm.

"Don't—" I gasped, but Blake's grip on my mind tightened, and he *pushed.* The push came from inside my body, like a parasite forcing its way out through my ears. My feet teetered on the edge, struggling to keep their grip. Flynn reached for me, his mouth moving as he yelled something, but the void swallowed all sound. Bright light filled my eyes, rolling toward me like a train coming into station.

I fell.

I toppled backwards and the world flipped around me, the grass falling over my head and the dark sky becoming a blanket beneath me. I toppled head over heels, my stomach lurching.

I slammed into something hard and sat up with a start. Darkness surrounded me. I rubbed my eyes, and gradually, the room came into view – dark wood ceiling. Swords hanging from wrought-iron chandeliers, bare wattle and daub walls and iron hooks for tapestries. I was back in Briarwood, back in the real world.

I glanced down at the bundle in my arms, peeling away the top layer of blanket. Connor's big eyes stared back at me. His face was all scrunched up, and a tiny fist flailed out from one corner of the blanket.

"Hey, little one," I whispered, cradling him against my chest. "You're home again. We're gonna get you back to your mommy as soon as we can."

Bodies scuffled and couches creaked as the guys started to wake up. Flynn sat up and stretched one arm in the air, his lean body extending like a cat. The second baby in his arms mashed a tiny fist into his chest. Rowan's dark lashes flickered open, and he rubbed his cheek where a long cut marred his dark skin. Arthur rolled over and narrowly managed to avoid impaling himself on his own sword, which he once again gripped in his trembling fingers.

"We did it," I grinned. "We actually fucking traveled to the fae realm in a dream and lived to tell the tale."

"*You* did it," Arthur said, wincing as he touched a finger to a long tear across his shoulder. "That was some seriously powerful magic you pulled off, bringing us all into the dream with you and pulling us out right at that exact moment."

"I guess we know what your power is now," Flynn said. "You are one badass dreamwalker."

I beamed. "So crisis averted?"

"For now." Arthur prodded Corbin's still-sleeping figure with the toe of his boot. "After the damage we did, I doubt the fae will be coming back for more children any time soon—"

"Um, guys." Flynn said, his gaze focused on a dark shape on the floor. "We have a problem."

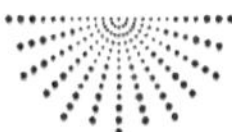

I whirled around. There, on the floor next to Flynn's couch, his hands crossed behind his head and a flirtatious smile on his face, was Blake.

"What the hell are you doing here?" *This is impossible, and since everything that already happened today was already impossible, this is impossible on a monumental scale.*

"*How* the hell are you here?" Arthur said. "You can't break our protection spells."

Blake grinned. He placed a boot on the corner of the table. "Maybe because I'm not fae."

"What? But—" Arthur looked totally lost.

"Look," Blake sighed. "I can explain it all, and I will. But right now you've got more important problems."

"Oh yeah? Global warming? Peak oil? Publican strike?"

Blake pointed at the babies. "You need to give those babies a protection spell and return them to their mothers. And *then* you need to give the bossy one over there something to wake him up."

"How the hell are we going to do a protection spell

without Corbin?" Flynn demanded. "He's the only one who can find what we need in the library—"

"Oh, for pity's sake. Let me do it." Before I could protest, Blake grabbed Connor from my arms and pressed his hand against his forehead.

"Don't hurt him!" I tried to grab his arm, but Blake flung me away. He muttered some words in the strange, singsong tongue of his. Connor whimpered, but didn't cry out.

After a few moments, Blake handed Connor back to me. "There. Now I suggest you call the mother and the police and say you found the babies dumped in the forest. Then go outside and roll them around in the dirt and leaves. The fae won't leave fingerprints, so the only evidence they'll find on him is from you guys, which will make you prime suspects in his kidnapping for a while."

"We can't go to jail for this," I said.

"No one's going to jail," Blake said, as he pressed his palm to the other baby's forehead. "Not with spirit users in our group."

I didn't know what he meant by that, but Blake's confidence was infectious, and I was desperate to return Connor to Jane.

"Right," Flynn glanced from me to Blake and back again. "I'll take care of the wee babies." I handed Connor off to Flynn, admiring the way his eyes lit up as he juggled both babies in his arms. Flynn made for the garden, making funny faces and voices until Connor was cooing and laughing again.

He'd make a great dad.

Rowan was already bent over Corbin, a vial of some sweet-smelling poultice in his hands. He smeared some of it over Corbin's lips, then sat back on his heels, his expression worried.

Blake paced around the perimeter of the room, his boots

crunching over the salt on the floor. He trailed his hands along the walls, pressing into the cracks between the stones. He stared up at the rafters and out the windows into the valley beyond. "So this is what it looks like from the inside," he said.

"Stop touching our castle! You're not supposed to be here!" Arthur yelled.

Corbin moaned. I ran to his side, practically shoving Rowan out of the way. "Corbin? Corbin, can you hear me?"

Blake yawned loudly just as Corbin's eyes flickered open. "Am I... am I dead?" he asked.

Tears brimmed at the corners of my eyes. Fuck, we nearly lost him. I nearly lost him. "No, you are very definitely not dead."

"I feel dead," he moaned, lifting his hand slowly and clenching and unclenching his fist. "I feel all... bollocksed up."

"You're perfect." I threw my arms around him, drinking in the distinctive smell of him. *You're not getting away from me that easy, Corbin Harris.*

"This is so beautiful, I think I'm going to cry," Blake grimaced.

I whipped my head around. "Leave us alone. It's partly your fault this happened."

Corbin's eyes grew wide as he took in Blake's presence. "But how..."

"Don't worry about it," Rowan tried to push his shoulder back into the couch. "It's some kind of accident. We'll figure it out as soon as you're strong enough."

Blake shrugged. "No accident. I followed you guys out."

"But you can't do that!" Arthur growled.

Blake shrugged again. "Empirical evidence suggests that I can, unless the scientist can come up with an alternative hypothesis."

The guys turned to stare at me. "Um, based on what we know about fae, this is impossible. Which either means that the magical protection surrounding the castle is destroyed, or that he's telling the truth and he really isn't a fae."

Blake blew me a kiss. "Got it in one, Princess."

"So if you're not a fae, why did you follow us? What do you want?"

"I've already told you. I want to help." Blake lifted his hands, palms facing up, a gesture of appeal. "Allow me to introduce myself properly. My name is Blake Beckett. I am born of the human realm to Colleen and Darren Beckett. I am the newest member of your coven."

TO BE CONTINUED

∼

Need to know what happens next? Grab book 2, *The Castle of Fire and Fable*.

(Turn the page for a sizzling excerpt).

∼

Can't get enough of Maeve and her boys? Get *The Summer Court* – a Briarwood short story – for free in *Cabinet of Curiosities*, a Steffanie Holmes compendium of short stories and bonus scenes. To get this collection, all you need to do is sign up for updates with the Steffanie Holmes newsletter.

If you turn the page, you'll find an excerpt of book 2, but I wanted to say a few words first. (As if I haven't already said enough words on the pages of this book!)

Maeve's story is close to my heart, even though as a character, she and I are very different. She comes from a world of science, where everything is logical and sensible. I live in a world of ideas and fantasy. What we have in common – and I think what we all have in common with Maeve – is that we've experienced traumatic events that have changed us irrevocably, and that we're all searching for our home.

More than her discovery of magic, it's the loss of her parents that throws Maeve off her axis. But her grief also becomes her strength, because she's able to process what she discovers at Briarwood through the lens of her own pain.

What happens when you encounter something so radical that it shatters the world? Do you curl up into a ball and rock slowly back and forth? Do you lash out? Do you try to continue by feigning ignorance? Or do you try to find a way to reconcile these conflicting ideas? Do you draw strength from the people who care about you, and the place where your feet land?

Throughout this series, Maeve comes up against this wall of her own making again and again. She's human. She doesn't always get things right. But she always tries to be better. I think we can all relate to that.

One of the big themes in the Briarwood Witches series, and indeed in all my books, is the meaning of home. How a place can get under your skin in such a way that it becomes part of you, how we connect with nature and architecture in ways that mirror our connections to people, but also how a home can be inside your heart, as well as in a building.

Briarwood Castle is an enormous, cold, damp, strange place – a fortification that was never meant to be lived in. And yet with love and care and compassion, the guys have made it a home.

In 2009, my husband and I, newly married, embarked on our Epic Adventure. We rented a camper van with two friends and spent four months driving around Europe and the Middle East.

We stopped at every castle we came across, and we let the cumulative history of war and intrigue and passion and power wash over us. What struck me about these buildings was how history built up in layers, each person adding their own story.

We came back to New Zealand and decided to take some of our memories – some of our story – and pour them into designing and building our own home. We borrowed from castle architecture to create a space that would make us happy and celebrate the things we valued – friendship, and family, and books, and good food, and creativity.

With help from my dad – a qualified builder – we purchased a plot of land and built our home with our own two hands. It's the craziest, most rewarding, and most difficult thing we ever did. It took four years, all of our money, and most of our sanity, but we did it.

I don't believe it's a coincidence that we finished our castle just as the first Briarwood book came out. We hosted our first medieval feast in our newly christened Great Hall. Just as Maeve's home was been torn from her, we were celebrating the joy of creating a home for ourselves, together.

My home may not have turrets, or a moat, or five hot guys at my beck and call, but it's built with love and passion and filled with books and music and things that light up my heart. Wherever you can find that for yourself, you are home.

Will Maeve find her home at Briarwood? Or is her home with her only living relative, her father? You're going to have to keep reading to find out.

Happy reading!

Steff

"Allow me to introduce myself properly. My name is Blake Beckett. I was born of the human realm to Colleen and Darren Beckett. I'm the new member of your coven."

Four pairs of eyes glared back at me like I'd just told them the world was really a giant wedge of cheese. There was Maeve – her beauty radiant even through the crackled marks my spirit magic made across her face. Her three witch boyfriends glowered at me, all fire and brimstone and "kill the outsider." At least the red-haired one had gone to the garden with the babies – he was more ready than the others to run me through with a blade. As it was, there were a ton of swords hanging conveniently above my head, should any of the others feel the desire.

It would be a damn shame, especially since I hadn't had a curry yet.

"Colleen and Darren?" The one they called Corbin asked, his breath throaty from the knockout draught the guards had forced down him. He scrambled upright, his dark eyes swimming with pain and confusion. That was good. That was better than anger. As I'd just seen, when these witches got angry, they also got stabby. "But... the murder suicide..."

I waved a hand. "Is that how he covered it up? Very classy. Make it a bloodbath – that's the Unseelie way. If you want the truth, Daigh took me from my parents before their coven sealed off the gateway. That's how he managed to get me through – and even then, it cost him much of his power for many years. That's why I hadn't been able to leave *Tir Na Nog* until recently."

"Haven't been able to leave, or didn't want to leave?" the particularly stabby blonde one with arms like tree trunks – whose name I think was Arnold – demanded.

I spied a door on the far wall, and started inching my way toward it. Better to be close to an escape route should this conversation not go my way. Although with Daigh's fae prowling around outside the castle walls, I was probably safer inside with the stabby witches.

"Oh, sure," I said breezily, meeting Maeve's eyes and trying to plant the thought in her head that I was trustworthy, that I was telling the truth. Now that she knew what I could do, I wasn't sure she'd trust her thoughts. "I just *love* living in a world that's only five miles square, where the weather never changes, the food will poison me if I eat it, and the inhabitants are like horny teenagers cooped up indoors with nothing to do, only they have magic and a penchant for sticking sharp things into their pet human for shits and giggles. No, I *never* wanted to leave."

"But you've come through the gateway twice before," Maeve demanded. "Once when you took Connor and once when you accosted me in Jane's bathroom."

"Even when Daigh was strong enough to send a human through the gateway again, he didn't want to use that power on me, in case I ran away as soon as my feet hit home soil." I shrugged, scuffing the edge of the salt circle with my boot.

"Turns out he was right, but I had to pretend he wasn't. It took me years to earn Daigh's total trust so he'd send me through."

Now was probably not the time to tell them I had to betray my own adopted cousin in order to finally get the King's approval.

"Daigh gave me that assignment and I could not refuse it. While the sprites were collecting Connor, I was trying to figure out how to get a message to you. I was going to plant something in the red-haired one's dreams, but you popped out from behind the wall and clobbered me before I had a chance. That's why I came back the second time."

"What assignment were you on then?" Maeve demanded.

"Nothing. I knocked out one of the Far Darrigs assigned to the next mission and used a glamour to take his place. That's why I couldn't stay in the bathroom and chat. I had to get back before they noticed I was out of formation."

"Glamour is fae magic," Arnold spat. "Humans can't do that."

"You can if you've spent twenty-one years learning from the fae." My eyes bore into Maeve's. "Your coven didn't exactly leave any color TVs or magazines or record players for me to enjoy in my prison. I didn't have anything else to *do but* practice magic."

"He is really powerful," Maeve said to the others. "I've read about all kinds of spirit magic in one of Corbin's books, but Blake can do stuff beyond even that. He can speak inside your head and—"

"Yeah, while he was *torturing* you," Arnold growled.

"Arthur," Maeve warned. Ah, his name was Arthur. I probably wouldn't remember that.

"Wait, *what?*" Corbin glared at me.

I held up my hands. "Whoa, there. I didn't torture her. She needed to wake up. All I did was influence her dream to make her see something she wouldn't want to face. It's nothing Maeve can't do herself."

"Sure." Maeve ran her hand through her short hair. A streak of pink slashed across her forehead – the color playing against her hazel eyes, making them seem deeper, like pools of rippling water. "I crossed through the gateway in my dream, and pulled the guys through after me, but you took things from *inside my head.* I heard your voice. The book says that only the most powerful spirit users can do that."

"And *she's* the Priestess and has no idea what she's capable of, so now you've got two of the most powerful spirit users in your coven. You should be dancing a jig, not interrogating me. Especially since we don't have time for any of this. The gateway is weakened and Daigh's fae will be swarming through as fast as they can." I pointed out the window in the direction of the sidhe. From this vantage point, I could see the castle gardens – bursting with bright flowers and weird statues – stretching down to a small wood. "The first thing we should do is fix that. We have to—"

"There's no *we*," Arnold – no, *Arthur* – shot at me. "What you're telling us is ludicrous. It's—"

"It's actually not," Corbin leaned forward. I noticed Maeve's eyes darting toward him, and her whole body shifted when he started to speak; a slight shudder echoing through her at the sound of his voice. My mind – still collecting the residue of her deepest thoughts – flooded with happiness that he was alive.

So they have a thing, then. Again, not a surprise, given that Maeve's powers – like my own – were stimulated by sexual encounters. Corbin was the one all the fae knew, the one who had collected the other witches, who had kept up the rituals that had held the gateway closed for so many years after his parents abandoned the castle, the one who'd dedicated his life to the study of magic. It made perfect sense that they would fall into bed with each other.

That was okay. I wasn't worried. If I knew one thing about spirit magic (and I knew a lot of things) it was that one person – even if they were another powerful magic user – was never going to be enough to satisfy Maeve's hunger.

But *two* spirit users… that was going to be more delicious than a curry.

~

Need to know what happens next? Grab book 2, *The Castle of Fire and Fable.*

PREORDER THE CASTLE OF FIRE AND FABLE TODAY

Five beautiful witches … one painful choice.

Now that the secrets of Maeve's past have been revealed, she begins to embrace her newfound powers. Being a witch and a science geek makes her head hurt at times, but luckily she's got Corbin, Arthur, Flynn, Rowan, and Blake to awaken her powers and tend her broken heart.

The only way the coven will be strong enough to battle the fae is if Maeve chooses a consort. But how can she choose when each of the guys need and want her? How can she accept only one when they all fill the empty void inside her?

Maeve is still reeling from the death of her parents when another tragedy strikes. This time, she must face her grief head on, and find strength in her bond with her five broken witches to battle an impossible foe.

The Castle of Fire and Fable is the second in a brand new steamy reverse harem romance series by *USA Today* bestselling author, Steffanie Holmes. This full-length book glitters with love, heartache, hope, grief, dark magic, fairy trickery, steamy scenes, British slang, meat pies, second chances, and the healing powers of a good cup of tea. Read on only if you believe one just isn't enough.

ABOUT THE AUTHOR

Steffanie Holmes is a *USA Today* bestselling author of paranormal romance, urban fantasy, and supernatural mysteries. Her books feature clever, witty heroines, dark and haunted settings, cunning witches, and a dash of sadistic humor.

Before becoming a writer, Steffanie worked as an archaeologist and museum curator. From Dark Age Europe to crumbling gothic estates, Steffanie is fascinated with how love can blossom between the most unlikely characters.

Steffanie lives in New Zealand with her husband, a horde of cantankerous cats, and their medieval sword collection.

STEFFANIE HOLMES NEWSLETTER

Can't get enough of Maeve and her boys? Get *The Summer Court* – a Briarwood short story – for free in *Cabinet of Curiosities*, a Steffanie Holmes compendium of short stories and bonus scenes. To get this collection, all you need to do is sign up for updates with the Steffanie Holmes newsletter.

Come hang with Steffanie
www.steffanieholmes.com
hello@steffanieholmes.com

www.ingramcontent.com/pod-product-compliance
Lightning Source LLC
Chambersburg PA
CBHW051321190726
48290CB00001B/259